Praise for Jane

'A sparkling story about the bittersweet relationships we have with our nearest and dearest, which will keep you turning the pages' *Prima*

'Sparks fly as secrets tumble from the closet in this deftly observed novel' *Woman and Home*

'This emotional read about family deceit and betrayal is a real page-turner. Prepare yourself for an all-nighter. 5 stars' *Heat*

'Forget *Dallas*, forget *Dynasty*. This is a thrilling, outstanding family saga for the new millennium that demands to be made into a TV drama' *Daily Record*

'Varley's absorbing follow-up to *Wives and Lovers* is a dark tale of modern relationships' *Bella*

'A lovely, romantic, intriguing novel' Penny Vincenzi

'A great page-turner which brings to mind the landscape of Joanna Trollope' *Daily Express*

Jane Elizabeth Varley's novels are inspired by the events of her own life. She was married and divorced by the time she was thirty and spent several tough but fulfilling years as a single parent. Now remarried, Jane had a baby daughter at the age of forty and lives with her husband, daughter and teenage son in the USA. She is the author of three previous novels, *Wives and Lovers*, *Husbands and Other Lovers*, and *The Truth About Love*, all available in Orion paperback. Visit her website at www.janevarley.com.

By Jane Elizabeth Varley

Wives and Lovers
Husbands and Other Lovers
The Truth About Love
Dearest Rivals

DEAREST RIVALS

Jane Elizabeth Varley

An Orion paperback

First published in Great Britain in 2008
by Orion
This paperback edition published in 2009
by Orion Books Ltd,
Orion House, 5 Upper Saint Martin's Lane
London WC2H 9EA

An Hachette UK company

1 3 5 7 9 10 8 6 4 2

A CIP catalogue record for this book
is available from the British Library.

ISBN 978-0-7528-8445-5

Typeset by Deltatype Ltd, Birkenhead, Merseyside

Printed and bound in Great Britain by
Clays Ltd, St Ives plc

The Orion Publishing Group's policy is to use papers that
are natural, renewable and recyclable products and made
from wood grown in sustainable forests. The logging and
manufacturing processes are expected to conform to the
environmental regulations of the country of origin.

www.orionbooks.co.uk

For Vivien

ACKNOWLEDGEMENTS

Thank you to Clare Alexander, Susan Lamb, Jane Wood, Sophie Hutton-Squire and everyone at Orion. Also to Alison Baguley, Fiona Lindblom and Sarah Graham. As always, a huge thank you to my husband and son.

Summer

Chapter 1

A wash of rain flowed down the outside of the kitchen window. It was a Gloucestershire monsoon. Peering out into the waterlogged garden, where she was barely able to make out the colours of the staked sweet peas planted against the far brick wall, Nina postponed a decision on tonight's barbecue. Nothing this weekend was going according to plan.

It felt to Nina as though her house guests had been here for ever. Already she had cooked one elaborate dinner for six – which had been stretched into eight at the last minute – and one full-scale cooked breakfast plus two loaves of banana bread for tea. It had been her husband Alex's idea to hold a weekend house party, to invite two people they barely knew – three if you counted her sister's boyfriend, Gerry – and to suggest everyone came down on Friday night.

'Why not Saturday morning?'

'Because that way they'll be more relaxed.'

'It would be much easier to have them arrive on—'

He had cut her off. 'It's business,' he said conclusively. He meant business with Howard, a new and rich holiday acquaintance.

The clouds overhead were so black that at three o'clock on a July afternoon it was necessary to have all the kitchen lights blazing. They were recessed halogens, the kitchen a recent extension to the original house, parts of which dated back to the seventeenth century. Alex had surprised her by throwing himself into the design of the kitchen: a royal blue Aga, an oversized butler's sink, pale blue hand-painted cupboard doors, the worktops a combination of marble and oak, and the floor reclaimed terracotta. Around her, the house was still. Muffin lay under the kitchen table. Alex was in his office. Jemma and Howard were presumably now asleep, having gone back to bed after a very late breakfast.

'It's the country air. Leave the washing-up, Nina. We'll help out later, won't we, Howie?'

'Mmm. Lovely bit of bacon. Shall I leave my plate in the sink?'

And her sister, Susan, was out with her party on an impromptu trip to the Cotswold Wildlife Park.

Nina put the kettle on the Aga and rinsed out the cafetiere to make a fresh pot. While she waited for the kettle to boil she lit a Marlboro Light. Now would be the time to take her coffee, a book and sit in the drawing room accompanied by Muffin, her aged brown and white shih tzu. But instead there was the dishwasher to be reloaded, the frying pans to be washed up, salads to be prepared, cream to be whipped and a pile of children's clothes to be washed.

The children's clothes belonged to Harry and Samantha, aged two and five respectively, the offspring of Gerry the boyfriend. Harry and Samantha had not been invited. In fact, they had been specifically excluded.

'No kids,' Alex had said.

'Could you let Gerry know it's just adults?' she had repeated to Susan a week earlier.

But they had come anyway, arriving two hours late in Gerry's Peugeot estate, Alex making no effort to conceal his dismay as they pulled up next to Howard's Lexus and piled out of the car onto the gravelled driveway. Samantha clung to Gerry while Harry clutched a scrap of tartan fabric later identified as The Blanket. Only Muffin, circling frantically, had seemed pleased to see them.

Susan looked thunderous. Striding away from the car she had abandoned Gerry with the luggage, grabbed Nina by the

4

hand and led them purposefully upstairs where she erupted in the seclusion of Nina's bedroom.

'That fucking bitch!'

Nina presumed Susan meant Gerry's ex-wife. Susan had mentioned her before. 'Linda?'

'Lisa. It's her weekend; it's marked on the schedule in black and white. And then she calls Gerry yesterday afternoon and says he has to have the kids because she's got to work.'

'The whole weekend?' Nina asked, more in faint hope than expectation.

Susan ignored the question. 'She knew. She fucking knew because Samantha blurted it out, I expect. And she can't bear the fact that Gerry's found someone else so she has to ruin everything for him.'

Susan threw herself onto the bed. She was wearing an elegant sleeveless red linen shift dress that Nina had bought her from LK Bennett for her birthday last year, teamed inelegantly with Birkenstocks.

Nina wondered why Gerry had agreed to this. Or why it had not been possible to call and forewarn them. But with Susan one had to tread carefully, framing all observations as neutrally as possible. 'It wasn't possible to make alternative arrangements?'

Susan counted off the points on her fingers. 'He feels he has to because she manipulated him into feeling guilty. He feels he has to because she makes him feel that whatever he does it's not good enough. He is at the mercy of her narcissistic personality.'

Nina needed to get back to Jemma and Howie, who had been abandoned in the drawing room, though contentedly enough with a bottle of champagne and a tray of crudités.

'The thing is …'

'It's a classic dynamic. Their marriage fell into a textbook pattern.' Susan looked at her as if she should anticipate what she was going to say next.

'Textbook?'

'Critical parent and obedient child,' Susan said as if it was self-evident. 'And now that he's broken free she can't bear to let go of her control over him.'

The thought came to Nina that Gerry, a lanky and rather unkempt man with a wild shock of ginger hair, walking into the house clutching two children and a booster seat, had not looked like a man who had reclaimed his power. And wasn't it his wife who had been the one to leave – for another man? She had not met Gerry before, but she had heard thrilling reports from Susan. It was usually like that in the beginning. Gerry was a newly divorced chartered surveyor with a passion for writing science fiction.

But this left the question of what they were going to do with the children that evening. 'The thing is, Alex wanted to have a quiet dinner. We quite understand about the children …' This was not exactly true. 'But can you make sure they're …' She struggled for a tactful word. Out of the way? Silent? 'Settled.' She looked at her watch. 'We ought to make up a bed for them. I'm afraid they'll have to share the fold-up.'

Susan appeared not to have heard her. 'I want to help Gerry,' she said earnestly. 'I want him to become the man that he is inside, the man who has been suppressed and ridiculed and marginalised by her. I want him to live his potential. He is such a creative person. He writes film scripts, you know.'

'You've mentioned that before.'

'And he's turning around the Chiltern Writers' Group. He's got them a regular room at High Wycombe Library.'

Nina moved towards the door. 'The children will have to sleep in your room.'

This remark brought Susan back to the present. 'Haven't you got a room they can go in?'

'No.'

'Oh.' For a moment Susan seemed nonplussed. But this condition rarely lasted. Her expression brightened. 'There's Alex's office. That would be much better! And if it's a fold-up bed we can carry it down there.'

Nina hesitated, mentally anticipating Alex's reaction.

Susan pressed on. 'It'll be perfect. It's just for the night-time. We can fold up the bed during the day. Alex won't even know they've been in there.'

Nina couldn't imagine that Alex would be blind to the presence of two small children asleep next to his desk.

'And if we're in the attic room,' Susan continued, 'there isn't going to be enough space anyway, is there? Unless you've given it to that couple.'

Now Nina felt on the back foot. 'No. Jemma and Howard are in the guest room. They arrived first,' she added by way of explanation. This wasn't exactly true, either. They had arrived first but Alex had already allocated them the larger first-floor bedroom with the view of the garden.

'Well, then,' Susan said, getting up. 'That's settled then.'

And it was. Susan had as always secured the last word, the final decision, her own way. Nina had, as ever, let her – over-whelmed by a mix of emotions that she was never quite able to identify but which included long-standing guilt, a measure of embarrassment at the difference in their respective finan-cial positions and a desire to put right all that was wrong in her sister's life.

Overlaying all of the discomfiture on this occasion was the fact that Susan and Gerry had been far down the list of couples considered for the weekend. Alex's first choice – his solicitor, Simon, and his wife, Carole – had cancelled two weeks ago. 'The au pair's mother's died. She's got to go back to Krakow.' Then, sotto voce, Carole added, 'It's bloody inconvenient, actually. We'll have to do Carcassonne without her.'

Nina's second- and third-choice couples had been rejected by Alex as too snobbish and too dull respectively. Howard was, in Alex's words, a bit of a rough diamond. It was important that Howard felt comfortable, which meant no public-school or Oxbridge conversation and definitely no opera talk. Their fourth couple, their American neighbours in London, were going to be away on holiday.

At this rate her brother would be joining the list. So Susan and Gerry had been their fifth choice.

With barely a week to go to the house party, Alex had reluctantly agreed. 'Just don't let your sister in the bloody kitchen!'

'Alex, that's not fair.'

'Christ, two customers ended up in hospital!'

'Salmonella isn't that unusual.'

'The woman literally can't boil an egg.'

Now, as the kettle whistled, Nina put out her cigarette, poured boiling water into the cafetiere and waited a minute to plunge it. She looked out on to the garden and saw that the rain was still pouring determinedly. The garden was much the same as when they had bought it: a good-sized lawn bordered with mixed beds and to the side what was optimistically referred to in the agent's particulars as a summerhouse, really a shed-like structure of peeling timbers with a small porch at the front and windows on either side of the door.

She poured out two mugs and took them along to Alex's study, trailed by Muffin. The door was closed. Grasping the two mugs in one hand, she turned the brass doorknob.

Alex looked up as if startled, then raised a tired smile. This year there had been so many late nights and long weekends of working.

'Coffee?'

'Thanks.' He pushed back his office chair and straightened the papers.

She leaned against the desk. 'You should take a break.'

'Yep.' He didn't sound as if he meant it. 'Howard up yet?'

'No.'

'I'm going to take him down the pub.'

'Without Gerry, I presume.'

Alex raised an eyebrow. 'Yes.'

At least he had calmed down since last night when they went to bed. Alex had been fuming: 'That fucking loser! Who in God's name talks about *Star Trek* over dinner?' He

8

mimicked Gerry. 'Episode forty-two, set in the intergalactic boredom zone, is the only one where Spock is seen to blow his nose.'

She had laughed. 'Jemma and Howard didn't mind.'

But Alex continued to sound riled. 'Christ. It was supposed to be relaxed and sophisticated. We couldn't even see each other.'

It had been necessary to blow out the candles after Harry had made repeated lunges for the silver candelabra. The children had finally fallen asleep at ten, after countless trips downstairs and exits by Gerry from the table for glasses of water and adjustments to the night light. Gerry struck Nina as a kind man, struggling to come to terms with what had clearly been a traumatic divorce. Over dinner he had seemed embarrassed at the interruptions from his children. 'Sorry. It's been a tough time for them.' He looked down at his plate. 'None of us saw it coming.'

Susan had chipped in: 'I think it's criminal. Gerry's ex-wife ran off with another man,' she proclaimed, seemingly oblivious to Gerry's discomfiture, 'and she still got the house and all the money.' She took a drink of wine. 'She got all the rights with none of the responsibilities.'

Privately, Nina could not see that Susan was the woman to help Gerry shoulder his parental duties. After her sister had moved back to Marlow, the dearth of single men in the town had been Susan's foremost topic of conversation. 'Everyone's married.' She had met Gerry at a Monday-night pub quiz, telephoning Nina the next day to tell her triumphantly, 'He's got a really good job and he's divorced, but his wife has the kids most of the time.' Susan's enthusiasms had a habit of fading quickly. Nina could not help but notice that over dinner Susan had ignored Gerry in favour of Howard, asking him a stream of fascinated questions about his business. She could only hope that Jemma hadn't noticed.

Now, Alex picked up his mug of coffee from his desk. He looked washed out despite his naturally tanned skin, the legacy of his Italian mother, who had named him Alessandro. The purchase of the Gloucestershire house was supposed to have provided a respite from the punishing work week. But the reality was that they had hardly been down this year and their plans to spend most of August there had been abandoned when Alex looked at his schedule of business meetings.

He had always worked hard. And she had too: painting and cleaning alongside him in the early days. There were staff to do that now and office staff – two, including his PA, Sasha. Sasha headed up the office, kept Alex's diary and featured in every late-night row between them.

In the old days it had been fun. But Alex had changed in his mid-thirties. He, and in consequence the business, had grown more serious. He had expanded the business dramatically, negotiating a new deal hard on the heels of the last, each with larger buildings and bigger loans.

And now there was Howard to consider, whom Alex had been courting for the last three months since they had hit it off on holiday in Las Vegas. On their return to the UK, Alex had taken him to dinner at his club, gambling at a London casino and in between trailed up to Howard's office in Radlett for a couple of pub lunches.

'It just makes so much more sense to involve private investors at this growth stage of the business,' Alex had explained to her. 'I'm outgrowing bank finance. The bank takes too long to make decisions. By the time I've got an answer on a loan, the building's been sold to someone else.'

Now she moved over to stand closer to Alex. Gently she said, 'Would it really be so terrible if he didn't want to invest? I mean, it's not as if you need the money.'

'No, of course not,' Alex said quickly.

'There are always alternatives. I know it takes longer, but you could just ask the bank.'

Alex's gaze had fallen out of the window onto the back garden lawn. 'Yes,' he said distractedly. 'I could always ask the bank.'

Susan reached for her glass of champagne and inhaled on a Marlboro Light before replacing both and tipping a further hefty dose of amber and lavender oil into the bath. There was a shower on her attic floor but, as she had pointed out to Nina, a bath would be so much nicer.

Nina had rolled her eyes. 'Just don't use all the hot water.'

'Definitely not. You'll never know I've been in there! Any chance of a ciggie?'

It was like staying in a luxury hotel. Alex had planned the master bathroom extension over the kitchen, incorporating the modern conveniences of marble tiling, a double vanity unit and under-floor heating. Two huge plush white towels were draped over the ceiling-height chrome towel rail and to the end of the claw-footed bath an assortment of Jo Malone bath products and candles were clustered on a small mahogany chest.

One had to concede that Alex, for all his faults, knew about property.

Beneath her she could hear the sounds of dinner preparations. Corks popping, Howard and Alex laughing and the aroma of sirloin, which Nina, abandoning the barbecue plans on account of the intermittent drizzle, had decided to casserole in a red-wine sauce for an informal kitchen supper.

Now Susan stilled herself to pick up the low hum of Howard's voice. Howard – tanned with the physique of a boxer, his hair cropped in a crew cut – had a lot to recommend him: two car dealerships, a yacht and a fat wife whom, after more than twenty years, he was surely ready to trade in? Furthermore Howard's two children were at university. And he drove a Lexus.

Howard wouldn't have got lost on the way to the Cotswold Wildlife Park or missed the exit on the way home or made them share two sandwiches in the café because it was 'a week to pay day and things are a little tight fiscally'. Howard wouldn't ask her for petrol money. Howard would have screwed her last night instead of letting a five-year-old climb into bed between them.

It would be perfect to have a joint right now, but she couldn't risk Alex detecting it. Maybe later in the garden. Sometimes Alex could be slightly scary which was why, for example with the children's sleeping arrangements, it was safer to work on Nina. Instead, Susan allowed the champagne to anaesthetise the afternoon's trip: the whining for juice, the endless trips to the lavatory, the melting ice-creams, Samantha's blister, Harry dropping The Blanket in the rain-sodden car park.

She could not quell her rapidly growing disillusion with Gerry, a man whose passive temperament she now realised she had misjudged as untapped creative genius. Why did this keep happening to her? Why did men represent themselves as one thing – in Gerry's case a man who was at least solvent – and then reveal themselves to be totally broke? Why did wonderful jobs turn into legal minefields? Why, in fact, did every man, flat, job, car and further education course start out so well only to end up in sour disappointment?

She took another gulp of champagne to head off the simultaneous depression and resentment that struck more and more frequently these days, coinciding with her move back home to her mother after the Swansea tea-room debacle. Once the environmental health officer had mentioned prosecution it had seemed prudent to move on without leaving a forwarding address.

It wasn't fair. It wasn't fair that someone should keep trying so hard and get knocked back at every turn. It wasn't deserved that at thirty-four she had nothing to her name but a bicycle, two duffel bags of clothes and the contents of her childhood bedroom. It wasn't right that she had been deprived of the basics of thirty-something life, particularly when someone like Nina – who was only two years older and who couldn't in all honesty be described as pretty or talented – had so much.

Susan now wanted with fervour all that she had spent her

twenties despising: a home, a car and a credit card. In short, she wanted a husband.

She reached forward and turned on the tap to let more near-scorching water run in. There was no point in rushing. If she got up Gerry would only want her to help put the children to bed. No. She would relax for a little longer, take her time putting up her hair and applying Nina's make-up, select something silky and clinging from Nina's wardrobe and descend the stairs just before eight. All that would be required would be to help Nina move the serving dishes onto the kitchen table, allowing her to deftly ease herself into position for dinner – next to Howard.

'Why don't you let me have him, sweetie? Then you can eat your dinner.'

Gerry cast Jemma a grateful glance. 'If you're sure.'

'Come on, Harry. Come and sit on Auntie Jemma's lap.'

Harry looked uncertain. 'Bring your blanket,' Jemma said encouragingly. 'That's right.' In response Harry, clad in Superman pyjamas, took a firm hold of it and scuttled round to her, silently lifting up his arms to be hoisted onto her lap.

'There. Isn't that nice?'

Harry was tired. He had spent the last half-hour clinging to his father and grizzling. Samantha meanwhile had circled the table in her nightdress, alternately lugging Muffin around and pulling at her father's arm. Gerry needed to get the kids into a routine. Maybe she would say something to him tomorrow. Years of childminding had taught Jemma a thing or two. But for now, the poor man needed to have a square meal and a nice glass of wine and relax a bit.

There was no childminding now. Those had been the days when Howard was just starting out. Howard had begun by repossessing cars. She would get up in the morning, pull back the curtains on the Dagenham flat and see if there was a car on the trailer. If there was, the bills would get paid that week. But Howard was good and there was usually a car. He was tough and wily and patient. After a few years the business had expanded into debt collection. Or debt management solutions as Howard called it now. Same thing – taking things off people who didn't want to give them to you. And then the first dealership, flogging second-hand cars from a dusty lot in a side road in Chingford. And then the new cars and the proper showroom on the High Street and in time the yacht chartering in Marbella and the half-share in Italian restaurants.

And all the while the other business that didn't have a name or an SA number or a UK bank account.

She pulled Harry to her and listened to the conversation around her. Alex was talking to Howard.

'People have been forecasting the collapse of the UK property market for years. But they overlook the importance that fixed interest rates play in stabilising downturns.'

'But there are some danger signs—' Howard said evenly, his eyes fixed on his plate.

Alex, who had barely touched his food, interrupted Howard. 'Yes. But any problems will be localised. That's why location is so important. London property is fail-safe.'

Jemma had noticed that Alex only really came alive when he was talking about work. He had been like that in Las Vegas, lying on the sun-lounger by the side of the pool at the Four Seasons Hotel talking on his mobile. He didn't even take Nina shopping! She wouldn't have let Howard get away with that.

Besides, as she and Howard had always known, you had to enjoy the ride while it lasted.

Opposite her, Nina was talking to Gerry. 'Are you taking the children away this summer?'

Gerry pulled a face. 'Things are a little tight … fiscally.'

'You're very welcome to come here. Next weekend we've got Alex's office staff coming down for their summer party. But after that we won't be down for weeks. Alex has meetings in London.'

Nina was all right. On holiday, after Alex had first struck up a conversation with Howard by the towel stand, the two women had fallen into a routine of having lunch by the pool while the men went off for an afternoon poker game. There, under the palm trees, waited on by tanned young men in khaki shorts and sparkling white polo shirts, they worked their way through the pool menu and too many Long Island ice teas. Nina, like Jemma, had thought it hilarious that every hour one such young man would come round with a white duster and offer to clean their sunglasses. Nina was down to earth. Not like Alex. Nina had told her about her work as a caterer, her new venture as a food writer and her plans for the garden in Gloucestershire. But she never talked about Alex's business.

It was Howard who told Jemma about that.

'He's a property developer. He wants investors for a block he's refurbishing on the edge of Putney.'

'Has he asked you for money?'

'No. But he will.'

Alex hadn't directly asked so far. But Howard, who had let Alex make all the running, had predicted he would this weekend.

She gave Harry a piece of bread roll. He stuffed it into his mouth, then brought his hand to rest on her breast. She was wearing a low-cut black crêpe dress from the Marina Rinaldi collection at Harrods. She might be heavy but she still had good boobs.

She pulled Harry close. Jemma had resigned herself to waiting for grandchildren. Jason and Elliott both wanted degrees and then MBAs. Howard had made it clear that they would have to make their own way in the world. Not that that stopped her slipping them a generous wad of cash every time they came home.

Nina was trying again with Gerry. 'And Susan tells me that you're planning a writers' workshop.'

Gerry sighed. 'It's not definite. Library health and safety regulations limit numbers and catering arrangements.'

Bloody hell! If Howard had worried about regulations they'd still be in the Dagenham flat.

She reached forward for her glass of wine, letting her eye fall on Susan. She was pretty enough if you liked her sort. Arty-looking, with her dark frizzy hair piled up in some sort of knobbly wooden clip that looked like it came from Oxfam. She had the type of skin that tanned easily, the same as Nina's, and the same dark brown eyes and good cheekbones. But whereas Jemma suspected that Susan was older than she appeared, Nina was the opposite. It had been a surprise on holiday when Nina had mentioned that she was thirty-six. Jemma had assumed she was closer to forty. Later Jemma realised that this was not because of her features or complexion but the way she dressed: longish shorts with crisp polo shirts or round-necked white T-shirts, her swimsuit a conservative black one-piece. Nina had come to say goodbye on the morning of their departure: she had flown back in sensible jeans and Tods loafers and a short-sleeved white seersucker shirt.

Susan, in contrast, dressed like a teenager going through a hippie phase: today she had skipped about in three-quarter-length olive-green linen trousers, a low-cut purple vest and leather flip flops. Tonight she had made a lot more effort. In fact she was overdressed and showing a lot of flesh in a thin-strapped pink number. Sitting next to Howard, she was hanging on his every word. When the men broke into laughter she joined in a fraction of a second late, touching Howard's arm and leaving her hand there too long.

No matter. Howard hadn't gone anywhere so far and he certainly wasn't going anywhere now. Like all couples they had had their ups and downs. And a nasty moment all those years ago with the receptionist at the Chingford showroom. Jemma had had to put her foot down over her. Howard had fallen into line, sacked her and nothing more had been said.

They had a history and it wasn't all picture-perfect. But when they got into bed at night – when Howard told her what was on his mind, when he spilt the beans and got down to the details – each knew that they could trust the other. Whatever the secrets and tales Howard spun the world, she was confident that there was nothing she didn't know about the business. Last night, as they lay in bed, he had told her all about Alex.

'He wants half a mill for Putney.'

'What?'

'He hasn't talked figures. But that's what he's going to ask for ...' Howard paused. 'Because that's what he needs. He's six months behind with the payments to Allied Bank on his central London properties. The business is sinking. He made some bad investments and the interest rate is killing him. And he spends too much. He's holding off the bank but any day now they're going to call in the loans.'

She hadn't asked him how he knew. Howard had a contact, a financial private investigator with great connections and no respect for the law, who for an envelope of cash would tell you all you needed to know about your business associate's bank accounts, credit cards and mortgage.

'So what are you going to do?'

Howard put his arms round her. 'I'm going to make him an offer. His entire business.' He began kissing the back of her neck. 'For a knock-down price.'

Susan sat on the kitchen step and watched the first rays of the dawn rise. She leaned back against the door, closed lest any smoke linger in the kitchen, and inhaled on the joint. She felt at a perfect pitch of physical and emotional wellbeing, a state all the sweeter for having been so long coming. After so long struggling and getting nowhere she reflected with elation that she could still pull it off.

Her success she put down to her ability to change plans according to circumstances, to pull triumph out of the most unpromising scenario. After dinner her plans for engaging Howard had been derailed when he had been dragged into the garden by Alex for cigars. Gerry, complaining of 'a long day', had gone to bed. She had been marooned in the living room with fat Jemma and boring Nina reminiscing about their luxury holiday in Las Vegas.

'Howard liked that Cirque du Soleil. But I made sure we got to see Céline.'

Listening to them had made her sick, the casual way they talked about spending money she could only dream of. Jemma, it was clear, liked to shop.

'You have to be careful, mind. I like to go for the classics. You can't go wrong with Louis Vuitton.'

There was more talk of the hot stone massage at the Four Seasons Spa and the merits of the different luxury malls.

'We used to go to Vegas every year. But now that Howie's got the yachts in Marbella it's more difficult to get away.'

Poor Jemma. It must be so fucking hard when you can't holiday in the USA on account of all the money you're making in Spain.

Susan had looked discontentedly around the room. Since she had last come Alex had bought a Victorian watercolour, which now hung next to the door. Over dinner he had explained that he got it from Christie's in South Kensington – which had got Howard talking about buying classic cars at auction. It had also emerged that Howard and Jemma lived in Radlett in a house with an indoor pool, a home cinema and a gym.

Nina and Alex were always buying things. The room was furnished with good antiques and big sofas. The doorway was made of old Cotswold stone and because it was from the seventeenth century you had to bend slightly to go through. The house had other old things like that: there was a wig-hole next to the huge fireplace and the flagstones were worn from hundreds of years of people treading on them.

Nina had tried to involve her in the conversation.

'Susan's spending the summer in Marlow with our family,' she explained to Jemma. 'She's got a stand at the farmers' market.'

'I'm selling soy soap and candles,' Susan explained brightly. But she didn't want to talk about living with her mother or her dead-end job or her God-awful brother. Nor did she want to be reminded that tomorrow she would have to leave this nice house, squash into the car with Gerry and go back to it all. She felt a surge of resentment. She was too old to be living in other people's houses, obeying other people's rules, eating what they allowed her to eat.

Before Wales she had been reduced to taking a nannying job, something she had sworn she would never go back to. The Phillipses lived in a five-storey house in Argyll Road off Kensington High Street. They had two children – Clemmie, who went to Norland Place and did as she was told, and Hamish, who was two and whined a lot and reminded Susan of her brother. Caro Phillips's husband was something in the City: she didn't even work. Instead Caro Phillips spent her time going to the gym, having coffee with her friends and making lists. 'We're going to be in Palm Springs for a week – it's the firm's fifty-year anniversary conference and I can't miss it. We'll be staying at the Ritz-Carlton. You'll be in sole charge while we're away. So you need to be up to speed before we go.'

The lists were mostly don'ts. don't answer the door without checking the entryphone; don't give Hamish any sugar; don't allow Clemmie more than one hour of television after homework; don't tumble-dry Clemmie's Kent & Carey silk-trim smock dress.

Susan had broken all the rules. What did Caro Phillips expect when she even told Susan what not to eat – 'Susan, that carrot cake was supposed to be kept for Sunday!'

Was it any wonder that these people couldn't keep nannies when they treated them so abysmally?

Susan half-listened to the conversation, which had moved on to London restaurants. Jemma was talking. 'I don't think you can beat Harvey Nic's Fifth Floor for lunch ...'

Susan looked from Nina to Jemma. Like Caro Phillips,

they didn't possess any special qualities that she didn't have: they weren't pretty or clever or talented. No, they had just got lucky and hooked up with the right man.

After a little while she made her excuses and retreated upstairs, only to be greeted by Gerry's open-mouthed snoring and the kids spread out across the bed. Perched on the edge, intermittently kicked by Harry, eventually she drifted off to sleep only to be woken up by the sounds of loud goodnights and the clatter of footsteps on the wooden staircase. At three o'clock she gave up trying to get back to sleep and decided to go downstairs for a joint. It was as she was coming down the stairs that she had first caught the whiff of cigar smoke from the drawing room and the sound of a glass being replaced on the table.

Howard? Or Alex? In a split second she realised that it didn't really matter.

So she had paused, retreated silently upstairs, splashed her face with water and swapped her faded nightdress for the pink silk dress discarded on the floor. But she had left off her bra and knickers.

Alex was in the drawing room. He looked up as she came in. Immediately she noticed that he looked downcast in a way that he never had before.

'Hey,' she said softly. 'Greetings, fellow insomniac!'

He lifted a hand as if in reply. She picked up Nina's Marlboro Lights from the table. 'Light?'

He leaned forward and lit her cigarette. She caught the scent of his aftershave and the aroma of cigars. She loved those mingled smells. Alex sat with a cigar and a near-empty crystal brandy glass. She picked up the bottle and refilled his glass.

And then threw him the line, 'What's happened?'

He shook his head. 'Sometimes the best laid plans go awry.'

She waited for him to say more. Sure enough after thirty seconds or so he spoke. 'Tonight I made Howard an offer.' He grimaced. 'And he made me an unexpected counter-offer.'

She had no idea what he was talking about. But that didn't matter. It was a question of validating people's feelings – she recalled that from Counselling Basics – in other words telling people what they wanted to hear.

'Alex. You are a business genius!'

He gave a hollow laugh. But she was right. Hell, Alex could pay all her bills out of petty cash.

Undaunted by Alex's grim expression as he stared into his glass, she pressed on. 'It's obvious how talented you are. Look at all you've accomplished.'

'All that I'm about to—' He stopped short. 'Sometimes holding it together can be tough.'

'Well, yes,' she said simply. 'Whoever told you it would be easy? Of course there are going to be tough times when you set out to do something exceptional. But what separates someone like you from the crowd – what makes you one in a million – is that you can pull it off.' She searched in her mind for the right metaphor. 'Any idiot can fly a plane on autopilot. What takes real skill and guts is to pull it out of a tailspin.'

She could see from the flicker in his eyes that she had caught his attention now. She took the opportunity to move over to the sofa where he was sitting. 'You just have to keep your nerve.'

She moved her hand against his shoulders. 'You're very tense.'

'I have a constant fucking headache.'

That remark was a very good sign. She could never remember Alex admitting any vulnerability before. She took the initiative, tucking her legs underneath her so that she was kneeling next to him on the sofa. She began massaging his shoulders. She could remember what to do from the Introduction to Massage Therapy course.

'It's your trapezius muscles,' she said confidently.

He didn't put up any resistance. Instead, as she worked in

silence, she felt him weaken with every minute that passed until she felt safe enough to gently unbutton his shirt and slip it from his back. They must have sat there for close to twenty minutes, in silence, Susan moving so that the inside of her thigh was pressed up close to his leg.

Softly she asked, 'Does Nina know how you feel?'

He shook his head. 'I don't want to worry her.'

She murmured in agreement. 'I think it's very noble of you to protect her. But you need someone to talk to – a sounding board. Someone to support you.'

He gave a humourless laugh. 'Are you saying I need to see a shrink?'

'No, of course not. You're not that weak type of person. You're a winner. But I think you need a friend. Someone who is on your side.'

He said nothing. She pushed her fingers up into his hair and he arched his head back with pleasure. 'Alex, you need an ally. A confidante.'

A mistress.

She took his continued silence as a sign of assent. 'And you need some pleasure in your life,' she concluded.

It was time to test him. She moved closer so that her breast was pressed against his bare back with just the thin silk of Nina's dress separating them. When he didn't resist she knew that it was time to strike.

It was ironic. The lowest three months of her life, the job she still pretended to herself she had not taken, the men who had only wanted to escort her to one place for one purpose, had taught her all she needed to know – it pays to be direct. She pulled down the straps of the dress, pressing her naked flesh to his, and eased her hand onto Alex's crotch. He was already hard. She felt the thrill of victory close at hand. Deftly she undid his belt.

'We can't,' he protested. He placed a hand on hers as if to stop her.

She ignored him. 'Alex, you need this. Let me give this to

you.' His hand relaxed but stayed in place. It was a dangerous moment. It was time to call his bluff.

So she pulled up the straps of the dress and stood up. He could not hide the dash of disappointment that crossed his face. She let him feel it. And then, standing in front of him, she slowly pulled off her dress so that she was naked. She saw his eyes fall on her full breasts, her flat stomach and then down. She saw his hunger, let him look but stood so that his hand was just out of reach. And then she dropped to her knees in front of him.

'Alex, you deserve this.'

He was lost to her now. She took his hard cock in her mouth and began teasing him, taking him to the brink but never far enough, until she could sense that he was growing angry with thwarted desire. She brought him the closest yet, almost to the point of climax and pulled away. Then, before he had a moment to think, let alone consider the consequences, she pushed him back and sat astride him. She fucked him hard and quickly, left no chance that he might have time to move or think or resist.

He came and she didn't. Afterwards, as she eased herself off him, she could see that he didn't know what to say or how to react. She did.

She handed him his shirt. 'You need to get to bed.'

He looked struck with doubt and fear.

'Shh,' she said soothingly. 'Go to bed. Go on.'

He hesitated, picked up his shirt off the floor, then placing a kiss lightly on her forehead, he departed. She stayed on the sofa, her legs up on the armrest, too intoxicated to sleep. She waited half an hour then went to roll a joint on the kitchen table.

And so it was that she was sitting on the kitchen step as dawn rose, in position overlooking the driveway, to hear the sound of tyres on the gravel and to watch as two police cars and a large black Vauxhall saloon pulled up outside the house.

Chapter 2

Detective Inspector Peter Taylor gave an appreciative nod.

'Very good. Banana bread, did you say?'

Nina was unsure of the etiquette surrounding the treatment of police officers searching one's house. But given that Inspector Peter Taylor – 'Call me Peter' – and his team had been there for three hours now, there didn't seem much alternative but to offer him coffee and cake when she made breakfast for herself.

It was another unreal element to a sequence of events that would have possessed a dreamlike quality had they not now been going on for three hours, beginning with Susan pounding on their bedroom door at just after five a.m.

'Nina! Alex! Get up. It's the police.'

Nina had shaken Alex. 'Alex, wake up. Susan's outside on the landing.'

He had looked horrified. 'Susan?'

'Yes. She says the police are downstairs.'

They had come with a warrant for the arrest of Alessandro Burnett, removed the entire contents of his office and then taken Alex himself for questioning in London.

She had seen that Alex was determined to show no emotion. He was preoccupied with trying to get hold of his solicitor. 'If Simon calls, tell him to call me straight away,' had been his parting words.

Howard had sped off in his Lexus within minutes of being alerted to the presence in the house of a joint team from the

Fraud Squad and HM Revenue and Customs. Gerry had shifted from foot to foot on the driveway.

'Perhaps, in the circumstances, it might be better if we left you to it.'

Susan had looked distraught in an excited sort of way. She had flung herself on Nina. 'If there is anything I can do. Anything at all.' And with that she had got in the car and left.

Now, Peter leaned forward in his chair towards her. 'I don't want you to be alarmed.'

'By a dawn raid in my house?' she said incredulously.

He gave an apologetic shrug. 'That's the Customs boys for you. Very keen. Personally, I'm not one for early arrivals. I'm more of a night person myself.' He took a last mouthful of cake and replaced his plate on the coffee table. 'The point is,' he continued, 'that we both want the same thing.'

This statement appeared as hugely inaccurate as the last. But she decided to hear him out. She lit a cigarette.

'Nina, it would help your husband and us if you could answer a few questions. An informal chat. All off the record,' he said with a casual wave of his hand. 'No one is accusing you of anything.'

It was hard to know what to do next. What she did know was that Alex was absolutely straight, that he would never do anything to risk the business – and that somehow Howard was involved in this whole affair. She knew that because when she had come down to the kitchen at dawn to be greeted by the sight of a policeman carrying Alex's computer to a waiting police car it was clear that Howard and Peter, talking in low voices in the corner, had met before.

If answering Peter's questions would help Alex then that was surely the right thing to do?

But first she wanted some answers. 'When am I going to see my husband?'

'As soon as you like. We can drive you to London as soon as we're finished here. We're just finishing up the paperwork.

Forms – they're the bane of modern policing,' he added with a shrug.

She felt miserably powerless. 'This is ridiculous! We're not criminals. My husband is a businessman. Not some drug dealer. How can you justify bursting in like this?'

'As I say, Customs ...'

'Oh, for God's sake!' She had had enough. 'What proof have you got that Alex has done anything wrong?' she said, her voice raised insistently.

Peter, dressed in a dark business suit and white shirt on a Sunday morning, did not miss a beat. 'Your husband came to our attention as a result of an investigation into another individual—'

'Howard,' she interrupted bitterly.

'I'm not at liberty to say,' Peter said, but blithely, as if he was making no real effort to counter her assumption. 'And when we took a closer look at your husband's business we uncovered some irregularities both in his accounts and in his SA return. Hence the involvement of Customs.'

'Irregularities?'

'Mortgage fraud. SA fraud. And your husband's considerable financial difficulties.' His matter-of-fact tone assumed that this was something she was aware of.

'He doesn't have any financial difficulties!'

'I'm talking about the arrears on the loan repayments.'

'Fraud? Arrears? There are no arrears.'

He shot her a hard appraising glance. Now he spoke more slowly. 'Nina, your husband is six months behind with his payments to his creditors. Seven months next week. That's when the main payment to Allied Bank falls due.'

She felt as though she was falling. Stunned by all that had happened, she was struggling to make any sense of it all. Random thoughts and connections flooded her mind. It was hard not to feel utterly overwhelmed. How had a weekend house party, centred on purely domestic drama, turned into a scene from a television crime series?

A thought sprang to mind. 'Why haven't you arrested Howard?'

He ignored this. Instead, he said, 'What do you know about Sasha Fleming?'

The mention of Sasha's name made her stomach turn over. 'She's Alex's PA.'

There was so much else she could say: I distrust her and suspect that she may be having an affair with my husband – all my friends have warned me – but every time I confront him he denies it so convincingly that I end up thinking I'm a jealous, paranoid wife.

She said nothing.

He prompted her. 'Sasha Fleming is responsible for keeping your husband's diary and the overall running of the office.'

'Yes.'

'She is a signatory on the business chequebook.'

The sick feeling in her stomach intensified. 'I didn't know that.'

'And this year she has made multiple five-figure deposits into a Cayman Islands bank account.'

'That's impossible. That cannot be true.'

He gave her a look that was sympathetic and all the more disturbing for it. 'Yes. It is.'

She believed him. 'Did Alex know about that?'

'What do you think?' he countered.

'I'm sure he didn't.' She held her head in her hands. 'She must have been siphoning off that money without his knowledge.'

He did not react. She could sense his scepticism.

She looked up at him. 'I know Alex. The business is the most important thing to him.' As she said this she realised how it must sound: shouldn't that be his wife? She backtracked. 'It's hard to explain.'

'Why don't you tell me?' Peter leaned forward, pulled a packet of Benson and Hedges from his pocket and raised his eyebrow as if to ask for permission to light one. She nodded.

He lit it, inhaled and sat back indicating that he had all the time in the world. 'Why don't you take your time and tell me, Nina?'

She struggled to focus, aware that whatever she said could be highly significant. Her head was swimming. How could she find the right words that would explain to this stranger all the complexities of her husband's character?

She began slowly. 'Most people go into business to make money. Why else would you? Well, in Alex's case it's the excitement of pulling it off. He doesn't actually care about spending the money he makes. It's the challenge of making the deal. Do you understand what I'm saying?'

'Yes. The thrill of the chase.'

'Exactly.' She felt encouraged by his remark. 'Don't be fooled by all this,' she said, waving her hand around the room. 'Alex doesn't care about a house in the country or what car he drives.' No, she was the one who had wanted the house. Maybe, she had reasoned, if she could get him away from the office then things between them would improve. But she wasn't about to share her thinking on that point with Peter. Instead, she paused. Peter did not prompt her.

'Alex started at the bottom. His family were working-class shopkeepers. They owned a delicatessen in Hammersmith, in King Street. His mother's Italian; his father's English. They met at the end of the war when his father was stationed in Salerno. For twenty-five years they ploughed every penny into paying off the mortgage on their shop. There were no luxuries, no private school, no foreign holidays. When I met him Alex was working in the shop.'

Nina had loved the shop, a few hundred yards from the flat she shared with two other girls at the catering college. She would call in on a Saturday morning to stock up on bread and pasta, stretching to Cerignola olives and ripe Gorgonzola when she found casual work and money was freer. Around her the conversation was largely Italian, people travelling from all around to buy there.

His mother was a permanent fixture in the shop, her wiry figure darting from the counter to the back room. Alex would look over his shoulder to see if his mother was watching.

'Something extra, just for you.'

It went on like that for weeks, the banter between them growing friendlier until one day, ignoring the queue, he slipped around to the front of the counter.

'Can I take you to dinner?'

She had liked that about him: his directness. That and his dark looks and his engaging smile. And for her part she was susceptible to a man who gave her his full and undivided attention.

Over dinner at Pizza Express on the Earls Court Road he told her more about his family.

'It wasn't easy for her,' Alex explained, describing his mother. 'She was eighteen when she arrived in England, knowing no one and hardly speaking the language. My father's family wasn't exactly welcoming. They were East End people, suspicious of foreigners.'

Alex was their only son: his mother had him when she was forty-two. They'd all but given up hope. Nina would have supposed that a late, only son born to an Italian mother would be adored. But this assumption did not take into account the character of Alex's mother.

Alex spoke as if choosing his words carefully. 'It was a big romance in Italy. But the dashing soldier she had met in Salerno was a different man back home. My father would have been happy to get a nine-to-five job. It was my mother who had the dream. She was the one who found the shop, negotiated the lease and searched out suppliers. She's had a hard life, away from her family. It's made her ...'

He did not finish the sentence.

Instead, Nina spoke. 'Do you plan to take over the shop?'

'No!' he sounded aghast. 'I'm taking classes at night school. Accounting, Business Law and Business English.'

She had hesitated. 'Did you think about going to university?'

He gave a hollow laugh. 'Yes. And my teachers wanted me to. But my mother ...' His voice trailed off. 'She needs me in the shop,' he concluded loyally. Then his tone hardened. 'But not for ever.'

In time, over walks around Kew Gardens and concerts at the Hammersmith Palais and after three months a trip to Marlow to meet her parents, he had opened up about his plans for the future. One night, walking in the summer evening in Holland Park, he had gestured for them to sit down on a park bench.

'My father owns the shop. And the three flats above.' He gave a sad smile. 'It's ironic really. It was my mother's idea to buy the shop but in those days the bank wouldn't lend to an Italian woman.'

She could tell from his serious expression that confiding this information to her was a significant step for him.

He put his arm round her. 'They're a gold mine, Nina,' he said excitedly. 'They're big flats, one on each floor.' He opened his other arm expansively. 'I want to convert them into nine bedsits and rent them out to young people who want to be a bus ride from Kensington High Street.'

She had an inkling of the possible flaw in this plan. 'What does your mother say?'

He gave an exasperated sigh. 'She says no. We have to leave them as they are.' He exhaled, looking up at the sky. 'Nina, I've studied property. There's so much potential in London. People say that the market's peaked. It's only just started!'

Over the months their relationship intensified and Alex's frustration with his situation grew. One day, over dinner with his parents at their 1930s semi in Chiswick, she witnessed the conflict at first hand.

Alex had made a passing comment about the flats. One of the tenants had given notice. 'It would be an ideal opportunity—'

His mother cut him off. Her tone was contemptuous. 'You are just a boy! What do you know about property? You would never succeed!'

Alex tried to defend himself. 'There's nothing to it. We should give notice to the other tenants, add a few dividing walls and relet the entire place. How difficult would it be?'

In her accented English, she said, 'Nine tenants! Three are too much trouble. Our business is the shop!'

His father chipped in to try to help Alex's cause. 'Reg could help him.' His father's brother Reg was a builder.

Alex's mother placed a basket of bread on the table. 'No.'

Nina wondered if it would go on like this for ever. Alex never directly criticised her. He always tried to explain away her faults, excusing her latest sharp rebuke or sarcastic put-down. But if Nina thought that meant he would take his mother's behaviour lying down she was to discover that she had underestimated Alex's ambition.

One night he turned up at her flat. 'I've left the shop,' he said simply. 'I'm going to get a job as an estate agent. Work my way up.'

And he did, walking out of the shop and his parents' house with a bag of clothes and his week's wages which his mother had thrown down at him.

'You'll be back,' she had spat at him.

Instead, he slept on a friend's floor, knocking on doors until he got a job at one of the lower-end agents.

And things might have continued like that if fate had not intervened. A year later Alex's father died. In his will he left the shop to his wife. And the three flats to his son.

Alex returned from the reading of the will ashen-faced. As he told her his voice broke.

'My father thought that I could do it. My father believed in me.'

Now, sitting with Peter, Nina's mind went back to that time. 'It was insane. We were both working full-time. I was cooking in the City by then and Alex was working crazy hours showing flats in Fulham. After a year he was the top negotiator in the office. If you wanted to view a flat at midnight on a Sunday that was fine by Alex. He'd be there waiting for you.'

Alex was intoxicating. She was swept up in his energy and vision and passion. Other men were pale imitations next to him. Most importantly, Alex had made her forget Michael. Michael Fellows, whom she believed she would always yearn for. But that was a subject, pushed deep down and buried further with every passing year, that she would never discuss.

She lit another cigarette. 'People see the trappings,' she told the policeman, 'but they don't see the years of hard work that went into acquiring them.' She thought of Howard. He and Alex were two of a kind. But it would be wiser not to point out too many comparisons between the two men.

'And then we would go to work on the flats in the evenings and at the weekends. Never once did his mother come upstairs to see. At least not when we were there. Pride, I suppose.' She paused. 'Alex proposed to me in one of the top-floor bedsits the day we finished the job.'

He had gone down on one knee. 'I've wanted to ask you for so long. But I had to do this first. I did it for us, Nina. For us.'

Their honeymoon was a long weekend in Paris travelling by coach from Victoria Station. Alex couldn't spare any more time. He was arranging to borrow money against the newly converted bedsits and he had to get back to deal with the paperwork. No one could say that she hadn't been warned of how life was to be. Alex used that money to buy a run-down house in Wandsworth Town, which he converted into three flats. Then came Ramsden Road in Balham swiftly followed by Isis Street in Southfields. The addresses were imprinted on her mind together with the memories of the long hours, the agonising waits for the bank's decision, the anxious period until the flats were let or sold. But by and large Alex preferred not to sell. Now he owned property all over London, affordable studios and one-bedroom flats, identically decorated with wood-laminate floors and cream-painted walls, all situated within a ten-minute walk of a tube or train station.

And currently there was Putney. She put that location out of her mind. It was better that Peter didn't hear more about that than he already knew. It was Alex's new venture into the luxury market, a break with the solid and successful brick-by-brick investment strategy that he had adhered to so far with such success.

Instead, she leaned forward and looked Peter hard in the eye. 'So you see, I can't believe that Alex would do anything to risk the business. It's his heart and soul. That's why I know he didn't set up this Cayman Islands account. Sasha must have done that without his knowledge. Alex would never divert money from the business. He'd pour every penny back in.'

Peter looked as though he was considering this point. 'When did his mother die?'

'Just over two years ago.' She picked up on his train of thought. 'You're saying that his mother's death provoked Alex into some change of behaviour.' Instantly, she regretted saying this, because it was true. In the months that followed his mother's death, Alex had thrown himself into his work with even greater intensity, taking on more loans, buying more property and expanding his staff. There had been awful rows.

'I can't wait for ever for a baby,' she kept telling him.

He had fobbed her off. They would have a child sometime soon when the latest deal had been done. She had been listening to the same speech for five years now.

Peter sat back and looked thoughtful. 'About the time that Sasha came to work for him?'

'Yes,' she said, hoping to disguise the hostility she felt towards the woman.

'And the SA Holdings account was opened a year later.'

'SA!' she exclaimed.

SA Holdings.

She got there before he said it. SA: Sasha and Alex.

*

SA Holdings! That was a bit cheeky!

Jemma levered herself up from the floor of the guest bedroom where she had been lying for the past hour, her ear pressed against the thin floorboards, conveniently widely spaced to allow her to listen to Nina's conversation with Inspector Taylor. She staggered slightly as she replaced the Turkish rug. Her left foot had gone to sleep and she had terrible pins and needles. She sat on the side of the bed rotating her foot.

Anyway, it had been worth it. Nina hadn't given anything away. How could she? Alex obviously didn't tell her anything. At the mention of SA Holdings there had been a few seconds of silence and then the sound of Nina bursting into tears. Inspector Taylor had ended the interview then.

'Let's leave it for now, Nina.'

Jemma hoped Nina did realise it was an interview. Informal chat, that's what he called it. There was no such thing with a copper, though to be fair this one didn't seem too bad.

Jemma sat mulling over in her mind what she had heard. Personally, she wasn't sure the SA Holdings name meant anything. If Nina was right, and this cow Sasha was nicking Alex's money, then it stood to reason Sasha would call the account something that made it seem as though Alex was involved – that would be her defence if it all went belly-up: my boss told me to do it, m'Lord.

Bursting into tears was no good. What Nina needed to do was march into Alex's office, sack Sasha and get as much money back as possible, preferably paid into an account in Nina's sole name. Sasha would have to make a deal: repay the money direct to Nina or go to prison for theft.

Jemma realised that everyone seemed to have forgotten all about her. It was safe to call Directory Enquiries for the number of a local taxi firm. As a precaution she would order it to go to their home address in Radlett. But when they got to the end of the lane she would lean forward and tell the driver that there had been a change of plan and give him the name of a small airfield in Kent. Howard was already there, the plane fuelled up and ready for take-off, waiting to whisk them away to Marbella for a month's impromptu holiday. Just long enough for Howard's lawyers to get to work and smooth things over until it was time to return home for business as usual.

Not that she was happy about it. She had been on at Howard to drop the ciggie run for months. Howard owned three yachts now, berthed in Marbella and chartered out for summer jaunts around the Med and hops across the Channel. On the Channel runs, the boxes would be quickly and quietly loaded at night-time. She was sure that this was what it was all about: Customs had caught on that he was bringing contraband cigarettes into the UK in the yachts, then selling them through the Italian restaurants and pocketing the duty. They had let him go today, which probably meant they wanted to make a deal with him: immunity from prosecution in return for the names of his Spanish contacts. As if Howard would ever make a deal like that!

'Why d'you have to do it?' she had hissed at him that morning as he hurriedly pulled on his clothes. 'We don't need the money.'

Howard had looked sheepish. 'Dunno.' Then, 'It's a nice earner, Jem. Cash.' Then he lowered his voice. 'I'm going to slip out. You stay here, see what you can find out.'

He had been the same as a kid – always up for a dare. He got a kick out of it. But it had gone far enough. She would put a stop to the cigarettes. They weren't getting any younger and she wasn't about to spend her old age visiting him in Ford Open Prison.

She got up from the bed, zipped up her Louis Vuitton Keepall 60 overnight bag and reached for her mobile.

It would all turn out OK. Howard would slip the net. Howard always had a Plan B: money in the bank for the best lawyers and a safe place to hole up until the heat was off.

Listening to Nina, though, it didn't sound as though Alex had a Plan A, let alone a Plan B.

Chapter 3

Richard's eyes were shining with excitement. 'They may just take him straight to prison.' His voice assumed an irritatingly knowledgeable tone. 'They're clamping down on white-collar crime. We watched a programme about it. And it's a good thing too,' he added sagely. 'It's about time someone stood up for the victims.'

Susan decided to reclaim centre stage. If she wasn't careful her brother, Richard, would start pontificating – ignorance of a subject had never stopped him before – watched dotingly by her mother. Then everyone would forget that she was the only one present at her mother's kitchen table in Marlow who had actually witnessed the events of that morning unfold.

'So,' she interrupted, 'I was the first person to be handed the warrant.'

She had not actually read it. She had pretended to, dashed upstairs to beat on Nina and Alex's bedroom door, then sped downstairs to wait with the police in the kitchen.

Alex had come down and read the warrant in silence. 'I'm going to call my lawyer.'

He had not even acknowledged her.

But she put that uncomfortable thought out of her mind.

Her mother got up slowly and went over to pour a cup of tea from the earthenware pot that stood on a cork mat on the chipped counter. The counter was stained brown with rings from mugs, littered with crumbs from the toaster, dusted with cat hair and scattered with junk mail, newspapers, seed packets and a stack of out-of-date telephone directories. It was a large kitchen, built on the corner of Orchard House to give views of what once had been an immaculately kept formal front garden and to the side a gravelled parking area giving way to the orchard beyond. Her parents had proudly updated it in the 1970s and seen no reason to change anything since. It showed: pale grey Formica with stainless-steel trim, a four-ring cooker and no dishwasher.

Susan had been shocked by the deterioration in her mother when she had seen her at Christmas. Her last visit home had been over a year before that. Through no fault of hers it had been difficult to make it down between times. Anne had opened the door wearing loose grey tracksuit bottoms and a large grubby white T-shirt under a man's thick plaid work shirt. Later Susan found out that her mother had taken to buying her clothes from Milletts. Her hair, which she had once taken such care of, was grey-white and needed washing; it lay lank against her scalp. Her limp, the result of a horse-riding accident years earlier, was more pronounced. And she had gained weight so that she wheezed every time she stood up.

'What do you want?' had been her words of greeting.

It was still possible, when her mother turned at a certain angle, or her features lightened for a moment, to be reminded of the beautiful woman she had once been – in the bright blue of her eyes, the well-defined cheekbones and the hint that remained of full and sensuous lips. Anne had always been made-up and carefully dressed on every public occasion. She had drawn looks of admiration from the men, sharp-eyed glances from the women and inspired pride in Archie, his arm more often than not drawing Anne close to him.

But there was much else that had been lost for ever: the hour-glass figure, the hip-swaying walk, the joie de vivre of the natural hostess. On the evenings of her parents' frequent parties, Susan, listening from upstairs, would hear their mother call out, 'Let's dance!', catch the first bars of the music and know that everyone would be preparing to follow Anne's lead.

A twenty-a-day cigarette habit had caught up with Anne in the last few years. The doctor had confidently diagnosed emphysema. Anne had equally emphatically dismissed his opinion: 'They just want to put you on pills you don't need. They get back-handers from the drug companies, you know.' Throughout their childhood their mother had been an active woman, athletic in fact. Susan's clearest memory of her mother from those days was watching from her bedroom window as Anne strode off over the fields to Fellows Farm, where she stabled her horses, sometimes not returning until the light was failing. When Anne came home, Richard would be the first to greet her, scrambling downstairs to get to her first, hungrily holding up his arms for hugs and kisses. After he had taken his fill there never seemed to be any left over. After the last, worst fall Archie had forbidden her to ride any more. And after Archie's death she barely went out at all.

The reason for the weight gain had been made clear to Susan when they had gone shopping. Her mother bought cat food, two plastic-wrapped Swiss rolls filled with bright white synthetic cream, a family pack of chocolate bourbons, two packs of frozen cod in parsley sauce and several tins of spaghetti. Her only fresh purchases had been a carton of milk and a small sliced Hovis loaf.

'There's no point in cooking just for me.'

Susan had had no idea that three years on, her stepfather Archie's death would have continued to have such a devastating effect.

Today her mother was dressed in the same white T-shirt paired with a pair of khaki shorts. Heavily she sat down. 'I'll phone Nina later.'

Another woman – a normal mother – might have run to the telephone when first told the news of her son-in-law's arrest. But Anne had never been one to cosset her children, as she put it. At least, not her two girls. And she never made telephone calls until after six o'clock. Susan had lost count of the number of times she had told her mother that the cheap rate extended all weekend. Her mother ignored her, stuck in a time warp of her own construction, her life constrained by a host of superstitions and rituals. So it was that she never ate cheese at night lest it keep her awake, never switched on the oil-fired central heating until November, never took the cats to a vet – there were four of them now, their cheap canned fishy food congealing in a dirty plastic bowl on the floor – and refused to see the GP: 'You'd be better off going to the vet. The training's longer, you know.'

Anne had also become averse to opening windows. The house stank of cats and cigarette smoke overlaid by an unidentifiable but generally unwashed smell. This was in depressing contrast to the imposing exterior of Orchard House, which was in the style of a substantial late-Victorian rectory: red brick with elegant white-looped gables, large sash windows and a grand stone entrance porch to the front door, which her mother now kept permanently locked and bolted, using instead the kitchen door. At the heart of the house was the drawing room, a high-ceilinged chamber to the rear where the two generous bay windows, accented by cushioned window seats, gave out on to the gently sloping rear lawn and the fields of Fellows Farm beyond, the farmhouse itself located in the valley. It was a house reminiscent of Victorian children's stories: of attic rooms and cavernous wardrobes, curved oak banisters and polished parquet floors, draughty bathrooms with deep white porcelain baths and bedrooms that in winter never quite got warm enough. The wide staircase, built in a broad arc, had once been the perfect foil for her mother to descend in evening dress, her hair rigidly set and lacquered, a fox-fur stole around her shoulders and long white gloves in her hand, off to the annual Rotary Dinner or the Thames Valley Law Society Christmas Dance.

Those days felt to Susan like another age.

'I thought you were keeping an eye on her,' Susan had said accusingly to Richard on the day of her arrival.

'I do,' he retorted. 'I come up every day!'

'It needs fucking fumigating in there.'

'Well get on with it.'

Christ, it was as if they were kids again, their childhood played out against a backdrop of petty fights and non-stop bickering.

It had been gratifying to see Richard's face when he had first walked into the kitchen of his mother's house six months earlier and seen Susan sitting there at the kitchen table reading the *Bucks Free Press*.

'What are you doing here?' Richard had asked suspiciously.

She had decided to play with him. 'Visiting.'

'Oh.' He sat down. 'Just for the weekend?'

'Hmm.' She had turned the pages of the newspaper. 'Maybe.' Then she had reached for the jobs section. 'Maybe longer.'

He spoke too quickly. 'What happened to the Swansea job?'

Susan had felt a surge of discomfort. In retrospect she regretted going on about it quite so much – 'It's an organic café. With a healing centre upstairs. I'm going to start off in the kitchen. But I'll also be offering complementary therapies. Wales is where I need to be right now. I need to have that spirit and energy around me – that magic!'

She chose her words carefully. 'The owner just didn't have the vision to take the place where it needed to go.'

That had been at Christmas – the cinnamon egg nog and the subsequent official investigation being the precise cause of her dismissal – and since then she had done a spell stacking shelves in Waitrose before moving onto the farmers' market.

Waitrose had been mortifying, all her old schoolfriends coming in with their designer-clad kids and peering down at her. 'Susan? Is it you?'

'Yes.' She had put on as brave a face as it was possible to do while kneeling in a Waitrose brown polyester uniform. 'Just supplementing my income. I've gone back to college,' she lied. The so-called promotion to the deli had been the final straw – serving stuck-up women half a pound of prosciutto ('I want it cut very thin; let me see a slice first') wearing a hairnet and a white mesh pork-pie hat.

At least at the farmers' market she could pretend she owned the stall.

Now Richard took up the thread of the conversation. 'And if he does go to prison he almost certainly won't get bail,' he said optimistically.

That thought had crossed Susan's mind earlier. She, just as much as Nina, wanted Alex out and about. As soon as Richard left she would call Nina for an update. But she wasn't seriously worried. Alex was a born survivor, unlike Richard. She looked across the table at her younger brother. He was going on about legal aid.

'It's not right that these fat cats get it and ordinary people don't.'

She tuned him out. He still had a baby face but it was looking worn now; at thirty he no longer had the teenage looks that he had enjoyed through his twenties. At school he had been the star cricketer, the feted fly half of the rugby team and he had set a new school record for the hundred metres. Now he was gaining weight, a beer belly was settling around his middle and his cheeks were gaining the ruddy colour of the habitual drinker. Several times, leaving her Waitrose job, she had encountered him slipping into the Crown. Richard would not age well; his round baby cheeks were already turning puffy.

No, she and Nina, the offspring of a different father, had the height and the cheekbones and a metabolism that burned fat.

'He may lose the business,' Richard concluded.

Richard would love that. He had always been jealous of Alex, the feelings growing worse after Alex had sacked him from a building job in Chiswick.

Richard had been fuming. 'Someone should have told me there were water pipes in that wall!'

It was always the same story. Richard, allegedly a builder,

41

never finished a job and regularly ended up getting sued. When he lived at home there would be endless telephone messages from annoyed clients asking when he would add the architrave or put up the guttering. She couldn't imagine that it was any different now that he was married to Kate.

But Alex wouldn't lose the business, Susan was confident of that. He couldn't. Things were finally turning her way, life was on an upward trajectory and this was her time to enjoy the good things in life that had for so long been denied her. Earlier that afternoon Gerry had dropped her off.

'See you later,' he had said nervously.

It was her birthday next week – no one wanted to be single on their birthday – and next weekend he definitely wouldn't have the kids. And he would have got paid. Besides, it would be wise to give Alex time to regroup before giving him a call.

'Yeah. Sure. I've got a really busy week at work,' she said earnestly. 'But we could go out on Saturday.'

Yes, Gerry was there for the time being.

Sasha Fleming took her crystal tumbler of San Pellegrino, drank the last few drops of water and washed and dried the glass. No wine, however tempting it may be to have just one celebratory glass, however much she would like to break her self-imposed rule.

Tonight had marked a turning point. It was so often like that: the break when it came was both unexpected and unprompted. When she had least expected it, on today of all days, Alex had whispered the words that she knew were so significant.

'Christ, I need you. I couldn't have done it without you. No one else comes close to you.'

She had felt a surge of excitement so strong she had worried that Alex, lying wrapped around her, would feel the swift beat of her heart. This was the first time that he had made a direct comparison between her and Nina. Now, replaying the afternoon in her mind, she saw how events were working to her advantage. Sasha could see how it could unfold perfectly: as the pressures on Alex grew more intense over the next few months he would rely on her all the more. There would be longer hours, the two of them alone together, and probably all the while complaints from Nina when he got home about the inevitable economies they would be forced to make. At a guess it would take three months for him to realise that he needed to leave. Maybe less, depending on how tedious Nina chose to be.

But Sasha knew it was important not to lose her head in the meantime. That was another rule: never take anything for granted.

She replaced the glass in its position in the cupboard. On one side of the cupboard were rows of six glasses arranged in a two-by-three formation: wine, tumblers, highballs, champagne and brandy. They were all hand-washed because dishwasher powder manufacturers lied when they said that their products didn't leave water marks. On the other side of the cupboard were the white china plates and bowls and the neatly stacked oval serving dishes. She liked to keep the counters bare, the black-grey marble polished with orange-oil cleaner. She had carefully tested a range of products to find the most effective. There were no unhygienic hanging utensils or copper pans to gather dust. Nor was there a bin in sight. It was hidden neatly in its own cupboard, and any rubbish was taken out at the end of the evening and pushed down the chute next to the lift, even if it was only an empty water bottle.

It would be impossible to get where she had got now without the rules. For example, there were times when the hand you were dealt was simply not worth playing. The rule in that situation was to move on: get up from the table and find another game. She had learned that with Tony. He was rich and doting and very generous – the loft was testament to that – but it was clear after the first few months that he would never leave his wife. Her condition, though debilitating and deteriorating year by year, was unfortunately not terminal, at least not for a very long time, and Tony with his Catholic background would only ever be released from his marriage by his wife's death. So Sasha had provided what he had sought – discreet relief from his sickbed marriage – and having secured a car and flat she had departed after three very happy years together.

'It's the guilt,' she told him. 'I can't live with it any longer. Your place is at home by Bridget's side.'

How could he argue with that?

Three years was a long time to play the game. Many women tried, but they were amateurs, playing it cool for the first few dates before descending into a dreary whine of demands. Take Nina. She was probably pretty good fun at the start. But look at her now, relocating City-loving Alex to the country, dragging him round garden centres and nagging him incessantly for a baby. It was clear that Alex was not the baby type. You only had to listen to him talk about his hard-nosed mother!

If women wilfully refused to face facts then they only had themselves to blame for the consequences. That was another essential rule: play the hand you're dealt. Instead women wheedled and blackmailed and tried to cheat the odds – he'll love the baby when it arrives – only to be terribly shocked and wounded when he walks out two or five or ten years later to have some bloody fun. Then they cried and spat and had breakdowns, bitching to their fat-faced girlfriends over bottles of Sainsbury's plonk about the woman who had stolen their husband. Stolen? Really? Did she walk into your home, wrap him up and pack him up in a box? No, I didn't think so. I think you'll find that he packed his own bag and called a taxi all by himself.

She walked back into the bedroom to pick up her gym bag. Like the rest of the flat it had plain white walls but here she had introduced a little texture: a brown suede headboard, vertical bamboo-coloured blinds and Indonesian hardwood bedside tables. But the sheets could only ever be white 800-thread-count Egyptian cotton from Harrods and the floor was the same limed oak that had been laid throughout the flat: rugs and carpets were disgustingly unhygienic. Sasha straightened the bed. She could smell Alex on the disarray of sheets where he had lain moments earlier. She could climb on there and wrap them round her. But instead she plumped up the pillows and replaced the white Jacquard bedspread.

Alex had arrived unannounced that afternoon. It had been hard, after he buzzed the intercom, not to open the door of the flat and rush to greet him as he emerged from the lift. But she had resisted, waited for him to ring on the doorbell of the flat itself and opened the door with a suitably blank expression as if he was only one of a host of possible callers on a Sunday afternoon.

'Alex! What a surprise!'

In response he had all but fallen on her, holding her silently with a tight passion.

She had been desperate to know what had happened, but knew better than to pepper him with questions.

'I need a shower,' had been his first words.

She had fetched him clean white towels and waited for him to seek her out where she sat in the living room, working on her laptop at the dining table in front of the picture window overlooking Tate Britain. It was a large open-plan room, sparsely furnished in leather, glass and chrome, the only colour provided by three abstract blocks of striped shades of red mounted on the wall above the sofa.

He had sat down. As he did so she caught him looking at his watch. Of course, he would only stay for a couple of hours. Nina would be expecting him back, watching the clock, fretting away. Little Miss Mouse.

'Have you got anything to eat?'

'No. Sorry. We could order something.' She never kept proper food in the house. It was too much of a temptation.

She came and sat opposite him on one of the pair of black-upholstered Andrew Martin occasional chairs.

He shook his head. But his mood once he started talking had been almost elated. 'It's a fishing expedition,' he had said confidently. 'Fucking Howard.'

'What's he done?'

He had shrugged. 'They wouldn't say exactly. But from their questions I'd guess he's smuggling booze. Or cigarettes.'

'But why did they get onto you?'

Alex waved dismissively. 'The SA bill. And seeing me with Howard. They seemed to think I had some Mafia enterprise going with Howard providing the East End connection. Kept asking me about my so-called Adriatic contacts. Howard's obviously been under police surveillance for ages. They knew all about our meetings. Dates, locations, everything.'

So they knew about her.

She did not miss a beat. 'So what's going to happen now?'

'Nothing. As long as I pay that SA bill and get up to date with the loans it'll be fine. The crucial thing is to get Putney financed. Or sold.'

She felt a rush of relief. Since he had called her from the police car – 'Simon's gone to ground; get someone' – she had worried that Alex would blame her. She was the one who had encouraged him to take bigger chances. She was the one who had urged growth and told him to let the bills look after themselves. Putney had been Alex's idea, but without her pushing him on he would never have taken the risk. She had done as Alex had requested, pulling out her address book to locate the name of one of the best criminal solicitors in London. Not the very best: she would always hold that name and number in reserve, just in case.

But he showed no signs of blaming her. Instead he had taken her hand and led her into the bedroom, pushing her onto the low bed, snatching hungrily at her clothes.

He had not spoken and so neither had she. Most men found talking a distraction. Instead, she let him lose himself in her, the sex more animalistic than it had ever been, despite the fact that they had been lovers for a year.

It was afterwards, as they lay together, that he had said it.

'Christ, I need you. I couldn't have done it without you. No one else comes close to you.'

In his voice she had heard truth and guilt and his need for her.

In response, beneath the excitement and thrill of victory, she felt something new. She felt her need for him. In the past, no matter how long it had gone on or how much she liked them, Sasha had always known that she could walk away in a heartbeat. The balance in the bank account had provided sufficient consolation. But Alex had got to her and though she did not doubt that she could, if necessary, walk away, albeit a little more slowly and with more reluctance than before, this time she didn't want to. This time she wanted to be his wife.

And so it had taken a special effort to get up from the bed first, gather up her clothes and make a very deliberate show of packing her gym bag.

He had watched her. His voice was almost petulant. 'Going out?'

'Just to the gym.'

'And the bar afterwards?'

She laughed but did not reply.

Actually, she never went to the bar on a Sunday night. There were too many divorced men drowning their sorrows after their weekend access visit with the kids. No, it would be a two-hour gym session, a stop-off at Tesco Express to stock up on water and Diet Coke. Before she knew it, it would be eleven p.m. and time to take out the rubbish, lay out her clothes for the next day, polish her shoes and pop a temazepam.

And so it would go on, but only for a little while, until it was time to make the final play.

*

Nina's initial relief at hearing Alex's key in the door of their London flat quickly turned to mounting exasperation at Alex's continued refusal to tell her what exactly was going on.

'I need a shower. Police stations make you feel grubby,' he had said curtly.

She had waited impatiently. Questions and suspicions had raged in her mind, her mood growing ever more disturbed. That afternoon, arriving back at the flat, she had taken two aspirin and laid down on the bed, her limbs heavy with exhaustion and her head throbbing. There had been no word from Alex and his mobile was switched off. But she had not been able to sleep. Instead, she had tossed and turned, the face of Sasha Fleming and flashbacks from their past encounters dominating her thoughts.

Sasha was always unfailingly polite and attentive. At the staff Christmas lunch she had sat opposite Nina and asked a series of questions about Nina's business.

'How did you get started?'

'How do you meet clients?'

'How often do you update your menus?'

But Sasha herself gave little away. She had trained at an unnamed secretarial college, worked with unspecified agencies and said that she preferred to temp because it gave her time to travel, which was apparently her passion.

Nina could not help herself. 'But this job has lasted much longer.'

It was as if Sasha had anticipated Nina's question. 'I only planned to work for Alex for three months. But with the office being so busy I've had to stay.'

She made it sound as if she was reluctant to linger anywhere.

It was the feeling that she gave off, rather than anything that she said or did, that disturbed Nina. There was something about her that was unnatural and mannered. Her appearance – severe swept-back hair, manicured nails, matching shoes and bag – was too carefully put together. When she joined in with the laughter it was forced. Her questions seemed rehearsed. And she was too cool about Alex.

'He's certainly a hard task master,' was all she would say about him.

But Nina knew that Alex had a way of getting under your skin, of turning you to his world view, of persuading even the most hard-headed person to follow him. First he had done it to her. Then over the years she had seen him do it countless times over dinner with bank executives. Most telling of all her mother, who never had a good word to say about anyone, adored him.

'My other son!' she called Alex, much to Richard's annoyance.

Nina supposed Alex possessed what would best be termed charisma. And she didn't for one moment believe that Sasha was immune to it.

Alex emerged from the bathroom after what seemed like ages and opened the fridge. 'Christ, I'm starving.'

'Didn't they give you anything to eat?'

'A sandwich.'

He took out eggs, ham and cheese and began making an omelette. In between, in silence, he opened a bottle of Burgundy and poured himself a large glass.

'Do you want one?' he said distractedly.

'Thanks.'

She was growing tired of his failure to talk. 'So what are the police going to do?'

He shrugged. 'I don't know.' He reached into the cupboard and took out a tin of smoked almonds, snacking on them as he cooked.

'Surely they said something?'

'Nope. They didn't charge me. They just asked questions.'

'About what?'

'Howard, mainly.'

She felt relief flood over her. 'I knew it! I bloody knew that he was at the bottom of all this.'

But this feeling was quickly followed by the growing resentment she harboured towards Alex for getting involved with him. 'Didn't you suspect that Howard was trouble?'

Alex snapped back, 'No. Why should I?'

She was taken aback by his tone. He seemed edgy and uncomfortable, almost as though he didn't know what to do with himself, rifling through the cupboards and banging doors.

She defended herself as evenly as she could. 'You said yourself he was a rough diamond.'

Alex turned from the hob and shot her an irritated glance. 'He's a businessman. A very successful one. You don't get to make that kind of money without cutting some corners.'

The euphemism aggravated her. 'Cutting corners! You mean acting criminally.'

He laughed. 'Oh, for God's sake.' He gestured at the news-paper. 'Do you think that everyone in the *Sunday Times* Rich List has played it by the book?'

'I think it's possible to.'

'Get real, Nina. You don't get to make serious money play-ing by the rules. You have to be creative at the edges.'

He took his plate, sat down at the table and began to eat as if the conversation between them were at an end.

She had had enough. 'Does that creativity include the SA Holdings account situated in the Cayman Islands?'

It was hugely gratifying to see the look of shock on Alex's face. 'How do you know about that?'

'Peter told me.'

'Peter?'

'Inspector Taylor.'

Alex put down his fork. 'What exactly did he tell you?'

'Everything,' she said as confidently as she could. She had already worked out that the only way she would crack Alex was to make him think she already knew. 'About all the deposits. The amounts and the dates.' She decided to take advantage of his stunned expression to press on. 'I suppose SA stands for Sasha and Alex?'

Belatedly she realised that it was the significance of these initials, more than the raid or the carrying out of their property, or the staring of the village passers-by on their way to buy the Sunday papers, that had disturbed her the most.

'Alex, you need to be honest with me. How many times have we talked about Sasha? Nothing you can say is going to convince me that there's nothing going on between you.'

He said nothing for a few moments. 'Then there's nothing I can say that will make any difference, is there?'

She felt infuriated. 'Oh, for God's sake! Do you think that I'm a complete idiot?'

'No.'

'I deserve some answers!'

'You are completely overreacting.'

'Then how do you explain yours and Sasha's initials on a bank account that you have never told me about?'

'They're not "our" initials,' he said quietly. 'There is no "our". SA stands for Salerno, my mother's birthplace. I would have called it Salerno something but I didn't want an obvious connection between me and that account. And I didn't tell you because I didn't want to put you in a position where you might have to lie about it. Perjury,' he said heavily, 'can get you sent to prison.'

She couldn't think what to say to this.

He pressed on. 'As for Sasha, I think you need to put this into perspective. First, I need a secretary. Second, she happens to be very well qualified.'

'But—'

He cut her off. 'I know. All your friends think there's something going on. Maybe they need to look more at their own lives and less at other people's.'

He took a drink of his wine and a mouthful of food. 'Look. I haven't wanted to worry you. But trust me, Nina, this is a rough patch. We're not in a ... tailspin.'

'A rough patch!'

'Yes,' he said calmly. 'It's a stormy spell but it isn't going to last. We have a solid business. Yes, there are cash-flow problems. But we can ride those out.'

'But why did you open that account?'

'As a tax shelter.'

It didn't make sense. 'But how could you open that if you were behind with the payments?'

'Because I knew that otherwise I'd have a fucking outrageous tax bill to pay on that money. It made more sense to shelter it than hand it over to the Inland Revenue. And I knew that soon I'd have the money to get up to date with the loans. And I will.'

He sounded utterly unruffled. The food and wine seemed to have calmed him down. He pushed back his kitchen chair. 'Come on. I'm knackered. Let's go and sit down.'

She followed him into the drawing room. The flat was on the third floor of a converted white porticoed house in Russell Road, W14, a location variously described by London estate agents as on the borders of Kensington High Street, Olympia or Brook Green. Alex had spotted the flat six years ago, correctly predicting that the street was on the brink of a surge in popularity as buyers were driven westwards by the soaring prices in Kensington and Notting Hill. The room was framed by two sash windows looking out on to the rooftops of Olympia.

He gestured for her to come and sit beside him. 'OK. This is the plan. First we pay the SA bill. That will get Customs off my back. My guess is that they've got bigger fish to fry than me.' He put his arm round her. 'They'll probably charge me interest and a fine but as long as I pay it they won't prosecute.' Then he hesitated. 'If we sell Gloucestershire we could use that money to get back on track with the loans.'

She had suspected that Alex would come home saying exactly this. And she had already decided on her response. She had thought about the garden and her plans for the terracing. She had remembered the fun they had had designing the kitchen, Alex drawing up the plans himself. She recalled the first time they had gone there, Nina fearing that he would hate it. But actually he had fallen in love with the golden stone and the small doorways and once he found out that he could get planning permission to extend he had gone ahead and put in an offer, waiting until it was accepted to tell her. It had seemed like a new beginning.

But what was the point in having a house with no means of paying for it? She would do anything to avoid a repetition of the events of this morning. She shuddered at how much worse it could have been. Alex might not have come home at all. She had a vision of speaking to him for an hour every other week in some noisy prison visiting room.

'Do whatever it takes,' she said simply.

He looked stunned. 'What?'

She leaned forward and ran her hands through her hair. 'I don't think there's any alternative.'

He seemed at a loss for words. 'I thought ...' His voice trailed off. 'I thought you'd say no.'

She turned to him, confused. 'Alex. Why ever would you think I wouldn't help you?'

Instead of replying he continued as if speaking to himself, 'And I thought you'd be angry if you found out about the SA bill.'

'Alex, you can always talk to me. I thought we didn't have any secrets?'

She watched as his face crumpled. She thought that he might be close to tears. He kissed her. 'Christ, I'm sorry.' He paused. 'I mean, I know how much you love that house.'

'I do,' she said heavily. 'But we have to face facts. If we can't afford it then we need to sell it.'

His voice assumed a new urgency. Now he was holding her tighter, with more passion than he had done for months. 'I promise you – I absolutely promise you – that I will get it back. If not that house then something bigger and better.'

'Don't think about that now.'

'Yes.' He sounded resolved. 'I never, ever meant to let you down.'

Then he did break down. And she held him in her arms and let him weep, awful, harsh sounds until he looked away.

His voice when he finally spoke was choked. 'I wanted to provide for you.'

'You have!' she protested, bewildered at his assessment of himself.

'No. I haven't. I've fucked up. Christ, my parents never missed a bill!'

'That was different,' she tried to reason with him. 'Things were simpler back then.' They could not tiptoe around the subject any more. 'Isn't the Putney project what's caused the problems?'

Alex shook his head. 'It's caused a short-term cash-flow problem. But it's temporary. And what's the alternative? To stay small scale, to remain at this level for ever?'

She could not understand his reasoning. 'It's not like that, Alex. The strategy you've followed has worked well for us so far.'

'It's not enough,' he said resolutely. 'I can't stay small scale all my life.'

Where had this thinking come from? 'No one's saying that you have to. But it's obvious that now is not the right time to expand. Haven't you always said that you can't buck the market? Well, look at the market. Interest rates are going up and the economy isn't in great shape. It doesn't mean that you can't do a luxury development at some time in the future. Just not now.'

She could see that she had caught his attention. 'It would feel like such a failure – selling, I mean.'

'Alex,' she said resolutely. 'It's a sensible business decision. Doing the right thing to safeguard the business isn't failure.'

Belatedly, she realised that she had underestimated the

importance of the Putney project to him, the extent to which he felt emotionally tied to its success.

She decided to try a new approach. 'You have to stand back and imagine that you were giving advice to a friend in your situation. What would you tell them to do?'

He did not hesitate. 'Pay the bills, sell Putney and go back to running the business myself.'

She sensed that it was better not to say anything in response to this, to let him consider the implications of what he had said himself.

'You're right,' he said finally.

'And who cares? It's your business; no one else has an opinion.'

After a pause he said slowly, 'I'll call the agents tomorrow first thing. At the same time I'll cut back the office staff. And at least one of the maintenance guys. If I have to I'll go back to doing it all myself.'

'You can't do it all!'

'I can do the lettings and if I'm driving round the properties I can do some of the repairs and cleaning while I'm at it.'

'I'll help you. Don't you remember how well we worked together on the shop flats?'

He nodded. 'I don't deserve you,' he said with feeling.

She had not finished. 'When you said you'd cut back on the staff, did that include Sasha?'

He sighed. 'I swear to you she has done nothing wrong. All the accounting has been done with my full knowledge ...' His voice trailed off as if to allow her to back down.

Some instinct came to her. It was like all those times in her childhood when everything seemed right but was so very wrong. She felt her resolve harden. 'Alex, Sasha needs to go.'

He hesitated. 'Very well.'

Chapter 4

Kate considered waking Richard up and then thought better of it. He would only turn over and go back to sleep or blearily ask her for a cup of tea. So she downed the last of her own cold cup and plonked Emily in front of the television.

'Mummy's going to have a very quick shower. Don't move!'

Emily, already anticipating the start of the video, pointed at the screen. 'Mummy, make it start!'

Kate could shower, dry her short layered hair and apply her make-up in twenty minutes, assuming Richard hadn't locked himself in the bathroom even though there was a cloakroom downstairs, which was another reason not to wake him. He had come to bed at three that morning, waking her as he jolted the bed, and she had never properly got back to sleep, drifting in and out of consciousness until the alarm went off at six forty-five. Then it was time to fetch Emily, get her Rice Krispies, wash and dress her and then do it all over again for herself. That left fifteen minutes to get to Dawn, her childminder, five minutes for the drop-off and barring major traffic delays she would be at her desk at eight thirty.

If Richard got up in the morning she could sleep in until seven thirty. If Richard got up he could get Emily ready, drop her at nine o'clock and thereby save them five hours' worth of childminder fees a week. It was not that Richard was a bad father. In the early days he had doted on Emily, getting up in the night to help feed and change her, proudly pushing her through the park and taking her to baby swim classes. But though he would still on occasion play attentively with her, now he was a distant and increasingly absent figure in both their lives, walking around the house in a permanently pre-occupied state of mind.

She grabbed Emily and her briefcase, reversed her small Renault out of the driveway and turned in the cul de sac of eight semi-detached houses arranged in a semi-circle. The houses, built five years ago, reflected the price of land in Marlow: narrow three-storey brick, with fake gables and PVC sash windows, small rooms and a handkerchief-sized garden all wedged together on the site of what used to be just one Edwardian villa. But they were three-bedroom houses, albeit with no garage, which allowed them an office – intended as the focus of Richard's building business and where he currently spent most of the night playing online poker and buying things they didn't need from eBay. Prior to that he had been a dedicated member of an international group of dungeons and dragons gamers, as a wizard. Half the office was taken up by racks of metal shelving containing a fraction of Richard's vinyl LP collection.

Emily was chatting in the back of the car. 'Are we shopping?'

'Later.'

'There's a red car.' Emily was proud of knowing her colours. 'There's a blue car. There's a red car ...'

At three she was incredibly talkative, but for Kate this was a cause for concern. Kate suspected that Dawn, whose postcard in the newsagent had promised 'loving home care and home-cooked meals', spent much of her time chatting in the kitchen with her sister while her three charges watched television in between being fed chicken nuggets, potato faces and Angel Delight. Was Emily's garrulousness a response to her silent days? It hadn't been such a problem in the past, when Kate had had the luxury of working part-time.

Kate had begun scanning the *Bucks Free Press* and newsagents' boards for other childminders. But then she remembered that Dawn had twenty years' experience and did genuinely provide loving home care, and that no child had ever come to harm under her roof. Kate wasn't actually sure that she wanted the array of stimulating trips and activities promised by other childcare providers: she didn't want Emily taken out in some other woman's car to go and feed the ducks in Higginson Park – exposed to the riverbank and an array of bird diseases – or worse still, the Marlow Leisure Centre swimming pool. Dawn never took them anywhere.

Emily walked up the path and Dawn, who also possessed the advantages of never oversleeping or getting ill, opened the door of her small terraced house within seconds of Kate ringing the bell.

'We'll get the paddling pool out today.'

And Dawn always smothered them in plenty of sun cream.

So Kate felt better as she drove to AdTech, situated in a glass-domed building on the Globe Industrial Estate by the Marlow bypass, where she worked as the HR manager. She needed her morning drive. It gave her time to focus on the day ahead. Today she was running the payroll programme for the month and interviewing for the post of a new delivery driver. There had been over thirty applicants. People knew that AdTech, an American software company, paid well and gave generous benefits – which was just as well. Last year, after she went full-time, it had proved necessary to change the direct debit for the mortgage so that it came directly out of her account. And this year she had closed down the joint account altogether, clearing the overdraft with her end-of-year bonus – paid in April and previously earmarked for a summer holiday.

'Why are you writing cheques if there's no money in the account?' she had yelled at Richard, waving the latest bank letter in his face.

He had looked wide-eyed with innocence. 'I was expecting the cheque for the kitchen.'

'But you can't write cheques hoping that the money will come in to cover it!'

'It'll be fine,' he said, 'I promise.'

But she had grown tired of the promises. The cheque for the kitchen had never arrived. Instead, Richard had got sued after the plumbing leaked, flooded the kitchen, ruined the laminate floor (which it turned out was not suitable for kitchen use) and additionally caused several hundred pounds' worth of damage to the flat below. Now he worked sporadically, successfully enough when he put his mind to it, but more often than not leaving some detail of the job neglected. For weeks afterwards there would be ever-more irritable telephone calls from customers and the withholding of the final payment. It would be nice to pick up the telephone without first checking the caller display.

The only stable and regular commitment in Richard's life was his daily trip to see his mother. Since Susan had arrived home six months ago these trips had grown longer in duration. When Richard wasn't setting the world to rights, Susan's arrival and its implications was his favourite topic of conversation.

'It's not a coincidence, is it?' he had said repeatedly. 'Mummy's getting older, her health isn't getting any better and hey presto Susan turns up. Like a bad penny.'

The low point had been last month when Susan had persuaded her mother to pay for the two of them to drive down to Cornwall for three days' holiday in a St Mawes bed and breakfast.

'She's just fucking freeloading!'

'Richard. Your mother needs a holiday. It's not good for her to be stuck in that house all day.'

He had looked sour. 'That's not the point. Where will it end? Soon Susan's going to expect a summer holiday and a winter trip. A cruise! I bet she'd like that. And before long she's going to have Mummy paying for the house to be done up. She's probably planning to move that Gerry in. What are the legal implications of that? It wouldn't surprise me if he claims squatters' rights – he's a surveyor after all.'

'Richard, calm down.'

'Someone has to think of the long term. There's only so much money. And it has to be split three ways.'

But it was a lot of money. Orchard House and its large gardens, situated in a prime west Marlow location, was a developer's dream: a substantial five-bedroom Victorian house complete with a detached garage block and an orchard set on two acres of ground.

And, to be accurate, Richard thought it should be split not three ways but one. He had often elaborated on his thinking.

'Nina doesn't need the money. Susan would only give it to some ashram. And I am the only legitimate heir: blood's thicker than water.'

He meant that Nina and Susan were Archie's step-daughters.

'Your father legally adopted them,' Kate pointed out.

But he was unmoved. 'Blood will out,' he declared dramatically.

These days Richard's focus on his mother's will was intensifying. Often she would see on the computer log of visited internet sites a list of names connected with wills, probate and obscure inheritance law. He was preoccupied with the fear that Nina and Susan were plotting to defraud him.

Last night, sitting in the garden after Emily had gone to bed, Richard had given her a word-by-word account of the events of the afternoon. His pleasure at Alex's arrest had been overshadowed by concern at what it might mean for his inheritance.

'If the business goes down they might ask Mummy to help them out. Alex has always had a hold over her. Christ, he could need a fortune for some top brief.'

Richard worried not only about his two sisters but also about outsiders gaining a hold over his mother. Alex – together with Michael Fellows – regularly topped the list of individuals he suspected of being likely to defraud his mother or persuade her to change her will in their favour. Sure enough, Richard followed his usual train of thought.

'Alex could even cut a deal with Fellows. Nina could engineer it. And Fellows would kill to get his hands on that land.'

She couldn't stand listening to him any longer. She got up from the table. 'Michael Fellows lives in France! He hasn't been back for years.'

But he had continued to look preoccupied.

'Richard,' she said forcefully, 'don't you think you should put it out of your mind? There's nothing to say that the money is going to come to any of you for ages. Your mother could go on for years.'

He nodded. But his gaze was far away. Kate now understood that this obsession was only going to grow as his mother got older. Richard, she had belatedly realised, was controlled by his sense of entitlement. As a child it was clear that Anne had openly favoured him and she continued to do so now he was an adult. So it was perhaps no surprise that Richard felt specially deserving of his parents' money, which Archie had accumulated over a lifetime of hard work as a respected local solicitor.

Kate's mother had tried to warn her from the early days. 'He's a mummy's boy, Kate. I hope you know what you're letting yourself in for.'

Now, with bitter hindsight, Kate realised that she hadn't had a clue. Her parents had only relented in their opposition when Richard enrolled on a law degree course. He had sounded so genuine when he explained to them his plans to join Archie's firm when he graduated.

She pulled into her allocated space in the car park. Already she was thinking ahead. If she got the payroll programme running quickly she could do the interview preparation this morning ready for the five candidates she was seeing that afternoon. That would give her an hour at lunchtime to dash to Waitrose, pick up something for dinner, throw it in the office fridge and in between times eat a sandwich in the car. She felt exhausted before she had even walked into the office. She got out of the car, locked it and entered the building. There was, after all, no alternative but to get up every day, go to work and provide for her family.

Sasha looked at Alex as he sat in his office on the first floor of the Notting Hill mews, hoping that the shock did not show on her face.

'I'm meeting with the bank tomorrow,' he told her. 'And I've arranged for three of the commercial agents to value Putney.' He reeled off their names. 'I've got the first appointment this afternoon at two o'clock.'

No, no, no! It was all Sasha could do not to kick the wall. Alex was not supposed to have done any of this. The whole point of the whole fucking plan was to prolong the financial difficulties so that he could divorce Nina when it looked as though he had no money. Not solve them overnight!

The last thing he was supposed to do was raid the Cayman Islands account. She had earmarked that as their secret running-away money. And the second-last thing he was supposed to do was sell Gloucestershire – in the divorce he was going to give that to Nina in a clean break settlement with no maintenance payable.

He was sorting it out far too quickly. As for selling Putney, that might be a good business strategy right now, but it was going to kill him later. What he needed to do was to fix the books in such a way as to maximise his debts and minimise his assets.

Didn't the man know anything?

Of course, he could be one of those husbands who, ridden by guilt, threw money at his wife to make good his escape. There were a few of them like that, though not many.

She flashed him a bright smile. 'Congratulations! I knew you'd get it all under control.'

He replied distractedly, 'I haven't got much choice. I can hardly go cap in hand to the bank for more money when I'm still officially under investigation by the police.'

She sensed that it was pointless to argue. He was turning the pages of his office diary. Instead she ladled on the praise. 'You've acted really decisively. That's just what's needed.'

Praise was Alex's weak spot. It had been simple enough to work that one out: denied all affection or appreciation from his mother, he needed it desperately.

But though he acknowledged her with a small smile his eyes were far away. She felt a growing sense of unease. An instinct, deep down, gnawed at her. Had she put too much emphasis on his words of yesterday? *I need you. I couldn't have done it without you. No one else comes close to you.*

She knew she hadn't. To compare her unfavourably with his wife was a breakthrough; there was no doubt about it. To be on the safe side it would be prudent to withdraw a little, to look around for another benefactor, to clear the exit route for a fast getaway.

But as she looked at Alex, the sun falling across his face and his clothed body still able to make her ache with desire, that instinct for survival deserted her. This time she knew she couldn't walk away.

Nina sat with her ex-business partner, Maria, in the Gloucester Road branch of Vineyard, one of a newly launched chain of casual Italian restaurants owned by the largest brewery in the country. But there were no indications, Nina noted, of corporate ownership. The walls, finished in rough plaster, were hung with old photographs and antique maps of the Italian provinces interspersed with brass lamps. The tables, small and close together, had white paper tablecloths, but good quality ones, and the staff were kitted out in black uniforms over which they wore wrap-around white aprons.

At Nina's job interview in April, Paula Nicholson, the editor, had briefed her on the concept behind *Capital Letter*.

'We launch in September. The magazine is going to be handed out free at tube stations on a Monday morning. *Capital Letter* tells commuters everything they need to know to get through the week. People are feeling the pinch. Every week the price of a paper goes up. We want to position ourselves as the magazine that's relevant to the lives of ordinary Londoners. And free.'

Paula had sat in silence scanning the three sample articles she had asked Nina to write. Nina had spent two weeks writing five hundred words each on simple children's parties, supermarket short-cut meals and how to spend an hour in the kitchen making three meals for the freezer.

'Have you done this before?'

'No.'

Paula raised an eyebrow. 'You're a natural. You've got a nice down-to-earth style. Conversational. Of course, it needs editing.'

Nina had spent hours rereading every line. But she nodded as if the point was obvious. Paula went on to ask her a few short sharp questions before apparently deciding on the spot to give her the job. But it was not the job Nina had envisaged.

'We want you to do a weekly restaurant review. And we want someone fresh who actually knows something about food. But not the la-di-da expense account places. We want to cover restaurant chains. Pizza, pasta – the kind you go to for a chit-chat with your best friend.' Paula reeled off a list of names from a typed list in front of her. 'We want to focus on value for money.'

Paula was not the chic editor of magazine clichés. She wore black trousers, the jacket hanging over the back of her office chair having been discarded in favour of a thick-knit pale blue cardigan jacket.

'It's what the magazine is all about.' Paula reached for another sheet of paper. 'Real life. We've just signed up a cab driver to do traffic tips – how to avoid the roadworks and find the shortcuts.'

Nina was thinking. 'Maybe leading up to Christmas you could do a series on cheap party entertaining.'

Paula looked pleased. 'Yep. That's the thing.' She got up. 'This is the list of restaurants. Take the first two and if we like them we'll go from there.'

Paula, beneath her mumsy exterior, was certainly decisive.

This was Nina's second review. She had taken Alex on the first one, but he had been scathing about Pronto Panini. 'It's all lousy. Just write that the chef ought to be fired.' Alex, brought up on good food since childhood, appreciated well-cooked simple meals.

So for her second review she had invited Maria in the hope that she would provide a better selection of adjectives than Alex had.

At seven o'clock, Vineyard was filling up fast.

Maria picked up the menu.

'We have to choose things that most people will order,' Nina prompted her.

Maria scanned it quickly, then put it down resignedly. 'That'll be tomato and mozzarella salad and lasagne, then.'

Nina took more time, rejecting her first choice of melon and Parma ham in favour of bruschetta al pomodoro followed by pollo della casa, chicken filled with pancetta in a cream and Marsala sauce. The waitress arrived to take their order carrying two large glasses of Pinot Grigio and a basket of ciabatta.

Maria, who seemed to be entering into the spirit of things, picked up a piece, squeezed it and took a tentative bite. 'Not bad. Hmm. Tastes almost home-made.'

Nina wrote that down.

'So, how are things?' Maria enquired.

Nina knew that 'things' meant Alex and Sasha. She leaned forward conspiratorially. 'He's agreed to sack her.'

Maria looked astounded. 'What? How did you manage that?'

'Well, the police arriving on our doorstep at dawn on Sunday seems to have concentrated his mind.'

Maria put down her bread and picked up her glass of wine. 'Police?'

'Let's just say one of Alex's new business associates wasn't quite what he seemed.' As concisely as she could she filled Maria in on Howard, Jemma and the events of Sunday.

'So last night I sat up with Alex sketching out a plan. He's agreed to sell Putney.'

'Wow! His precious baby.'

'Yep. And he's going to pay the SA bill. And he's going to cut the staff.' She paused for effect. 'Including Sasha.'

Maria raised her glass. 'Here's to the end of the Wicked Witch!'

Nina decided to leave it at that, omitting the part about the Cayman Islands account. Maria had been gunning for Sasha from the start, her bad impressions of her garnered from Nina's account of the cool, immaculately turned-out brunette who seemed to have no problem working late into the night with Alex. Maria's opinion of Sasha had worsened after she met Sasha at last year's office summer party, which Maria had catered. After that she had been vocal in urging Nina to take a stand. 'You can tell by the way she looks at him!' But then was Maria the best judge of character? Despite her petite and elfin good looks, and her good business sense, Maria had a knack for finding the most unreliable men. She was currently single, her last boyfriend having just returned to his ex-girlfriend.

'Are the police going to charge Alex?' asked Maria.

Nina shrugged. 'He doesn't seem to think so. It's Howard they're after.'

Last night Alex had been alternately scathing about Howard and angry with himself. 'I should have checked him out. It was all too good to be true.'

In fact, Alex's mood as they had talked into the night had grown unusually introspective, with the help of a good measure of a bottle of whisky. By two o'clock he had become positively philosophical. 'Maybe it's all for the best. It'll take me back to the real business. Back to what I actually enjoyed – getting out there and doing it instead of being stuck in meetings with accountants for days on end.'

He had taken her in his arms and shocked her with what he said next. 'Over the last few months, as things got heavy, I thought you might leave when you found out. That's why I didn't tell you.'

She had been almost insulted. 'Hey! I was with you at the start, remember? Why would you think I would do that?'

He shrugged. 'I don't know. I just thought you would.'

He obviously felt awful about the events of the day. He seemed almost consumed with guilt and self-loathing.

'I got so wrapped up in it all, in doing things that weren't ...' He stopped. 'Important. I should never have let things go this far.'

'Alex, stop saying that. You can catch up with the payments.'

But he continued to look bereft. 'I promise you – I swear to you – I will always look after you.' His voice faltered. 'I lost my way. But I'm going to make it up to you.'

Only when they talked about how they would work together again had his mood seemed to lift. 'We can go round again on a Sunday, like we used to do, doing the repairs. Do you remember that? You used to clean and I would fix things. Christ, I don't even know where my toolbox is!'

He had held her as if he couldn't let her go. And at the end of the evening he had said the words she had waited so long to hear.

'And we'll try for a baby.'

Maria, listening to Nina's account, looked as if she was impressed despite herself. Though she had never said anything directly, Nina knew that she didn't like Alex. Maria confined herself to the very occasional double-edged comment – 'He's a cool customer' or 'He's certainly a hard worker' – but Nina guessed that Maria thought Alex was a cold and unfeeling workaholic.

'A baby! Well, the leopard can change his spots after all.'

Maria took another mouthful of her lasagne. Nina, belatedly remembering that she was there to write an article, broke off from her chicken and picked up her pen. 'This is very rich. The sauce is too salty next to the pancetta. How's the lasagne?'

'Good sauce, too much cheese, soggy pasta. Good enough to eat after a long day in the office, but nothing gourmet.'

Maria was doing a whole lot better at this reviewing game than Alex. She and Maria had met at catering school and fallen into a partnership almost by accident when they both realised that working single-handedly on bigger jobs was becoming impossible. After eight profitable years together Maria had taken the news of Nina's departure badly. She had blamed Alex for Nina's decision to leave. 'Is it that girl Sasha who's making you do this?'

'No! Well, maybe,' Nina had admitted. But it was more than that. Alex worked all day and she worked every evening and plenty of weekends. Maria, who flitted between boyfriends, couldn't understand what it was like to go for days snatching an hour together with your husband at the end of the evening. Nina would have been a fool not to recognise that Alex's new PA was spending more time with her husband in a week than she did in a month. How would they ever find time to conceive a baby, even if Alex agreed to try?

But it was more than Sasha. The baby and thoughts of family had assumed a compelling quality. Archie's death, followed a year later by Alex's mother, had made her think more about family and less about the business that had always been her passion.

By then the success she had worked so hard for had in many ways become a burden. There were too many clients, too many casual staff and too much paperwork. She had agreed a knock-down price with Maria for her share of the business, taken a month off and gone back to picking up work that suited her: small in house lunches and a surprisingly lucrative line in upmarket children's parties: cake and shaped sandwiches for the children and canapés and wine for the mothers. It was amazing how some of them knocked it back – but very profitable.

In the weeks that followed she had shifted between relief at being free from the business and missing it terribly. Once or twice she had almost called Maria to go back. But then fate had intervened. At a City lunch she had got talking to Hal Green, the managing director of the publisher of *Capital Letter*. After raving about her chocolate soufflés he had persuaded her to sit down after the other guests had left. Over coffee he quizzed her about trends in catering and restaurants, her work experience and what she liked to cook. Then he suggested he send in her CV to Paula Nicholson.

'We need some young blood. Someone with a new perspective.'

She had never imagined she would even get an interview.

Now, as she sat swapping mouthfuls with Maria, it seemed as though things were on the turn.

'Maybe all marriages go through rough patches.'

Maria cut across her. 'The important thing is that you've seen off the threat from Sasha. It might have been just in time,' Maria added darkly.

'And at least she won't be at the party.' Alex had decided that the annual office summer party should go ahead as normal.

Maria reached into her handbag. 'Which reminds me, here's what I had in mind.' She handed Nina two typed sheets of menus. 'One for the children and the other for the adults.'

Although Alex only employed a staff of eight, the summer party included husbands, wives, partners and children. So last year they had ended up with thirty-five people brought down on a coach from London. Alex had hired entertainers and a bouncy castle. Nina had been run ragged.

'Let's hope it doesn't rain.'

And then she realised that it was the last time they would be at the house before it went up for sale.

'It's our swansong,' she said sadly. But that was surely a small price to pay for saving the business – and her marriage?

Chapter 5

Anne Carruthers waited until she heard the sound of Susan's van pulling away from the house before taking a deep breath and heaving herself out of bed. A few years ago they had had to replace the old, high, bedknobs and broomsticks bed when the mattress springs began to break through the wadding. She and Archie had gone to John Lewis in High Wycombe and been talked into buying a divan. She regretted it now; it was too low. But there was no point wasting more money and changing it.

She pulled on her summer rosebud dressing gown, a present from Archie from Caleys in Windsor. The fabric was thin and faded but she would never give it up. She needed every one of her reminders of Archie. Grasping the banister rail hard she descended the stairs. With Susan's departure the house was mercifully quiet. Anne didn't like to talk in the morning or listen to Capital Gold. First thing, all she wanted was a strong cup of tea, a cigarette and the *Daily Mail*. Susan seemed to think that she was entertaining her by providing a blow-by-blow description of her forthcoming day. Susan acted as if she was gasping for her company, as if encroaching old age had of itself changed the habits and personality traits of a lifetime, when all Anne really wanted was to be left alone.

She boiled the kettle, lit a cigarette and held on to the kitchen counter as the first inhalations reached her lungs and she began to cough. That was another reason for avoiding Susan, who, despite smoking herself, relentlessly nagged her mother to stop. On holiday, in the bed and breakfast in St Mawes, Anne had been forced to hang out of the bedroom window and get the morning coughing bout over with so as to avoid a breakfast lecture in the communal dining room.

Susan insisted that the coughing had got worse. Maybe. But it always passed so it couldn't be that important. Once it was over she took her mug of tea, sat down at the kitchen table and reached for the paper, immediately irritated by the fact that Susan had filled in three-quarters of the quick crossword. Susan's presence had its advantages – she fed the cats and emptied the kitchen bin – but a little of her second daughter had always gone a long way. That was the problem with children: once you had them you couldn't send them back.

She scanned the front page and began methodically to work her way through the paper. Around her feet, the cats circled. She liked cats. Like horses, they weren't needy or demanding. They let you be.

She turned the pages, savouring the stillness of the house, hoping that Susan would not be back from the stall until the afternoon. Susan had told her last night which market she was doing today but Anne had forgotten. Susan had always talked too much; it was impossible to remember it all. She had been exactly the same as a child: trailing her, pestering her, wanting more and more attention.

'Mummy, look at my dolls' house!'

'Mummy, come and see my tent! I made it out of my sheets.'

'Mummy, I want to do papier-mâché!'

It was always Mummy. Anne's own family said Ma or even the shudderingly common Mum, but once Anne moved into Archie's world she had faultlessly learned the language of the English upper-middle classes. So Susan had cried Mummy, Mummy, Mummy and in response Anne had fled the house. Nina was so good and quiet and Richard was – well, a boy. But Susan had been suffocating. Over the years Anne had hoped that Susan might by some psychic process one day grasp the fact that she was lucky to be alive at all, that she had been a catastrophic accident, that all Anne's carefully laid plans had been destroyed on her account. Her dream of freedom – so very close – was dashed and she was stuck in a rented High Wycombe two-up two-down terrace with that drunken fool, a man who worked for cash and lived for beer, all because of Susan's accidental conception. Never rely on a Dutch cap. She had had no choice but to turn down the BOAC air hostess job and forget the speech she had worked out in which she would ask her mother to take Nina 'for a little while'.

Anne closed up the paper and focused her mind for the climb upstairs and the slow process of washing and dressing. Richard would be over at lunchtime. They would watch the news and then the afternoon television quizzes and more likely than not he would bring a Bakewell tart or a cream horn for their tea. Richard talked, but not in a way that demanded any response from her. Richard was confident enough to just be: he was her love-child, her lucky charm, the precious child who had sealed her relationship with Archie in every way. She had made sure that his first word was Daddy. Richard had never demanded attention because from the earliest age he knew he had it, happy to let her go because he was assured that his was the face she sought first, that his little-boy hugs were the most welcome, that his mistakes and errors were the most quickly forgiven and forgotten. He would always be her baby boy, her unspoken favourite – and both of them knew it.

The Thames Valley Organic Farmers' Market, held twice a month on a Thursday, was busier than normal. But not with people buying anything from Valley Candles. The customers were, as usual, clustered around the pie stall, the cheese van and the table set up by the old bloke who sold organic straw-berries. Susan, like the fat woman in the tie-dye sundress who sold nuts and spices, was having a quiet day. Roger, the owner of Valley Candles, said that business was good around Mother's Day and through the winter with Christmas accounting for half their annual sales. Susan had no intention of being here in December to find out.

Roger was OK but always hounding her with new ideas. For an ex-hippie he was dead set on making more profit. He started the stall after he sold his High Wycombe gift shop: when it first opened thirty-odd years ago Roger's shop was the only place you could buy joss sticks in the town. Now nudging sixty, short and stout, Roger still sported a greying ponytail, wore fairtrade sweatshirts and spent the winter on an Osho retreat in India.

Instead of paying customers, child after sticky-fingered child came up to the stall where Susan was sweltering underneath the white plastic canopy to grab the tea-lights and votives laid out at the front. There was a handwritten sign: 'Please do not touch the goods – we are here to serve you!' But no one paid any attention to it.

Now a two-year-old boy with a close-cropped haircut wearing a replica Manchester United football shirt was pushing a vanilla-scented candle into his mouth. His mother snatched it from him, replacing it in the wrong box.

Another sign said that all the candles were handmade by women in Wales but Susan had seen amongst the Welsh supplies stacked in Roger's garage the occasional box marked 'Made in China'. Roger had been unapologetic. 'You have to keep the customers happy; that's the main thing.' She had said nothing. She didn't care as long as she got paid every week. Questions about the provenance of her products were another reason to avoid the other stallholders. They were all really into this local organic thing. The cheese man who had told her at length how he had left his job as a civil engineer to start Say Cheese! even had a booklet explaining how his cheeses were made. He had a creepy beard and she caught him looking at her from time to time, but at least he was useful in helping her set up the metal frame of the canopy.

It was tempting to start packing up. It was nearly eleven fifteen and the market finished at noon, but sometimes Roger popped by unexpectedly. So she sat down on the fold-up picnic chair and picked up her book.

At least she would be home in time for Nina's visit – she was planning to use the fact that it was her birthday tomorrow to ask her for a small loan. And she wanted to find out about Alex. On the telephone last Sunday when Susan had called to ask if Alex was home, Nina had been cagey.

'Yes. He's back. Everything's under control.'

And then there was the other question that Susan planned to ask Nina. Ignoring a customer, she sat back in her chair, rested her open book in her lap and went over in her mind for the umpteenth time exactly how she would phrase it.

'You're looking thin,' her father said disapprovingly, eyeing her up and down as if she were a racehorse. 'You need to get some meat on your bones.'

Sasha ignored him, beginning her weekly visit as she always did by taking a sheaf of twenty-pound notes out of her purse, folding them over and putting them in the beefeater Toby jug which stood in the centre of the green-tiled mantelpiece. There was no fire, just a two-bar electric heater.

'Put those on the table,' he said. He meant the packs of Golden Virginia rolling tobacco and Rizlas which she also brought every week, along with a bag of coins for the electric meter.

Today at least he had a window open. The curtains were drawn, though, stained yellow like the walls. Despite the heat he wore his usual slacks and a white shirt with the sleeves rolled up. She had come to his fifth-floor Feltham council flat early this afternoon, anxious to avoid an encounter with Pat, her sister, who called in every evening with shopping and asked too many questions. But she had waited until after the horse racing had finished on Channel 4. He wouldn't talk to her while that was on.

Sasha sat down in one of the two matching high-backed armchairs with narrow wooden arms and sagging cushions. She had suggested countless times that she buy him a new pair but he always refused. He didn't like change. The flat was the same as it had been since childhood. Her mother had died twenty years ago, when Sasha had been thirteen, but he still kept her hairbrush, red-bound Collins address book and handbag in his bedside cabinet.

He had the *Racing Post* and the *Daily Mirror* on the floor. These days he phoned in his bets. But he still won.

'You have to do your homework, Angie,' he always said.

Alex didn't know that her real name was Angie – she had changed it by deed poll – or that she had a sister called Pat and a brother called Keith who was a roofer and lived in Hounslow with his wife and two kids. Alex thought she was an only child and her father lived in a home on account of his Alzheimer's. That would be why he wouldn't be able to come to the wedding which, in any case, Sasha had decided would take place quickly and quietly in a register office. Not overseas, though – there would be a British marriage certificate to rely on in court if things went wrong, not some dodgy piece of paper from a Pacific island.

Her father did not have Alzheimer's. Forty years working in a bookies had provided him with ample mental exercise. Those were the days when bookies existed to take bets on horse races from men in cloth caps who smoked roll-ups.

Her father looked at her. 'What's the matter?'

'Nothing.'

'Boyfriend?'

'No.' It wasn't Alex. In fact, tomorrow they would be going out to dinner. They always did on a Friday. Alex and she had barely exchanged a word all week on account of him being out of the office.

Her father reached for a large plastic tumbler full of Lucozade. Pat was in despair at how little he ate now and had taken to filling him up on Complan and sports drinks.

He took a sip. 'You be careful,' he said.

She had not told her father, but he had guessed, that Alex was married.

'It's fine,' she said. But she felt unaccountably weary. It was as if the natural energy that had propelled her through her twenties was starting to seep away. At thirty-three she was getting the first inklings that she was growing jaded.

She knew what was coming next.

'You can always go back to the tables.'

She raised her eyebrow. 'No.'

He began to argue with her. 'It's a good living, girl. Don't knock it. People will always want to gamble. And look at a pretty woman while they're doing it.'

It was her father who had taught her how to shuffle and deal. So it had been easy with her looks to get taken on by Dauphins, an exclusive membership by invitation only casino with a five-figure joining fee and a reputation for discretion, located off Park Lane. She had been drilled in blackjack, poker and roulette for six weeks by a sixty-something bleached-blonde East End tyrant, then sent to a shop in Covent Garden and fitted for three close-fitting evening dresses. That was when she had met Kelly, a girl who had spent the last five years of her life in children's homes. They were put on six weeks' probation handing out free drinks and having passes made at them by an international clientele used to buying what they wanted.

Then she was moved to dealing and the money was particularly good, because she had a way of talking to the punters as if she really liked them, making them think she gave them luck and causing them to stay longer at her table.

'I'm not going back there. I'm too old for it.'

He laughed. 'Girls work till their forties. You've just got to look after yourself. Then you can go back of house.'

'No.' She stood up. 'I've got to go.'

Her father didn't know that she could never go back to Dauphins – it had been necessary to take a new career path.

Just because the police hadn't pressed charges didn't mean that Dauphins would have her back. In fact she had been blacklisted at every London casino. It was a small world and it would require more than a different name to work the tables again. Kelly had been afraid to meet her for a while. After a few months they had met up in Kew Gardens.

As they walked Kelly had kept looking behind her. 'God, what did you do to Sir Christopher? They had us all in. It was like that Spanish Inquisition thingy.'

She had told Kelly the whole story. Kelly was a girl like her – someone who understood that when you are close to friendless in the world, you look after the ones you've got.

Kelly had whistled. 'That policeman was steaming mad. He thought he had you good and proper.'

Kelly no longer worked at Dauphins. She had married one of the back-office boys and lived in Caterham now with her new baby. But Sasha didn't have any regrets about leaving. Tony, a Dauphins regular, had given her the loft. The casino officially forbade such relationships, but in practice turned a blind eye. And after she broke up with Tony, Sir Christopher had provided her with working capital. Not willingly, it was true. But capital nonetheless.

After Dauphins fired her it had been time for a new career. Like her father said, you had to do your homework. Most people met through work. And most rich men had businesses. So she got her secretarial skills up to speed, fixed some references and signed up with London's most exclusive secretarial agency off Hanover Square. After a change of name, plenty of research and a few false starts she had arrived at Alex's office. And then the game had begun for real.

She stood up, reached for her bag and kissed her father.

'See you next week. Call me if you need anything.'

He sniffed. 'I'm going over to Pat's for my dinner on Sunday.'

He meant that he wanted her to come to Sunday lunch. Pat, who took after their mother, would cook a roast.

'I've got the office party,' she lied. The party was on Saturday but on Sunday Alex would be with her. He always told Nina that he was going into the office on a Sunday afternoon to catch up on paperwork.

'Right you are.'

And then she left before he could make her feel bad, taking the stairs and walking five hundred yards to where she had parked her black 3-series BMW on the main road, safely off the estate. Her father was the only person in the world who could do that. So she pushed any guilty thoughts out of her mind. It was only six o'clock. Still time to get into the West End for late-night Thursday shopping. She had already bought her dress for Saturday's party: a floaty jade Alice Temperley number with a plunging neckline that would knock Alex dead. Next to that dress, Nina, who wore capris last year, would look like a librarian. But it might be as well to get something new for tomorrow night as well. Something tight and low cut that would make Alex utterly miserable at the thought of having to leave her bed in the morning and head to Gloucestershire.

Kate reviewed her shortlist of five candidates for a second interview. The front runner was a local man who had been doing an identical job for five years until the Japanese firm he worked for relocated to Norwich.

'I can't move,' he had explained. 'My daughter's just coming up to GCSEs.'

The second choice was well qualified but had a patchy work history. Two others would be competent but no more. And then there was Daniel, who shouldn't be on the list at all.

She sat with her pen poised, ready to put the cross by his name that indicated the sending of a rejection letter. She was in no rush to leave work. The days of clock-watching to go home were long gone. Now, if she did leave early, she collected Emily and went to the park with her. There was only so much of a long evening in her husband's company that she could take.

Last night she had arrived home, holding Emily with one hand and carrying two bags of shopping in the other, to find Richard standing in a scattered mass of metal parts, discarded cardboard packaging and bubble wrap strewn across the floor.

'It's a mitre guillotine,' he explained. 'I ordered it online.'

'A mitre guillotine,' she repeated, confused. As he unwrapped the package, an invoice slip floated to the ground. She picked it up and looked at the total. 'What?'

'Relax. It's an investment. It'll pay for itself in no time.'

'How?'

He sighed. 'Picture framing. I told you.'

She had no recollection of him telling her anything. She looked at the sink. A frying pan, plate and several mugs were piled up.

'It was Mummy's idea. People always want pictures framed. And Susan said that if I framed some prints she could sell them on the stall.'

'That's after you've bought the prints, the mounting and the lengths of frame?'

'You have to speculate to accumulate.'

She had had enough. 'You have to work. What's wrong with going and getting building work? You already have the tools for that.'

Just in time she resisted pointing out that if he hadn't dropped out of college he would have a law degree by now. That would have been unfair: the law degree had been Anne's idea, an essential part of her long-held plan to get Richard to follow in Archie's footsteps. At family gatherings Kate had observed Richard trying to look and sound enthusiastic about it while at home there had been endless late nights of studying. But at the end of the summer term she had come home to find Richard sitting silently in the living room.

He had looked up at her, his expression defeated. 'I failed the first-year exams.'

She touched his shoulder. 'You'll pass the resits!'

He shook his head. 'Kate, I hate it at college. Half the time I haven't got a bloody clue what the lecturer's talking about.' His eye fell on the photograph of his school's first-eleven cricket team, which Richard had captained in his final year. 'I never was any good at exams.'

He gestured to the results letter on the coffee table. 'Susan's going to have a good laugh about this.' He turned to her anxiously. 'And what the hell am I going to tell my mother?'

Between them, they had formulated a plan. Anne would be told that his studies would be postponed and in the meantime he would carry on with the building business. Only that too had turned sour.

Now, Kate watched as Richard continued to unpack the mitre kit. 'The bottom's dropped out of the building trade. People want everything cut price. It's migrant workers.' These days Richard always found someone to blame. 'Framing's much better. I can work from home and I'd get paid up front. Virtually no outlay and no bad debts.'

'Richard, we can't go on like this.'

He ignored her, swearing as a piece that he was trying to fix came loose and bounced on the floor. 'Fuck!'

Emily, playing on the floor, looked up.

'Richard!'

He was distracted by trying to wedge a piece into another. 'Blasted thing doesn't fit.'

She looked through the packaging on the floor for the assembly instructions. Quickly she scanned them. 'It's upside down.'

'Oh. They should make that clear.'

Not for the first time recently it struck her that life as a single parent would be easier. She was already paying the mortgage and most of the bills. If Richard was gone she had a suspicion that her parents would be more willing to pitch in and help. And there would be no bad debts, no more awkward telephone calls and no knot of fear in her stomach when she opened the Visa bill at the end of the month.

'It'll get better,' he said reassuringly every time she raised the subject of their finances. 'I promise.' Sometimes, after they had had a particularly nasty row, he would come home with some cash and press it into her hand. 'I got some paving work.' And he always seemed to have cash for petrol, a lottery ticket and a trip down the pub.

She didn't believe it really would get better. It had taken her a little while to work it out. But now she timed the beginnings of their problems from the date of Richard's father's death. Archie had been Richard's guardian angel. When Anne had threatened to overwhelm him, Archie had restrained her. When Richard dropped the ball, his father had been there to catch it. How many letters had Archie written, how many writs had he defended, how many idiotic schemes had he dissuaded his son from pursuing? Plenty. And now that Archie was gone, she was left to fill that role.

Richard had eventually got the mitre kit assembled, carting it off into their small living room, where it lay in the middle of the floor. Today he was off to buy more supplies.

In her office she scanned the list again, pen in hand. Daniel Lovell had arrived at his interview wearing jeans, a loose-cut polo shirt and brown suede Converse trainers. But that was not so bad. Actually, to be fair, this represented an effort on his part because, as he explained, he had just returned from a year teaching sailing in New Zealand. A graduate of Bristol University, where he had studied zoology, he had a clean driver's licence and wanted a day job while he studied at night.

'It's time to get serious about my career,' he had explained. 'I'm doing a part-time masters at Wycombe College. The programme's designed for people who are working.'

She had looked at his CV. He had held one job in New Zealand, for which his employers had provided a glowing reference. He was reliable, a self-starter and able to see a job through without any supervision. In other words the exact opposite of her husband.

Ordinarily, knowing that he would not stay beyond a couple of years, and maybe less if his studies became too time-consuming, she would have sent him the standard rejection letter. But now she thought of reasons to keep him. He was intelligent and charming, with a warm manner. Customers would like him. He had a great tan and an outdoors athletic figure. He had been the last candidate on her list, so they had ended up talking for an hour about things other than the delivery route, inventory requirements and pay and conditions. Instead they discussed growing up in Marlow, the fact that they had never met but had so many people in common, how they both learned as children to sail lasers on the Thames and last night's television.

Perhaps she should call and check the situation with the other candidates before rejecting him? It might be prudent to have a stand-by candidate.

The first and second choice candidates were eager and available. But the third choice had been offered another job. That settled it. She picked up the telephone and dialled the number of the Bourne End house, a couple of miles down the river from Marlow, which he was sharing with friends.

'Daniel. It's Kate Carruthers from AdTech. I'm phoning to ask you to come for a second interview.'

'Great! Thanks.' He sounded genuinely pleased. 'When do you want me to come in?'

She looked at her diary. 'Four thirty tomorrow?' The last appointment of the day.

Chapter 6

'I'll try to get the five fifteen,' Alex said. 'We can go out to dinner.'

He put the last of the party supplies in the boot of Nina's car. He didn't seem to be able to do enough for her. He had carried out their overnight bags, the party bags for the children, Muffin's basket and Susan's birthday present of a Jo Malone gift basket – which seemed a good choice given how much of Nina's bath oil she'd used last weekend.

'Drive carefully.'

Nina pulled out onto High Street Kensington and headed west for the M4. She was travelling to Gloucestershire via Marlow, calling in to see her mother and drop off Susan's present.

Since the events of last Sunday Alex had been a changed man. They had eaten together every night, bar the evening of her restaurant review. Twice he came home with flowers. He had displayed more interest in her work than he had done for ages. He had even asked to read the first draft of her Vineyard piece for *Capital Letter*. And most surprisingly of all they had made love with a new enthusiasm. She had been shocked to realise how cursory their lovemaking had become in the last year: quick, often drunken exchanges reserved for a Saturday night. But now Alex touched her with a new appreciation for her body, his lovemaking attentive.

It was as it had always been with Alex: he made love in a way that was deliberate and practised, as if he was slightly self-conscious, never quite letting himself go completely. But she

84

had grown used to that now. In the early days Nina thought that in time Alex would relax totally, that it would be as it had been with Michael, but that had never happened. Alex had refused outright to talk about it and in time she had dropped the subject, accepting that his reserve was an intrinsic part of his character and that he was almost certainly incapable of change.

It was one of the compromises necessary for a good marriage, one that was undoubtedly successful – mutually supportive, companionable and secure.

The only cloud on the horizon was Sasha.

They had almost had a row when Nina found out that Alex had not, as she had assumed he would, gone into the office on Monday morning and sacked her.

'I can't,' he said and his voice seemed genuine enough. 'She's the only one who knows all the computer stuff inside out.'

'What about Harriet?' Harriet was the office assistant.

'Harriet needs constant supervision. And she's careless. Sasha never makes a mistake on the figures.' He went on to explain how they were raising the rents of everyone who had not had an increase for eighteen months. 'Sasha needs to run the programme that generates the notice of a rent increase.'

'But how long will that take?' Nina persisted.

'All this week. And then I need her for the day of the party to come down on the coach with them. Left to their own devices they'll probably end up in Birmingham.'

It was an uncomfortable truth to see how much Alex had come to rely on Sasha. Nina had listened as Alex explained how she ran all the computer programmes, signed off on all the tenancies, administered the payroll and was the informal head of the office.

'Anyway,' he said tersely, 'I can't sack anyone till after the party. It'll put a damper on the whole thing if I do.'

It was a fair point. Alex had already decided to fire half

the staff: one from the office, one girl who did lettings, one handyman – and Sasha.

So there seemed no alternative but to continue as they were until after the weekend.

Nina arrived in Marlow and pulled into the Orchard House driveway. Richard's van was parked outside the front door. Didn't he have any work to do? She pulled up behind him and walked round to the back door, Muffin running excitedly by her side.

The garden was unkempt. The once lush beds on either side of the front door were overgrown with weeds, where formerly dense lavender and hardy scarlet fuchsias had jostled for space. The grass was overtaken with dandelions, and thistles dotted the dusty driveway. As children they had scrunched through thick, raked gravel. It was depressing to see the deterioration: the garden had been magnificent, Archie's passion. The driveway was still lined with Grace de Monaco rose bushes bearing pale pink fragrant blooms, but their once glossy leaves were speckled and they were growing ragged in shape.

She turned the corner and saw her mother and Richard sitting in deckchairs on the back lawn.

Her mother looked up. 'I was expecting you an hour earlier.'

'Sorry. Awful traffic.' Nina leaned over and kissed her mother on the cheek. 'I brought you these.' She handed her mother a tied arrangement of Acapulco lilies, cream roses and eucalyptus.

She raised a flicker of a smile. Richard had said nothing. 'Hello,' she said brightly.

He raised his hand in greeting. 'Hi.'

He did not offer to get her a chair.

Nina took the flowers back from her mother. 'I'll put those in water.' She stepped into the kitchen, searching for a vase, finally locating one in the under-sink cupboard. It was chock-a-block with empty containers of cleaning supplies and ancient Scotch-brite sponges. The kitchen was a sight. A pile of washing-up lay in the sink; the table was covered with newspapers; and the floor, plastered with cat paw prints, looked as though it hadn't been washed for weeks. When Archie was alive her mother had kept the house immaculately clean. Probably this was down to Mrs Baxter. But her mother had sacked her, along with Jim, who helped in the garden. Simultaneously she had dropped her membership of the Lawn Bowls League, the Women's Institute and the Round Table Club of which Archie was a past president.

She took the flowers to the drawing room and placed them on the Victorian oak card table to the side of one of the pair of chintz sofas. A mahogany sideboard stood along the wall facing the two bay windows, a pair of giltwood green and gold striped Louis chairs to each side, and at the far end of the room was Archie's pride and joy, the French walnut escritoire. It was all good furniture, now covered with a layer of dust. The room still had the power to impress, but the air of neglect was unmistakable. It was hard to believe there had once been parties in this room, the women in cocktail dresses, the men laughing too loud, everyone smoking – and Jack Tyler's white Rolls Royce parked on the driveway outside, the engine starting up at three or four o'clock in the morning. Jack was the local colour, a tycoon with a taste for all the good things in life. His voice was always the loudest. Nina would be woken up by noisy goodbyes and the slam of car doors, in the years when no disgrace was attached to driving drunk. Mrs Baxter would purse her lips the next day, emptying the ashtrays of cigar ends, saying under her breath that Jack Tyler was a bad penny. There was a time when Nina had come to agree bitterly with Mrs Baxter's assessment, almost hating Jack for the influence he had wielded over Michael. If Michael hadn't gone to work for Jack during that last summer, who knows how things might have turned out?

Over it all hung the painting of Monty, commissioned by Archie. He had been painted in a formal style, unsaddled, against a stylised background of green pasture and oaks. Anne had taught all her children to ride, but none had her talent or enthusiasm. Nina knew that she was merely competent while Susan was a liability and Richard had no interest. None of them had ever been allowed on Monty, a seventeen-hand stallion sired from a racing line with the speed and temperament to match.

Those had been the days when her mother had spent most of her time out of the house, tending Monty or riding at point to points. Not hunting, though. They weren't her crowd, she used to say.

Nina took a moment to pick up the messy pile of newspapers from the floor and straightened the squashed sofa cushions. As she stood up she regarded the neat brick of Fellows Farm in the distance. She tried to pop in to see Edward Fellows at least a couple of times a year. But not today. He was in hospital receiving his latest round of chemotherapy and she knew he was not the type of man to receive visitors in a weakened and vulnerable state.

It was hard to believe that he had cancer: at Christmas, when she had last seen him, he looked as vigorous as ever, six foot and thickset with a farmer's colouring. He was still working: ploughing and harvesting and doing all the paperwork, though he had been forced to employ a farm manager and two labourers.

The manager was by all accounts perfectly competent, but this did not stop Edward sounding off. 'Man's a bloody idiot. He must be – who goes to college to learn about farming?'

They had been sitting, as they always did, in the kitchen. It was unchanged from when Nina had visited as a child: the Rayburn in the old chimney breast, the oak tabletop scrubbed hard over the years so that it was near-white, the linoleum patched and lifting at the edges. He passed her a strong cup of tea, pausing to put three spoonfuls of sugar in his own.

She knew what was coming next.

'The only way to learn is to get out there and do it.' He

gestured out of the window. The farm stretched towards Henley, one of the largest and, thanks to Edward, the most profitable in the area. Every year there were ever higher offers from developers, but he sent each of them away saying that they'd have to come up with a damned sight better offer than that. He looked out of the window at a tractor on the horizon. 'That's what my son should be doing.'

It used to hurt her when he talked this way. For the first few years after Michael left she had avoided Edward and the farm altogether, even after she had married Alex. Because of course, that was what she had thought, too.

'He's still in France?' she prompted him.

'Yes. Wants me to go over.'

'Oh.' She could not conceal the surprise in her voice. The rift between father and son had gone on for so long now that she thought it would never end. Michael had last come over for his mother's funeral, staying a few days and then departing abruptly. She had mentioned the funeral to Alex. 'I don't want you to go,' had been his reply, his tone vexed. Any mention of Michael or his family had that effect on Alex.

'I'm not going to France,' Edward said stubbornly. 'He needs to come here.'

Perhaps then the rift would go on for ever. Edward had never forgiven Michael's decision to leave. It was always the same. Sure enough, his features hardened. 'How can I approve of it? He's abandoned his parents, his duty and the land that's been in this family for generations.'

But that day there was an unexpected follow-up. He looked across at her and said, apparently casually, 'Maybe you could speak to him?'

'Me?' She was caught off guard.

'Yes. You are the best daughter-in-law I never had.'

She had blushed at that, known that it had been his dream to hand the farm on to her and Michael – and also known that the time for dreams was gone.

So she had changed the subject and it was only afterwards

that she wondered if he might have had some inkling that he was ill and that the knowledge had made him mellow a little.

She had not contacted Michael. She didn't have his number. She knew only that he lived and worked in the south of France. If she went on the internet she could track him down – his photographs were widely published – but instinct told her that this would be unwise. Instead, when her mother had called to tell her the news about Edward's illness, she had sent flowers and a card to Edward promising to visit as soon as he was home.

Her mother had been sombre. 'It's in his stomach,' she said flatly. More depressing medical detail had followed. Then, 'I expect Michael will come home now.'

Nina had said nothing to that.

'We're all on our way out,' her mother had concluded. 'Archie, Jack and now Edward. Then it'll be me.'

'Mummy!'

Her mother needed to get out more. Briskly Nina pulled her mind back to the task at hand. She went out into the garden.

'I thought we could go to lunch at Burgers,' she said brightly, carrying out her chair and hoping it was clear that the invitation was directed solely to her mother.

Her mother sniffed. 'Friday will be packed in Marlow. You'll never park.'

'And you'll have to queue,' added Richard.

Nina persisted. 'We could get a cake for Susan.'

'If you want to,' said her mother doubtfully. 'I suppose you want me to get changed.'

She did, actually. Her mother looked down-at-heel in an unironed golf shirt and shorts. When had she taken to wearing these scruffy clothes? Muffin was sniffing at her mother's feet, but she ignored him. Her mother liked cats and all through their childhood their pleas for a dog had been refused.

There was an awkward silence.

'How's Kate?' Nina asked Richard. 'And Emily?'

'I never see her. She's always at the office. They take advantage of her.' He seemed reluctant to say more. Then, 'So how's the police investigation going?'

Nina had wondered how long it would take for the subject to come up.

One of the reasons that she had married Alex, though she had not recognised it at the time, was that he was an inherently optimistic person. In every situation, Alex would look for the best. Her family, on the other hand, were determinedly downbeat. She could remember as a child her mother reading the *Bucks Free Press*, occasionally commenting happily on some bad piece of news: a neighbour's son caught for drink driving or the closure of a local business. She even read the legal notices of bankruptcy.

'It was all a misunderstanding. One of Alex's business associates was doing something he shouldn't have been and Alex got caught up in the net.'

'What was he doing?' asked her mother.

'So they're telling you he's in the clear?' said Richard, speaking at the same time.

'Yes.'

Richard shook his head. 'You have to be careful with that. The police lead you on, hoping to lure you into a false sense of security. Then you let something slip and before you know it you're banged up. Look at all these innocent people in jail. It can take you years to get out.'

'Most of them are guilty,' cut in her mother. 'They're too soft on them.'

'And that's if they get out at all,' Richard continued.

'Alex is not going to prison!' exclaimed Nina.

Richard nodded as if in reluctant agreement. 'Let's hope not.'

'Anyhow, we're having the office summer party tomorrow,' she reminded them, hoping to change the subject.

Richard gave a whistle of surprise. 'So you're going ahead with that. Wow, Alex has got some guts,' he said, shaking his head. 'I would have thought he'd want to keep a low profile.'

It was impossible not to respond. 'Richard! Alex has done nothing wrong.'

'I'm sure. Still, sometimes it pays to be discreet.'

It was infuriating. What did her brother know about discretion? Richard – who since he turned eighteen had never been able to get paid without splurging his money on a set of wheels for his car, some stupid piece of clothing and rounds of drinks for his idiotic friends in the pub. Richard – who had lost more than one building job by boasting loudly to anyone who would listen about a nice little earner he had just quoted for, only to find that some so-called friend had tipped off a relative with the result that the job was swiped from under his nose. Richard – who had on several occasions badgered their father to show him the contents of his will, complaining later to Nina that the old man was being fucking unreasonable and he had a right to know.

Richard was still talking. 'I expect you're wishing you hadn't taken that Las Vegas trip. You might need the money for a fancy lawyer.'

It was so tempting to ask Richard what had happened to his plans to become a lawyer himself. There had been a big flurry at the time: piles of books were purchased and announcements made about how they would all have to allow him undisturbed study time.

Now Nina restrained herself and instead turned to her mother. 'Why don't you get changed and we'll get off?'

Her mother got up. As she did so the sound of a car could be heard.

'Susan,' her mother explained. 'Her boss lets her use the van.'

'She has to put the petrol in,' Richard added. 'He doesn't pay for that.'

A car door slammed shut and Susan rounded the corner. She greeted Nina with delight, embracing her with a warmth that was slightly disconcerting.

Richard looked up. 'You're just in time. Nina's taking us all to lunch at Burgers.'

'Actually ...'

'Fabulous!' said Susan. 'A birthday treat! That is the nicest thing. Thanks!'

Nina had intended to have a talk to her mother, at the end of which she was hoping to persuade her to go and see the GP. The more she thought about it, the more she was convinced that her mother was seriously depressed. She refused to go anywhere or speak to anyone except her three children. It had taken all of Nina's powers of persuasion to get her to go on holiday with Susan. As for the house, it was decaying before their eyes, a process that had begun in the last years of her father's life as the cancer took hold and had continued since. It wasn't a shortage of money. Each month a trust fund set up by her father paid a generous amount of money into her mother's bank account. But she clearly wasn't spending much of it. Nina made a mental note to speak to her about transferring the balance from her current account to a savings account.

Susan said, 'I'm starving. I have to get up at six these days.'

'Do you good,' said Richard.

'How's business?' Susan retorted.

Susan turned to Nina. 'So, you've got the office party tomorrow?'

She was surprised that Susan had remembered.

And she was even more surprised by Susan's next solicitous remark. 'I expect that's an awful lot of work. I hope you've got some help organised?'

Susan liked Burgers. It was cosy and old-fashioned. Since Nina was paying, she ordered a proper lunch: home-made quiche Lorraine and a salad and afterwards she would have a slice of chocolate ganache cake. They sat on the raised upper floor around a small, round wooden table, the ceiling beamed and the walls dotted with prints of antique serving plates and classic patisserie desserts.

Richard was talking about the price of gold. 'I'm not so sure it's peaked.'

Where did he get this stuff from? Susan had noticed that Richard watched a lot of television programmes, then came round and repeated what he had learned to their mother.

She ignored him and began talking to Nina.

'Thanks so much for my present! I love it.' She did. Nina was good at stuff like that. And in her birthday card there had been cash, too.

'So, is Gerry taking you somewhere nice for your birthday?'

She pulled a face. 'He can't make it tomorrow. He said he would.'

'Is there a problem?'

'He has to look after the children.' Susan tried to sound disappointed. 'So I'm not sure what my plans are.'

Nina did not comment.

Sometimes with Nina it paid to be direct. 'Why don't you let me come down and help you with the party?'

Nina looked surprised. 'Oh, don't worry. Maria's coming down to do the catering.'

'But what about the kids?' Susan persisted. 'I could do games with them.'

'We've got a bouncy castle.'

'Well, then you definitely need someone to supervise that. That's the last thing you want – an injured child.'

Nina was wavering. 'Wouldn't you rather spend some time with Gerry?'

'We see each other all the time,' she pressed on. 'I'd love to help. You worked so hard last weekend – you deserve a rest. This way you can sit back and enjoy the day.'

Nina sounded doubtful. 'If you're sure …'

'I'd love to!' It was settled. Gerry was scheduled to take her out to Zitti's tomorrow night, but that could be put off until next week. She had gone round to his flat last night. It was close to the industrial estate and if you opened the bedroom window you heard the constant sound of the traffic on the by-pass. She'd taken a bottle of wine and Gerry had cooked them half a bag of economy pasta twirls with a tin of tuna and a tin of tomatoes. After the ten o'clock news she'd made her excuses and left.

No, this was a much better idea. A nice ride down in the car, a hot bath and dinner with a good bottle of wine from Alex's supply. Alex would presumably come down late, but that was OK. They would have all day together on Saturday at the party – and later on.

Happily she returned to her lunch. Richard had moved on to the subject of a Bank of England interest rate increase. 'It's very bad,' he said in an expert tone. 'It could slow down the whole economy. Who knows, even push us into recession.'

'Do you think so?' asked her mother. She always listened to Richard in preference to either of her daughters. Even when he was wrong. Even when he was lying.

Susan had hated him when they were children and she still hated him now. When they were small they had all gone on holiday to Bournemouth. She was eleven and Richard was nine. It was a cool and overcast week, the beach windy and too chilly to stay all day, but the hotel had a small, kidney-shaped pool. It was early evening and the other guests had gone in to get ready for dinner. That night, though, Archie was taking them to a proper restaurant. Now, looking back, she appreciated that the Bournemouth holiday must have been dull for their father, who was a cultured and bookish man. So there were just the four of them by the pool: Archie had gone upstairs to bathe. Her mother was supervising them, lying on a sun-lounger fully clothed with her eyes closed; Nina was as usual reading a book; she and Richard were in the water.

Richard suggested that they play a game. 'I'll stand in the shallow end and you swim between my legs.'

It was fun. She was good at it. Susan was a strong swimmer,

daring and confident. They took turns. Richard was less skilled in the water.

'I'm faster!' she shouted. 'I'm faster!'

'Try again. Best of three.'

She was underwater now and as she was moving through his legs she felt them clamp hard around her body. His hand grasped the back of her one-piece swimming costume, pushing her down. She was two years older but he was strong. She began to panic. Her chest began to hurt, really hurt and she tried desperately to break free. Still he held her, for what seemed like a very long time and she thought she was going to die. Then, as if he knew it was the last second, he released her, pulling her up.

She heard his voice. 'Mummy! Mummy! Susan couldn't swim. I pulled her up.'

She was choking and spluttering. She couldn't speak. All she could do was cough, her body almost convulsing from the effort, while she took heaving, gasping breaths.

He was thumping her back hard. 'I think she tried to go too fast and took in water.'

Her mother turned to her. 'Showing off!'

'She was shouting about going faster,' Richard pointed out.

'I heard her.'

Finally, her eyes stinging and her chest aching, Susan managed to speak. 'He held me, Mummy!'

Richard's voice was louder and sounded truthful. 'I was pulling her up, but she was fighting me. That's what drowning people do. They try to pull the other person under.'

'And very selfish they are too,' her mother commented.

That night she was banned from the pool for the rest of the holiday. There was talk over dinner of telephoning the *Bucks Free Press* to get a reporter to write a story about the brave little boy who saved his elder sister. On the walk back to the hotel along the promenade Richard was rewarded for his actions with a Mr Whippy 99, turning round to grin at her as he shoved the Flake into his mouth.

Later she had told Nina the truth. 'He held me under.'

And at that moment it had meant so much that Nina had believed her. 'I know,' Nina had said sadly. 'But they won't believe us. It's too late now. Mummy was there and she's already told Daddy.'

It was just a moment. They were divided siblings. Richard was her mother's favourite and Nina was her father's. Susan had no one. It was so unfair.

Now the conversation had shifted. Nina had taken up the subject of the banks. 'That reminds me, Mummy. I wanted to ask you about your current account. You need to make sure you're earning interest on your balance. It must be quite a lot of money.'

Her mother was preoccupied with finishing her Cornish pasty. Before she could speak Richard cut in. 'The bank takes care of all that.'

But her mother talked over him. 'No they don't. You do,' she said, patting his hand. 'Richard's got all the banking set up online. That way he can monitor what the bank is doing every day. It's much safer.' She looked at him proudly.

This was news to Susan. Now she realised that in six months she had never seen a bank statement arrive in the post. She looked to Nina for guidance on how to react.

Nina's face was set hard and her voice had an edge to it. 'I see. Well, it's always a good idea to have paper statements as well. Computers can crash,' she said to her mother.

Richard spoke too quickly. 'Fine. Good idea. I'll take care of it.' As if to end the conversation he pushed back his chair and looked around for the waitress. Catching her eye he lifted his hand. Then, as if he was the one paying for the lunch, he said coolly to her, 'Shall we order pudding?'

Nina listened hard and looked at her watch. It was too early for Alex, the time just gone six o'clock. But from where she was standing at the sink washing fruit for tomorrow she could see the taxi turning in the driveway.

'He must have caught the early train.' Alex, to give him credit, was certainly making an effort to be attentive. Over the last few months he had fallen into the habit of taking the last train from London on a Friday night or, if he had a lot of paperwork to catch up with, not making it down until Saturday morning.

Susan was leaning in the centre kitchen island picking at a bowl of olives and drinking a glass of Merlot.

The kitchen door opened with a bound and Alex walked in. 'Hi!'

There was no time to warn him. He strode into the kitchen. 'God, I'm parched. I need—' There was a silence. 'Susan?'

'Hi, Alex.' Susan went up to him and embraced him warmly. 'Surprise!'

Nina hurriedly offered an explanation. 'It's Susan's birthday tomorrow and Gerry's got the kids and Susan said she wanted to help with the party, so she came down with me.'

Alex had walked over to the counter and was pouring himself a glass of wine. 'Really.'

'Yes,' Susan said. 'I was saying to Nina that she worked so hard last weekend – and I had such a nice time – and I wanted to return the favour.'

Nina was feeling increasingly uncomfortable. Alex was being very rude. She should have warned him that Susan was coming, but she hadn't had a minute to herself since lunch. First she had had to shepherd her family out of Burgers – her mother telling Richard to choose a birthday cake for Susan, which Nina paid for – then drive them back home. While Susan packed she had endured twenty minutes of Richard talking about some new idea for a picture-framing business. And then she had had Susan in the car with her on the drive to Gloucestershire talking non-stop about how awful it was living at home, her plans to teach yoga – and Richard.

'I think Richard has a very controlling personality,' Susan had said. 'Controlling and narcissistic.'

'Do you see much of him?'

Susan gave a loud sigh. 'He's there all the time. Mummy says it's because he's unhappy at home. She says it's a refuge for him.'

'From Kate?' This seemed unlikely. Kate had always struck her as the weaker one of the partnership.

'Actually Mummy says she takes advantage of him.'

'What?'

'Hmm. Mummy says that Kate's turned him into a househusband. He can't work because someone has to be at home. She's always at the office.'

Kate had never appeared domineering. If anything, she had seemed naïve and childlike. She recalled that Kate's parents had been unhappy about the whole thing.

Susan continued. 'Mummy says he should put his foot down. But he's too nice.' She gave a bitter laugh.

Nina said nothing. She understood Susan's frustration. Their mother, so sharp and unforgiving in her assessments of other people, was blinded when it came to Richard. In his case, events were always portrayed to show him in the best light – the victim of circumstance or misfortune in which no blame could be attached to him. She recalled the conversation that had taken place a few months after Archie's death when Richard revealed that he had dropped out of his muchvaunted law degree. He did not, of course, actually use those words. 'I've decided to take a sabbatical and look at other institutions.'

Her mother chipped in then. 'The tutors weren't the quality that he expected.'

Richard took up the thread. 'It isn't my fault if they set questions on topics they've barely covered! I need a more high-powered college.'

Nina had been privately furious. A pile of expensive law textbooks, no doubt paid for by Archie, lay in pristine condition on the dining-room table. She had cleared her throat. 'Wouldn't it be better to stay put and make a go of it where you are? You've already paid the fees and enrolled there.' As she said this she realised that Archie had doubtless paid the fees, as well. 'Who's to say that another college is going to be any different?'

Richard had shaken his head. 'Not a good strategy, Nina. That's like throwing good money after bad.' He had turned back to their mother. 'The firm is too important to take any chances with.'

Her mother had nodded in agreement. But three years later he had yet to enrol elsewhere and all talk of Richard joining Carruthers & Kirkpatrick had been forgotten. Nowadays when she looked at Richard, Nina saw the face of a disappointed man, a boy spoiled from birth who was in consequence a man still struggling to find his place in the world.

But Susan continued to rail at the unfairness of it all. 'He says he works, but I don't believe him. I think he's down the pub every day.'

There was much more of the same followed by an update on Gerry.

'He's decided to go in for this BBC competition. You have to be an unpublished writer and you submit an idea for a six-part series plus the whole first episode. It's going to take him ages.' Susan sounded resentful about this.

Then it was on to the subjects of Gerry's spoiled children, her overtime issues with Roger at Valley Candles and her money problems. 'It's so fucking unfair. The landlord in Swansea won't give me my deposit back. There's no way it could cost that much to replace a bit of carpet. It was one tiny cigarette burn!'

By the time they arrived in Gloucestershire, Nina felt drained. Every time she saw her family she told herself it would be different. And on every occasion it was exactly the same mix of tense exchanges, bickering and point-scoring. Leaving Susan in the guestroom she had disappeared up to the bedroom for a cigarette and some peace and quiet.

Now, there was an undeniable atmosphere in the kitchen. 'I thought we could all go out to dinner,' Nina said brightly. 'To the Gardener's Arms.'

Alex did not reply.

'My favourite!' exclaimed Susan. 'It's so ... intimate.'

'I'll go and change,' said Alex, picking up his glass and with that he was gone.

'Is Alex all right?' asked Susan worriedly.

After a few minutes Nina followed him upstairs. He was lying on the bed staring at the ceiling. 'What the fuck is she doing here?'

'She wanted to come and help.'

'Help! That's a first. Is she planning to poison our guests or just bore them to death?'

'What could I do? She hasn't got anywhere else to go.'

'She's got a room at your mother's house.'

'I mean for her birthday.'

He leaned on one elbow and reached for his drink. 'Hell, Nina. You don't have to look after her. She's a grown woman.'

Didn't she? She sat down on the edge of the bed. 'I didn't feel I could say no. Listen, let's have a quick dinner together and then we can have an early night.'

Now, seeing Alex's grim expression, Nina realised that it had been a big mistake to allow her sister to come. Alex and Susan had always had a strange relationship. In the early days Nina would look across at Susan, posed with her legs tucked coquettishly under her, and wonder if Alex was attracted to her. But over the years he had had plenty to say that was far from admiring.

Sure enough, now he let rip. 'She's a fucking disaster area. She can't hold down a job or a boyfriend.'

'Keep your voice down!'

'She's a user, Nina.'

'She just needs some stability.'

'She needs to grow up. She's an adult who thinks it's OK to act like a kid, sponging off you and your mother.'

That reminded her. 'Actually, I think it's Richard who might be doing that.'

Grateful to change the subject, she relayed the conversation about Richard's management of her mother's bank account.

Alex was always good in these sorts of situations. He thought for a moment, then said, 'Take your mother to the bank. Then she can sign for copy statements. And get them sent to our address.'

Nina reached across and touched his shoulder. 'I'm sorry about Susan. I didn't realise you had such a problem with her.'

'I don't,' he said quickly. He paused. 'God, your family. What a shower.' He kissed her and got up, headed towards the wardrobe. His back was to her as he thumbed through his shirts. 'How did you turn out so normal?'

She did not answer. Instead she lay back. If she had answered him it would have been a concise reply: Archie, the source of all the good things in her childhood.

Things were not going according to Susan's plan. Alex was not reacting at all as she expected. Admittedly, she had antici-pated a little awkwardness. But there was no need for him to be acting almost as if he wished she wasn't there. They were seated in a window seat of the Gardener's Arms, now at eight o'clock packed with locals and weekenders. You could tell the weekenders because the women were thinner and much better dressed in expensive jeans, wearing strappy sandals on their tanned, pedicured feet.

She had been really, really nice to Alex and he wasn't being at all nice back.

'Nina tells me that you've already had an offer on Putney.'

He sounded bored. 'Not an offer. An expression of interest.'

'But that's a good start,' she persisted.

'Nothing's good until the ink's dry on the contract.' He turned to Nina. 'Darling, please pass the salt. You could do a London pub review,' he said to her. 'Maybe the lunch menu?'

Nina nodded. And she started talking about the menu for tomorrow's party. 'So it's chocolate lime cheesecake, summer pudding or grilled figs with mascarpone.'

Alex pulled a face. 'Figs? You'd have been better off with strawberries and cream.'

Nina shook her head. 'People are more sophisticated than you think.'

He shrugged. 'If you say so.'

And then they started talking about the drinks.

It was very rude. Susan was the guest and they should be involving her in the conversation. She picked at her pan-fried salmon. The food here was really good; the pub had been bought a couple of years ago by a couple from London who changed the menu every month. She should be able to come to places like this all the time.

Eventually, Nina brought the subject back to Susan. 'Susan's thinking about going back to college,' Nina told Alex, 'so she can teach yoga.'

Alex grunted but he didn't look at her.

'Maybe,' commented Susan. 'Actually I was wondering about getting my massage qualifications. People say I'm very good.'

There was a rewarding flicker across Alex's face.

She continued. 'And massage therapy is a very flexible way to work. You can do it in people's homes at times to suit them.'

Alex was now focused on extracting bones from his grilled trout.

'Well, I think it's a very good idea,' said Nina. 'You could live at home, save your money and study.' She nudged Alex. 'What do you think?'

'Yes.'

Nina turned back to Susan. 'Alex has had a really busy week at the office,' she said apologetically.

Susan leaned across the table and shook his arm. 'You see! You're exactly the type of client I would appeal to. I could come to your home and set up the table in your living room.'

She paused to give Alex the opportunity to respond.

'Yes,' he said after a moment.

'In fact,' added Susan, 'any time you feel like letting me practise on you just say the word!'

And with that Alex had put down his knife and fork. 'Excuse me.' He got up and headed for the bathroom.

'Sorry,' said Nina. 'Like I said, it's been a tough week.'

Susan exhaled and took a big gulp of wine. Alex was behaving in a very immature manner. If he wasn't prepared to accept the consequences of his actions then he shouldn't do them in the first place. The correct response to this kind of acting out on Alex's part was to set a boundary with him. She would do this just as soon as they were alone together.

She looked across at Nina. There was no reason why Nina would ever know anything about it. And besides, there would be some very undesirable consequences if she ever did find out. An end to the presents, the meals out, the weekends away, the occasional loans and, to further complicate matters, the certainty that their mother would take Nina's side.

She regarded her sister. It wasn't that there was anything nasty or unpleasant about Nina. It was simply that Nina, just because she was two years older, got all the things that Susan should have had. Her mother had occasionally paid some attention to Nina – when she wasn't fawning over Richard – and Archie had always favoured her. Nina had always had too much, always got things that should have been shared. A new tennis racquet when she made the school tennis team; a gift token from WH Smith when she got the form prize – and Archie probably gave her money to start her business. As Nina had got older it had got worse. She had so much it was unbearable. Susan thought about her birthday present. What was a stupid gift basket and a few quid compared to two houses stuffed full of expensive things? So anything Susan did get, however it was come by, was just a small fraction of what she should have had. It was compensation for all that had been wrong in the past.

Chapter 7

Sasha stared out of the coach window. She sat at the front, her bag on the seat beside her to discourage anyone from sitting there. The sprawling, congested suburbs beside the A4 went past as they left London: Brentford, Chiswick, Feltham, Hounslow and then Heathrow Airport. Even as a child, standing on the patch of scuffed council grass outside their flat, she had looked up at the planes on their noisy flight path and wondered where they were going – and known that one day she would leave behind the brick walkways and rusting cars of the estate and be a passenger going far, far away.

She could hear Sean, who looked after maintenance of the properties, at the back of the coach, talking loudly in his ignorant south London accent about the coming football season.

'Chelsea are up for the double.'

Her family spoke like Sean. And she would have, too, if she had not realised that there was a world out there which offered more than four weeks' paid holiday – when the boss said it was convenient for you to go – and an annual office party. Pat was grateful for the five- and ten-pound notes slipped into her Christmas cards by her Chiswick house-cleaning clients. When Sasha was fourteen she had started working on the checkout at Budgens. It had not taken her long to notice that she could add up the customers' purchases in her head as quickly as inputting them on the till. She had mentioned this to Pat, who had looked unimpressed.

'I suppose you think you ought to have the supervisor's job.'

She did, actually. If she was the supervisor she would put a stop to the deli staff pocketing five per cent of the take from their till and correct the security cameras so there wasn't a convenient blind spot for shoplifters located at the end of the wine and spirits aisle.

From the back of the coach came the sound of cans being opened and kids whining, and Marjorie, who did the books, calling over to her husband. 'Just one! I don't want you showing me up.'

And then more stupid laughter. Sasha felt a mix of contempt for them and relief that she had escaped that fate. Sometimes she looked at Harriet, the office assistant, and wondered if she would have looked like her if she had stayed in Feltham. Harriet, at twenty-one, was already getting heavy, her fat fingers tapping her office keyboard, her hair lank and loose, her short frame squeezed into cheap trouser suits. She wore too much make-up and didn't know how to apply lipstick properly. Sometimes she looked at Harriet and thought about giving her some advice, but she had learned over the years that most people had no desire to better themselves.

Besides, after yesterday it was her mission to get her sacked.

Yesterday afternoon, when Sasha had arrived back at the office from depositing the day's cheques at the bank, she had started to go up the stairs to Alex's office.

Harriet called after her. 'He's left for the day.'

Sasha stopped dead on the stairs, then came down. 'What?'

'He caught the early train to Gloucestershire.'

She could not conceal her shock. He hadn't even called her to say they wouldn't be going to dinner.

And then Harriet had given her a sly glance. 'Didn't you know? I thought he would have told you. I thought he told you everything.' She smirked. 'I don't suppose it's anything I can help you with.'

Sasha could have slapped her then, hard across the face, like she had done with the cloakroom girl at Dauphins, a little bitch who'd seen her leave with a client and the next day made a smart remark – 'So you're a proper working girl, Angie.'

Kelly had pulled her off and she'd got away with it. She made too much money for Dauphins to be fired for that.

Her father had always been on at her about her temper. 'It'll get you into trouble, girl. There are better ways of getting even.'

Sasha got angry when she felt used, taken for granted and patronised. She got angry when people treated her like she didn't matter. Sir Christopher had been like that. Oh, he was polite enough. But he had a way of talking to her that made her feel like the hired help. She would get out of bed and he'd gesture to the minibar.

'Get me a brandy, will you?'

He never ordered room service. Too scared to be seen with her.

God, it had felt so good when she finally took him. It wasn't just the amount of money. It was the fact that she was taking it off him – one hundred and three thousand pounds to be exact, carried out of the hotel room at four a.m. in his own briefcase as he lay drunkenly asleep, and deposited at nine thirty the next morning in a bank account they never found. What a fool! Sir Christopher was too keen to save tax and conceal his gambling habit from his wife to take a cheque – and too desperate to get laid to put it in the hotel safe. Ordinarily he lost but that night he was celebrating his big win.

He deserved to lose it.

And besides, though she had been surprised when Sir Christopher had gone to the police, she had known it was a bluff and he could never press charges.

She had been taken in for questioning by an ambitious young detective, DC Cannon. As the interview stumbled along she had felt like giving him some advice: if you want to get ahead, get a decent haircut and do your homework in advance.

He had tried amateurishly to trip her up. 'So you admit that you know Sir Christopher!'

She had stayed cool. 'Of course I do.' She had paused to play with him a little. 'I know him as a customer. But not outside of work. I was never with him. You must have the wrong person.'

DC Cannon had not been able to conceal his frustration as the interview progressed. 'We know you were having an affair! If it wasn't you, who was it?'

'That's your job to find out, not mine.'

She knew she was safe. Sir Christopher had a wife who sat on the board of trustees of the Royal Ballet and a son who had just been selected as a Conservative parliamentary candidate. Sir Christopher had a reputation in the City for being whiter than white. He could never explain in court what he was doing in a hotel room with a croupier half his age.

'So what exactly does he say we were doing together?' she had asked, wide-eyed.

Before she left his hotel room she had taken the remains of her bag of coke and liberally powdered every surface.

'I've heard rumours that Sir Christopher's got a habit. Have you dusted that hotel room? He may be hallucinating.'

At that DC Cannon had laughed bitterly. 'You're a pro,' he said grudgingly, letting her go. She hadn't even asked for a lawyer. She didn't need one. She knew exactly how it would play out: the police would let her go, Dauphins would sack her and it would be time for a new career.

So few people quit when they were ahead. All gamblers talked about it, but most stayed until the house wiped them out. Then they borrowed money and came back for more of the same. Now, sitting on the coach, she acknowledged that

Alex was slipping away from her. You couldn't make excuses for men: he's too busy or his wife's just had a baby or he's under a lot of pressure at work.

No. The only reason he doesn't call, doesn't take you to dinner and doesn't fuck you afterwards is because he doesn't want to.

Alex had gone back to Nina.

She closed her eyes. The next step was obvious: stay cool, transfer the remains of the Cayman Islands account and walk away.

But she couldn't. She felt too damned angry. And besides, she wasn't ready to give up on Alex yet. You have to play the hand that you're dealt – her father had drummed that into her a thousand times – and so she sat back, closed her eyes and blocked out the noise of raucous laughter coming from the back of the coach to work out how she would use the whole day in Alex's company to regain the initiative.

Nina had mentioned someone called Sasha, but only in passing. Susan, not paying much attention, had assumed that Alex's secretary would be a rather mousy figure. So it had been a shock to see Sasha leading the office party across the lawn wearing a dress that must have cost a bomb and carrying that season's Anya Hindmarch bag. It had been in all the magazines. Nina hadn't mentioned that Sasha had a figure like a model, legs to die for and a fashion budget that must take all her salary.

Susan found that she couldn't take her eyes off her. She must have had a boob job. It might be Nina's house but Sasha was the centre of attention. While Nina ran around with drinks for the children, checking that everyone had food and giving directions to the downstairs cloakroom, Sasha moved around the party, chatting to everyone with equal ease.

At lunch, Susan had rather hoped to sit next to Alex. But he had wedged himself between two members of staff from his office. It was really aggravating. Every time she had tried to be alone with him he had found some excuse to run away. Last night he'd feigned a headache and gone straight to bed.

Now, all the places at the other groups of chairs taken, she had had no option but to sit next to a woman called Alison, who was pregnant.

'My husband, Steve, shows the properties to people,' explained Alison ponderously, pointing to a young man with gelled hair at a nearby table holding a bottle of Budweiser. 'That means he gets a company car. Then when they move in he does the inventory. Then at the end of the tenancy he checks them out.'

Susan sat balancing a plate on her knees, struggling to think of something to say next. 'Do you live in London?'

'Acton.'

'Right.'

At that point Sasha had come and sat down next to them. 'Hi! I'm Sasha. Do you mind if I join you?'

Susan nodded. 'No, be our guest.' Sasha carried a glass of water and no food. Susan felt her spirits instantly fall. Sasha was one of those people who made you feel unfashionable and ungroomed, however much effort you had made and however good you had been feeling until then.

'Not eating?' asked Alison, leaning awkwardly over her plate, her knees jammed together. 'It's really good.'

'I just had something.'

Personally Susan found all pregnant women really boring. But Sasha seemed genuinely interested in Alison. 'So how many weeks are you?'

'Twenty-two.'

Twenty-two! God, she was huge. Alison needed to stop eating as a matter of urgency. Next to Sasha she looked like a troll. Sasha's hands were immaculately manicured with three rings: two diamond and one sapphire. Her arms were really toned, shown off in her sleeveless dress. Susan always began by assessing women when she met them: more or less thin and attractive than herself?

Sasha paused. 'So the baby's due in November?'

Alison came alive. 'Yes. I don't know how we're going to get everything done. We can't start the nursery until we find out whether we're having a boy or a girl.'

'Have you got any ideas for colour schemes?'

Unfortunately Alison had. 'Blue walls and stars and planets if it's a boy. And pink walls and daisies if it's a girl. With pink gingham curtains. But if you get those you need a blackout blind as well because they let in the light.'

Who cared?

Sasha obviously. 'And just in time for Christmas! What a lovely time to have a newborn.'

'Hmm. I'm not sure about a real tree, though. I don't want to be clearing up lots of mess.'

Susan just couldn't think of anything to say. It wasn't as if the baby would know it was Christmas.

But Sasha seemed to find this whole conversation scintillating. 'Do you have family nearby?'

'In Nottingham. My mum's going to come down to help.'

'It's so important to have family around you,' commented Sasha warmly.

Susan had had enough. 'I'll go and see if Nina needs any help.'

At this there was a flicker of interest from Sasha. 'Nina?'

'I'm her sister.'

'Oh. So you're Alex's sister-in-law. I've heard so much about you!'

Susan didn't know what to say to this. It was slightly unnerving.

But Sasha took up the thread. 'Oh, yes. Alex has mentioned you several times.' She gave a little laugh. 'Something about some trouble with egg nog?'

She pronounced *egg nog* with exaggerated curiosity.

As if on cue, Alison looked up, confused. 'Egg nog?'

It felt to Susan at that moment as if she was seven years old and at the mercy of the coolest, cruellest girl in the playground. Sasha put her head on one side. 'Why don't you tell us, Susan? It sounded quite a drama.'

Yes, it was definitely that playground feeling. She wanted to run. She struggled to think of what to say. 'It was nothing.'

'Really?' Sasha raised her eyebrows. 'That's not what Alex said. Didn't you have to leave?'

It was unbearable. She would do anything at that moment to take that supercilious half-smile off Sasha's face. She decided to play the insider card. 'I'm very happy to be back home. It gives me more opportunity to spend time with Nina and Alex.'

Sasha looked unimpressed.

'In fact, I was here last weekend.' She turned to Alison. 'They had a house party. For friends and family.' She fixed Sasha hard in the eyes. 'Alex and I spent quite a lot of time together. Funny, he never mentioned you.'

Sasha's expression was unmoved but her eyes betrayed a hint of confusion at where this conversation was leading.

'But it was late at night. Nina had gone to bed. Alex and I often get together to talk like that.'

She held Sasha's eyes until the other woman looked away.

She turned to Alison. 'Alex is one of those men who likes to forget all about the office at the weekend. All those day-to-day worries.' She looked at Sasha. 'He can leave all of that in the hands of his staff.'

At the mention of the word *staff*, Sasha bristled. Only very slightly and not so that Alison would have noticed. But Susan did. And having scored a substantial victory she turned on her heel. 'So if you'll excuse me, I must go and find my sister.'

Maria handed Nina a plate. 'Go and sit down,' she ordered. 'We can manage.'

They could. Maria and her assistant chef had put on a fabulous spread, laid out buffet-style in the kitchen, main courses on the kitchen table and desserts on the centre island. There was a centrepiece of cold beef Wellington, plus dishes of spiced chicken with almonds and Thai noodle salad with seared tiger prawns, surrounded by an assortment of side dishes, bread and salsa. Most people had taken something of everything.

'Looks like we'll need that other chocolate lime cheesecake,' Maria said to her assistant. 'They've hardly touched the figs.'

Nina rolled her eyes. 'Just don't tell Alex.'

Nina went outside. She would have been happier to stay in the kitchen. Alex was far better at this sort of thing than she was: she had watched him play croquet with the office girls, organise a badminton tournament and move effortlessly between groups making inconsequential small talk. Alex didn't especially enjoy socialising, but you would never know it. And for a man who had been so reluctant to try for a baby he was a natural with the children, even climbing onto the bouncy castle with them.

Alex was talking to the men. Susan was with Sasha and Steve's pregnant wife whose name she had forgotten. But she was saved from deciding where to sit by a loud 'Yoo hoo!' from Marjorie.

'Come and join the girls.'

Marjorie, Alex's part-time book-keeper whom Nina had always thought of as rather reserved, sounded as if she had had at least one too many glasses of wine.

'Lovely food, Nina,' said Harriet. She turned to Christine, who was new. 'Nina has a catering business.'

'So we're in professional hands,' chipped in Marjorie.

Nina found it difficult to meet Christine's eye. Alex had told her that Christine was one of the members of staff earmarked for the sack.

'The garden looks very nice,' commented Christine politely.

'Oh, thank you. Of course we haven't done much to it.'

'I'm sure Alex has got plans,' interrupted Marjorie. 'Are you going to get landscapers in?'

Oh, God. She hated having to lie.

'We haven't decided,' she said distractedly.

'Alex told us all about the extension,' said Marjorie. 'He designed it himself,' she told Christine. 'He's very talented.'

And then Marjorie was off. She talked about Alex with a kind of maternal pride: what a good eye he had, how much the tenants liked him and how the agents described him as the best in the business.

And Nina, allowing herself to relax, felt a vicarious pride in all that Marjorie was saying. Because she was right: Alex was one of the best. All that had happened was that he had taken a wrong turning; in his desire to be the best he had pushed a little too hard, a little too quickly.

Archie used to say that the darkest hour was before the dawn. But now, on an English summer afternoon, with scents from the garden carried on the breeze, it was clear that the sun was rising on their fortunes. Even seeing Sasha had been bearable, with the knowledge that her presence in their lives would soon be over.

Alex had been very clear that morning. 'I promise you. I'll tell her to leave on Monday.'

She had nodded her assent.

He had hesitated. 'I think we should ask a couple of the local agents to come and give us a valuation on Monday morning. I'll stay if you want me to.'

'No. I'll do it. You catch the train in.'

Nina had a motive for getting him back: the sooner Alex got into the office, the quicker he could sack Sasha. She had made a resolution which she now repeated in her mind: in return she would never mention Sasha again. It would be a new start, the past forgotten – as if none of this had ever happened.

Even the children seemed to have lost some of their energy. At past four o'clock the talk amongst the adults was more subdued. And Marjorie was lying flat out on the lawn fast asleep.

But Susan remained watchful. She was waiting for an opportunity to speak to Alex. Which was how she had observed, five minutes earlier, Sasha walk up to Alex where he was playing croquet with a teenage boy and girl. It looked like a casual approach, as if they just happened to bump into each other. And they had exchanged only a few words. But then they had both simultaneously looked at their watches.

A rendezvous?

Sure enough, five minutes later, Alex ambled towards the summerhouse. And a little while later Sasha followed.

Susan got up and walked into the kitchen. Nina was having a cigarette, watching Maria wash up.

'I've banned her from picking up a tea-towel,' commented Maria.

'Come and join us,' added Nina.

'Just a minute.' Susan pointed towards the bathroom. But at the end of the corridor she turned into the far door of the living room, silently doubled back and let herself out through the front door.

As she approached the back of the summerhouse she took off her shoes. Drawing closer, she could hear voices and as she kneeled down silently, her ear pressed to the thin wooden wall, she could hear everything.

They were having a row in urgent, hushed voices.

'I didn't have any option. Christ, Sasha! You can see how much we've had to organise. I had to get down here.'

Sasha sounded cool but angry. 'Alex, I understand. I'm just asking you to tell me what's happening.'

'Do we have to talk about this now?'

'No. But I think you need to be clear with me. About everything.'

'There is nothing going on with her!'

Who were they talking about? One of the girls in the office?

'Alex, all I'm asking for is the truth.' Sasha sounded very calm, Alex not at all.

'She's just a fucking troublemaker,' he said. 'She always has been.'

He sounded totally dismissive of this unnamed person. Was it that young girl Harriet? It couldn't be the other two women in the office; they were far too old.

'So there's nothing?'

'No.' Alex sounded genuine. 'There's no way I'd get involved with her. She's just a little tart.'

Sasha gave a laugh. 'Not a very nice way to talk about your sister-in-law.' Her tone of voice was familiar and intimate.

Susan, kneeling against the wall, felt a jolt of shock.

'Believe me, it's justified. Look, it's some sister thing. She wants what Nina's got. She's eaten up with jealousy because her own life's such a bloody mess. It's always been like that, since they were kids.'

It was hard to know what was worse: listening to Alex talk about her like that or knowing that he was saying these things to Sasha.

There was no reply. Then Alex's voice was quieter. 'Let's have dinner after work on Monday. Then we can talk.' He sounded uneasy. 'I need to get back to them. Nina will be wondering where I've got to.'

Sasha spoke as if she hadn't heard him. 'All I'm asking is that you treat me with the same consideration that you treat your wife.'

'Fine. Yes.' There was a pause. 'Look, I'm sorry. I just need some time.'

Sasha's voice was warmer now. 'OK.'

Then the voices stopped. She could hear shuffling and rustling. But she didn't dare stand up to look through the small dust-coated window.

'Stop! We can't. Are you trying to get caught?' It was Alex.

Sasha laughed. 'Relax. No one would guess we were in here.' Her voice was low and seductive. 'I've missed you, Alex. And I know you've missed me. Haven't you?'

Susan couldn't hear his reply, just the odd whisper and movement.

Susan exhaled.

'Stop.' It was Alex again. 'We have to stop.'

'But we can't. Not really. Oh, we can stay apart for a little while. But we'll always be drawn together. We understand each other, Alex. I know you think you're doing the right thing.' Her voice was confident. 'Staying small. Playing it safe – in everything. But ultimately you'll hate it. And you'll resent Nina for taking away your dreams. For stopping you being all that you can be. For all the missed chances and lost opportunities. And then the bitterness seeps in. You'll feel it every time you see someone with less talent pass you because they had the nerve to press on – and the right person next to them.' Her voice was quiet but impassioned.

Susan was immobile, fixed to the spot, hanging on to Sasha's every word.

'One road leads to the mountains. It's steep and treacherous and it takes nerve to follow it. But it takes you to the top of the mountain, to the cleanest air and the very best view where you can see the ocean. The other road takes you inland. It's slow and safe and you'll never come to any harm. But take that road and you'll never see the view. You'll spend your life in the valley, in the shade, deprived of the light.'

For a while there was silence. Then Alex spoke. 'It's not that simple.'

'Yes, it is. Do you think we met by accident? Do you think it was just coincidence that I walked into your office?'

There was no reply.

Sasha forged on. 'No. We met for a reason, Alex. We met because we need each other. Because together we can do what we couldn't do alone.' Now there was the sound of short, sharp footsteps and the door opening. 'Because there aren't many people like us out there. We need each other.'

And then she was gone. Susan sat back and heard a minute later the sound of Alex's footsteps as he left the summerhouse.

It was all she could do not to walk round and confront him. She could have done, she reassured herself: he would have deserved it. Only the thought of Sasha stopped her. Whatever she had to say to Alex would have to wait until they were alone together, when Sasha was safely gone for ever. There was something about Sasha that was ... scary. Instinctively she didn't want to face her again.

It was obvious they were having an affair. That was why Alex had to be so horrible and untruthful about her – he needed to placate that bitch Sasha. And there was only one sure way to get rid of her. She sat back and thought about it. It was undoubtedly the right thing to do: Nina had a right to know that Alex was having an affair. In fact, it would be wrong not to tell her. If she kept quiet then she would actually be – what was that word? – yes, colluding in the deception. So the moral thing to do was clear. The more she thought about it, the more convinced she was that she had no choice but to tell Nina in no uncertain terms exactly what was going on.

The coach left just after six o'clock. Maria had already packed up and left. All that remained was to clear up the garden.

'We'll do it,' Susan volunteered insistently. 'You need to sit down. Doesn't she, Alex?'

Nina sat on the terrace watching as Susan and Alex folded up the chairs and tables, hired from a local firm.

'Shall we take them inside?' Susan asked.

'No. Just leave them against the wall.'

'What about the bouncy castle?'

'I'll do it later,' Alex called across to her. 'Nina, I'm going to get the papers.'

Susan looked up. 'I'll come! I need some cigarettes.'

'No, you stay here and relax. I'll get them for you. Didn't you say you wanted to have a bath?'

In the aftermath of a successful party it felt to Nina like the old days. She had worked hard to persuade Alex to invite the office staff to their home, copying Archie's tradition.

Throughout her childhood Archie had invited his office staff to the Marlow house for a summer party. To Nina, it had felt like Christmas: tables and chairs set up, games laid out and a spread of food put on by a firm from Henley. In those days it had been sausage rolls, egg sandwiches and trifle. Anne, who always loved a party, would buy a new summer dress for the occasion. Archie would retrieve the badminton set from the outhouse and she would run to help him, holding the smooth wooden poles as he hammered them in with a mallet, the two of them hanging the much-repaired net.

Archie was a generous-spirited and popular man. Their housekeeper, Mrs Baxter, worshipped him.

'He's a proper gentleman. And there aren't many of them left.'

For years, Mrs Baxter had come every day, cycling from her terraced cottage in West Street. She shopped, cooked, cleaned and ironed until one day Anne made an announcement that they had to make some economies – the reason for which was never explained – after which Mrs Baxter was demoted to a cleaning lady coming in on Mondays and Fridays, donning her print housecoat over a stout frame. There were other economies that year: Archie turned the heating down so that the upstairs of the house was even colder, the summer holiday was spent at home and all talk of a new car was quietly dropped.

It was Mrs Baxter who, during her years as their housekeeper, had taught Nina to cook. Her mother had been in service, 'a cook to the gentry' as Mrs Baxter proudly put it, and hers was the cooking of the previous generation. Suet-crust steak and kidney puddings, milk custards prepared gently in a bain-marie, shortbread rounds and homemade preserves. Mrs Baxter's shortcrust pastry melted in the mouth – 'Don't add any more water; it'll be tough if you do' – and Nina had never since found marmalade with the same fresh sweet-sharp taste.

Mrs Baxter would shoo Susan away, telling her that she

could help when she was older. Then she would set Nina shelling peas, kneading dough, whipping cream and only if she had performed these tasks particularly well would she grant her a hold of the icing bag or a turn of the rolling pin.

It was during these hours in the kitchen, when she and Nina were alone together, that Mrs Baxter's comments grew more ambiguous. The conversation would turn to Archie.

'He's had a hard time of it.'

'It was a tragedy.'

'Oh, if you had seen her.'

Nina had been mad with impatience. 'Seen who?'

Mrs Baxter, who knew everyone in Marlow and divulged all their secrets, shook her head. 'I'm not one to gossip.'

'Please, Mrs Baxter. I won't tell anyone.'

'Hear no evil, speak no evil.'

Finally, one day there was an unpleasant scene with her mother. Mrs Baxter had, her mother alleged, failed to clean the bathroom properly.

Her mother had clicked into the kitchen, dressed in her black jodhpurs, pulling on her weather-beaten riding gloves. Mrs Baxter was washing up.

'There's Vim on the bottom of our bath. You'll have to rinse it out again.'

Nina knew that Mrs Baxter hated to be criticised. Her mouth turned down and her face flushed red.

Next, there was the slam of the door as her mother left for the stables.

Mrs Baxter cracked. 'Some people are born with good manners. And others aren't.'

'Who?'

Mrs Baxter turned round from the sink. 'You have to promise not to tell anyone. Do you promise?'

'Cross my heart, hope to die, stick a needle in my eye.'

'Well, there's no need for that.'

She paused to let the water drain out of the sink. 'I mean the first Mrs Carruthers. Oh, she was lovely. So sweet-natured.

She was a real lady.' Mrs Baxter was still now. 'It was a love match. They met at the tennis club.' Mrs Baxter assumed a respectful tone. 'Her father used to be mayor. And she was sent to private school. So you see they were the same class.' At the time Nina had not recognised the implied comparison. 'His father gave them some money and they bought a little house down by the lock. She used to grow roses at the front. Pink ones, the same kind as what you've got on the drive.'

Nina hadn't known what to make of that coincidence. 'And then what happened?' she asked urgently.

Even though they were alone in the house, Richard and Susan out in the garden playing, Mrs Baxter lowered her voice. 'Cancer. Oh, it was quick. It ate her up.'

Nina shuddered. She had an image of a beautiful woman who looked like Disney's Snow White being eaten alive.

Mrs Baxter tapped her chest. 'Up here. That's where it was. But then it got into her bones.' She paused as if in remembrance. 'He was a broken man. Oh, he went into the office every day. But you could see that he wasn't the same. People said she was the love of his life.'

'And then what happened?'

'Well, dear. He met your mother, didn't he? She was a typist in his office.'

Her mother had said that they met at the office. Somehow Nina had got the idea that her mother had gone to see him for legal advice, not that she had worked there. She had a feeling that a typist wasn't as good as a secretary.

Mrs Baxter gave her an odd look. 'He did the honourable thing by your mother. Plenty wouldn't have. That's the kind of man he is, you see.'

Nina had felt such a fool when a couple of years later, researching a family tree for a school project, she had looked through the family certificates and seen that Richard's birthday was five months after the marriage.

It had never been mentioned.

And she knew instinctively that she should not draw

attention to it. So she had replaced the certificates, closed the bureau drawer and mentioned the family tree to no one. On her project sheet she had put the year but no month.

After a year or so money got easier again: Nina resumed her private tennis lessons, the thermostat was raised and one day Archie turned up in a brand new racing-green Rover saloon. But Mrs Baxter never came back full-time – 'I told your mother I had another job! They give me paid holiday. She's ever such a nice woman.'

Nina had never had the courage to ask her mother about the first Mrs Carruthers. Besides, she knew that she would never get a proper answer. It would be the same as the questions she had asked about her real father.

'He's gone and he's not coming back. And good riddance.' Her mother had been angry. 'Don't you go stirring anything up, young lady.'

'But who was he?'

'He was a drunk and a liar and a womaniser.'

And with that her mother had shaken her roughly by the arm. 'Just be grateful I didn't make the same mistake twice. You don't want to go stirring up the past.'

Her mother made her feel that asking questions was dangerous. It was the same with other mysteries in their childhood, the questions that were never answered. Why did they go occasionally to visit their mother's family, but the family never came to visit them? Why did Archie's mother only buy a birthday present for Richard? And why, if Jack Tyler was a bad penny, did their parents keep inviting him to parties?

It was Susan who found their father: her then therapist had advised her that it would be a healing experience, assisting with closure. She came back and presented Nina with a photograph of his headstone. 'He died ten years ago,' she said sadly. Susan had made efforts to contact his second family but her overtures had not been welcomed and after a little while Nina persuaded her to drop the idea.

And that had been the end of it. Nina had not mourned

for him. It had been her stepfather that she had grieved for – and all the things she wished she had said to him. Even as he lay dying she had been unable to talk to him in the way she should have.

She had colluded in her mother's denial. 'The doctor says he's doing very well.'

Besides, it was too painful to acknowledge he was dying.

Now she bitterly regretted her lack of courage. She would have thanked him for treating her like his own flesh and blood, for teaching her to ride a bicycle and play chess and cook bacon and eggs. She would have thanked him for the long boring hours he spent patiently testing her on French vocabulary, for encouraging her to try for the school tennis team and for urging her to stay on for A-levels. Without him pushing her she wondered if she would even have started the business.

'You can do anything you set your mind to, Nina.'

And she would have thanked him for his speech at her wedding.

'I am a very lucky man to have such a beautiful daughter.'

It was she who was the lucky one.

Chapter 8

James Fennell, from the Winchcombe branch of Houghton's estate agents, stood in Nina's kitchen barely an hour after her nine o'clock telephone call to his office. Whether it was a natural enthusiasm to gain the business, or prurient curiosity to see the house that was the location for last weekend's police raid, James had said he would come right away. But James, wearing what she presumed was a Guards tie, was not the type to ask indiscreet questions. Part of his job, she realised, was sensitively to assist distressed homeowners forced to sell their houses as a result of marriage breakdown, bankruptcy or criminal activity.

He scanned the kitchen. 'Very good.' He jotted a few notes. 'We'll need to send a photographer for internal shots.'

'Any time.'

Susan, fortunately, was asleep. She had a habit of saying too much on these occasions. They had peered silently into the guest bedroom, Nina carefully closing the door behind them.

Nina, showing James around the rest of the house, had been determinedly casual.

'We're thinking about selling. We really don't use the house as much as we had hoped to.' This at least was true. 'But we haven't made a firm decision.'

If buyers sensed desperation, Alex always said, they deducted five per cent from their offer.

James had nodded appreciatively at the new master bathroom. 'Bathrooms are so important these days. Almost as important as kitchens.' And he had reassured her about the garden. 'Maybe you could add some containers at the front for colour. But it's fine. People tend to come in and do their own thing anyway.' He looked up from his notes. 'Perhaps I could take some measurements?'

'Of course.'

'Then I'll go back to my office and consult with my colleagues on prices.'

Nina worked out that she would have to come back down that week, get another couple of quotes and let in the Houghton's photographer. For now she needed to head off to Marlow. She was anxious, if at all possible, to arrive before lunchtime. Richard, Susan had explained, usually called in then. Nina's plan was to persuade her mother to go to lunch, call in at the bank and then drive her unannounced to the doctor's surgery. It would all be much easier, she was sure, if she could get her mother on her own.

Showing James out, she felt curiously detached about the sale. Perhaps it was because they had not had the house long enough to become attached to it – or maybe she was just being realistic.

It was as she was clearing out the fridge, packing food into the coolbox to take to London, that she heard the guest bedroom door open and the sound of footsteps. Susan sauntered into the kitchen.

Nina looked pointedly at her watch. 'We need to leave in half an hour.'

Susan yawned and stretched slowly. 'I have to make a phone call. Any chance of a cup of coffee?'

And then she was gone to Alex's office. Nina could just make out what she was saying. 'Roger.' She sounded very faint. 'It's Susan. Look, I can't come in today.' There was a pause while Roger was speaking. 'I know. I'm really sorry. I just couldn't get out of bed. I've been up half the night. I've had terrible food poisoning.' There was another pause.

'Honestly, I can hardly stand up. I think it was the prawns. Nina used caterers.'

Nina felt a surge of annoyance. Her sister was the limit – and she shouldn't be here at all. Last night. Nina, sensing that Susan was really getting on Alex's nerves, had offered to pay her train fare home.

'No. I'll come back with you.'

'Don't you have to go in to work tomorrow?'

'No. Roger owes me heaps of time off.'

Who knew if that were true? Resignedly, Nina had gone back to clearing up the house while Alex had taken the portable television from his office up to the bedroom.

Susan had always lied, though not in the carefully constructed way that Richard did. About homework and exam revision – 'I've done it all!' – and then when she was a teenager about money and boys. Susan insisted that she was off to the Wimpy on a Saturday lunchtime, even after Archie bumped into her coming out of the pub reeking of shandy and cigarettes.

'You're underage! It's a criminal offence.'

'But I was just there with some friends. It was them. They didn't serve me anything.'

She could recall Archie's exasperated voice on innumerable occasions. 'Why can't you just tell us the truth?'

And Susan would stare back innocently. 'But I am!'

It was almost as if Susan could reach a state whereby she believed her own lies. At fifteen she had got a lucrative job babysitting for the Palmers – the owners of Palmer's Marina off the Henley Road. All went well for six weeks until fifty pounds disappeared from a jar in the Palmers' kitchen.

Nina had listened on the stairs as Susan, Archie and Mrs Palmer convened in the drawing room. Mrs Palmer had been firm. 'It was five crisp ten-pound notes, straight from the bank. I need it for the gardener.'

Archie found the money in Susan's khaki rucksack.

'I don't know how it got there,' was Susan's repeated

explanation. She never cracked. In fact, with each denial she sounded more wounded. Archie gave Mrs Palmer the money. 'I am truly sorry.'

The woman had been tight-lipped as she left. 'I feel I'm owed an apology by Susan.'

A little while later Mr Palmer moved his business to a solicitor in Henley.

Susan always said that their mother put Richard first. But Nina did not completely agree. Her mother put Archie first, less concerned about Richard's behaviour because he was Archie's son too and therefore not her sole liability.

It was clear to Nina that it was time to put some distance between her and Susan. And for the first time she began to see that Alex might after all be right. Last night he had looked as if he wanted to say more but had instead said, 'You'll never be able to do enough for her. She'll always come back for more.'

So when Susan came back into the kitchen after making her telephone call Nina told her brusquely that they needed to leave straight away.

'I thought we could have breakfast.'

'Susan, let's go.'

Later, having waited impatiently in the kitchen for Susan to pack, she pulled swiftly out of the driveway and put on Radio 4.

'Let's talk!'

'Actually, I'm going to concentrate on driving.'

And with that she turned up the volume to make further conversation impossible.

It had only been a week and already Jemma was bored. There were only so many walks you could take down to the old town to buy milk and the weekly international edition of the *Daily Express* – and half the time they didn't have that.

'No arrive! Come next week.'

She wished she knew the Spanish for 'you should sort it out with your wholesaler or find a new one'.

Howard had left to play golf. But she would need to wait a little longer. He was always forgetting something and tearing up the drive unexpectedly. Leaving that morning he had kissed her on the cheek. 'See you at lunchtime.'

She would join him at noon at the club. But even going there wasn't much fun since she started the diet. It was day five and this time she was serious. Jemma had got up at seven that morning and done the whole of the workout tape before sitting down to half a grapefruit, a slice of melon and two poached eggs. Then she had written it down in her food diary. All wheat products, sugar and alcohol were forbidden until week four, when there was a limited reintroduction of wholegrain.

She sat by the pool and tried to get back into her book, a novel she had picked up at the airport which was set amongst the expatriate community in Spain. All the women were thin, snorted cocaine and were bitches to their young Spanish maids. She put it down: it made her think of Barbara.

The house, set high up on the hill, had a far-reaching view of the bay. Howard had had the foresight to purchase the land in front of their plot so as to secure the view. He had plans to plant oranges and irrigate it, but for now it was dried-up scrub. She hated that about Spain – there was no green. Just like there were no proper cafés where you could get a cake and a cup of tea. And no WH Smith or Boots or Ocado home delivery. Sometimes Jemma wished they could sell up and stay at home. But Howard liked it here and the golf was good exercise for him.

The large pool was edged with Ali Baba pots, each containing a miniature palm tree and surrounded by a tiled area big enough for umpteen loungers. Dimitri, an eager young Russian employed by all the expats, looked after the pool and kept an eye on the house while they were away. Along the back of the house a row of white arches bordered a covered terrace with patio doors leading into the open-plan kitchen, dining area and living room. Howard had the television hooked up to all the British channels. He wouldn't have come if he couldn't watch the Premiership football.

At nine o'clock it was too early to ring the kids. They were at home, still on holiday, getting up to God knows what, and she should be there with them. She felt a pang of disquiet. Her relationship with Jason and Elliott was a subject on which she and Howard increasingly did not see eye to eye.

'Jem, they're grown men! At their age I was running the business.'

'It's different now. The world's changed.'

'You've got to let them go. You can't run their lives for ever.'

But that was exactly what she wanted to do. At the thought of backing away she was always overtaken by a feeling of miserable fear. If she let the boys go, what would she be left with? Her family was her whole life. Other women in Radlett filled their days shopping and lunching and getting treatments at the spa in the town's new state-of-the-art gym and tennis club. But though she had a Gold pass membership – Howard had got it for her for Christmas – she had never felt comfortable there. Those type of places, with their stick-thin Lycra-clad clientele, low-fat menus and Grecian-pillared pools, the tanned beauticians in white doctor's coats and layers of make-up, always made her feel fat and frumpy. It had been different in Las Vegas – there were loads of fat people there.

She had so much to be grateful for. She looked out at the sea, a view that most people back in Britain, stuffed on rush-hour trains and stuck in dead-end jobs, would die for. But it did nothing to raise her spirits. Not for the first time she wondered if she was having a mid-life crisis. Around her, everyone seemed to be happily moving ahead with their lives, leaving her behind. Howard had his work and his golf. The boys had their girlfriends. She thought of Nina with her proper career, the type of thing you needed qualifications for, not a handful of GCSEs. Even her sister didn't have time any more to meet up for a coffee – she'd only gone and started a house cleaning business. 'It's easy. You get the Polish girls to do the work for you. And it's all cash.'

In public she always put on a front. She was good old down-to-earth Jemma, contented wife and mother, always bright and cheery. Inside, she felt fat and stupid, depressed and homesick. But there was no going home yet. Howard had been firm. 'I need to stay here while the lawyers deal with it. And we'll be back in a tick.'

She had read him the riot act. 'No more cigarettes!' She had been furious on the plane over. 'How could you risk everything for a bit of cash? It's got to stop.'

He had nodded meekly. 'Whatever you say, Jem.'

She could have gone back alone – there was no reason why she should get into any trouble with the authorities. But she hadn't stayed married for more than twenty years by leaving her husband alone with the type of woman who became an expat in Spain and hung out all day at the club. A woman like Barbara. At the thought of that woman her mood sank still lower.

Barbara also had a husband. But that had been little comfort last week when over lunch in the club room, Barbara had touched Howard's hand and leaned over so that he could see right down her sequinned halter-neck top. Brian, her husband, a retired builder from Wilmslow who'd already had three beers, didn't appear to notice.

Barbara was talking about her newfound calling as an artist. 'I've always had a dream to paint. So Brian built me a studio. It's the light here! And the seclusion of the hills. So inspiring! We're going to have an exhibition of my work. You must come!'

Barbara, who wasn't a day under forty-five, was Brian's second wife, had no children and – it was no surprise to learn – used to own her own beauty salon. Later Barbara had suggested tennis.

'Do you play, Jemma?'

'No.'

'Oh. Well, there's a wonderful pro here. You could take lessons.' She turned to Howard. 'We should play sometime.'

That was why Jemma would go to the club, even though she felt fat and unfashionable and wouldn't be able to order a chicken and bacon club sandwich, chips and a nice glass of wine.

She looked at her watch, a gold diamond-edged Cartier Santos, Howard's present to her for their twentieth anniversary. It was half an hour since he'd left. She went into his office, which overlooked the pool, and logged on to the computer. She put his password into his email account – their children's names plus their wedding anniversary. He always used the same one; it was the only one he could remember.

There was nothing. She checked the sent messages to be sure, but they were all business. Next she looked in his briefcase. Nothing, just as there had been no unfamiliar numbers and no messages on his mobile, which she had checked when he was in the shower that morning.

It wasn't that she didn't trust Howard. She trusted him insofar as any woman would be wise to trust their husband. It was a question of vigilance, of never taking anything for granted, of understanding that an awful lot of women would like what she had and wouldn't have any qualms about taking it from her.

Reassured now that there had been no contact with Barbara, but just to be doubly sure, she went through the filing cabinet.

It was there, at the back, tucked out of sight, that she saw the brown envelope.

She pulled it out, feeling the weight of it. She took the envelope over to the desk so that she could pull out the contents without anything falling to the floor and ending up in the wrong order. In fact, the papers inside were fastened together with a paperclip. At the front was an invoice from DTS Business Services whose address was a PO box in London.

It was for 'professional services' and dated one month earlier, but there was no clue as to the nature of the services.

She looked through. It was information on Alex from Howard's private detective: bank statements, a credit report and information about the Putney building.

It was standard stuff. Howard had used DTS for a few years now to gather information on business associates. DTS was a retired Special Branch officer. Jemma didn't know his name and suspected that Howard didn't either. According to Howard he was in his fifties with dark hair and he wore a black leather jacket, hardly a description that narrowed the field. Officially, DTS carried out legitimate surveillance work. But for cash, a range of unofficial services was available: telephone taps, bugs and tracker devices on cars. As Howard had explained, it was easy: turn up at someone's office in a British Gas boiler suit with a toolbox and a photo ID round your neck: 'Your neighbour has reported a gas leak. You might want to take an early lunch break. Better safe than sorry.' No one ever checked.

Jemma sifted through the papers. She couldn't see that the information was important now anyway. Howard had said he wouldn't touch Alex with a bargepole. But then, at the back, she reached a set of photographs. It showed Alex with a woman whom Jemma did not recognise. She was tall and thin with her hair swept back. They were shown leaving a building she assumed was his office, going to various restaurants, holding hands as they walked along what looked to Jemma like Bond Street and gazing at the window of a jeweller's shop. There were some thirty photographs. The last five showed Alex entering a block of flats and then emerging at night. She turned the final photograph over. On the back someone had stuck a typed label: 'Friday, 11th February. Departed 0013.'

And then lastly there was a report headed 'Sasha Fleming AKA Angela Taylor'. Jemma sat down to read it. It was clear that whoever DTS was, he had really gone to town on

133

Sasha/Angela: 'We conducted forty-four hours of surveillance and spoke to two current neighbours, two former neighbours, a former work colleague at Dauphins Casino and obtained further information from other sources.'

Other sources meant the police. Howard had explained it. 'It isn't exactly illegal, Jem. He takes one of his old mates for a drink, has a chat off the record and maybe some cash gets passed under the table.'

Sasha, Jemma read, was born Angela Laura Taylor. The report went on to give her date of birth, address, schools attended, work history and family details. She had never been married, had no children and her family consisted of her father, who lived in Feltham, and a brother and sister. Her mother had died in Ashford General Hospital of ovarian cancer when the girl was thirteen. Jemma paused: that would have been a hard age to lose your mother.

DTS had found out that Sasha owned a flat in London, a BMW 3-series sports car paid for in cash and had two British and two overseas bank accounts. Jemma scanned the figures in surprise: for a PA she seemed to have an awful lot of money.

She turned to the final page. It was headed 'Criminal Activity'. There was a list: as a teenager Angela had been cautioned for shoplifting from Woolworths, cautioned for affray outside a nightclub in Leicester Square and arrested for actual bodily harm. The victim, Jemma read, was a former girlfriend of her then boyfriend. The victim declined to press charges.

Then there were two more recent incidents, each within the last three years:

'Arrested in connection with a forged cheque drawn on the account of Tony Marchant. Charges dropped.'

'Arrested in connection with the theft of cash from Sir Christopher Chatton. Charges dropped.'

This Sasha/Angela certainly had a way of getting out of trouble.

Jemma carefully replaced the papers. She knew why Howard hadn't told her about this woman: she wouldn't have been able to be nice to Alex if she had known.

Thoughts of her own concerns over Barbara were now dispelled. She wondered if Nina knew that Alex was having an affair – and then understood that she didn't. She had seen the way Nina looked at Alex during the weekend they had spent in Gloucestershire. There was no tension there and none of the signs of a couple putting on a brave face in public. Jemma could always spot them because however hard couples tried they couldn't resist sniping at each other after a few drinks. And she recalled the conversation she had overheard between Nina and Inspector Taylor. His revelations about Sasha had been a shock to Nina.

Jemma got up and put the envelope back in the filing cabinet. It was none of her business. She knew exactly what Howard would say: you stay out of it, Jem. Still, she could not help but think that someone ought to warn Nina about this woman, who was something more than the run-of-the-mill girlfriend, who had danger written all over her. Nina, though she did not know it, was way out of her depth.

Anne was impossible. Nina had suspected that her mother might be awkward. But in the event she had refused even to get out of the car. They had sat arguing in the car park of the doctor's surgery.

'I'm not going in.'

'Mummy!'

Her mother's face was determined. 'I don't need to.'

Nina had struggled to control her anxiety. 'Mummy, I can hear you wheezing now! You need to see a doctor. You should have a check-up.'

'I go for my repeat prescription,' her mother objected.

'You need a proper examination. Emphysema is very serious.'

Anne ignored this point. 'You get more germs sitting in

that waiting room than you had when you went in. Most of these doctors don't even wash their hands.'

'If that were true no one would ever go to the doctor.'

'And they'd be a damned sight healthier for it.'

Nina tried another tack. 'I'm really worried about you. You're not socialising. You're not doing any of the things that you used to do. You never go out.'

'I see Richard. And Susan's there.'

'I mean with other people.'

'Why would I want to mix with a lot of idiots?'

'I think you're depressed. I think you're isolated and unhappy. You don't do anything!'

Her mother rounded on her. 'That's not because I'm depressed. It's because I don't want to. What do you think it's like, going everywhere on my own?'

'I don't know. I'm sure it must be very hard. But you can't avoid the world for ever.'

'Oh yes I can.'

Nina, emboldened by her success so far, had not anticipated that her mother would be so stubborn. She and Susan had arrived in Marlow after a silent journey. As she pulled into the driveway Nina was pleased to note the welcome absence of Richard's van.

'I'm going to take Mummy out.'

'I'll come.'

'No. There's something I need to talk to her about.'

'Oh. What?'

Susan would only go on and on if she refused to tell her. So instead she said, 'I'm going to sort out the bank statements. Don't tell Richard.'

For once Susan did not argue. Nina had gone in and extracted her mother from where she was sitting, predictably, at the kitchen table.

'Right. We're going out.'

Her mother looked up. 'Out?'

'Yes. For lunch. Just the two of us,' she said pointedly as

Susan came in with her holdall. And mindful that Richard was probably on his way over she added, 'No need to get changed.'

'So what is it?' her mother asked querulously in the car.

Nina paused. She had never been good at spinning a tale. 'We need to go to the bank to get paper statements for the account.'

'But Richard takes care of all that.'

'Yes. But you have to have paper statements as well. For legal purposes.'

Her mother sounded worried. 'Legal purposes?'

'It's for the trust. There need to be records.' She endeavoured to sound very serious. 'If Richard doesn't keep them he may be in trouble.'

It worked. Her mother frowned. 'We better get them, then.'

'Yes, we'll have them sent to my address. Then I can file them safely.'

'And he won't get into trouble?'

'Not if we do this now, no.'

So her mother had dutifully gone into the bank and signed the forms. Over lunch, Nina had tried to get more information out of her.

'So what are your monthly expenses?'

'Richard takes care of all of that. He pays everything online. He gives me cash for the shopping.'

'But do you know how much he's spending?'

'I'm sure it's all fine.'

Finally, after arguing about the doctor's appointment for five minutes, Nina had given up and driven her mother home. Today, as she started the car to drive home, even more than usual her visit felt like a failure. She never felt that she did enough. Even though neither Susan nor Richard appeared to do anything around the house, let alone look after the garden beyond sporadically mowing the lawn, Nina still felt at a disadvantage, because they were there all the time.

She could resolve to come down more often. But when she left it was always with this feeling of disappointment, of never having achieved the connection with her mother that she hoped for. More often than not she ended up spinning out the time by occupying herself with household tasks that her mother appeared not to care about anyway. Today she had cleaned the kitchen windows, instructing her mother to leave them open.

'You need some fresh air in here.'

She was beginning to get a headache and what felt as though it might be the start of a summer cold. She wound down the front windows to clear her head. She needed to get home, take Muffin for a quick walk in Holland Park and then settle down for a quiet night in. Muffin, eschewing his basket in the footwell, jumped into the front seat and put his paws on the window edge to sniff the breeze.

As she was reversing the car in the drive, Susan came running out of the house. Her heart sank.

'Nina! Nina!'

'I must get off. Otherwise I'll hit the rush-hour traffic on the M4.'

Susan took no notice. Instead, she ran round the front of the car, opened the passenger door and climbed in, picking up Muffin and putting him in the back. Then, before Nina had a chance to object, she moved his basket, too. 'We need to talk.'

It was hard not to roll her eyes. 'Can't it wait? Why don't you ring me?'

Susan shook her head dramatically. 'No. It can't. I couldn't forgive myself if I let you go without talking to you.'

This seemed unlikely. Susan always gave herself the benefit of the smallest doubt.

Nina looked pointedly at her watch. 'It will have to wait.'

'It's about Alex.'

If this was some recitation of Alex's alleged mistreatment of Susan over the weekend then she needed to get Susan out of the car. It could take for ever. There had been episodes like this in the past, most recently at New Year when Nina had relayed to Susan Alex's refusal to offer her a job.

'But I don't understand! I'm very well qualified, and if you can't trust family, then who can you rely on? It just doesn't make sense to me, Nina. And I wouldn't ask if I didn't really, really need the job. Alex is always saying how much work he has. Can't you persuade him just to give me a chance?'

Now Nina kept the engine running. 'Susan, it's nothing to do with me.'

'Yes it is.'

'This is between you and Alex. I can't referee things between you. You have to work out your own relationship.'

Susan sighed. 'That's the word, Nina. Relationship.'

Nina was unclear where this was going. She looked at her watch. She remembered now that they had no milk or fresh fruit. She needed to get to Marks & Spencer as well.

'But it's not my relationship with Alex.' Susan looked out of the window into the far distance. Then she shook her head sadly. 'I wish it was that simple.'

'I'm sorry?'

Susan turned back. Deliberately she laid a hand on Nina's arm. 'But we have to live in the real world.'

Muffin, dislodged from his favourite front-seat position and frustrated that the car wasn't moving, began to whimper.

'Nina, I want you to know that whatever happens you will always have your family.'

'Shh, Muffin. Susan, I don't know what you're talking about.'

Susan's expression was unchanged. Her voice was now slow and grave. She moved her hand from Nina's arm, picked up Nina's hand and placed her other hand over it. Her head was tilted to one side and her expression was one of deep sympathy. 'Alex is having an affair with Sasha.'

Nina let out a deep sigh and withdrew her hand from Susan's grasp. 'No he's not.'

Susan shook her head. 'I'm afraid it's true. I have proof.'

'Proof?'

'At the party. I was suspicious from the start. It was quite clear to me that they were lovers.' Anticipating Nina's objection she held a hand up. 'You can't be expected to see that,' she said authoritatively. 'You're too emotionally involved. Technically we call it denial – a psychological refusal to acknowledge the truth. It's not your fault.'

It was hard to know where to begin. 'Susan, you're not the first person to suggest this.'

'Really?'

'Yes. No, I don't mean it like that.' Too late she realised that this would only add credibility to Susan's story. 'Look, she's his PA. They spend a lot of time together. That arouses suspicion. And I have asked him time and time again and I've never had any proof that there's anything going on.'

'And he's always said no.'

'Yes.'

'But he would, wouldn't he?' said Susan dismissively. 'And I do have proof. They were in the summerhouse together.'

Now Nina felt unsettled. 'What?'

'Yes. They arranged an assignation and I followed them.'

It sounded as if Susan had rehearsed this explanation. 'Assignation?'

'Don't worry, they didn't see me. But I heard everything.'

Nina reminded herself that with Susan, the master story-teller, it was important to remain objective. 'Which was what?'

'Sasha was telling him to keep Putney,' Susan said confidently. 'She told him that if he scaled down the business he'd be unhappy for the rest of his life. She's obviously got a real hold over him. Some women have that power.' Susan paused for effect. 'Then they arranged to have dinner on Monday. That's tonight,' she added portentously. There was another, longer pause. 'And then there were noises.'

'Noises? What kind of noises?'

Susan looked surprised by the question. She faltered. 'Shuffling noises. And some groans.'

Nina gave Susan a hard look. Up until that point what she had said had rung true. But Alex never groaned.

'Who was groaning?'

'Both of them.'

'Really.' Nina looked out of the open window. It was typical of Susan to create a drama out of nothing. She tried to keep her voice even. 'Look, Sasha has played an important role in the business. She's encouraged Alex to do bigger deals. And that's what they were talking about.'

'Then why did they need to slink off to do it?'

'Presumably because Alex doesn't discuss sensitive business strategy in front of his staff. And because Sasha is smart enough to realise that her plans have been a disaster. And because she's trying to save her own skin before he sacks her – which is what he's going to do tonight.'

Actually, Nina had presumed he would deal with Sasha in the office. But now she understood that for such a sensitive conversation and the likely scene that would ensue he would want to be away from the other staff. 'That's why they're having dinner.'

'How do you know?'

'Because we discussed it. Like we discuss everything. Because we don't have secrets, Susan.'

Susan cast her a resentful glance. 'How can you be so sure?'

'Because I've been married to Alex for enough years.'

Nina could believe that Sasha engineered that conversation. It made sense that they would slip away to the summerhouse. But what she absolutely knew without a shadow of a doubt was that Alex would never, ever indulge in a sexual encounter with another woman in the middle of an office party, in the presence of his wife in his own home. He would never be so recklessly stupid.

Susan's mouth was set in a hard line. Despite all the

evidence that proved that this was a harmless business conversation she sounded utterly sure of her silly story. 'You're wrong.'

It was infuriating. 'No, I'm not. And I think you ought to be very sure of your facts before you accuse Alex of anything. You didn't see anything, Susan. You didn't hear anything significant. God knows what you heard, but if you seriously think Alex would be stupid enough to have sex with another woman while I'm a few feet away then you must be insane.'

Susan had flushed red. She seemed to want to say something.

Nina found herself filled with fury. 'Well, go on. What else have you got to say?'

'You're wrong, Nina.'

Something in the defiant tone of Susan's last statement made Nina lose control. She had had enough. Unable to stop herself, she flung open the car door and stormed round to open the passenger door.

'Get out!'

'No.' Susan looked as if she was afraid to leave the safety of the car.

She grabbed Susan's arm. 'Get out!' She pulled her from the car, Susan stumbling and virtually losing her balance on the driveway. Then Nina let rip. 'You make me sick. After all I've tried to do for you, this is how you behave.' She had some vague consciousness of talking in clichés but she didn't care. 'I have tried to help you, over and over again. And so has Alex. And now I can see that he's been right about you all along. You're lazy and unreliable and dishonest.'

'No I'm not!'

It was incredible. 'You stole money from the Palmers!'

'No I didn't.'

'Yes you did; Dad found it!'

'Well, he was wrong.'

It was all the proof that Nina needed: Susan would lie even when the evidence contradicted her story.

There was the sound of slow footsteps as their mother, presumably drawn out by the commotion, came out onto the driveway. 'What's going on?' She sounded breathless.

'Go inside, Mummy,' Nina said.

Their mother did not move.

'You're upsetting Mummy,' Susan said accusingly.

It was as if with each successive statement, Susan was intent on making Nina angrier.

'Since when have you cared about anyone except yourself?'

'I do care! I came down to help with the party!'

'You came down to have a free weekend away. And this is how you repay our hospitality!' Nina gave a hollow laugh. 'You're jealous of me.' All that Alex had told her over the years came back to her with the ring of truth. 'Why don't you just admit it? You can't bear to see that I have a good life – and a husband who loves me and looks after me – so you have to try to ruin it. Well, that isn't going to happen.'

Susan was trying to interrupt but Nina refused to give way. She shouted, 'You need to stand on your own two feet. Don't come to me for handouts any more. In fact, don't come to me for anything. Hell, why don't you try working for a change? That might solve your financial problems.' The memory of that morning's telephone conversation came to mind. 'I've a good mind to ring Roger and tell him that there was nothing wrong with the food at my house. How dare you! I put you up and give you the best of everything and then you lie about Maria.'

'I did feel sick—'

'Oh, shut up!'

She went up to Susan so that they were almost touching. Susan took a step back. Nina slowed her voice. 'Alex and I are married. We're going to stay married.' She saved the best for last. 'And we're planning to have a baby together.'

A flicker of shock passed over Susan's face.

Nina looked over at their mother, who was observing them with a detached expression. 'Mummy, go inside.'

She did not move. Instead, their mother turned to Susan. 'It's about time someone told you some home truths. Richard's been saying you need to knuckle down and stand on your own two feet.'

'Fuck Richard!' Susan burst into tears and ran for the house. Before she turned the corner she stopped and shouted back at Nina with passionate indignation, 'I am telling the truth!'

And Nina at that moment, hearing the passion in her sister's voice, could almost have believed her. But just then she caught her mother's eye. Her mother's voice was dismissive. 'No she's not. She wouldn't know how to.' She pulled Nina to her. 'You're a good girl, Nina. You've done well for yourself. Now listen to me. There'll always be people who want to take away what you have, or criticise you for how you got it. But you hang on to it.'

As her mother held her, speaking with a resolve Nina had not heard for years, there was fleetingly that connection that had for so long eluded them. And then her mother let go and went inside.

Nina turned and went slowly back to the car. Taking a few seconds to regain her composure, she started the engine and went cautiously up the driveway.

As she turned on to the road, Richard sped in without acknowledging her.

Susan crashed upstairs and slammed her bedroom door, just as she had done countless times as a teenager.

'What's up with her?' Richard said, intrigued.

Anne for once didn't feel like having a conversation with Richard. 'Some set-to with Nina. Nothing important.' She felt winded and sore in her leg from hurrying out to the car. She sat down hard on the kitchen chair.

'Oh.' He looked as if he wanted to ask more but looked at

his watch instead. 'I'll go and switch on the television.' Their current favourite quiz show was about to start.

Anne lingered in the kitchen, stretching out her leg to try to ease the pain. She listened to the theme music start up, waiting for the tightness in her chest to ease before reaching for her packet of cigarettes. She was disturbed. She had heard everything that had just passed between her two daughters through the open kitchen window and, notwithstanding her reassurances to Nina, she wouldn't be surprised if for once her younger daughter was right. Susan hadn't sounded as if she was lying and God knows they had had enough practice over the years learning to differentiate the truth from fanciful stories where that girl was concerned.

Archie had had misgivings about Alex from the start. 'There's something about him I don't like. Something ... unfeeling. I think the business will always come first for him.' They had been sitting having a late-night whisky in the drawing room. He frowned, which was unlike him. Archie naturally wore the imperturbable expression of the family solicitor. He was not especially good-looking. Rather he had a kind face, his receding hair brushed back, his wardrobe consisting of good suits, pullovers and corduroys.

'But he's an estate agent!' Anne objected. 'Of course he's working hard. He'll be a good provider.'

And she had had no doubt that was the most important thing. What good had marrying for love done her the first time round? Her own mother had been right – when poverty comes through the door, love goes out of the window. But she had been young and stupid. At least Nina would be spared that fate.

She pressed on. 'He's got a sensible head on his shoulders.'

Archie had gestured towards the window at Fellows Farm. 'It's all very sudden. You're not telling me she's got over Michael? She's on the rebound.'

Archie had made no effort to conceal his disappointment

when things went sour with Michael Fellows. But Anne saw no point in crying over spilt milk. She continued to promote Alex's cause. 'He comes from a good family.'

Archie snorted. 'The mother's a tyrant.'

'She's set a good example for him.'

In the months leading up to the wedding Anne had worked hard to promote the marriage to Archie and to head off any plans he might have of dissuading Nina. The last thing they needed was Nina backing out on the wedding day, leaving two hundred guests in the church. Anne's acceptance into Marlow society had been hard-won and she wasn't about to be humiliated in front of those people now. She had made Archie promise not to say anything. 'Don't go telling her it's not too late to pull out because it damn well is!'

Reluctantly, eventually persuaded by Anne's forceful argument that he would only confuse and upset Nina by expressing his doubts, he had promised.

Now she put out her cigarette and resolved to put the matter out of her mind. A married couple had to work things out between themselves, just as she and Archie had done. If there was another woman, Nina would have to roll up her sleeves and see her off – just as Anne had had to weather the reminders of the first Mrs Carruthers. She sat still for a moment, the unwelcome recollections of decades earlier returning to her, still with the power to hurt after all those years: the pointed reminiscences of her mother-in-law, the asides of Mrs Baxter, the snide remarks of the old guard at the WI – and the love letters Archie kept hidden in a mahogany box in the attic. She never told him she knew.

Anne was not quite sure if she had loved Archie on their wedding day. It had been hard to differentiate love from all the other emotions she had felt that day at High Wycombe Register Office: relief, hopefulness and a degree of triumph that she had carried off one of Marlow's most eligible bachelors. Archie's mother had cut her dead on the steps but there was nothing she could do and both women knew it.

She had been dreading the wedding reception, held at Archie's parents' house on the river at Bisham, an Edwardian pile of a house which her family had loudly oohed and aahed over like day-trippers touring a stately home. She had instantly regretted inviting them, her sister in a print miniskirt, her brother asking for a beer, her mother acting with exaggerated deference as though the lady of the manor had invited her for tea, which in a sense she had.

'Thank you very much, Mrs Carruthers. Is there anything I can do to help?'

'I don't believe so. The staff have everything in hand.'

Her father spent all of his working life as a groom at Cliveden, touching his cap to the owners, the Astor family. He taught Anne to ride, but only when the family wasn't there. He was a man of few words and never once was one wasted on praise. A brief nod was all that she ever got. But Anne knew that she was good. As a teenage girl she mastered with ease the horses that the other grooms shied away from. She was lithe and balanced, fearless and instinctive. Years later, watching the Horse of the Year Show, she knew that one of those riders could have been her. All she lacked was money, education and connections.

In the years that followed Anne had seen less and less of her family until the time came when they did not come to the house at all. Instead, Anne preferred to visit her mother from time to time. It was simpler that way. When they came to Orchard House her parents perched uncomfortably on the sofas and made comments about how much everything cost. There had been a particularly embarrassing incident when her mother had insisted on helping Mrs Baxter with the washing-up, chatting to her a little too freely about Anne's childhood. After that she had resolved to keep the two sides of her life firmly separate.

There had been a buffet at the wedding, Archie's mother previously looking pointedly at her stomach. 'In your condition a sit-down meal would be a little over the top, don't you agree, Annie?' She always called her Annie, even though no one else did. But later there was a band and dancing and everyone let their hair down. That day she had been grateful for Jack Tyler: best man, property developer, wheeler-dealer, local millionaire and, in time, Archie's biggest client. Three times married and twice declared bankrupt, Jack had gone on to rebuild his fortunes on each occasion. Already on his second wife at that stage, an Italian girl who lasted a couple of years, he had encouraged everyone onto the dance floor and made a speech that had everyone laughing. He was a five-foot-six bundle of energy, dangerous but irresistible, predictably making several passes at Anne over the years, all of which she easily rebuffed. It was hard to take offence; it was almost as if he couldn't help himself. And afterwards they had departed in Jack's chauffeur-driven Rolls to spend the night at the Randolph in Oxford. That part of things she knew would be all right.

Had she loved Archie on that day? She thought she probably had. But what Anne did know without doubt was that love had budded and grown stronger year by year, that the shadow of his first wife, which in the early days had tortured her, had grown fainter, that she had found the passion of Archie's early embraces grow to real affection. Did he love her? Yes, he did – in time. She remembered the first time she had felt it for sure. It was a summer's day and they had been sitting in the back garden as Richard, dressed in a blue and white striped romper suit, practised his first unsteady steps. Archie had reached over and taken her hand.

'I love you, Anne.'

Yes, Richard had been their love-child in the truest sense. That was when she had known that it was all going to be all right, that Archie was a man who would make the most of their unpromising start, that all her efforts were paying off. Richard was the tie that bound them, the son and heir. She would whisper to him, 'One day you'll grow up to be just like

Daddy. One day you'll go to the office just like Daddy. You're Daddy's special little boy.'

It had been an effort. When they said you had to work at a marriage it was true – young people these days didn't understand that, especially the girls. When Archie came home from work it was to a quiet and orderly house, the newspaper ready for him, a glass of sherry in her hand. They ate alone. Archie would read the children a bedtime story – he liked to do that – but after seven o'clock there had better be a very good reason for any child slipping downstairs. Then they would watch television or sit outside or sometimes put an LP on. And finally it was bedtime, when she didn't have to make any effort at all, when the passion that never faded between them took over, when she was at her happiest: lying in Archie's arms, just the two of them.

Chapter 9

All her life Sasha had survived, or more accurately prospered, by keeping the lid tightly closed on each of the painful and unpleasant episodes of her past. She had moved forward, never lingering long enough to feel anything much at all. There was always a new job, man, flat or place to take her mind off whatever pained her.

But right now, standing in her white-tiled bathroom, there was nothing to distract her.

She felt as though she was unravelling – she who had always been so tightly, perfectly coiled. She stared at herself in the mirror. The face that stared back at her was alone, unanchored in the world, and growing older.

She was distanced from her family, she had no true friends and she was jobless. If she died tonight there would be four people at her funeral: Dad, Pat, Keith and Kelly.

But not Alex.

At the thought of him she took several deep breaths to stop herself getting angry again. She had expected more of him and had every right to do so. She had behaved with perfect dignity, self-control and understanding. She had been more than generous in her willingness to play a long game.

And Alex had behaved like a gutless, self-serving, cowardly fool.

If only he had confined his comments to himself.

She had known that he wanted it to be over. His suggestion of dinner had been reluctant, his eyes averted and in his choice of the Wolseley he had chosen a public and bustling restaurant. She guessed that he was afraid she would make a scene and felt affronted that he would so underestimate her.

When they had sat down, Alex, to his credit, had surprised her. She had thought he would wait at least until the main course before raising the subject. Men, after all, liked to minimise their discomfort. But he had leaned forward shortly after the waitress had brought them drinks.

'We have to stop.'

Sasha took a sip of her Martini. 'Stop?'

'We have to stop seeing each other. It can't go on.' He paused. 'And you need to leave the office.'

He certainly wasn't sugar-coating the pill.

She sighed. 'What's brought this on?'

He looked around the Wolseley, at the high ceilings and grand columns of the former bank building, as if to gain inspiration. They were early and the restaurant had just a scattering of diners.

'I'm sorry, Sasha.'

He looked as if he thought that this explanation would be sufficient.

'Does Nina know?'

'No,' he said urgently.

'Does she suspect?'

He shrugged. 'Probably.'

Belatedly, he seemed to realise that he needed to say more. 'I just can't. It's not you. You're ... fabulous. You're an inspiration. Any man would be proud to have you by his side.'

At that moment they were interrupted by the waitress, who came to take their order.

Sasha took the opportunity to appraise the situation. It was all going according to plan. Clearly Alex didn't really want to end it at all; he was just going through a temporary crisis of confidence.

She waited until the waitress had left.

'Alex, I understand your position. Truly I do. I can't imagine the strain you've been under.'

But he second-guessed her. 'Sasha, I mean it,' he interrupted. 'We have to end it.'

'I think we have to take a break.'

He shook his head. 'No.' He looked up at her and then away. 'Sasha, I'm married.'

She was unable to hide the note of impatience from her voice. 'Yes, I know that. You were married when we met.'

'And I have to stay married. I'm Catholic, for God's sake.'

He was being ridiculous, but at least she had drawn him out. 'So God wants you to stay in a miserable marriage for the rest of your life.'

'No. It means I have to make a go of it.' He downed his drink and looked around for the waitress. 'I have to think about Nina as well. She's been very … supportive.'

It was important to keep him talking. 'Supportive?'

Alex continued haltingly. 'I owe Nina a lot. She was with me at the start. I can't just forget all that and ride off into the sunset.'

'Alex, she would get very adequate financial provision.'

He gave her a hard glance. 'It's not all about money.'

She backtracked. 'No, of course not. But if that is one of your concerns then it can be addressed. How is it going to help Nina or make her happy if you stay out of some sense of obligation? You'll both end up unhappy. This way she has time to make a new start, too.'

'I have to try.'

There was another interruption as Alex ordered a second gin and tonic. And even though she knew it would be better not to, she asked for another Martini. She was beginning to feel just a little rattled.

She gathered her thoughts. 'You say you need to try. But you tried before! Alex, you didn't have an affair because your marriage was so blissfully happy. You came to me because something, lots of things, were lacking in your life. And those problems in your marriage will still be there tomorrow.'

But he was not conceding. 'I can't just walk away,' he said stubbornly.

'Alex, if you go back things will be exactly as they were before. Actually, they will be worse because now you know what it's like to really be able to share your feelings with someone. Our relationship isn't just physical.'

She stopped to give him a chance to respond. But he sat silently, rotating his tumbler and staring at his drink.

It was useless to argue with him. The guilt had taken hold of him and men in that condition were hopeless. She had experienced it with Tony: he tried to break it off with her after some test result of his wife's had been especially bad. But he had come back – and so would Alex.

'OK,' she said. 'I'm not going to argue with you. You must do what you think is right.'

She recalled that Tony – when she had said this same sentence at roughly the same point in their conversation – had looked up worriedly: 'Will you be OK?'

'Don't worry about me. I'll take a holiday. Maybe New York. Some time away will do me good.'

Two days later Tony had called. 'Have you booked your ticket?' was his first nervous question. 'When can I see you?' was the second.

But Alex, far from looking anxious, visibly relaxed. He even took a mouthful of his soup. 'Christ, I'm sorry, Sasha. I just can't go on. I have to think of Nina.'

He really needed to stop talking about Nina as if she was important in all this! Nina was a little person, a pawn, who didn't have a clue that she was in the game, let alone what the rules were. Nina was irrelevant.

But he went on. 'It's a question of doing what's right. I know it's late in the day but I have to try.'

And then something wholly unexpected and unwelcome began to happen. For some unaccountable reason she began to feel short of breath.

She took a good, long gulp of her first Martini, emptying the glass.

Alex did not appear to notice anything amiss. As she struggled to regain control, taking a gulp from her second drink, he continued talking.

'You have so many options, Sasha. And no baggage.' He opened his hands expansively. 'You're a free spirit. And I will never forget our time together ...'

She blocked out his words, focusing on maintaining her composure. It was a question of mind over matter. She fixed her eye on a far spot and breathed slowly in and out.

Alex was still talking, something about her being very important in his life, but she wasn't listening now. It was taking every ounce of her energy and concentration not to explode with emotion.

Finally, she couldn't take it any more. 'And what about me, Alex? Don't I matter too?' She took another drink. In front of her, her food was untouched.

He looked surprised. 'Of course you do. But hell, Sasha. You're not exactly the girl next door.' He shot her a half-smile. 'You've got the biggest fridge in London and it never has any food in it.'

He was ruining everything. Why was he saying these things? He was ending it because of needy Nina, because he couldn't afford an expensive divorce, because he'd lost his nerve with the business expansion and because, apparently, he'd developed some late-in-the-day spiritual principles.

He wasn't leaving because of her. None of this was about her. She was just fine as she was. And there was no reason why, after a little while, they couldn't resume where they had left off.

But he had more to say. 'Sasha, you're ... independent. Self-assured. You're a girl who can take care of herself.'

'Not the marrying kind?'

'I didn't say that. I just think that what works in a relationship doesn't necessarily work in a marriage.'

'And when did you come to this conclusion?'

'I don't know.' He sounded impatient now. After all, she had never before posed awkward questions. 'I didn't think this out in advance, Sasha. You and me – the situation – it just happened. I couldn't stop it.'

The situation. Was that what he was calling it now? How could he deny all that they had had together, making her seem like some bit on the side? She thought back to the intimate dinners, the long talks about his childhood, the way he had confided in her more and more.

'Even though I knew I could never please her,' he had once said about his mother, 'I still kept trying.'

She should have been a psychiatrist. She was much better at reading people than most of them. 'How do you know you didn't get it?' she had responded. 'Just because she didn't say so doesn't mean she wasn't proud of you.'

Their relationship had been about so much more than sex. They shopped and went to galleries and did all the things that married couples did. Hell, Alex even put up the birch shelves in her living room and fixed the bath panel that had come away from the side of the bath months ago. She had left it, hating to have strange tradesmen wandering about the flat.

'It just needed the nut tightening,' he'd said, getting off the floor.

Now she was filled with fury that he could demean her and their relationship in this way. 'So I was the fun bit on the side when you never had any intention of leaving your wife.'

She knew it was the wrong thing to say: men hated to be told the truth.

Sure enough he retaliated. 'I never said I would,' he hissed. 'If you got that idea then it wasn't because of anything I said.'

It was a row now. 'So it's all my fault.'

His mouth was set hard. 'Look, I don't think there's any point in this. I'm going to get the bill.'

Before she could stop him he raised his hand. The couple

on an adjacent table gave each other a knowing look. And then the waitress came over.

She looked worriedly at Sasha's uneaten food. 'Was everything all right?'

'Yes,' Alex said testily. 'The bill, please.'

'You don't want to re-order?' She turned to Sasha. 'I can get the manager if it was not right.'

Alex intervened. 'The bill. Please. Now.'

It appeared to take for ever. They sat wordlessly as she cleared their plates, Sasha inwardly burning with anger and humiliation. He had no right to end their dinner, to cut off the conversation, to dismiss her like this as if she meant nothing. The couple at the adjacent table kept stealing glances at them. She felt like telling them to mind their own fucking business.

She focused on getting out of there without losing control.

But Alex cleared his throat. 'I need your key.'

'What?'

'Your office key.'

She did not want to deal with it. 'I'll bring it in tomorrow.'

His voice had taken on a new tone that she had never heard before. It was hard and detached and emotionless. It was the same voice, she realised, that he must have used all those years ago when he told his mother that he was leaving. 'I think it's better if you don't come back to the office. It would be difficult for everyone. I'll make the final payment by bank transfer tomorrow. And I'll get your personal things packed up and sent over by courier.'

Sasha had a vision: Harriet – fat, snickering, ignorant Harriet – would be instructed to go through her things. And the whole office would pile in to watch. After Harriet had touched her belongings she would need to throw them all away.

'Don't bother. I don't want any of it.'

Slowly she undid her handbag, took the key from the key-ring and slipped it under her palm across the table.

She couldn't take it any more. It was very fortunate that the couple on the adjacent table were at that moment pre-occupied with ordering from the dessert menu. Otherwise, who knows what she might have said if they had cast her one more of those prurient looks. As it was she got up, carefully placed her white linen napkin on the table and without look-ing at Alex she walked out of the restaurant.

Now, back at home, she took a temazepam and went into the living room. Outside, the lights of London, illuminating the city, served only to make her feel lonelier.

It was unbearable. She could get drunk, but she knew it wouldn't work. She would wake up at three o'clock in the morning, alone and depressed and hungover. She could call Kelly. But as she recalled their last conversation she already knew what she would say.

'You need to get out, Angie. He's married.'

They had met for a drink in the bar of One Aldwych. Kelly had come up to London on a rare night away from her husband and baby. She had looked around the bar like a girl who had never seen the inside of an upmarket hotel before.

Kelly had leaned forward. 'Someone's been asking ques-tions about you at Dauphins.'

'Who?'

Kelly had shrugged. 'Copper or an ex-copper.' Kelly went on to provide a vague description of a man in his fifties with short brown hair wearing a black leather jacket, as provided to her by her husband who still worked in the Dauphins back office. 'He was handing out twenties like they were going out of fashion.'

If he was throwing cash about then it was more likely a private investigator. She had not been unduly worried. They couldn't prove anything.

But Kelly had had more to say. 'Is it about this fella?'

'Alex? I don't think so.' It was probably Tony or Sir Christopher trying to get some of their money back.

'But you don't know that,' Kelly persisted. 'I don't like the sound of him. He's a property developer. Which probably means he's up to all sorts.' Kelly counted off on her fingers. 'Dodgy planning permissions. Tax evasion. Salting money away in some Swiss bank account.' She took a sip of her drink. 'And he's married.'

'Not for long.'

Kelly rolled her eyes. 'That's what they all say. Angie, I don't want to see you get hurt. Get out now while you can. You've still got time to find yourself a nice single bloke.'

'I don't want a nice single bloke.'

Kelly had shaken her arm. 'Angie. Married men are all the same. They want to have their cake and eat it.'

Kelly had been right. Calling her would only result in one of those all-things-work-out-for-the-best conversations, at the end of which Kelly would pronounce that Alex leaving was a blessing in disguise and she should go and book herself a nice holiday.

No, something else, different and foolproof, was needed this time. She paced up and down, glancing at the telephone, instinctively understanding that even in the lifting of the receiver and the dialling of the number she would find relief.

She always knew how to find relief. As a child, after her mother had died, it had been in cigarettes, cider, loud music, sex and staying thin. She would write down, in neat columns in a notebook, exactly how many calories she had eaten that day.

People also provided relief. People could be knocked into or pinched or shoved or slapped or kicked. Or straight-out hit. Of course, you had to find someone smaller. But it was not risky, especially not if you did it in games. They played hockey at her school, after all. And after a while the other kids knew to stay away and that in itself worked pretty well too, that look of wary fear in their eyes.

It was all in the eyes. Like Nina's sister at the party when she started to toy with her, that look of someone who knows they're trapped and they've got no means of escape. You could get it easily from shoe shop assistants: make the girl bring out twenty boxes. Take them out, help her, take them back. And then, at the end, walk away. Waitresses could be sent back and forth. Manicurists could start that nail again so that it was absolutely right. And all hotel staff were easy game.

But there was no one and nothing now to distract her. She looked at the telephone, understanding that the call would place her there – with them – instead of here alone.

She sat down, then got up, impatient for the pill to take effect.

It was unbearable. She picked up the receiver and dialled his home number: there was no risk. Her number was blocked.

After three rings Nina answered. 'Hello.'

She held on to the receiver, feeling the calm descend, feeling the power and the control return.

'Hello. Hello?' A note of confusion and a hint of anxiety had entered Nina's voice.

And then the receiver went down.

She waited for five minutes and called again.

It was Alex. 'Who is this?'

He knew. He sounded like a second-rate actor feigning confusion. She replaced the receiver before he had the chance to and felt the sense of security intensify. Now she knew she would sleep and tomorrow – at nine thirty a.m. sharp – she would make the next telephone call.

Nina watched Alex replace the receiver. His expression unsettled her. His composure was seldom disturbed. They were standing in the drawing room.

'It was her, wasn't it?'

For a moment he stood motionless, his hand resting on the receiver. Then he nodded.

Her voice rose accusingly. 'But you said she took it very well.'

He snapped back defensively. 'She did.'

'Then why is she calling?'

He spread his hands. 'Probably because she got home, had a couple of drinks and began to feel sorry for herself.'

That seemed plausible enough.

He continued, 'She's just lost her job. What do you expect her to do, throw a party?'

'And she's not coming back to the office?'

'No. I told you. She gave me her key.'

It was a cause of irritation that Alex had given Sasha a key to the office. No one else had one. But Alex, who had let this fact slip some months ago, had said that it was necessary for her to be able to let the staff in and set the alarm.

Now, he pulled off his tie, slumped on the sofa and clicked on the television remote control to watch the end of the news bulletin. Clearly he considered their conversation at an end.

But Nina continued to feel unsettled. Susan's words reverberated in her mind as they had done since she left Marlow.

Alex had, predictably, been dismissive when on his arrival home that evening she had recounted that afternoon's conversation with Susan.

'Look. Sasha's no fool. She knew what was coming. And yes, she did ask to speak to me on my own – to tell me how important she was to the business. That's all.'

'Then why did Susan say there were noises?'

He had sparked at that. 'Because I was bringing out some more chairs!'

Nervously she had pressed on. 'But why would she say it?'

Alex had rounded on her then. 'Because she's a trouble-maker. Open your eyes. Because she loves to stir things up.' He corrected himself. 'To make trouble where there isn't any. This is hardly new, is it?'

She had conceded the point by saying nothing in response.

But now Nina continued to ponder the silent calls. Sasha didn't seem the type to make drunken calls – she was the kind of person who would let rip with some pretty unpleasant invective. Nina walked over to Alex, took the remote from where it lay on the side table and switched off the television.

Alex responded by laying his head back on the sofa, letting out a deep breath. 'For God's sake.'

She ignored him. 'Look at me.'

Reluctantly he did so. His voice was impatient. 'What?'

He seemed to have no conception that this whole situation, and the accusations and suspicions that had resulted, was entirely of his own making.

She spoke as forcefully as she could. 'I want you to promise me – I want you to swear to me – that you never slept with that woman.'

He held her gaze. She searched his face, looking for the trace of a lie, some flicker or movement of the eyes, some touching of the face, some sign that could betray him.

Alex was motionless. His eyes did not leave hers. 'I swear to you, Nina. Nothing at all ever happened.'

Then he stood up. He took hold of her shoulders. 'Darling, I love you. You're my wife.' He paused. 'Don't tear us apart over something that never happened.' He kissed her on the forehead. 'Now, I don't want to discuss this again.'

She knew that he was right. 'OK.'

It was nine thirty a.m. Sasha had showered, dressed in a business suit and was sitting at her dining-room table with a cup of black coffee. She felt much better as she turned to the telephone listings in her Filofax. She had not used this number before but Tony, who knew about these things, had once said that they were the best for this type of case.

After two rings the clipped-voiced receptionist answered. 'Masterson, Ryder and Jardine.'

'Good morning. I would like to speak to one of your

employment law specialists. Someone who deals with claims for sexual harassment. And it's urgent: I need to see someone today.'

'Certainly. I'll put you through.'

Autumn

Chapter 10

Lady Harnford, dressed in a purple bouclé wool suit and cream silk shirt, delivered the same speech that she had given for the last six years.

'Nothing too spicy. Nothing Oriental. And none of those new-fangled miniature beefburgers.'

Nina nodded attentively. She made a note in her hardcover A4 notebook. 'Menu the same as last year.'

'And please make sure that there are plenty of those cheese straws.'

She had already pencilled in the date before her meeting: Lady Harnford's Christmas drinks party was always held on the third Thursday of December. There would be some twenty-five guests in the drawing room and spilling out into the hallway. It was a beautiful first-floor drawing room, looking out over Cadogan Gardens, yellow silk curtains elegantly draped to the side of the floor-to-ceiling windows.

They sat on aged horsehair chintz sofas surrounded by elegant cherry and walnut side tables. Family photographs in heavy silver frames dotted the room, including one of Lady Harnford's late father with Winston Churchill and another of her late husband in evening dress standing next to Harold Macmillan.

Lady Harnford got up and clicked across the polished parquet floor, dotted with worn Oriental rugs, in a pair of old but immaculate Ferragamo patent leather court shoes.

The flat, like Lady Harnford, had remained unchanged for the six years that Nina had been coming. Unfortunately so too had the kitchen, with its temperamental 1970s cooker and too-small sink. Like many of the old aristocracy hanging on in these London flats, Nina suspected that Lady Harnford lived on a relatively small pension and memories of better days. She had not increased her charge for the party for the last three years and didn't mark up the wine. Really it was hardly worth doing it.

But her annual visit was a chance to experience a world fast disappearing. On her death, Lady Harnford's large and highly sought-after flat would be gutted and luxuriously refurbished by a City banker and his wife. They would bring with them a four-wheel drive, a Bugaboo and a Polish daily nanny.

Lady Harnford poured another cup of tea from her engraved Victorian silver teapot. She liked to chat and Nina had allowed an hour for their appointment.

'My daughter will be coming and the grandchildren. Both the girls are at Cambridge now but they'll be home for the holidays. And I have new neighbours, so I have to ask them. Ground floor. They're Canadian.' She paused. 'But perhaps they'll be busy.'

She proffered Nina a plate of Rich Tea fingers.

'No, thank you.'

And then Lady Harnford was off, talking about the goings-on in the local Conservative Association, her August holiday in Perthshire and the wicked increase in the service charge for her flat.

'It's not as if we even get hot water! We each have our own boiler.'

Then there was more talk of the new Canadian neighbours and the building work that started at seven thirty a.m.

'Of course I'm up and dressed by then. But it's such an uncivilised start to the day. I haven't been in there, but apparently they're taking down all the ceilings. Why ever would you want to do that?'

Nina, who normally enjoyed their conversations, felt her mind begin to wander. Lately it had been difficult to concentrate on anything much at all. Last week she had got caught out in an editorial meeting at *Capital Letter*.

Paula Nicholson, whom she had not seen since her interview, had come in to address the features staff. 'After four weeks advertising revenue has flatlined.' She pressed a switch and a Powerpoint slide of the London underground zones overlaid with different coloured sections flashed up on the overhead screen.

'The sections represent *Zut!* distribution numbers. You can see that *Zut!* is making a very strong showing in Zone 1.'

And then she started on a page-by-page comparison of each magazine. Privately, Nina liked *Zut!* It's mix of showbusiness news and celebrity gossip was just what she liked at the end of the day.

Belatedly, after Paula Nicholson had stopped talking, Nina realised that they were now going round the room. She had no idea for what reason. And her turn was fast approaching.

She turned to Diana, the features editor sitting to her side. 'I think I've missed something.'

Diana didn't miss a beat. 'Say that it lacks contemporary edge,' she whispered.

There was no time to ask more. It was her turn. 'It lacks contemporary edge,' she said authoritatively.

Paula Nicholson looked happy enough with this response. 'Yep. Exactly what I thought.'

Listening to the other participants she grasped that they were being asked to comment on their rival feature in *Zut!*

Afterwards Diana had given her a strange look. 'Everything OK?'

'Oh. Yes. Fine. Sorry about that. Late night.'

How could she explain? It all sounded so ridiculously far-fetched.

At worst she felt hounded. And at best, when she was able to rationalise the strange events of the past few weeks, it felt to Nina as if she was living under a permanent cloud, which would only be lifted when Sasha Fleming settled her court case against Alex for unfair dismissal. Alex insisted that Sasha would drop the case at the eleventh hour.

'You've got to see it for what it is, Nina. She's doing it to get attention. This is exactly what she wants – to get a reaction from you. You've got to carry on as normal.'

As for Alex, he was barely at home. And when he was there he spent the evening crashed out in front of the television. At ten o'clock she would gently shake him awake. He was working crazy hours, leaving the flat at seven a.m. to show properties, carry out repairs and check tenants in and out. Then he would go back to the office to help Harriet with the paperwork.

It was hopeless to tell him to slow down. She had persuaded him to take last Sunday off only to return from a shopping trip to find him seated at the kitchen table poring over spreadsheets.

'It's temporary,' he said. 'Until we get to full occupancy and the rent increase kicks in.'

At least he had squared things with the tax authorities regarding the SA and negotiated a payment schedule with the bank. For a while she had privately worried that they would lose the London flat as well.

And in between times there was the unresolved issue of all the money that Richard had taken out of the cashpoint with her mother's bank card, the purchases and payments to online gambling sites and eBay from her account, and her mother's continued refusal to admit that there might be something wrong. Finally, getting nowhere, Nina had telephoned the family solicitor, John Kirkpatrick, who had suggested a meeting. The prospect of being in the same room with Susan, Richard and her mother in a week's time made her feel permanently stressed out.

Now Alex refused to discuss Sasha. She had pressed him time and time again. 'I just don't understand. You made her redundant – her and three other staff – and you haven't replaced any of them. How can she possibly have a case for unfair dismissal?'

With each successive attempt to press him on this point Alex had grown more exasperated. 'That's the way the law is these days. These lawyers can argue that night is day. You don't have to have any evidence.'

Several times she had gone through his desk, but there was nothing. He must be keeping all the papers at the office where Harriet and Marjorie had moved in to cover for Sasha.

Now, listening to Lady Harnford, she wished she could stay all afternoon. It was like stepping back in time to a less complicated world. Watching as Lady Harnford poured boiling water into the teapot she envied her ordered, structured life with its rituals and certainties. Her own life seemed to be spinning out of control. She glanced again at the cluster of family photographs, smartly posed pictures in which people who looked as though they would never behave badly gave carefree smiles to the camera. The men made her think of Archie. It had been three years now, but she missed him as much as ever, and appreciated how much she had relied upon his wise counsel. And as for the rest of her family, without Archie to keep them in line they seemed to have entirely forgotten how to behave.

Archie's death had made her hunger all the more for a family of her own. Alex had been supportive but uncomprehending.

'We've got plenty of time, darling.'

His mother's death a year later, far from promoting parallel thoughts of family in Alex's mind, had taken him in an opposite direction. He had become consumed with the business, buying up properties one after the other, pursuing expansion it seemed to her almost for the sake of it. She had given up trying to reason with him or persuade him to spend less time at the office. Besides, when they did spend time together all he wanted to talk about was the business, drumming his fingers impatiently on the table.

It was comforting to blame Sasha. But the fact was that the problems between them had already started before she arrived.

Sasha was the catalyst, not the cause of their estrangement. Sometimes, in her darkest moments, Nina needed to push away the thought that perhaps she and Alex had always held different values and desires – their incompatibility masked by work and socialising and a relationship in which they seemed so well suited – until time and circumstances conspired to reveal the truth. And often at these times her mind turned to Michael. She would see him in her mind's eye, holding her hand as they walked along the riverbank or cheering at the Henley Regatta or standing on the Statue of Liberty ferry, the New York skyline behind him, their last summer together. Even after all these years she could be driving in London and feel a jolt at the sight of a stranger who resembled him, or a pang of remembrance as she passed a place they had visited.

They had known each other since they were children. Michael would come up to the house for hide and seek or rainy-day board games. Susan trailed him, Richard tried desperately to beat him and Nina stood apart, slightly in awe of this clever, funny, sometimes wilful boy who had a worldliness about him surprising in someone who had grown up on a Marlow farm with his destiny mapped out for him. But Michael, as she later found out, read voraciously, listened attentively and when he passed the 11+ to go to the William Borlase School, seized this chance of a gateway to the outside world.

When Michael came back from his first year at art school in London, the headstrong boy had become a confident young man. She was at Wycombe College then, doing a foundation catering course and still living at home. She had bumped into him one Saturday afternoon as he got out of a red Triumph sports car parked in Marlow High Street. He was still the same figure, tall and well built, but his hair was longer now and he wore a dark T-shirt, Levi's and sunglasses. She was wearing a red cotton sundress, the type that was fashionable at the time, sleeveless with an elasticated smocked top. She had almost walked straight past him.

'Nina!' He had pulled off the sunglasses and given her an appraising look. 'Do you need a lift?'

Only afterwards did she realise that this was a strange question given that he had just parked the car. 'Thanks.'

He had taken her shopping and piled it in the small back seat, mostly groceries. With Mrs Baxter working part-time Nina had taken on most of the cooking, supplemented by Marks & Spencer's ready meals. Her mother's recent accident was to provide her with a permanent excuse not to cook.

She sank into the worn leather of the passenger seat. 'New car?'

'It's very old, actually. I rescued it from the scrapheap. But I've been working on it.' He started the engine. 'I've been doing some assistant work for a photographer. As you can imagine, Dad loves it.'

She laughed. Later she would hear Edward's opinion on the car first hand. 'Bloody piece of junk. Red! What's wrong with the Land Rover?'

The car was a declaration of independence, a sign of things to come between Michael and his father.

When he dropped her at the house he turned to her casually. 'I was going to go up to the National Portrait Gallery next week. I'm doing a Hockney assignment. Would you like to come?'

'I'd love to!' And again it was only later that she had asked herself why she had felt quite so excited about going to a museum with a boy she had known since childhood.

They had spent an hour at the gallery, been hushed several times because they were laughing too loud and escaped into the June sun. It had been natural for Michael to take her hand and for them to walk to Covent Garden, where they sat outside an Italian cafe sharing pizza slices. They talked about his father and the farm and then about her mother and Monty and the accident.

'Archie wants to send him to a home for retired race-horses.'

Michael raised an eyebrow. 'What does your mother say about that?'

She gave an exasperated sigh. 'You can imagine. She thinks you're going to ride him over the summer.'

'I can do,' he said quickly.

'Thanks. But the problem is finding someone after that. She keeps finding people, then she spies on them from the house and sacks them a week later because they're not good enough. Poor Monty doesn't know if he's coming or going.'

'Will she ride again?'

Nina shook her head. 'I don't know.'

And Michael, who was always honest to a fault, said, 'I don't think she will. If she can't do it perfectly she won't want to do it at all.'

It was like talking to someone who knew you inside out. She never felt that she had to put on a show or make excuses for her family or do anything other than be herself.

Afterwards they had walked back to the car and when he drove her home he had stopped in the driveway where they were secluded by the beech trees.

He hesitated for a moment. 'If you like, we could see a film at the weekend.' In those days Marlow had a cinema in Station Road with crushed red velvet seats and tired Pearl & Dean advertisements for local car dealers.

'I'd love to.'

He reached over and took her hand.

She wanted to ask him then if he had a girlfriend at college. There was a pause.

'Have you got a boyfriend?' he asked. That was to happen so many times in the future, the two of them thinking parallel thoughts.

'No.' She was surprised by the question. But she took the opportunity. 'Have you got a girlfriend?'

'No.' And she knew then that he wasn't playing games or looking for some temporary summer fun.

'I've always liked you, Nina. Didn't you know?'

She shook her head.

'You're special. I've thought about you a lot while I've been away.'

And then he put the car into gear and pulled up to the front door – and she would have done anything at that moment for the afternoon to have continued into night, to have spent it with him, instead of creeping into the house to face the disapproving questions of her mother.

Richard was steaming. He waved a letter at Kate. 'It came this morning. We all have to go to that bloody solicitor's office.'

Kate put down her handbag on the kitchen table and began to take off her coat. She spoke to Emily. 'Go and play, Emmie.' She turned back to Richard. 'Why?'

'To talk about the trust. Nina's called a meeting.' He took a beer out of the fridge. 'It's fine for her. All she has to do is sit around all day filing her nails and living off her rich husband.'

'But what exactly is it all about?'

'Nothing,' he said angrily. 'First she stirs up trouble with the bank and now this. She's got nothing better to do with her time.'

Kate had always got the impression that Nina worked pretty hard.

'This is all Dad's fault,' Richard continued. 'He should have divided up the estate on his death.'

Kate had heard this time and time again. Archie's will stipulated that on his death all his money went into a trust which was administered by one of the partners of his old law firm, Carruthers & Kirkpatrick. Worse still, the exact terms of the trust were a secret. No one knew exactly what it said. There had been a very embarrassing incident a couple of years ago when Richard had discovered that one of their new neighbours worked as a secretary in the Carruthers & Kirkpatrick office. The neighbour had refused to tell him anything. Kate still felt awkward when they crossed paths.

'But instead he has to set up some complicated trust,' Richard continued. 'We can't sneeze without asking the solicitor's permission.'

Kate couldn't understand why he was so worked up. 'But if there's nothing wrong, and this meeting is just to talk about the terms of the trust, then what's the problem? Your mother isn't going to do anything to hurt you.'

Richard was so obviously the favourite. But he seemed to gain no reassurance from this position. If anything, it made him paranoid that Nina and Susan were conspiring to gang up and usurp him.

'There doesn't have to be anything wrong,' he said, agitated. 'I have to be on guard, that's the point. If Nina and Susan get together then they've got a majority vote after Mummy dies.'

Kate could not be bothered to respond to this. She looked at him, unshaven and dressed in a grey tracksuit. He had spent the last two days, as far as she could make out, listening to Pink Floyd's *Wish You Were Here*. 'It's in mint condition,' he had said excitedly, showing her the LP. He had bought it on eBay. 'I slipped in a bid right at the last second!'

She no longer asked where he had been all day or what he had been doing. In fact, she could no longer stand even to listen to him. She walked out of the kitchen and into the living room where a stack of framing supplies stood in the corner. Emily was playing with her Barbie dolls. She sat down and closed her eyes.

There was an open race at the sailing club this weekend, one of the last of the season. 'It'll be cold,' Daniel had warned her.

She and Daniel had been eating lunch at a café on the river in Maidenhead. Kate had driven out to see one of their major customers, timing her meeting to coincide with Daniel's Friday delivery. It was, after all, important to see that the job was being done properly so that she could write an accurate appraisal for his three-month review. And afterwards she had suggested that they look over the new planned delivery route

– and since it was lunchtime it would be a sensible use of the firm's time to do this in their lunch break.

Daniel had scanned the new routes, taken out a pen and made a couple of swift notes in the margin. 'Just a suggestion,' he had said, pushing them back across the table to her. 'It would cut about half an hour off.'

'Thanks.' God, it was absolutely impossible not to compare him to Richard. He was so positive and go-getting. The customers loved him. He had on more than one occasion run back to AdTech after hours to collect a missing box or urgently needed supply. She had hesitated in response to his comment about the sailing, searching his face to see how serious he was. Encountering Daniel at work was one thing – sitting at the same group table in the canteen, most days catching each other first thing by the coffee machine – but arranging to meet him out of hours was quite another.

'Maybe,' she had said, not able to bring herself to say no.

He had nodded. 'I'll look out for you.'

At that she had felt a ridiculous thrill at the thought of him watching the riverbank for her. But immediately she forced herself to discount the idea. She had fallen into a silence, her mind on the reality of her activities for the weekend. At the thought of it she felt suddenly depressed at the miserable predictability of it all: on Saturday Richard would take Emily swimming while she shopped and cleaned; on Sunday they would visit one set of parents. There would probably be an argument between her and Richard over which. He would want to see his mother and if, for the sake of a quiet life, she agreed, she would be compelled to sit in a fug of cigarette smoke all afternoon while Anne ignored her, virtually ignored Emily and instead tackled the *Mail on Sunday* giant crossword with Richard. And as for Susan, Kate always had to watch her step there: the girlish confidences the two had exchanged during the early days of her engagement to Richard had all, she subsequently discovered, been repeated to Anne and Richard. 'Mummy says you don't like her suggestions for the church music!'

'Is everything all right?' Daniel was looking at her with concern.

'Oh. Yes. Fine.'

'You don't look fine.'

She picked up her spoon and used it to stir her coffee distractedly. He did not jump in.

'I was thinking about the weekend.' She let her voice fall off, hoping that he would change the subject. But still he did not prompt her. 'Richard and I,' she paused, aware that she was entering dangerous ground, 'have different ideas about how we should spend our free time.' She hoped that sounded suitably diplomatic, as she had tried to be on the few occasions Richard came up in conversation between them.

He's working very hard at his new business.

Looking after his mother takes up quite a bit of his time.

It had become second nature to put the best presentation on the reality of her marriage, not just to Daniel but also with her family and friends. To the outside world they were a busy young married couple. The truth was that they lived as strangers, teetered perpetually on the brink of an argument and Richard no longer came to company events, not because he was working, far from it, but on account of his surly demeanour and penchant for taking full advantage of the free bar.

Daniel looked at her appraisingly. 'It might do you good to have a break.'

She said nothing, not trusting herself to take advantage of the opening. God knows what might come out if she started telling him the truth. Instead she looked up and caught the eye of the waitress. When she left them the bill for lunch, Daniel reached for it decisively. 'I'll get this.' And then they had stepped out into the sunlight of the afternoon and nothing more had been said.

Now from the kitchen she heard the sound of Richard

cracking open another can of beer. She knew how the evening would play out. It was a Friday so he would shower, change, then slip out to the pub 'for a couple of hours', returning late when he would jolt her awake climbing into bed.

Tomorrow she and Emily could dress warmly, drive to Spade Oak, park the car and walk along the towpath. It would be fun for Emily to see the boats, and for her a distraction in a weekend that would otherwise be filled with Richard ranting on about this meeting. And they might not even speak to Daniel – they would simply be two of many spectators on the riverbank.

And she suspected that Richard wouldn't notice the absence of his wife and daughter anyway.

Howard wasn't himself. When Howard had something on his mind he went all quiet, staring at the television blankly and sitting through dinner not saying a word. He had been like this for weeks now and Jemma had had enough. Most worrying of all, it had started up since they got back from Spain.

At the moment Howard was in his office. Jemma turned her attention to the spaghetti bolognese sauce bubbling on the range, a Smeg six-ring burner. It was a relief to be out of that Spanish kitchen with the propane cooker that was always running out and the tap that drizzled brown water. Here in Radlett she had real oak cabinets, a centre island with its own sink and imported American appliances.

In total they had been marooned in Spain for a month until Howard's lawyer had given them the all-clear. And every day of that long month Barbara had been there too, in her bare-midriff tops and tight white shorts and little strappy sundresses. They couldn't avoid her in the club, they ran into her in the shops and once or twice she and Brian had been in the same restaurant having dinner.

It had been impossible to avoid the invitation to their house to see the studio.

Barbara, wearing skin-tight white jeans and an Escada

Sport T-shirt, had served them very strong gin and tonics while Brian got started on the barbecue.

The studio, to the rear of the house, had white roughly plastered walls, a high ceiling and a window looking out over the valley. Two fans whirred overhead. Mounted on the walls and stacked up against them were Barbara's paintings.

'I like to choose spiritual themes,' said Barbara, pointing to a four-by-six canvas of doves in flight from an olive grove.

Howard knelt down and began looking through some of the smaller pictures.

Jemma peered at the large ones on the wall. There were lots of churches and mountains and angels.

Howard was asking her a question. 'Where did you do this?'

'At the church. The one on the other side of the valley. I went in and took some photos – I know you're not supposed to, but no one saw me – and then I came back and painted them.'

Howard sounded really impressed. 'They're very good.'

Jemma was damned if she was going to go rushing over to admire whatever it was. She stole a look over her shoulder at a small painting of a white church on a hill. Personally, whilst Jemma had to concede that Barbara could draw, she didn't think much of her choice of subjects. She paused in front of a group of angels, arranged on a pile of rocks by the side of a black seashore, looking down on a dead seagull.

Barbara saw her looking. 'It's called *The Price of Oil*,' she said, not leaving Howard's side. 'I think it's very important to have the courage to tackle difficult subjects. That's what all the major artists do.'

The seagull had creepy glistening eyes. It was definitely not the type of thing you'd want to have on your living-room wall.

But Howard had been full of compliments. 'You're very talented, Barbara.'

Over dinner, things had taken a more ominous turn. In

between the light conversation and the standard expatriate boasting – the square footage of the house, the length of the pool – Barbara had begun to snipe.

'Brian likes to stay here for the summer. But we have to go back to Manchester for Christmas. When it's freezing!' She took a drink of wine, then glared at him. 'We've got a flat. Of course it's not big enough for all his family. So Brian goes over to his ex-wife's house on Christmas morning.'

Brian cast her an exasperated glance. 'It's only for the morning.'

'Last year you stayed for Christmas dinner!' Barbara turned back to Jemma. 'And I'm left on my own.'

There had been an awkward silence at that point. Howard had turned to Brian.

'Still, good to keep an eye on the properties.'

Brian, it turned out, had sold up and bought himself a collection of terraced houses, which he rented out to students.

Barbara continued to talk to Jemma. 'Of course, when we moved here I had to give up the salon. I think it's very important for a woman to have her own money.'

Jemma nodded, even though it was years since she had earned any herself. It didn't bother her – Howard never kept tabs on her spending. But recalling how Brian never left much of a tip at the club she saw how he might be the type of man to keep his wife short of money, the kind who wanted to see receipts. She couldn't have put up with that.

Brian, overhearing Barbara, had called across the table, 'You could always go back to work.'

And she had shot back, 'Maybe I will.'

Howard and Jemma had left shortly after.

They had no plans to return to Spain. But that was no comfort, given that Brian and Barbara would be arriving in Manchester at the beginning of December. Jemma knew this because Barbara had called her to tell her.

'We'll come down for the weekend! We can have dinner and take in a show!'

Jemma had played for time. 'I'll need to check my calendar.'

'We'll be staying at the Dorchester. You could come! We could have a spa day.'

Jemma could think of nothing worse than the prospect of sharing a sauna with Barbara clad only in some inadequate towel. In Spain, she had lost eight pounds in total. But then on their return to Radlett there had been meals out with the kids, Howard's birthday chocolate cheesecake and a disastrous buffet at their neighbour's son's eighteenth. It had taken only a month to put it all back on again and add another two pounds.

She mixed cherry tomatoes into a bowl of lettuce. Howard never used to eat salad, but if she doused it in enough bluecheese dressing he'd have a bowl now and then.

Howard wandered into the kitchen. He said nothing and he had a face like a wet weekend. She was getting really pissed off with it. He loved spaghetti bolognese; there was a nice bottle of red on the side and she'd bought profiteroles for afters. They'd have a TV dinner in front of *Coronation Street*, watch that American police drama he liked and then bed. There was nothing wrong with a routine: Wednesdays and Saturdays and sometimes an afternoon when they were on holiday.

He leaned back against the counter, his arms folded.

'For Pete's sake, Howie. What's the matter with you? Are you still running those cigarettes?' she said suspiciously.

'No. Cross my heart, Jem.'

She had let it ride for long enough. It was time to make a stand. 'Maybe you're missing Spain.'

He shook his head. 'I've got plenty to do here.'

'I meant the company.'

He looked up, startled. 'What?'

'You've been like this since we got back. Ever since you don't get to see Barbara every day.'

'Barbara?' He looked genuinely surprised. 'It's not Spain, Jem. There's nothing wrong there. It's Alex.'

'Alex who's married to Nina?' She had imagined that Howard had forgotten all about him.

He nodded. He went over to the fridge and took out a can. Everyone else drank bottled designer beers these days but Howard liked a can of Sainsbury's Pale Ale.

'Alex is seeing a lawyer,' he said slowly.

She didn't bother asking Howard how he knew. 'So? That doesn't mean anything.'

'He's seeing a lot of this lawyer. Three times this week. Pricey firm in the West End.'

Jemma pondered this. Maybe it was a divorce lawyer he was seeing. But she couldn't admit to rifling through Howard's filing cabinet and in consequence knowing why Alex and Nina's marriage would be in trouble.

'Something's up, Jem. You don't pay out the money for that kind of firm unless you've got trouble.'

'Maybe the police have got something on him?'

'Maybe.'

'Well, how does that affect us?'

'It doesn't. But if he's about to go down, he might need to make some money quick.'

'You mean sell the business?' She took a good handful of spaghetti and tossed it into a pan of boiling water. 'You said he wasn't interested in selling.'

'That was then. But this is now.'

She thought about this. Most people would have run from Alex – as Howard had initially – but the scent of money always drew him back. At least it would explain why he had been so withdrawn. Howard got preoccupied when he was setting up a deal, working out every possible move and countermove in his mind before he acted.

'So what are you going to do?'

He moved closer to her. 'I think you should ring Nina.'

'No.'

'You've had lunch with her.'

She said nothing to this. Howard might not appear to be listening to her accounts of how she spent her day, but nothing got past him. She felt suddenly defensive. Her friendship with Nina was nothing to do with Howard. They had met up a couple of times since the summer but Howard had never taken any notice or asked her what they had talked about. She was glad.

She thought back to their last meeting. Nina had invited her to come along on one of her restaurant reviews – a new pizza place in Lancaster Gate. Jemma had been flattered and worried at the same time. She had gone to the newsagent, bought every magazine with a restaurant review column and read each one several times. A new vocabulary was needed: *simple*, *sumptuous*, *delectable*.

Over lunch, under bright lights, seated on uncomfortable moulded plastic chairs, they read the menu.

'I think the pizza toppings are a modern twist on classic themes,' commented Jemma.

Gratifyingly, Nina wrote that down. 'It's always hard to find a different way of saying the same thing.'

Jemma couldn't imagine Nina would find that hard. She had, after all, been to college.

They had ordered. Whether it was because she was technically working or some other distraction Nina didn't seem quite herself. She looked ill at ease and tired.

'How are things with the business?' enquired Jemma. Fortunately Nina didn't seem to bear any grudges about the events of the summer.

'Oh. Fine.' Nina looked away. 'Alex is working all hours. I hardly see him …' Her voice trailed off as if there was more to say. But instead she changed the subject. 'How are the boys?'

'Oh, we hardly see them either. They've got a studying week coming up but then they're both off to Ibiza with their girlfriends. I suppose that's what you have to expect once they fly the nest.' She tried to sound as if she believed this. But at least it was an opening. 'Did Alex go to university, then?' she asked Nina, keen to keep the topic focused on higher education.

Nina rolled her eyes. 'Nope. He wanted to. But his mother insisted he worked in the shop.' She reached for a piece of garlic bread. 'Still, it hasn't done him any harm.'

Jemma wondered though if Alex sometimes felt like she did – at a disadvantage, when everyone these days seemed to have a qualification. Even Barbara had gone to beauty college. She thought of Jason's girlfriend, who was studying to be a lawyer, and Elliott's, who was training to be an accountant. Both girls must think she was stupid, only fit for cooking and clearing away the dishes.

For dessert, Nina ordered ice-cream and Jemma, seeing as it was for research purposes, went for tiramisu. 'Sickly,' she blurted out.

Nina leaned over and took a bite. 'Yep, that's exactly the right word.'

Finally, over watery cappuccino, Jemma steeled herself. 'Actually, I was thinking of taking some classes.'

'Oh.' Nina didn't look surprised or amused or any of the things Jemma had feared. 'What in?'

'Nothing fancy. Book-keeping, maybe. At the local college. Just part time.'

And at that Nina had nodded. 'Good idea. Are you thinking of going back to work, then?'

God, it was so different from what the boys and Howard would have said.

Why do you want to waste your time doing that?

We don't need the money.

You, Mum?

Emboldened, Jemma continued, 'I think it's time to do something for me.' And then she voiced what she had been thinking for a long time. 'Maybe I will go back to work.'

Now, standing in the kitchen recalling Nina's enthusiasm for her educational ideas, Jemma felt irritated that her new, discreet friendship was in Howard's sights.

'I'm sure there are other ways of finding out about Alex,' she said briskly.

But Howard was not to be put off. He moved over and put his hands on her waist. 'Ask her out for lunch again. Go somewhere nice.'

'No. It's nothing to do with me.'

'Just see what she's got to say.'

'Isn't she going to think it's a bit bloody strange – me cross-examining her about her husband?'

'You'll think of something to say.' He stepped back. 'Take her up the West End. She's not going to say no to a bit of shopping and a chinwag. You had a good time in Vegas, didn't you?'

Actually, they had. 'That was different. We were on holiday! I wasn't pretending to be a private eye.'

Howard persisted. 'Come on, Jem. Call her. What harm can it do?'

She knew that when he was like this it was pointless to argue. Once Howard got an idea into his head he wouldn't let go. He'd be on at her until she said yes.

The best thing in the circumstances was to get something out of him in return. If they went to Harvey Nics they could go for a walk down Sloane Street afterwards. 'All right, then. But don't start complaining if I buy myself something nice.'

He grinned. 'Whatever you like.'

Chapter 11

The midwife frowned. 'You're about fourteen weeks.' She put the wheel back in its plastic folder. 'Which makes your due date the end of March. But since you're not sure of your dates,' she said mildly disapprovingly as she made a note on Susan's file, 'they'll have to get a better idea at your scan. Then we can tell you the exact day.'

Susan was sure of her dates. There was only one possible date on which the baby could have been conceived – in the early hours of the Sunday morning of Nina's house party. It wasn't as if she and Gerry had what you would call an active sex life; he preferred to work on his script. She just wasn't sure of the precise date of the first day of her last period: what kind of person wrote that down anyway?

The woman Susan had sat next to in the waiting room – where she'd spent forty-five minutes – had told her that you never saw the same midwife twice. As far as Susan was concerned this was a good thing. This one was old and grey-haired and needed to retire. She kept talking about Susan's husband and about 'baby' and telling her what to do, or more precisely what not to do.

'No cigarettes. No alcohol is best but one glass of wine at the most. If you must, coffee in moderation. No contact sports and none of these foods.' She handed her a list.

This was Susan's second visit. She had arrived early, glad to get out of the house. Richard spent most of the day there now. Richard wouldn't tell her what was going on, but it had to have something to do with those bank statements. She was looking forward to the meeting: it would be fun to see Nina and Richard going at each other.

Next time, however, she made a mental note to come late, because the woman in the waiting room had also said they booked everyone at half-hour intervals. At least they weren't going to examine her this time.

Then the midwife stood up. 'Now, then. Let's have you up on the bed.'

Or maybe they were.

'No need to undress. Just pull your top up so I can feel for baby.' She did this, her hand dexterously passing over Susan's skin, standing in a silent pose of concentration. 'Now, let's listen to the baby's heartbeat.'

'Already?' Surely they couldn't detect anything now. She didn't even have the trace of a bump.

'Oh, yes. Sometimes you can pick it up much earlier.'

She took out a small machine with a wand attached to it. 'It's a Doppler, dear.'

She began passing it over Susan's stomach. It was a good thing she wasn't showing, since she hadn't yet told her mother. Only Gerry knew. He would have come today, except he had a site meeting in Chesham.

It took for ever. The midwife smiled at her. 'Don't worry. The placenta may be in the way.'

And then Susan heard it. Loud, amplified throughout the room, fast and furious, the sound of a real person. It was incredible that a heart could beat so fast. Somehow the frantic pace made it seem more fragile.

And Susan, to her shock, felt her eyes water. She began to cry. It was true. She really was having a baby. There was a difference, she realised, in knowing that you were having a baby and really understanding that you were. An unplanned, accidental baby admittedly – the consequence of years of her haphazard approach to contraception finally catching up with her – but a baby nonetheless. Everything changed in that one moment; something that had been abstract came to life, and she grasped that when they told you your life would never be the same again it was true. And then she felt glad that Gerry hadn't come. Because she would have had to pretend – to grasp his hand and smile eagerly at him – to share a moment that shouldn't be shared, at least not with him. For once in her life she was glad not to lie. Lying there, she was surprised at how pleased she felt about the baby: at long last a person of her very own.

The midwife, seeing her cry, squeezed her hand. 'It's a miracle, isn't it?'

And Susan looked up at her, not wanting to let go of her hand. 'Yes, it is.'

Richard slammed the back door. 'Good riddance!'

From outside Anne heard the sound of the community nurse's car starting up and, if she wasn't mistaken, the crunch of gravel as the car accelerated away.

He turned to Anne, annoyed. 'I've told you not to let these people in! What would you have done if I hadn't got here? They prey on vulnerable people – one minute some mother's letting the health visitor in to look at her baby, the next minute the social workers have grabbed it and she never sees it again.' With that he stomped off into the drawing room, switched on the television and she heard the muffled voice of the mid-afternoon news announcer.

Anne went into the kitchen, sat down at the kitchen table and lit a cigarette. She felt foolish and a little shaken, her breathing laboured. Richard was right – she should never have let the girl in. Just because someone wore a uniform didn't mean you could trust them. Richard was always warning her about old people getting burgled by men pretending to be from the water or the electric.

Besides, her health didn't interest her. Nina, Susan and the entire staff of the Marlow doctors' surgery could nag her until the cows came home, but none of them could make her care. What she had said to the nurse was true. The only dream she had left in her life was to ride again and that could never happen. It had been a crushing fall: over two hours in a watery ditch before help came in the form of Edward Fellows on his tractor. The pain had been excruciating, but she hadn't wanted to be lifted until Monty was taken care of. He had waited by her, which was how Edward had spotted her. Thank God Michael was at home. He had been summoned; he was one of the few who could handle Monty. Later she told Archie, as she lay in the hospital in plaster and traction, that she had taken the steep incline of the west field too fast.

'He just couldn't handle it.' She had looked at Archie for his reaction. His features were contorted with worry. 'I didn't realise it was so slippery.'

'I think he ought to go.'

'No!' She would have said anything at that moment to save Monty, her favourite. Monty was a thoroughbred, sold from a racing stable because he had a tendency to get spooked, taken in by Anne and patiently schooled and loved until she believed she had tamed him. She had been wrong. At the sound of the shotgun in the distance, an early morning rabbit hunter probably, Monty had bolted and thrown her with a casual ease that was almost contemptuous. She had landed hard, known that her hip was shattered and yet somehow levered herself to look up as she searched for him on the brow of the hill. Even in her pain she had prayed for Monty – please God don't let him run into the road.

He had returned after a few minutes. He looked chastened. So she had not scolded him as they waited together for help.

From her hospital bed she had understood it was vital to placate Archie. She was terrified that he would go home and get rid of Monty in a fit of anger.

'It was all my fault,' she said firmly. 'But just to be on the safe side I won't ride him any more. Not until I'm totally better. Just turn him out in the field and ask Nina to go down every day.'

Archie hesitated. He looked at her body, surveying her leg

and the bruise on her arm and the bandage applied to her head. Gently he touched her face.

'It's just a scratch,' she said dismissively. 'Promise me you won't get rid of Monty.'

He had sighed. 'All right.'

She had never ridden him again. There had been some gentle walks on a pony loaned to her by a friend from the point-to-point, even a canter for a little while, but she was finished and she knew it. She could barely get on using a mount and God knows how she'd handle Monty at a gallop. Another operation failed to make a difference. She hadn't lost her nerve, but the limp and the pain were permanent. So she put away her riding clothes in a cardboard box and told Jim to take them up to the attic. But she kept Monty, asking Michael to exercise him.

'Be careful.'

Michael had looked at her then and understood.

It had been hard, watching Michael and a succession of heavy-handed farm boys from the drawing room of the house, but it was best for Monty.

Part of her spirit died then – and the rest went with Archie.

The community nurse had caught her by surprise, arriving unannounced to do a statement of Anne's health needs, or something like that. 'I'm Nurse Deirdre. I have rung twice.' Nurse Deirdre looked about thirteen. Her hair was tied back in a loose ponytail and she wasn't wearing a hat. She didn't even have a proper uniform: instead she was wearing a purple V-neck tunic over matching trousers. She may just as well be working behind the butcher's counter at Tesco. 'It won't take a minute.'

She seemed nice enough and so Anne had let her in, careful to take her into the drawing room. There was a fog of smoke in the kitchen and with all the rain recently and the cats coming in and out the lino was the worse for wear.

Nurse Deirdre took a plastic file from her briefcase and

took out a sheaf of notes. 'It's nothing to worry about,' she said patronisingly. 'We work as part of the doctors' surgery multi-disciplinary team. We offer conventional and alternative therapies. Every two years we do an assessment of patients over the age of sixty who haven't had a full medical.'

'I go to the surgery!'

'Yes. For your repeat prescriptions.' Nurse Deirdre made this sound as if it didn't count. She read down her notes, then looked up earnestly. 'This is what we call a health appraisal.' She handed Anne three sheets. 'This is the health authority privacy notice – it covers access to your computer records. This is our mission statement. And this is a feedback questionnaire on the service you have received today.'

Anne took them without looking. She also didn't want to draw attention to the fact that without her glasses she couldn't read small print or, come to that, any print at all.

'Now. I see you take Mogadon for sleep problems.' Nurse Deirdre looked unhappy about this. 'Mogadon is a barbiturate. Have you considered alternative therapies?'

'No.'

'Many patients have been able to use non-drug alternatives to alleviate their symptoms and come off medication altogether. Massage, acupuncture and exercise classes. Lavender baths can be really helpful last thing at night, particularly when combined with a hot non-caffeinated drink.'

'That won't work for me.'

'Let's come back to that, shall we?' Nurse Deirdre said brightly. There followed a lot of talk about her medicines, directed as far as Anne could tell at getting her off them. Nurse Deirdre frowned at her notes. 'You started taking the tranquillisers after the death of your husband. But that was over three years ago.' She glanced up. 'Let's ask the doctor to review that on your next visit.'

'No.'

Then, predictably, it was on to her heart, her chest – 'Emphysema is a chronic, progressive condition' – and her bloody hip. 'There is quite a long waiting list for hip replacement. But that's all the more reason to go on a waiting list now. You did sustain a very serious injury, compounded by arthritis, and an x-ray may well show subsequent deterioration of—'

Anne cut her off. 'Could I ride a horse?'

'I'm sorry?'

'If I had a new hip. Could I get on a horse?'

Nurse Deirdre faltered. 'Well, that would be a question for your orthopaedic surgeon. Mr Jones at Wycombe General has a very good reputation.'

'Good for him. But he's not going to get me on a horse, is he?'

For the first time, the nurse looked perplexed. 'Is that a quality-of-life target for you?'

'It's the only reason I'd let them cut me open. They use a saw, you know. Like butchering a pig in an abattoir.'

Nurse Deirdre faltered, then said, 'The improvement in mobility that results from hip replacement makes it a very worthwhile procedure—'

Anne interrupted her. 'I'm fine as I am. I get about. I can climb the stairs. And I can get in and out of the bath.'

This was not true. She had to make do with a flannel and a basin full of water these days. But she wasn't going to admit that to anyone.

It was at that point that Richard had arrived. Things had got a little tense after Anne introduced them.

He had sat down and looked at Nurse Deirdre accusingly. 'I suppose this is a cost-cutting exercise?'

'I'm sorry?'

'Well, you're not a doctor, are you? These days the doctors find any excuse to get the nurses to do the work for them. Then they rake in money from the government and spend every afternoon on the golf course.'

Nurse Deirdre had flushed red. 'I can assure you that we work with the doctors, not in their place. In fact I was about to recommend that your mother come in for a full medical.'

'I suppose you get paid for that.' He shook his head at Anne. 'NHS targets,' he said knowingly, then looked back at the nurse. 'The more people you ship in and out, the more money you get.'

Nurse Deirdre recovered herself a little. 'I think targets have a valuable role to play in making sure the people who need help get it.'

He ignored her. 'It's all a con.' He looked at Anne confidently. 'The government wants the elderly out of their homes – bussed off to some old people's home. They make you sell your house and then they take all your money. You'll get left in your nightdress in front of the television all day – if they get you out of bed at all.'

Nurse Deirdre spoke up. 'I really don't think that's a fair—'

He gathered pace. 'They drug them to keep them quiet. Do you know how much they spend on food in these places? One pound fifty! That's less than a prison – and you have to share a room.'

Anne was beginning to feel quite alarmed. Thank goodness Richard had arrived. Now she came to think of it, there was no telling what this girl might say about her or where it all might lead. She didn't fear dying, but she was bloody terrified of ending up in a home. 'I think you'd better be going,' Anne said hastily.

Nurse Deirdre frowned. 'But I still have your nutrition questionnaire to fill in.'

'I eat very well, thank you. My daughter's got her own catering business. Write that down.'

Richard got up. 'You heard my mother. This interview is terminated. And I have to say that I think turning up unannounced is very unprofessional. I've a good mind to make a complaint.'

'Actually I rang twice. There was no reply.'

'Really?' Richard sounded as if he didn't believe her.

Nurse Deirdre packed up her papers. She turned back to Anne. 'Please think about coming into the surgery. You really should have a flu jab. Winter's coming and with your emphysema you could benefit from our Smoking Cessation clinic—'

But Richard had already stood up. 'We're fine as we are, thank you.'

Now Anne took her time over her cigarette. Richard could be funny when she did something he didn't like. It was better to give him time to cool off. Then he would relent and say, 'It's only because I care, Mummy,' and she would feel guilty for upsetting him and promise not to make the same mistake again.

She stared out of the window at the darkening afternoon sky. The fact of the matter was there was only one person living in this house who needed to see a doctor and she was currently at work. It would be interesting to see how long it would take for Susan to tell her – or whether she was going to keep the baby at all. Obviously Susan took her mother for a fool: she might not be showing, but she was eating like a horse, falling asleep at seven o'clock in the evening and her full bust was even more pronounced. Anne had been exactly the same. All her babies had been small. She assumed that Gerry was the father, nice enough but not the sort to satisfy Susan, who had ideas above her station when it came to men. Of course with Susan you could never be sure: she'd got an eye for the boys at thirteen and never looked back. That had been another aspect of her character to add to the list of things Anne didn't like about her, another threat to the respectable life she had worked so hard to construct, as if bunking off school, drinking and stealing wasn't enough. They should have shipped her off to boarding school, which was what Anne had wanted, preferably somewhere in Scotland, but Archie was too soft to go through with it.

All of a sudden she felt old and tired and depressed, unable to summon up any enthusiasm for a wedding or a christening.

It would have been different if Archie was still alive. His zest and enthusiasm would have inspired her. But he wasn't and so there was nothing left but to get up, sit in front of the television and wait for nothing to happen.

Jemma had secured a window table at the Fifth Floor restaurant at Harvey Nichols. She was, after all, a regular. The room was light and airy, white panelled walls offset by contrasting sharp turquoise around the sash windows. The cool effect was heightened by the stripped wood floor, modern cream-covered chairs and pristine white tablecloths. Around them, the noise levels rose as the tables filled up with well-dressed Knightsbridge shoppers interspersed with tables of business people.

Across from Jemma, Nina was knocking back the glass of champagne that she had carried with her to the table from the bar. It was her second. She was telling Jemma about Alex's mad work schedule. 'Last weekend he spent Sunday afternoon laying a new laminate floor in a studio in Earls Court.' She gave a wry smile. 'By the way, we've completed the sale on Gloucestershire.'

'Oh. Shame!' It seemed to Jemma that Howard's hopes of picking up Alex's business at a knock-down price were wide of the mark. From what Nina had told her, far from hurtling towards bankruptcy Alex was by sheer force of will and hard work succeeding in turning the business round.

Nina shrugged. 'I'd rather have the bills paid.'

Jemma nodded. 'You can't get too attached to things when your hubby's in business. You never know what's around the corner.'

It was like Las Vegas again. Jemma remembered one of the reasons why they had hit it off: it was nice to talk to someone who understood what it was really like to be married to a risk-taking workaholic – someone who didn't think it was all flash jewellery and fancy holidays and who knew that in business it could be easy come and easy go.

Jemma leaned forward. 'A few years back we had to sell up.' She shook her head. 'Never get involved in timeshares. Howard got us back on track, though.' She picked up the menu. 'You have to expect the unexpected.'

'Absolutely,' agreed Nina, emptying her glass. She seemed to be under a lot of strain. Her face was drawn, she looked tired and she had definitely lost weight.

All that behind them, her mission for Howard accomplished, Jemma decided to move the conversation on. 'I saw your article in the magazine. The restaurant one. We thought it was very good. I showed Howard.'

'Oh, thank you.' Nina sounded distracted. She was surveying the other diners as if she expected to see someone she knew. 'I've been really busy at work. They've got me doing another six reviews – we're covering gastro pubs – and I'm booked up with party work.'

'I thought you gave that up.'

'I did. I just do small functions. Still, it's good to keep busy...' Her voice trailed off as if there was much more to say about precisely why she needed to be occupied.

They were interrupted by the waiter taking their order. Jemma liked the menu here: you could get a proper meal. Lately a number of the Radlett crowd had dropped to a size six, in part by making it a rule to order two starters, both salads, each without dressing. What was the point in coming out to lunch and doing that? She turned to the waiter. 'I'll take the pan-fried scallops with the Jerusalem artichokes to start and then the duck confit.' She looked down at the menu. Pommes frites or pommes purée? 'With the chips.'

She handed back the menu and observed Nina order. She had barely scanned her menu. 'Roquefort salad and then the tomato risotto, please.' Jemma felt increasingly concerned.

After they had ordered a bottle of Sancerre from the wine waiter, Nina abruptly changed the conversation. 'So how are the boys?'

And then they talked about Jason's birthday party – they'd

all gone for dinner at Le Caprice – and Elliott's work placement and Howard's fears that Elliott was getting too distracted by his girlfriend. 'He's told him he can't get married. Not if he wants us to help him out financially. He's got to finish his studies first.'

Though Nina never looked less than attentive, she couldn't quite seem able to give Jemma all her attention. And when Jemma's mobile rang she jumped out of her skin. It was only Howard asking what time she wanted him home for dinner. These days he was good like that.

Nina hardly touched her food when it came, pushing the rice around her plate. Yet she knocked back her glass of Sancerre without blinking. After an hour, Jemma had had enough.

She leaned forward and shook Nina's arm. 'So what's the matter, love?'

Nina toyed with her glass. 'It's nothing really.'

'Well, it must be something.'

Nina sighed. 'You'll probably think it's all a fuss about nothing. That's what Alex thinks, though my friends say the complete opposite. I don't know who to listen to or what to think.'

It was like dealing with a small child. 'Why don't you just tell me what's happened?' said Jemma firmly.

Nina, as if to fortify herself, took the bottle from the ice-bucket and poured wine into her empty glass. 'Alex had a secretary. Her name's Sasha. She's got a very ... strong personality. Anyway, three months ago he sacked her. Over three months, actually.'

Jemma hoped she looked surprised. 'Oh. Why?'

'He decided to cut back on staff costs. And ... well, to be honest I wasn't comfortable with her. We had a few arguments about it. I don't mean they were having an affair,' Nina added hastily. 'I just thought that she was the type who'd like to.'

Jemma nodded sympathetically.

'Anyhow, she didn't take it very well.' Nina took a big gulp of wine. 'It started with telephone calls. The first night, actually, after Alex fired her. After that she would call at all hours, then say nothing. I didn't have any proof, but I just knew that it was her. After a week Alex changed the number.'

'Did you go to the police?'

Nina shook her head. 'Alex didn't want to. He said it would just make things more complicated.'

Complicated for whom? But Jemma resisted passing comment.

'But there were other things. The day after he sacked her Alex got his car scratched. It had been parked outside his office. It was a really deep scratch. There was no way it was accidental. The man at the bodywork shop said it was probably a key that had been used. It was right down the side.' Nina stopped as if to collect her thoughts. 'Then it went quiet for a while. And then, a month later, mine got done, too. I came out one morning and there it was. Right down one side, just the same as Alex's car.'

'So you went to the police?' Jemma prompted her.

Nina shook her head. 'We didn't have any evidence. Alex said she would only deny it.'

Jemma was beginning to feel worried herself. 'Then what? More calls?'

Nina shook her head. 'Nope. At least none that I know of. I'm sure she calls Alex's mobile. Now when he comes home he switches it off. He thinks I haven't noticed.' A trace of bitterness had crept into her voice. 'Anyway, it went quiet again. That's how it is. You think it's over and then it starts up again.'

'Starts up again?'

'Yes. That's when the post started.'

'Post?'

'Hmm. Odd things. Things that I didn't order. Restaurant menus. A catalogue from Tiffany. Holiday brochures for the Cayman Islands.'

'As if she was sending you a message,' said Jemma before she could stop herself.

Nina looked up sharply. 'That's exactly what I said! But Alex said they were just coincidental.' She looked earnestly at Jemma. 'Why would all these things just suddenly start arriving?'

Jemma shifted uneasily. 'Has there been anything else?'

Nina shook her head. 'It's probably nothing ...'

Jemma thought it was definitely something. 'What?'

Nina rolled her eyes. 'It's ridiculous. You remember my sister, Susan?'

'Yes.' How could she forget her, the one who'd flirted with Howard all through dinner.

'She works on a farmers' market in Marlow. Last week she said she saw Sasha down there.'

'In Marlow?' Jemma put down her glass.

Nina nodded. 'Of course, I can't be sure. She didn't speak to her. And Susan isn't totally reliable. But she must have been pretty sure because she called me and we hadn't spoken for a while ...' Nina's voice trailed off. There was clearly another story there with her sister that Nina didn't want to go into.

'Are you saying she's stalking you?'

Nina looked up. 'Yes! Oh, God, you can't imagine what it's like. I do think that, but Alex just won't take me seriously. I know she is. Like the time my first restaurant review came out in *Capital Letter*. Someone sent flowers to the house. And the card just said "Congratulations?" with a question mark. No name, nothing. The florist wouldn't say who had sent them.' Nina's voice ran on. 'And sometimes I just feel as though I'm being watched. As though she's tracking my every move. But each time I say something to Alex he just says I'm imagining it.' Nina's voice was close to breaking point. 'I know it must all sound so far-fetched. But it's this feeling I have all the time of not knowing what's going on.'

Jemma sat back.

She felt furious. Furious at Alex and Howard and all these

bloody men who went out and did exactly what they wanted and caused all this pain.

Furious that Nina had been taken for a fool – just like she had been.

Furious that Nina would be the last to know – just like her.

Her mind went back and even after all that time the pain returned. It was five years ago at the Chingford showroom Christmas party. Howard had booked the private room at an Italian restaurant. The girl had been there, of course, in a black number. Nothing had been said. But at the end of the evening Jemma had seen her go up to him and touch his arm and kiss him on the cheek. And she had known. It had all fallen into place: the pitying looks of the other staff; the awkwardness and change of subject when the girl's name had come up in conversation; Howard's behaviour – the way he veered from overly attentive to acting like she wasn't there – and all the late nights and two weekends away supposedly looking at business ventures in Paris. Paris! Howard had never had a good word to say about the French.

She had felt so stupid. And still he had denied it, so she had borrowed a leaf out of Howard's book and hired her own private detective. Poacher turned gamekeeper, that's what she'd been. The photographs had made her sick, literally, throwing up in the bathroom after she looked at the pictures of them strolling hand in hand into some Chigwell hotel in the middle of the afternoon – and emerging three hours later.

She had taken the boys to her mother. Then when he'd got home, she'd thrown the photos at him. She had heard of people going white but never seen it.

He hadn't known what to say. 'Jem …' Instead, he'd sat on the settee and held his head in his hands and then he'd started crying. 'Oh, God. Please, Jem. Please don't go.'

'Chigwell!' she had screamed at him. 'Did you think you could sneak around and I wouldn't find out? Do you think I'm stupid?'

'No ...'

'Why did you do it?'

They had talked long into the night.

'I swear to you, Jem, it didn't mean anything. You're everything to me – you and the kids.'

She had laid down her terms and he had agreed. The next day Howard had called the girl and arranged to meet her at a café. Oh, her face when they both walked in ...

Jemma had done all the talking. 'You're fired. Don't come back to the office. Don't call Howard. In fact, the best thing would be if you left Chingford.'

The girl had looked at Howard. He had nodded in silent agreement.

They left to get him a new mobile and to book a holiday.

And after that Jemma had stuck to her side of the bargain: it had never been mentioned again. There had been no one since, she was confident of that. She had learned from her mistakes. Looking back she realised that she had got too wrapped up in the kids, too complacent about letting him spend time without her and she had grown distant from the business and stopped talking to him about the ins and outs.

But Nina would have to work all of this out for herself. Perhaps if you didn't have children, you wouldn't be so inclined to stay. God knows it had been hard at times not to throw it back in his face – but the alternative, life without him, was worse.

Jemma knew Alex's game. He would deny it until the bitter end. He would hope against hope that he could keep the secret. But a woman like Sasha wouldn't stop until Nina knew, and in the meantime she would play with her rival like a cat with a mouse. But at the end, when she had had her fun, Sasha would make sure Nina heard all the details.

Sometimes, Jemma knew, you had to be cruel to be kind.

'All this makes sense if they've been having an affair.'

'I've asked him over and over again. He absolutely swears—'

Jemma interrupted, flicking her hand dismissively. 'That's what they all do. But there's one way to find out for sure, isn't there?'

'There is?'

'Why don't you ask her?'

Nina looked astounded.

Jemma pressed on. 'Ask her, Nina. And then you'll know for certain.'

Nina gave an ironic smile. 'I think that's what I'm afraid of.'

'Listen, just make sure you surprise her. And don't go off anywhere on your own with her. Do you understand?'

'We've been visiting a supplier.' It was a lame story but Kate couldn't come up with anything better on the spur of the moment.

It was three o'clock on a Friday afternoon and she had been walking down Cookham High Street with Daniel, having emerged from a pub lunch, window-shopping in the expensive boutiques and art galleries of the narrow picture-postcard street. It was a half-day at AdTech – the company gave them occasionally in lieu of American public holidays.

Susan shot her an amused look. 'Really? Aren't you going to introduce me?'

'Oh. Yes. Susan Carruthers, this is Daniel Lovell.'

Susan held his hand for a second too long. 'I'm Kate's sister-in-law.' She brushed a strand of hair from her face. 'Her husband's sister,' she added unnecessarily.

'Good to meet you.' His reply sounded casual enough, but Kate caught the note of tension in Daniel's voice.

There was an uncomfortable pause. Kate gestured to the expensive nursery shop from which Susan had just emerged. A cot, in white wood with a presumably hand-painted motif of a locomotive train, stood in pride of place surrounded by child-sized rocking chairs, old-fashioned teddy bears and artfully arranged piles of patchwork toddler quilts. 'Did you buy anything?' Kate asked brightly.

'Oh. No. Just looking. For a friend.' Susan, rather rudely, turned her attention full on to Daniel. 'So where's the supplier?'

'The supplier? Oh, just round the corner.'

'A name I would have heard of?'

Kate cut in. 'I doubt it.' She was desperate to get away. 'We ought to get going. Lots of work to do,' she said to Susan.

Susan still did not take her eyes off Daniel. She acted as if she hadn't heard Kate. 'So you're a work colleague of Kate's? What do you do?'

'Logistics.'

'Wow. That sounds interesting. How did you get into that?'

Daniel shifted. 'I just sort of fell into it.'

Susan was not to be put off. 'I think that's often the best way to get a job. Sometimes the things we least expect turn out the best.' She pulled her heavyweight grey wool poncho around her. 'God, it's cold. Why don't we go for a cup of tea?'

'We really have to get back,' Kate said firmly.

'Deadlines,' Daniel added in a resigned tone of voice.

Susan finally gave up when Kate took a step away. She addressed her goodbyes solely to Daniel. 'Great to have met you.' There was an undeniable flirtatiousness in the glance that she gave him. 'Hope to see you again.'

They made their escape, fortunately heading in the opposite direction. As they walked down the pavement, a chill afternoon wind cutting her face, Kate knew that she had flushed red and her heart was beating fast. She had always been a hopeless liar.

They walked in silence for a minute, then Daniel spoke. 'Will she tell Richard?'

'Yes.' Kate had no doubt about that. 'Susan always likes to stir it up.'

They had reached their respective cars parked by the common.

'You haven't done anything wrong,' Daniel said softly.

She gave an empty laugh. 'I doubt if Richard will see it that way.'

'Just stick to your story.' But she could tell from his expression that he was as uncomfortable with lying as she was. It was one of the character traits that she liked about him. 'You're allowed to have friends, Kate.'

Was she? Could a married woman have a friend about whom she daydreamed constantly, plotted to meet, conspired to sit next to at every opportunity? A friend whom she cheered from the riverbank and then joined for tea in the warm clubhouse of the Upper Thames Sailing Club? She hadn't kissed Daniel – but they were so close to that. She hadn't slept with him – but she would like to. And how could she keep pretending that this was a work relationship when last weekend she had told Richard she was going to her parents' – only to leave Emily there and slip away for a couple of hours to go to a Sunday lunch party at Daniel's house? Yes, there were lots of people there. No, nothing had happened. But that was no defence and deep down she knew it.

They stood by her car in silence. It was as if Susan's appearance had injected a blast of cold, harsh reality into their warm and private world.

Daniel looked anxious for her in a way that Richard never had. She couldn't share her problems with Richard – when she tried all she got was a barrage of his opinions or a raft of stupid advice. Or a reminder that he had been right.

'I told you that promotion was going to be too much.'

'Tell your boss where to stick it.'

'Call in sick if you don't want to go to the meeting.'

Daniel reached out and pulled her to him. It made her want to cry. She pushed her face into the softness of his ski jacket and allowed him to close his arms around her.

'What do you want to do?' he said gently.

And the tone of his voice made her realise that this was more than a friendship for him, too. He could so easily have brushed off the incident and acted as if they were only friends, as if there was nothing to be concerned about. But now, with his arms around her, he was acknowledging the truth of the attraction that existed between them.

'I don't know.' And that was the truth, too. She felt acutely the unhappiness and hopelessness of her situation. 'Sometimes I feel my life is over.'

He didn't contradict her or tell her she was exaggerating. 'Kate,' was all he said softly as he ran his hand gently over her face.

'I just don't know what to do. Richard is impossible. I don't think he'll ever change.' She felt a wave of relief wash over her as finally she let go of the secrets she had been keeping. 'Actually he's getting worse. Half the time he's not even sober. The only things he cares about are his stupid LPs and buying more of them. But every time I think about leaving I feel so guilty. I feel I have to stay for Emily's sake. He's not a bad father.' She struggled to hold back the tears. 'I'm sorry. You don't want to hear all this.'

'I want to hear everything,' he said firmly.

Now the words were unstoppable. 'I feel so overwhelmed. I feel like a one-man band – I work and pay all the bills. My parents don't think I should be working full-time. But what they don't know is that I don't have a choice. We'd lose the house otherwise. Richard seems to have given up. He doesn't make any effort to stick at anything. And I never know what sort of mood he's going to be in when I get home from work. Honestly, Daniel, I feel relieved when he goes to the pub. It's a break. And then I feel sick and anxious when I hear his key in the door.'

She felt his arms tighten around her.

'And all the time I feel I have to put on a brave face, to cover up for him.'

Now his voice was resolute. 'You don't have to put on a

front with me. What you're saying is hardly a surprise. It's obvious how unhappy you are.'

'Is it?' She was astounded.

He sighed. 'Kate. You hardly ever talk about Richard. And when you do it's obvious you're putting a spin on things.'

She was so tired of coping alone that it was almost a relief to hear him dismiss her pretences. 'I just don't know what to do.'

He continued to hold her tight. 'Well, the first thing you should do is to stop pretending. I think you should tell your parents what's really going on. They probably suspect anyway. You can't soldier on alone. And anything you want me to do, just say the word.'

She looked up at him to gauge his expression. She saw that he was utterly serious, that he meant all that he had said, that these were no mere lines to comfort her in the moment, only to be forgotten later.

'What about Emily?' she said slowly.

'Kate, you're a fabulous mother. Concentrate on getting yourself sorted out. If you do that, Emily will be fine whatever happens.' He shook her gently. 'You don't deserve to live like this.'

In that moment she realised that he was right. She nodded and instinctively they drew closer again. And then there was nothing left to think about. She lifted her face up to his, met his lips and felt the depth of his kiss, so long awaited and so much sweeter for that.

Chapter 12

It was done. The outcome Sasha had waited for and planned for – schemed and dreamed of – had happened. But when it came it wasn't how she had imagined it would be.

Sitting down on the cream leather sofa in her flat Sasha felt neither elated nor victorious – nor even satisfied. If anything, she felt depressed.

The game was over. It would play out a little longer, but in essence it was finished. She would have to find another way to pass her time. And she hadn't wanted it to end so quickly. She had planned for it to go on right up to the steps of the court when she would make Alex an offer he couldn't refuse: a six-figure sum and all her costs paid and in return she would drop the case. By then, his nerves shattered, he would agree.

In fact it had ended that morning, quite unexpectedly and not at a time or place of her choosing. She had returned from the gym to find Nina waiting for her on the steps to the communal entrance to her flat.

They had both started at a disadvantage: Sasha had been taken unawares, feeling exposed without make-up and dressed in her workout clothes. Nina, though, looked worse: haggard and ill at ease, dressed like a frigid Kensington housewife in a navy blue pea coat, jeans and loafers.

Nina was nervous: a red flush coloured her cheeks when she saw Sasha. Her voice when she spoke quavered. There was no preamble. 'I want you to leave us alone.' She was speaking too fast, her words pouring out and obviously rehearsed. 'I know it's you doing these things. Don't bother to deny it. Just leave us alone.'

Hearing Nina's silly little speech had given Sasha confidence. 'So he's told you, then?'

'Told me what?'

Sasha understood then that Nina still didn't know. But it wasn't the right time to tell her just yet. 'About the court case.'

Nina looked relieved. 'Of course he's told me about the case. Though what you expect to gain from it I don't know. You can't imagine that you'll win.' She could not hold Sasha's gaze. Instead, she kept meeting her eyes then looking away.

Sasha fixed her with an unflinching stare. 'Oh, I think I will. It's a sustained pattern of sexual harassment going back for over a year.'

'What!' Nina looked stunned. 'Sexual harassment.'

'What did you think it was?' Sasha adopted a tone of surprise. 'Didn't he tell you? Hasn't he shown you the paperwork? My affidavit makes very interesting reading. You must ask him to show it to you. You're not telling me that he doesn't take you to the meetings with his lawyer?'

Nina appeared to be struggling to take all this in. She looked utterly bemused.

Sasha put her head on one side. 'Why don't you come on up? We could sit down over a cup of coffee.'

'No,' Nina said quickly, almost recoiling.

'You'd prefer not to know?' Sasha exhaled slowly. 'More secrets, Nina. More lies.' She raised an eyebrow. 'What kind of a marriage do you have, exactly?'

Nina replied slowly as if thinking aloud, 'I don't believe Alex harassed you. You're just trying to cause trouble. Or get a payoff. Alex won't give you a penny.'

'But it isn't up to Alex, is it? It'll be the judge who decides. And I have a very persuasive lawyer.'

Nina sounded shrill. 'You can't expect to get away with this. Do you think anyone is going to take your word? What's that worth?' she asked contemptuously. 'Vandalising our cars, calling the house, sending us stupid post.'

'It's not stupid. It's all significant. Ask Alex. If you want to come up to the flat I can show you the necklace he bought me from Tiffany.'

Nina pursed her lips. 'So you say. But you're hardly the most reliable person, are you? In fact, judging from your behaviour, I would say you're unstable.'

Sasha felt her temper beginning to rise.

'You don't need a lawyer,' continued Nina now with more confidence. 'You need a psychiatrist.'

That did it. It would have been so much better, Sasha realised in retrospect, to have walked away at that point. Then they could have continued to play, perhaps for months. But the mention of needing help was too much.

'I need a psychiatrist! Is that what you think? You need to concentrate on your own problems. You've got enough of them.' Before Nina had a chance to reply she pushed on. 'Let's see. Your husband's business is stalled, he's about to lose a very public case for sexual harassment and all this has happened because he couldn't keep out of my knickers.'

Gratifyingly, Nina flinched at that.

Sasha gathered momentum. 'Still telling you it didn't happen, is he? God, how long are you going to keep hanging on to the pathetic idea that your husband is faithful to you? You think I need help. At least I'm living in the real world.' She laughed. 'Have you any idea how ridiculous you looked at your little party? Scurrying around Alex. Touching his arm. Jumping through hoops for your wonderful husband. Everyone at that party knew about Alex and me. Everyone except you.'

Nina raised her hand as if to hit her, a silver charm bracelet on her wrist glinting in the sharp morning sun. But Sasha was too quick. She caught Nina's wrist, holding it hard. 'You live in a fantasy world.' She mimicked her: 'My husband loves me and everything in my life is perfect.' Until that point Sasha had not realised how much she really hated Nina.

But Nina, to her surprise, twisted free and shot back. 'Why should I believe you? You wanted Alex and you didn't get him. And now you're set on some campaign of revenge. I don't believe for one moment that Alex would get involved with someone like you.'

Someone like you. That did it.

Sasha was shouting now. 'He screwed me for a year, you stupid bitch. Day and night, everywhere he could get his hands on me. He couldn't get enough. The only reason he came back to you – the only reason – is because he feels guilty and he can't afford a divorce. He doesn't love you. Personally, from the things he's said, I doubt he ever has.' She laughed. 'Oh, before I forget – your party. He couldn't even stay away from me there! He dragged me off to that shed at the back of the garden.'

At that, Nina looked too shocked to speak.

'Still don't know whether to believe me, do you?' Sasha moved closer. 'Because it might just be possible that all those Friday nights and all those Sunday afternoons he was actually at the office doing paperwork.' She pointed up at the building. 'Instead of up there, with me, fucking me. And loving every minute of it.' She lowered her voice. 'Do you want me to tell you what he likes? Would that help you make your mind up? Well, let's see. He likes black lace and stockings and occasionally soft porn. But that doesn't help you, does it? So does every man in the country. Let's see if I can be more specific … He likes it every way. But especially from behind – that's how he likes to finish. And in between times he pulls me on top, and he holds my hips like this and he tells me to touch my breasts and he calls me *baby*. He doesn't talk, though.' She gathered momentum. 'Now, let's see. He's got a small mole right between his shoulder blades and a scar on his left thigh where he caught a piece of barbed wire on a cross-country run when he was twelve. They had to stitch it. And then there's his appendix scar, of course. Not a good one; a junior doctor at Charing Cross sewed him up.'

'Shut up.'

'And afterwards he likes to—'

Nina shouted at her. Finally she had lost control. 'He's my husband. Mine. You had an affair with a married man and now he's left you – and you deserve it.' Her voice was gaining strength. 'What you need to do now is walk away and leave us alone.'

Nina was strong but Sasha knew she was stronger. As she took a step towards Nina, sure enough she backed away. 'Your husband? Believe me, he didn't act at all like your husband when he was with me.' She slowed her voice. 'Let's get this absolutely straight. I wanted him and he wanted me and if he didn't feel trapped with you we'd be together. Do you expect me to be happy about it? I deserve to be compensated – and I will be. This court case isn't going to go away, Nina. And I'm not going to go away, either.'

She picked up her gym bag and unzipped the side compartment, taking out her keys.

'But what are you worried about? Your husband has come home. Now all you have to do is stay married to him.'

She walked towards the front door of the block, turning back as she reached it. 'Think what you've got to look forward to. A lifetime with Alex. Except you'll always be wondering if he'd rather be with someone else. Or if he is with someone else. Or if one day you'll come home to find that he's finally had the guts to walk out.'

Next to Jemma, Howard was steering determinedly through the traffic inching into Lakeside shopping centre. It was two months to Christmas and already Lakeside at ten a.m. was packed.

He had been complaining about it all week. 'Why do you need me to come?'

'Because I want to get the boys' stuff and your mum's present and your sister's and anyway it'll be a nice day out. We'll have lunch in Debenhams.'

Howard would be OK for an hour. Then he'd start trying to hurry her along and she'd have to park him in Costa Coffee.

As they entered the car park her mobile rang. She clicked it open. It was Nina. 'Jemma …' Nina's voice trailed off.

From that one word, hearing the shock in Nina's choked voice, Jemma knew that something was terribly wrong. 'What is it?'

'I just saw her. I waited for her outside the flat.'

Jemma saw a space and gestured urgently to Howard to pull in. He was always fussy about where he parked in case someone scratched the Lexus opening their car door. She mouthed at him, 'Nina.'

But she didn't want him to hear what she suspected Nina was going to tell her. 'Nina, hang on a minute.'

She got out of the car and walked away. It was freezing, the autumnal Essex wind cutting across the car park.

It was hard to make out what Nina was saying. 'It's true, Jemma. He did have an affair with her. Oh, God, I can't believe I've been so stupid.'

'I'm sorry, love.'

'I just don't know what to do.'

'Where are you now?'

'I don't know. I've pulled in somewhere in Pimlico. I just got in the car and drove away.'

'Good. Now listen. Just calm down before you start driving. You don't want to have an accident, do you?'

Nina didn't appear to be listening. 'I just want to go home and pack my bags and go.'

'No! Don't do that.' Jemma had seen enough of her friends get divorced to set up in business as a matrimonial lawyer herself. 'You stay put, girl! Don't you dare move out. If anyone is going to leave it will be Alex.'

'But—'

'But nothing. Go home, have a nice cup of tea and see if you can get a friend to come round. I'd come myself but I'm up at Lakeside with Howie.'

'OK.'

'And then it's up to you.' She paused. 'Do you want him?'

And then Nina broke down. 'I don't know. It was going on for a year, Jemma! A year. And she's not going to go away.'

'What?'

'She said she wasn't going to go away. She said that the court case wasn't for unfair dismissal, it was for sexual harassment and that Alex was going to have to pay. He's lied to me about all of that as well. And she was really nasty. Like she hated me.' Nina cleared her throat. 'I think she might be a bit ... unhinged.'

Jemma sighed. Business was one thing. But there came a point when you had to stand up and do what was right.

She looked round at the car. Howard was reading the paper. She walked still further away from the Lexus to make doubly sure Howard could not hear her. 'Listen, Nina.' She struggled for a way to put it. 'I did a bit of asking around about this Sasha girl.' She hoped Nina wouldn't ask when or how. 'And it turns out that she's got quite a history. Sasha isn't even her real name ...'

Nina had searched every pocket, drawer, cupboard and then every other possible hiding place in the flat – his bathroom cabinet, the side compartment of his overnight bag – before going right through his desk again. She had found nothing. Whatever Alex had bought Sasha, and wherever he had taken her, he had paid cash. She didn't know whether to feel further demoralised by this evidence of his calculated deception or relieved that he had taken such care for her not to find out.

Maria had come round at lunchtime.

She had held her tight in the hallway. 'Oh, God. I am so sorry.'

'I should have listened to you.' She should have listened to Maria – and to Susan.

'No one wants to believe the worst.' Maria reached into her bag. 'Here, I bought you a sandwich.'

Nina shook her head.

'You need to eat! You're wasting away.'

After Nina had managed a couple of mouthfuls and half a cup of coffee, Maria had asked hesitantly, 'What are you going to do?'

Nina sounded shell-shocked. 'Do you think we could ever come back from this?'

Maria had been unable to answer. Instead she said inadequately, 'It just shows, you never really know someone, do you?'

Now, waiting for Alex in the darkening late afternoon, Nina got up and walked over to where their wedding photograph stood on the mantelpiece. She picked it up and looked at it, seeing in her own eyes the love she had felt for Alex on that day and all the hope she held for the future. She put it back. What a sham! Alex had destroyed not just the last year but everything that had gone before.

On the day of her wedding she had come downstairs to the drawing room where Archie stood waiting for her. She saw that there were tears in his eyes.

'You remind me of someone I used to know.' He hesitated. 'She was very beautiful. She was graceful – in every way.'

And then he had taken her arm and escorted her to the car to drive to the church in St Peter's Street.

She had been so sure. Alex was everything she needed in her life: strong, reliable, devoted – a man she could spend the rest of her life with. After the tumult she had endured over Michael it had been like coming home to a safe harbour from stormy waters. All the confusion and disappointment and pain went away when she was with Alex.

There had been no inkling at the beginning of her last summer with Michael of what was to come. He had returned from college to a summer job with Jack Tyler. At the end of the 1980s Jack had gone bust in the property crash. But he had lost no time in starting over. Before long he was back to his wheeler-dealer ways and busier than ever. Michael was to be his assistant for the summer: officially photographing the properties for Jack's new corporate brochure, but in reality acting as Jack's driver, messenger and all-round Boy Friday. Jack was generous. It was his money that allowed them to take a holiday in New York.

At the top of the Empire State Building, the wind gusting and the city laid out before them, Michael had taken her in his arms. 'I want to be with you for ever,' he had said.

And she had nodded and thought that nothing could separate them. That afternoon they had gone to Bloomingdales and he had bought her the silver charm bracelet. 'It's our for ever bracelet,' he said, fastening it on her wrist.

On their return home her mother had noticed it immediately. 'No ring then,' she said sarcastically. 'You see, Nina. He can't afford one, can he?'

And Nina was glad then that she had chosen the bracelet, that their pledge was secret, that her mother's cynicism would not taint all that they had.

A few weeks later it was all over.

A year later she was engaged to Alex. On her wedding day, taking Archie's arm as she walked down the aisle, she had had no doubts.

Her mother had resolutely promoted Alex's cause. 'Romance won't pay the bills.' Ever since Nina had started seeing Michael, Anne had never tried to conceal her disapproval. 'You're too young! You think you know it all, that you'll never want anyone else. But what do you know at your age?' Her face would contort with worry. 'He's at art school, for goodness' sake!' Perhaps if Michael had settled down on the farm it would have been different. But as it was Anne viewed him as an unreliable drifter. When Nina had announced – in a carefully pre-prepared and not entirely truthful speech – that they were going to New York, Anne had come up to find her in her bedroom.

'Don't go getting yourself pregnant! Are you on the pill?'
'Mummy!'

'Oh, for goodness' sake. Your father might think butter wouldn't melt in your mouth, but don't think you're fooling me. Going with a study group from the art class indeed! Do I look like I was born yesterday?' She had grasped Nina's arms. 'Take precautions and don't leave it up to him. What does the man care?' she said bitterly. 'You'll be the one left holding the baby.'

Nina had fled at that point, but she'd made sure she had her month's supply packed in her handbag for the flight.

Alex, in contrast, was viewed by Anne as the perfect husband. 'He'll be a good provider; one day he'll own that shop and the flats. That's a little gold mine. You can't beat property. He's steady. You know where you are with a man like that.'

Archie had been more circumspect. 'Just don't make any sudden decisions,' was the most he ever said. Right now she missed Archie so much: he would have known what to do. Knowing that she could not look at the photograph again, she took it down and put it away in a drawer. Then, she did what she had been considering all day: she took off her wedding ring and put it in the drawer as well. As she closed it, she heard Alex's key in the door.

'Hello!'

Immediately she understood that he did not know. She had imagined that Sasha would call him to gloat. But then she could do that any time.

He walked briskly into the living room. 'Why are you here in the dark?' He leaned over and switched on the table lamp. 'Hey. What's the matter?'

She had wanted to be so strong and dignified. Instead she burst into tears. 'I know. I know all about it.'

His expression said that he knew exactly what she was talking about. 'What's happened?'

He moved closer to her. She took a step back.

'I saw Sasha today. And I know, Alex. Don't lie about it,' she said urgently. More lies would be unbearable. 'She told me all the details. Everything.'

He stopped dead. He looked stunned. 'Where did you see her?'

'I went to her flat.'

'What?'

'I didn't go up. I waited for her outside.'

She remained standing, wanting to keep her distance from him. The memory of that morning's conversation came to the fore. 'A year, Alex. You slept with her for a year. And there's no way out of this or back from this for us. God, a one-night stand would have been bad enough. But you lied to me for a year.'

He looked as though he was in a state of shock. 'I need a drink.' He walked out towards the kitchen.

She followed him, the words spilling out now in an unstoppable torrent. 'I believed you. I believed you when you said that you were working late. I trusted you. And in return you betrayed me.'

She watched as, his hand shaking, he poured a whisky.

She was shouting at him now. 'And you did it over and over and over again.'

He took a drink.

A blind fury consumed her. 'How could you lie to me? How could you sleep with that bitch? How could you?'

Finally he looked over towards her. 'If I tell you it was nothing—'

She came further into the kitchen to stand in front of him. 'No. It wasn't nothing. Can't you tell the truth about anything? You were planning to run away with her. God, I should have listened to that policeman, Inspector Taylor. You even had the money salted away.'

'No! That's not true.' He sounded genuine. 'That was a tax shelter.'

'So what were you planning to do? Sleep with her behind my back indefinitely?'

'No. Look, it just got out of hand. And I broke it off.'

'After I insisted you sack her! Left to your own devices you would have carried on.'

'No. It wasn't like that.'

'What was it like?'

'It was a stupid fling, Nina. I just got drawn in. I didn't plan it that way.'

'So what did you plan?'

'Nothing. Look, we worked together. We got to know each other. And one thing led to another. I never set out to have an affair or for you to find out or any of this to happen.'

'You just thought you could get away with it.'

He paused. 'Yes. Probably I did.'

'And you thought she would settle for that,' she said contemptuously.

'Yes.'

'How could you be so naïve? How could you think that a woman like that would be content to be your mistress indefinitely?'

'Look, I didn't think. I didn't set up some master plan. I just sort of ... fell into it.'

'Like you fell into her bed?'

'Yes. No. Look, it wasn't calculated. And I never had any intention of leaving you.'

He sounded as if he thought he should get credit for that.

'So you just thought it was OK to lie to me and deceive me indefinitely. How many others have there been, Alex?'

'None! I swear to you. There hasn't been anyone.'

'Anyone else, you mean,' she said bitterly. She was filled with disgust for him. 'You even had sex with her at the office party!'

'What?'

'In the summerhouse. Don't bother to deny it!'

He sounded outraged. 'I didn't! I swear to you. If she told you that, she's lying.'

She gave a contemptuous laugh in response. 'Frankly, Alex, I can't believe a word you tell me.'

He turned round so that he was looking out of the kitchen window into the dark. 'Look, this is going nowhere. What do you want me to say?'

Nina wanted what she could never have – for them to turn the clock back and for it never to have happened.

'I think you ought to leave, Alex.'

He turned to face her. His expression was incredulous. 'You're not serious?'

'Yes. Why ever not?'

'Because we're married, for God's sake. This doesn't have to be the end. You can't just throw away fourteen years.'

'I haven't thrown anything away. You did that.' It was the lies that were as bad as the infidelity. The thought that he had taken all the love and trust that had existed between them, manipulating her unquestioning faith in him to cheat and deceive her. 'I can't forgive you.'

His expression was earnest. 'Not now. Of course not. But in time …' His voice tailed off. Then, 'Darling, we could get help. You should try.'

'Don't tell me what I should do!' It was the limit. 'Have you any idea what trouble you've caused? She's got a criminal record, Alex. Sasha isn't even her real name.'

He looked confused. 'No. I checked. She had perfect references.'

'Probably fake,' she said dismissively. 'She's a con artist, Alex. This whole court case is about getting money out of you. That's what she specialises in.'

'How do you know all this?' he said suspiciously.

'Jemma told me. I told her about Sasha and she did some asking about.'

He looked furious at this news. 'You told Jemma about our private life!'

His attitude was incredible. 'Yes! Given that I can't get an honest answer out of you I didn't have much choice.'

Alex had always adhered to the traditional Italian view that family matters were strictly private. 'You shouldn't have told her,' he said angrily.

'You shouldn't have given me a reason to!' she snapped back.

There was a pause. She could see that he was considering this new development. 'How did Jemma know?'

'I've no idea. Instead of worrying about Jemma, shouldn't you be thinking about this psycho you've brought into our lives? She's even been in trouble for assault.'

'Assault! Christ.' He took a good drink.

'You should never have gone near her.'

'I know!' He slammed down the glass. 'Hell, Nina. Do you think I'm proud of this?'

'Then why did you do it?'

It was rhetorical. He could never give answers that would satisfy her questions: why had he turned his back on her and their life together, shattered all that they had had, and brought them to this point? Why had their marriage not been enough for him? Why had she not been enough for him?

And how could she ever be sure that it would never happen again?

But in the silence still she felt driven to ask futile questions, whilst knowing there was nothing he could say that would be right. 'Was it about the sex? Is that what you wanted?'

'No! Look, it was just a terrible, stupid mistake. The whole thing.'

'Did you love her?'

'No!'

She was scathing. 'So it wasn't about sex and it wasn't about love. So why exactly did you sneak off to screw her for a year?'

'It wasn't a year; it was less than that.'

'Oh, shut up.' She leaned back and closed her eyes.

He came over to her. 'I'm sorry, darling. About everything. We should never have let this happen.'

'We?'

He put his hand on her shoulder but she pushed it roughly away. The sight of his hands made her think of him touching Sasha.

'I mean it's all my fault. But we should have spent more time together. I shouldn't have got so wrapped up in work.'

She had no patience for this. 'Other men work long hours and they don't have affairs.'

Or did they? Nothing she had once believed was certain any more. Maybe all men were unfaithful. She had a suspicion from her conversations with Jemma that Howard might not be whiter than white.

He said nothing in response to this last comment. Instead he slowly refilled his glass.

As she watched him, she imagined him pouring himself a drink in Sasha's flat. She thought about all the lies Alex had told her – *I've got a ton of paperwork, I'll catch the late train* – and all the times she had tried to call him but the mobile had been switched off. *Sorry, the battery went dead.* She thought about the places he had taken Sasha and what they had talked about – her, no doubt – and wondered what he had said when he had handed Sasha that Tiffany box.

She remembered Maria and Susan trying to warn her.

She pictured his entire office staff gossiping behind her back.

Eventually she broke the silence. 'What did you buy her from Tiffany?' She stood staring past him, unable to look at him.

He sighed. 'A necklace.' He sounded worn out. 'Look, she's my secretary. I would have got her a Christmas present anyway.'

'What kind?'

'I can't remember.'

'What kind, Alex?'

'A heart.'

It was hopeless. Her mind was flooded with images of

them together. It was an impossibility that they could ever share a bed again.

She got up and walked towards the door, still not looking at him. 'You need to leave.'

She heard him put down his glass.

'Nina. Please ...' he called after her.

'Now. Go!' And then she walked back to the living room and shut the door.

Chapter 13

As a way of spending a Saturday night this was about as bad as it got. Susan, tired and, unusually for her, nauseous, lay sprawled on Gerry's bed while he sat hunched over the computer desk that, along with the Ikea beech wardrobe, took up the rest of the available space in the undersized bedroom.

From the living room came the sound of Samantha and Harry screaming. On the weekends that they stayed they shared the pull-out sofa bed. There was barely room to walk round it to switch on the television. Gerry let them stay up late. Actually he let them do whatever they wanted. The only rule that he enforced was the one about them not touching Dad's papers. Or 'the Manuscript' as he referred to it.

Gerry was typing demonically. It was a week until the deadline for his BBC script-writing competition. Susan had grown sick of hearing about the plots, the characters and the input of the members of the Chiltern Writers' Group.

As if on cue, Gerry turned round. 'The group thought that at the end of scene eight it should be left unclear whether the Deobe spaceship made it through the atmosphere. That way there would be more tension at the start of the battle scene. The Deobes come in at the end as reinforcements.'

Susan stared at him blankly.

He turned back to the screen. 'That's the earth battle scene, obviously. Not the War of the Suns. They have to be there at the start of that otherwise the Kelset galaxy alliance doesn't make sense.'

Susan had been listening to this for weeks and she still

didn't have a clue what he was talking about. She wanted to cry with boredom. Tap, tap, tap he went at all hours. It was such a complete fucking waste of time when he could be working in a second job. They couldn't manage with the money he earned – and even that job didn't look too stable.

Gerry was still talking. 'It's the alliances that really add intrigue to the plot.'

Alliances. She needed to make a few herself. She looked down at her stomach and rested her hand there. She had a definite bump now.

It was all so expensive: the cot, the pushchair and the car seat. Come to think of it, the car. Then there was all that stuff that she really, really wanted now – a hand-sewn patchwork gingham cot bumper, a rocking chair and a designer changing bag, for example, and all the other nice mail-order things they advertised in the baby magazines hidden under the driver's seat of Roger's van. She remembered when she worked for Caro Phillips, Caro had ordered all of Clemmie and Hamish's furniture from Daisy & Tom. Clemmie's was white; Hamish's was French cherrywood. His cot bedding – sailing boats and steam ships – was matched by the fabric of the roman blinds and the blue and white rug, all of it specially imported from Pottery Barn. Clemmie and Hamish had both been born at the Portland, Caro had told her matter-of-factly. 'There's no nonsense there about having to beg for an epidural. You have your own doctor, your own room – and a fridge for champagne.'

When the time came for the baby to be born Susan knew she would be lucky if Gerry bought her a bunch of Tesco daffodils. Lately he had been talking about possible redundancies at his firm.

'It's the slowdown in the housing market,' he said resignedly. 'There isn't the work around. Still, something will come along.'

He had absolutely no get up and go. The only thing he showed any enthusiasm for was his script. He was happy enough about the baby but characteristically passive at the same time. 'We'll manage. Something will turn up.'

How? she wanted to scream. How will we manage in a one-bedroom rented flat when all your disposable income goes to your ex-wife?

It had been a foolish plan, she now realised, to imagine that it could ever have worked with Gerry. At the start of her pregnancy she had had some vague romantic notion about them forming a proper family. At least Gerry was single. But that was the only characteristic he had to recommend him. Aside from the fact that the baby was going to be a quarter Italian – and Gerry was pale and very ginger – he could never be the type of father that she wanted for her child.

She was sure it was Alex's baby. In the week before the Gloucestershire house party she hadn't seen Gerry, then they hadn't had sex that weekend thanks to the bloody kids, and she hadn't seen him for a week afterwards. Lest Gerry worked this out, she had been vague about the delivery date. He hadn't questioned her.

It was Alex's child and he would have to provide for it. The time had come to go to see him. She would be reasonable but firm. He could rely on her discretion and Nina need never know. But in return she would need money for the baby and money for herself. He couldn't expect the mother of his child to work on a market stall in winter! And once she finished work she would need a car, spending money and somewhere to live. She had started looking in the windows of Marlow estate agents. A flat in the old Wethered's Brewery development would be nice. Or perhaps a little cottage by the river with a garden. As for Nina, she was easily dealt with: the baby would be the result of a one-night stand with a dark-haired stranger.

She lay back and looked at the back of Gerry's head, bent over the computer, concentrating fiercely as if what he was doing actually mattered. She would have to make her own plans. In her mind Susan returned to the question she had been toying with since the news of the meeting with the solicitor: her encounter with Kate in Cookham High Street. God, it had been so tempting to run back, tell Richard and savour his reaction. Work colleagues, indeed! You could tell just by the way Kate looked at him. But on the other hand, telling Richard about Kate could well distract him from all the trouble he was stirring up for Nina. He was never good at handling more than one thing at once.

So she lay back and resolved to continue to say nothing – for the time being. Besides, she had an instinct that she might soon need his help. She passed her hand over her bump and rested it there; she couldn't stay quiet about the baby for much longer. When the time came to tell her mother, who could be funny about anything she thought wasn't respectable, Susan might be glad of an ally; was now the moment to make a tactical alliance with Richard?

Maria, who had plenty of experience with break-ups, said the crucial thing was to keep busy. Yesterday night Maria had dragged Nina out to help with a drinks party at an elegant mansion flat in St John's Wood. It was the client's seventieth birthday party.

'If you're going to be miserable at home, you may as well be miserable helping me.'

It had taken her mind off Alex, but only because Nina had stayed safely in the kitchen, away from the throng of happy couples and out of earshot of the speech. At the sound of the client's opening words she had shut the kitchen door.

'Seventy years is a milestone. But it is the forty-one I have shared with Eileen that are the real achievement ...'

Usually on a Sunday morning she and Alex got up late, took Muffin for a walk in Holland Park, then stopped off in High Street Kensington for the Sunday papers and a Starbucks. She had not dreamed that she could miss him so much. It was six days now since he had left and Maria was right when she said that the weekends were the worst.

Nina forced herself to get out of bed. Around her the house was deathly still. No sounds of the shower or banging of kitchen cupboards; no pot of tea waiting for her on the counter; no muffled news bulletin from the television in the drawing room. No life at all except for Muffin dozing on the bed where he had been promoted from his basket. She felt permanently shattered. Everything was an effort, from brushing her teeth to making the bed. A pile of post waited to be opened and soon she would have no clean clothes. She wanted to draw the curtains and go back to bed and never get up. She felt so raw, unable to listen to music on the radio or watch a television programme or read about a celebrity break-up without some triggered memory of Alex and their situation causing her to feel overwhelmed with grief.

Alex was at the Tara Hotel in Kensington, some five hundred yards up the road. He had texted her on the night he left. 'I'm sorry. Call me, please.'

She hadn't called him. In the morning there had been an email waiting for her.

She imagined he must have been up half the night writing it.

'God, I am so sorry. I know you have every right to hate me and never forgive me. I know all that. But please, please think about all we had together and all we can have. Don't let one stupid mistake spoil that ...'

But it wasn't one stupid mistake, was it? It was God knows how many lies and deceits and betrayals.

'... Truly, I do not deserve you. Any man would be proud to be married to you. We can still have a good life and a family and everything that you want. I will devote my life to making this up to you in any way I can.'

It went on in a similar vein for a page. Then it ended, 'I am off to the "breakfast buffet" now. I seem to be the only non-German resident of the hotel. Can I drop in later to collect clothes, etc.?'

She had typed back, 'Yes. After ten a.m.'

And unable to face another encounter she had left before he arrived.

Since then Alex had sent her a morning email and texts throughout the day, to which she had replied sporadically.

But she liked the texts and emails. And then she felt guilty for doing so. What kind of woman welcomed contact from her lying, cheating bastard of a husband?

She got up, put on the kettle and logged on.

'Hey, me again. I am worried about you. I wish you would let me talk to you. I know you need time – I understand that; I don't expect you to forgive and forget. Nina, I am willing to wait for as long as you need. But please don't rush into making any decisions. Can you at least consider the possibility that we may be able to get past this? Who knows, we could even emerge stronger. I don't mean that you have to overlook what has happened. But I believe we CAN recover from this. I am willing to do whatever it takes. If you want to see a professional that is fine by me …'

She stopped reading for a second. She could hardly believe that Alex would suggest that.

'… I am totally committed to doing whatever you want.'

She leaned back in her chair. It was impossible. Even agreeing to see him would feel as if in some way she was backing down, letting him off, saying that it was OK. That was the insurmountable problem: if she took him back then he would have got away with it. He would have lied to her, had his fun and then come back to all that he had had before. Instead of that she wanted him to suffer, to share in her pain and to understand that he wasn't going to get away with this.

It was so bloody unfair. She was the one who had been landed with the humiliating consequences of Alex's actions. How could she ever go again to another of his office functions? How exactly was she going to apologise to Susan? God knows what Richard would have to say. Plenty, that was for sure. And if she did take Alex back, surely everyone would think she was an utter fool? Before it happened to her, that's what she would have thought about any woman in her situation who hadn't already changed the locks and consulted a lawyer.

Yesterday she had bumped into their neighbour in the hallway. Sally, who was married to Jonathan, was an elegant and very social Californian.

'I was saying to Jonathan only the other day that we must have the two of you round for dinner! Catch up on all your news!'

'Oh. Yes. Thank you.' Nina felt a wave of secret shame wash over her. Pointedly she had looked at her watch. 'Sorry. I must dash. I have a meeting at work,' she lied.

'I'll call you!'

She had not told her family: the prospect of listening to Susan's and Richard's analyses of her situation was unbearable. Even though Nina had been so sure that none of this was her fault, she felt increasingly confused. Despite her anger, doubts had begun to surface in her mind: maybe she had had a part to play. If their marriage had been stronger, then Sasha wouldn't have gained a foothold. If she had been more alert, the affair would never have lasted as long as it had done. If only she had paid less attention to her work and more to the warning signs blasting out from all directions.

A debating society had set up camp in her head: on the one hand couples recovered from worse than this; Sasha wasn't pregnant and marriage was for better or worse. But on the other hand everyone knew that husbands who strayed invariably went on to do it again. People changed? People didn't change? Besides, what were the odds of her meeting someone else? Worse still, what were the odds of her meeting someone else in time to have a baby?

She had taken to downing most of a bottle of wine in the evening just to get to sleep. Maria called a couple of times a day and so did Jemma.

'Now don't do anything stupid! Do you promise?'

But she had not told anyone else. It was as if by keeping the whole damn thing a secret it would be less awful.

And in the midst of all of this there was the wretched trustee meeting to deal with next week. Now she regretted asking for it. The last thing she needed now was to see her family. She felt a stab of loneliness. If Alex had been here she would have talked it through with him: he would have made suggestions on how to handle the meeting, how to present the bank statements to the solicitor and what to expect from Richard. Alex was so good at that type of thing. She hadn't realised how much she relied on him. He had been her confidant, her chief supporter and her friend.

She sat in silence for a while then typed back a reply to Alex's email.

'Would you like to meet for a coffee?'

And then she stared at the sentence for a moment, deleted it and logged off.

The windows of the kitchen of Pat's Hounslow semi were steamed up. Pat always insisted on boiling three vegetables for Sunday lunch, just as she always overcooked the meat and never made enough gravy.

Pat jerked her head toward the oven. 'Check on the potatoes.'

Sasha picked up the oven gloves and opened the oven door, heat blasting out at her. 'They're done.'

Pat peered over her shoulder. 'All right. Get them out.'

Pat had been the same since they were children: asking Sasha to do things, then checking up on her. Pat had a permanently self-satisfied air, even though she had very little to be pleased about. Sasha glanced at her sister, standing at the cooker in her elasticated-waist jeans and her cheap polyester blouse, and considered asking if she was going back to Weight Watchers. But she wasn't in the mood for an argument.

The men were in the living room watching the football. Every couple of minutes Pat's two teenage sons erupted in cheers or obscenities directed towards the referee and players. In between there was the sound of her father's hacking cough.

'His chest's playing him up,' Pat had said. 'There's a bug going round. I took him for his flu jab yesterday.'

Sasha had felt a pang of guilt. Despite all the time on her hands she hadn't been to see him for a week. She'd got wrapped up in her new plan, spending hours on the internet and telephone calls to the States. She now spoke virtually daily to Gloria, the owner of a Miami estate agent specialising in upmarket lettings.

Pat was spooning the potatoes into a Pyrex dish. That was another annoying thing she did – getting the potatoes cooked too soon so they sat and got cold while she made the gravy.

'You still seeing that fella, then?' Pat asked.

'No.'

'Gone back to his wife, then, did he?'

Sasha did not reply.

Pat turned round. 'Angie, you need to find a nice single bloke.' She sounded worried.

'I know.' She had come to the same conclusion herself. She sat down at the table. Pat and her husband had knocked through to make a kitchen-diner but even so it would be cramped with the six of them around the table. 'I'm going to go travelling for a while,' she continued.

'Oh.'

'Miami. For the winter.'

'Very nice, I'm sure,' said Pat disapprovingly. She didn't like foreign travel.

Sasha, undaunted, filled Pat in on the details. 'I'll probably rent a high-rise apartment – with a porter and an ocean view. Or I could go further out to a gated development.' Then she told her about the shops and the nightlife.

Pat, of course, refused to say anything positive. 'Aren't there a lot of guns and drugs out there?'

Sasha ignored her. She had never listened to Pat's opinion and wasn't going to start now. If she had followed Pat's advice she'd still be working in the Feltham branch of Budgens. Miami was exactly the right place to go. It had good weather, excellent amenities and a high- net-worth population. Florida, her internet research had revealed, was one of the world's top retirement destinations for millionaires.

She would drop the court case the day before she left. They had set a trial date for January now: much as she would have liked to have waited until the day of the hearing and faced Alex on the steps of the court it would be too much of an inconvenience to fly back. By then she would be otherwise occupied. But she had not shared this information with her solicitor. In fact, she had instructed her to press ahead.

'Write to his solicitor and tell them that I'm not interested in settling. I want the truth to come out in court.'

Her solicitor, an impressionable feminist called Tricia, had sounded sympathetic. 'I understand. It's part of the psychological consequences of harassment. You need to be heard.'

Pat was stirring Bisto into the roasting pan. 'What are you going to do with your flat?'

'Leave it.' Whatever else would she do with it?

'You should rent it out!' Pat sounded horrified. 'It's a waste of money to leave it empty.'

That was just the kind of idiotic suggestion she would expect from Pat. Who in their right mind wanted a complete stranger sleeping in their bed, using their cutlery, standing in the shower? It was disgusting.

'Maybe.'

Ordinarily she would have told Pat what a stupid idea it was. But for some reason she had lost her appetite for a fight. These days she felt listless and unfocused. There had been times like that in the past. And the answer had always been to get up and move on; to find a new challenge and to play another game. But even as she thought this, there was a part of her that for the first time ever envied Pat her husband, her children and her hot, cramped kitchen.

*

'A baby.' Her mother didn't sound excited or even particularly surprised. 'I was wondering when you were going to tell me.'

Susan was taken aback. There had been no tell-tale morning sickness or premature purchase of maternity clothes, though she had been tempted. 'How did you know?'

Anne looked her up and down. 'All that weight you've put on.' She paused to light a cigarette. 'Who's the father?'

'Gerry is, of course.' Susan thought her mother really was the limit.

Anne leaned over slightly from where they were sitting at the kitchen table to take a look at Susan's stomach. 'When is it due?'

'March.'

It was the reaction Susan should have expected. Other mothers would have thrown their arms round their daughter – and if it had been Nina her mother probably would have, her expression delighted and full of pride. Instead, Anne was looking at her with disdain. 'You're not married.'

'I know. We'll get married.'

'He's already got two kiddies. And an ex-wife. How's he going to pay for you?'

Richard stepped in. 'Mummy, it'll be fine. He's got a good job. He's a professional man. And he's very steady. I like him.'

At this, Anne looked slightly mollified. 'Well, you're small, I'll say that for you. Of course I was the same.' Her mother sniffed. 'Don't be getting any ideas about me babysitting. I'm too old to be running after kids. You've made your bed and you'll have to lie on it.' With that she surveyed the Monopoly board. 'Where's the dice?'

Susan turned her attention back to the game. She was on a good run and had just bought up the last of the four utilities. Her mother was in the lead with a smattering of hotels. And Richard had just been wiped out when he landed on Park Lane. At least he didn't have tantrums any more, bursting into tears when he lost. All in all, breaking the news had not been too bad. A game of Monopoly might seem an unusual occasion to impart momentous news but experience had taught Susan that it was more important to catch her mother in the right mood, whenever that might be. So she had waited until Anne had drawn a good card from the community chest and then dropped it into the conversation. She had been anxious that her mother might take the moral high ground – she liked to do that where other people were concerned. The thought had crossed her mind that Anne might even throw her out. But there again it suited her mother to have her there: Susan cooked most nights and fed the cats and fetched her cups of tea so she didn't have to get up from her armchair.

Susan stole a glance at Richard, who held her gaze just long enough to acknowledge the arrangement that existed between them. Naturally, the new alliance had been Susan's idea. She had tackled him a few days earlier.

'I've got some good news,' she said brightly.

'Oh.' Richard looked wary.

'Hmm. Gerry and I are expecting a baby.'

He thought for a moment. 'Are you going to get married?'

'I expect so. Anyway, I'm going to be staying in Marlow.'

Richard looked less than delighted to hear this. 'Where are you going to live? How are you going to afford a place here?'

He was right, of course. 'Oh, something will come up,' she said breezily. 'Things are going very well for Gerry at work. Who knows, to begin with we might even move in here.'

He could not conceal his dismay at that. 'Have you told Mummy?'

'Not yet.'

'Well, good luck,' he said cheerfully. 'You know what she thinks about unmarried parents.' Susan could almost see the plan forming in his mind by which he would scupper her chances of living at home.

She spoke quickly before he had a chance to think further. 'Actually I'm more worried about Nina.'

'Nina?' He looked puzzled.

'Hmm. It's obvious she's trying to get into Mummy's good books. Look at the way she's making up all these stupid accusations about you stealing from Mummy's bank account.'

'I'm not stealing!'

'Of course you're not. We know that. But that's not what Nina is going to tell Mummy. It'll be the same with the baby – she'll use it to make me look bad. Just like she always does.'

Richard looked up, now understanding where this conversation was leading. 'What do you want?'

'I don't want anything. I just think that we should make more of an effort to get along. For Mummy's sake.' She paused. 'But there are ways that we could help each other.'

'For example?'

'For example. When I tell her about the baby you could say what a good piece of news it is. She listens to you.'

There was a trace of suspicion remaining in his voice. 'And?'

'And when it's the trustee meeting next week I could say that you've done nothing wrong. And I could persuade Mummy not to go.'

At that, Richard could not conceal the excitement in his voice. 'How are you going to do that?'

'I'll think of something.' And she would.

Richard was a good liar. He knew how to spin a story. But he was never good at thinking more than two steps ahead.

'The point is,' Susan continued confidently, 'that if Nina is going to start coming down here and stirring up trouble then we have to protect ourselves. Who knows what she'll think of next? You're the man of the house. She hasn't got any right to tell you what to do.'

'All to get herself in Mummy's good books.' Richard had clearly been pondering this. 'Have you noticed this sudden interest in Mummy's money has all started up since Alex got into trouble with the police? You're not telling me that it's a

234

coincidence. If you ask me, the business is on the rocks and they're paving the way to ask her for a loan.'

Susan didn't believe this for a moment. 'I think you're right,' she said firmly. 'Thank God you've worked it out.'

Richard looked at her with a newfound affection. 'What we need to do is nip this in the bud. Before Nina has any other bright ideas.'

'I knew you'd get it all under control.'

Susan shot him a worshipful smile. God, he was such a fool. No wonder Kate had had enough. But even that fact would work to her advantage: as soon as the meeting was over she would tell Richard about Kate and Daniel – 'You've no idea how sorry I am, Richard' – advise him that he needed to spend more time at home and send him off on a mission to save his marriage, leaving her comfortably in prime position at the house. The key to success, as so often the case, was all in the timing.

Chapter 14

Jemma sat at the kitchen table with *Introduction to Account-ancy I* opened at chapter three. It was too cold to sit out by the pool. Howard had left early to warm up for the club tournament, unfortunately extending over Saturday and Sunday. He had insisted on booking flights back to London on Monday morning, which meant she would miss her ten a.m. class: management basics. Howard hadn't said anything against her enrolling at college, but he wasn't bending over backwards to be supportive, either. Jemma had imagined, when she went in to see the student advisor, that she would have to wait until next year to enrol on business studies. But start dates or even term dates were old hat now in further education: it was all online supported learning in modular form, which meant you only went in twice a week and you could pick up sessions all through the year.

She was about to get started on unit two of basic principles of double-entry book-keeping when there was a knock on the glass of the patio door and the sound of it sliding open.

'Only me!' Jemma heard the clatter of Barbara's heels on the tiled floor. 'I was passing so I just thought I'd pop in.'

Jemma's eye caught the large shopping bag that Barbara was carrying. She knew what was coming next. Barbara had recently become Marbella's first sales rep – or consultant, as she called herself – for Rocco, a French cosmetics company specialising in home parties. 'My samples have just arrived. I knew you'd want some.'

So far Jemma had managed to evade Barbara's first party

by being in England, and then to dodge Barbara's suggestion of a one-on-one makeover with special tips for Christmas party make-up.

She closed up her book. 'Would you like a coffee?'

'Well, I can't stay long.' Barbara made it sound as if she was doing Jemma a favour in dropping in unannounced. 'I want to get this round before the Christmas parties. I've got two set up now. But it's not too late for you to host one.'

'I don't think we'll be here.'

'You get a fifty-euro hostess gift certificate towards any cosmetic product of your choice and a surprise gift,' said Barbara, appearing not to have heard her. 'And there's no post and packing because I deliver to your door.'

Jemma resisted pointing out that there wasn't any post or packing when she went to Lakeside, either. Instead she said, 'I'll look in the diary.'

Lately Jemma had relaxed a bit around Barbara. For a start she acknowledged to herself that Barbara wasn't Howard's type. As he put it, he liked a bit of meat on the bones. Today she was wearing a skinny rib T-shirt over Seven jeans, an outfit that made her arms and legs seem even more twig-like than usual. Then there was Barbara's unremitting friendliness. It was hard to be hostile when Barbara either didn't notice or carried on regardless issuing invitations for lunch at the club, dinner at their place and all her Rocco events. And finally Barbara was the only person apart from Nina who had been supportive of Jemma's new studies. 'I think it's good to expand the mind. That's what I love about my painting. Not that I've done much recently.'

Jemma put a cup of coffee in front of Barbara, who took it black, and didn't bother offering her a biscuit because she would only refuse.

'Is Brian playing?'

Barbara pulled a face. 'No. His back.' No additional explanation was needed. Brian's back gave out after plane journeys, car rides, golf games or come to that any form of physical movement. 'I had to get out of the house. He's run out of painkillers.'

Jemma was beginning to realise that life with Brian was something of a trial.

Barbara pulled out some samples of lipstick and eyeshadow. 'They came yesterday. Take what you like. I get more on account of being a top ten.'

'Top ten?'

'The top ten per cent of the Spanish consultants.'

Jemma put down her cup. 'But you've only been doing it a couple of months.'

'Hmm. I sell a lot when I go home. That helps.'

It was impossible not to admire Barbara: whatever her faults, laziness wasn't one of them.

'If I keep it up I'll go to the Top Ten Sales Conference in Nice next year. Of course Brian isn't very keen on it. It does take a lot of time.' She paused. 'To be honest I need the money.'

Jemma thought back to her early suspicions about Brian keeping Barbara short. 'You can't ask Brian?' He seemed to have plenty, driving around in a Mercedes.

'Credit cards,' Barbara said heavily. 'Brian gives me an allowance and I'm not supposed to spend more than that. But it's hard. When we came here I needed new clothes and then there was the studio to fit out. Not that I have much time for painting,' she added quickly. 'And you have to have spending money, don't you? Anyway,' she added in a confiding tone, 'I've got into a bit of trouble with the cards.'

'How much?' Jemma asked.

Barbara looked sheepish. Instead of answering she held up five fingers.

'Five thousand?' Jemma guessed.

Barbara shook her head. 'Five figures.'

'Oh. I see.'

'I've made an arrangement with the companies.'

'Companies?'

'MasterCard, Visa, Amex – and then there's the store cards.'

'But can't you tell Brian?'

Barbara shook her head. 'Nope. He'd go nuts. It's happened before, when we got married. God, there's so much stuff to buy when you get hitched. He cleared all the cards and made me promise I wouldn't do it again. He doesn't even know I got new ones.'

She pulled out a packet of cigarettes. 'Brian's funny about money. I mean, he's loaded but he's always worrying about not having enough. He's always online, checking his accounts, moving his money about. Every Sunday he gets the papers and reads the financial pages, all of them.' She lit her cigarette. 'And God help those tenants if they're late with the rent. He goes round there and has it out with them. He's not supposed to but he does anyway.'

Jemma realised that Barbara was a little frightened of Brian.

'So can you get it all straightened out?' she asked with genuine concern.

Barbara nodded. 'It'll take a while but I'll get there. I just have to make sure he doesn't get to the post before me.' She looked at Jemma. 'You're doing the right thing, getting a qualification. A woman needs to be able to stand on her own two feet. That was my mistake – selling the beauty salon when I married Brian. I should have got a manager in, but Brian didn't want the tie. And like a fool I listened to him.' She leaned across the table and nodded approvingly at Jemma's accountancy textbook. 'You keep going with that.'

Kate came downstairs to find Richard in the kitchen ironing a shirt. It was the day of the meeting at Carruthers & Kirkpatrick. She looked at her watch and saw that she had ten minutes before she had to leave with Emily. She stepped out into the hallway, looked into the living room where Emily was playing with her Barbie Magical Castle and stepped back into the kitchen.

She hesitated. 'Richard – about this meeting. Are there any problems with the bank account?' Lately she had begun to think more carefully about exactly where he got his cash. In asking questions, however, she knew she had to tread carefully. 'I mean, is there anything in the bank statements which could be misinterpreted?'

For a moment he looked up and caught her gaze, then his eyes flickered away. 'No. Only expenses for Mummy.' He continued to look determinedly at the shirt he was ironing. 'Not for me, for Mummy.'

From the expression on his face and the note of defiance in his voice she knew that he was lying.

'Richard, I know things haven't been easy financially. But …'

What she wanted to say was that that didn't justify stealing from his mother.

Instead she said, 'I think it's important that you tell me exactly what's been going on.'

He jabbed impatiently at the collar of his shirt with the point of the iron. 'Nothing. This is all about Nina. Susan doesn't think there's a problem.'

At the mention of Susan's name, Kate felt a twinge of unease. She knew she should mention their encounter in Cookham before Susan did. But it never seemed the right moment.

Richard continued, 'Susan's happy with the way things are and so am I. Susan's having a baby,' he added casually.

'Oh!' Kate was shocked. In her family news like that would have been a cause for celebration. But in Richard's family it hardly merited a mention. It had been exactly the same when she got pregnant with Emily. Archie had been delighted but Anne had barely raised a smile. 'Rather you than me. You'll miss your freedom,' had been her first response, followed later over tea and biscuits by, 'Be careful you don't pile on the weight or you'll never get it off.'

Kate watched as Richard gave up on the collar. She thought on her feet. 'Actually I saw Susan the other day. She was coming out of a baby shop in Cookham. I was there for a meeting.'

He appeared not to take any notice of this. 'Susan's going to tell Nina about the baby after the meeting. Nina is worked up enough without anything else winding her up.'

Kate felt a surge of sympathy for Nina. From family gatherings where Nina lavished attention on Emily she had guessed that Nina had been ready to have a baby for some time now.

But it was clear that Richard and Susan had worked everything out in advance. She felt uneasy about the whole affair – was Susan taking money, too? – and sorry for Nina, who was clearly being outmanoeuvred.

Richard unplugged the iron. He appeared to hesitate. 'I'm thinking about bringing up the furniture.'

Kate's heart sank. 'Why?'

'Because if Nina insists on dragging us in there we may as well discuss that as well.'

Kate could not be bothered to pretend that there was the slightest merit in this idea. The furniture – or more particularly its distribution after Anne's death – was a topic to which Richard returned infrequently but doggedly.

'Some of it is very valuable,' he said with exaggerated reasonableness.

Kate knew exactly what was coming next: the bloody French escritoire.

'What about the escritoire?' he said irritably. 'It's French. Maybe Louis the Fourteenth. It was in Dad's family for years and I should get it.'

'You probably will.'

'But what if it's not covered in the trust? What if he forgot to put it in? What if—'

She lost her patience. 'And what if we all get hit by a meteor tomorrow? For God's sake, Richard! We have to live in the present. What about the bills? What about the things we have to deal with today?' Her voice rose. 'The things *I* have to deal with!'

He rolled his eyes. 'Well, I'm sorry,' he said sarcastically. 'I have an extremely important legal meeting this morning, with potentially very serious consequences. But we have to talk about you.'

'About us! About our financial situation. About whether you are going to get a job.'

'I'm doing my best. I'm sorry if that's not good enough for you.'

'Richard!' She felt frustration overtake her. In all their discussions the truth constantly slipped away, confused by a combination of Richard's excuses and lies. She had to fight just to establish the facts of their situation. 'You could do more – read the ads in the paper, fill out more applications ...' *Pull your bloody finger out* was what she wanted to say. She stopped herself. 'You need to be more focused in your approach. The longer you stay out of work, the harder it is to find something.'

'I do work! I did that job in Lane End.'

'The paving? That was weeks ago.'

His voice grew more hostile. 'It was a job. Make your mind up. First you accuse me of not working and when I point out to you that I do work you ignore me.'

'It's not enough to work when you feel like it!'

'No,' he snapped. 'It's never enough, is it? Christ, Kate. Whatever I do is never right, is it? Maybe if you were more supportive things would be better.'

She tried to interrupt him. 'I—'

But his voice overrode hers. 'But no! You prefer to criticise me. Do you ever stop to think how that makes me feel?'

She shouted at him. 'How *you* feel! What about me, Richard?' She lost control. 'I don't feel like going to work every day. I don't feel like paying all the bills. But I don't have any choice. I have to keep us afloat.' She was shocked at the extent of her own anger, at the simmering resentment towards her husband which she thought she had under control. 'You've opted out and left me to pick up the pieces.'

Now he was angry, too. 'Christ. On and on. You've changed, Kate. Ever since Emily was born. You used to be fun to be around. Now all you do is nag like some old woman.' He looked at her with disdain. 'No wonder I need to get out of the house.'

'Oh, grow up!'

In response he mimicked her, his eyes rolling: 'Do this, Richard. Do that, Richard.'

She was so furious she could have hit him then. But just as she was preparing to tell him that she hoped he got exactly what he deserved at the meeting, she felt a tugging at her skirt. She looked down. Emily, holding her Princess Genevieve Barbie doll, was standing there. She looked up at Kate, confused, then hugged her doll. 'Mummy, why are you shouting?'

'Where's Mummy?' said Nina furiously, glaring at Richard.

'She's not well,' Susan cut in. She felt apprehensive but excited, too. This could be fun.

'Since when?' Nina looked astonished, which was understandable given that Susan had assured her on the telephone yesterday that she would be driving their mother to the meeting. But later that morning Susan had set about dissuading her from coming. 'You don't want to say the wrong thing, do you? You might get Richard into even more trouble!'

'Oh, no.'

'You know what these lawyers are like. They'll twist what you say.'

Anyhow, Susan knew that it was too late for Nina to do anything about it now. They were seated in the hushed waiting room of Carruthers & Kirkpatrick prior to their appointment with John Kirkpatrick. The offices were in Marlow High Street, opposite the old post-office building, on the first and second floors of a narrow red-brick town house. The ground floor was let to Lily's, a boutique specialising in cashmere. Lily herself was an ex-model, now in her fifties. None of the clothes in the boutique window were priced and Susan had never even dared go in there.

The waiting room of Carruthers & Kirkpatrick was furnished with reproduction antiques, watercolour prints and copies of *Country Life*. John Kirkpatrick's father, together with Archie, had founded the original firm. There were no Carruthers working there now, though Susan recalled that Richard had once talked about how in time he would become the senior partner.

Nina was looking back and forth between Susan and Richard. 'She should be here,' she said furiously.

'She's got a migraine,' explained Susan innocently.

'Probably brought on by the stress of this meeting,' continued Richard.

Nina, before she could reply to this, was interrupted by John Kirkpatrick stepping out of his office and calling them in. Susan remembered him from Archie's funeral and the meeting about the will held a couple of weeks later. He was not the stereotypical market- town solicitor. In fact, as he had explained at the time, he had spent several years in a City firm doing high-powered deals before returning to join the family firm.

'My wife wanted to leave London. So what choice did I have?' he had explained. The photograph of a pretty blonde on his desk had been a disappointment to Susan.

There had been five of them there at the meeting with John Kirkpatrick held three weeks after Archie's death: their mother, Susan, Richard, Nina and Alex. In the aftermath of their father's death, Nina had fallen to pieces and Alex had driven her down. There had been some debate, Susan recalled, about whether Alex should be allowed to be present in the meeting.

'Strictly speaking,' John had explained, 'it should be family members only. Unless you all agree for Alex to stay.'

'Fine,' said Richard. He had been almost cheerful. 'None of us has a problem with that.'

John had begun by speaking at length about their father. 'I want to begin by saying that it is our intention to keep the name of Carruthers. Your father was more than the joint founder of this firm. He was its heart and soul ...'

Next to her, Nina had begun to cry. Alex had reached over and held her hand.

'... and his portrait will continue to hang proudly in our hallway.'

John had gone on to talk about all that he had learned from Archie. 'He taught me that a lawyer doesn't just represent his clients. He's part of the fabric of the town. He showed me all the ways that it is possible to give back. For example ...'

After five minutes Richard had begun to fidget. Then John had reached for some papers in front of him.

'Now, sadly, we must turn to the matter at hand.' To begin with, Susan could understand what he was talking about: their father hadn't left just things in a will. He had set up a trust as well. But then John had started to go on and on about the testator's intentions and beneficiaries and from then on Susan had lost track. But Richard started to interrupt him.

'What? That can't be right! Explain that again!'

Finally John said he would summarise the position. 'Your father arranged for all his assets to be placed in a trust. While she is alive, your mother is the sole beneficiary. After her death, the estate will be distributed according to the terms of the trust which your father specified must remain confidential.'

Richard, when he finally realised that there would be no money that day for any of the three children, had been incandescent. 'You mean there's nothing now!'

'Your mother, I can assure you, is generously provided for.'

'I'm talking about me!'

Next, Richard had demanded to see the terms of the trust.

'It's secret,' John had said simply. 'It's all in order, I can assure you.'

'I'll sue you! You'll have to show me.'

John had remained unfazed in the face of Richard's temper. 'That is your prerogative. I should tell you, however, that your father took great care with the drafting of the trust. He was an excellent lawyer.'

Eventually, Alex and Susan had all but dragged Richard out of the meeting.

Today, Susan saw that John still had that slightly sharp City look in a well-cut suit. He gestured for them to sit down in a semi-circle of chairs set out in front of his desk. Susan saw that on a bookcase there was now a new photograph of his wife holding a baby. Instantly her spirits fell. Everywhere she went in Marlow she encountered well-heeled married couples and their designer babies. Today she had dressed carefully to conceal her bump in a tiered beige corduroy skirt, the top button undone, over which she wore a baggy Peruvian jumper. Nina didn't need to know about the baby just yet – she was clearly wound up enough as it was. Susan would drop that bombshell after the meeting.

'Please don't tell Nina!' she had been careful to instruct Anne. 'I want to tell her myself – and ask her to be a god-mother!'

John began with pleasantries and an offer of coffee. 'No, thank you,' said Nina in a businesslike tone, as if determined to take control and speak for all three of them. That was fine by Susan; the thought of coffee made her feel nauseous.

'I'd like some,' said Richard loudly. There was a delay while John buzzed his secretary.

Nina finally began quietly but confidently. She had clearly prepared what she was going to say. 'I'm very concerned about some irregularities in my mother's bank account. I have obtained her bank statements for the last six months.' She pulled out papers from a file. 'I've made copies for you, John.' She handed these to him and he began quickly to scan them. Nina waited a moment before saying, 'You'll see that there are a number of purchases that could not have been made by our mother.'

But before she could continue Richard interrupted her. 'My mother is very anxious to clear this up. She's extremely upset about the whole matter.' Richard took a paper out of his document folder. 'Which is why she has added my name to her account.' He looked over at Nina. 'So it is now a joint account. This is the bank paper she signed.'

John took the paper from Richard and read it. There was an interruption while John's secretary brought in coffee. In the awkward silence Susan stole a glance at Nina and then back at the solicitor. They looked equally unhappy at this development. 'I see,' he said heavily. 'Richard, I think it would have been preferable if this bank authorisation had been executed in this office and that your mother had had the benefit of prior independent legal advice.'

Richard looked unconcerned. 'That's your opinion.' He said this in such a tone as to imply that it was worthless. 'You're welcome to come round to the house and speak to her. I think you'll find her in sound mind and very happy with her decision.'

Nina exploded. 'It's Mummy's money, not yours. You have absolutely no right to steal from her bank account!' She looked back at John and gestured to the copies lying on his desk. 'That's the word for it. Stealing! Look at the statements. There are payments to internet poker sites! Can't you do anything about this?'

Richard cut in. 'I did make those payments. I asked her first. And then I paid her back from my winnings.'

'Oh, for goodness' sake,' snapped Nina. 'Do you expect anyone to believe that?'

'Can you prove it isn't true?' said Richard smugly.

Nina appealed to John. 'You must be able to do something.'

He sighed. 'We have the option of asking the court to take over your mother's affairs.'

Before he could explain what this involved, Nina cut in. 'Then that's what I want to do.'

Susan was stunned. She had imagined that Nina would roll over. But today there was something different about her, as though she was spoiling for a fight.

'It's not right,' exclaimed Nina. 'Dad left that money for Mummy. To make sure that she was cared for.'

Richard interrupted her. 'Cared for! What would you know about that! You only come down here once a month. Susan lives with Mummy and I come by every day to spend time with her and help around the house.' He looked at John. 'At the expense of spending time with my own family.' He turned back to Nina. 'If you really cared, you'd come and help look after her instead of stirring up trouble and making her ill with worry.'

'Oh, for goodness' sake! Mummy's not ill with worry. You've just told her a pack of lies to get her to sign that paper.'

Richard's tone was indignant. 'You should withdraw that comment unreservedly!'

John intervened. 'I think we all need to calm down. The next step, Nina, would be to apply to the court to administer your mother's affairs, including her bank accounts, if the court felt that she was unable to look after her own interests. The court would, in turn, appoint a professional to do this.'

'That professional would be you, I suppose,' interjected Richard bitterly.

'As the trustee charged with the day-to-day administration of your mother's affairs I would be the obvious choice.'

'More fees for you, then!' exclaimed Richard and then he was off. 'The problem with this whole trust is the secrecy. How do we know that the trust is just for my mother? We've only got your word for it. What if you've made a mistake? Solicitors get it wrong all the time. If what you say is true

– and Dad set this up to provide for Mummy – why can't we see the documentation to prove it?'

John did not miss a beat. 'Firstly, our fees are available for you to see. They are posted to your mother quarterly. I might add that since your father was a founder of this firm, the rate we charge is considerably lower than for our other clients. As for the terms of the trust, your father specifically declared that the terms were to be kept confidential. That is not unusual. It's designed to prevent disputes and infighting,' he added with what Susan thought was a suggestion of irony.

Richard did not pick this up. 'Well, it's caused a lot of problems!'

Nina cut across him. 'It was Dad's money and he had a perfect right to do whatever he wanted with it.'

'Well, you would say that. But he didn't mean as much to you as he did to me.'

'What! That is a disgusting thing to say!'

'Let's stop there,' John's voice rose above the commotion. He stood up. 'I don't think there is any more to be gained by debating this today. Nina, let me know if you want to go ahead with the court application.' From his tone of voice Susan could tell that he was keen to promote this idea to Nina.

Susan looked back at Richard to see his reaction.

'And line your own pockets in the process,' Richard said gracelessly.

John ignored this.

Nina looked embarrassed. 'I'm sorry. Thank you for your time.'

John shook her hand. 'Any time.'

This brought forward a harrumph from Richard, who, without another word, marched out of the door.

They reassembled on the pavement of Marlow High Street. It was already nearly dark at a quarter to five, the High Street choked with traffic.

Nina exhaled, then turned to Richard. 'You're not going to get away with this!'

'Just try me. Some of us have to live in the real world. We don't all have rich husbands to pay the bills.'

'So you think our mother should do that for you?'

'No. But I think you should mind your own business. I've done nothing wrong and you won't be able to prove that I have.' He sounded to Susan exactly as he had when they were children. 'If you care so much, move down here.'

'I shouldn't have to move to Marlow to make sure Mummy isn't being defrauded by her own son!'

And then Susan saw him.

She stopped listening to them. At first she wasn't sure. In the darkness and amid the throng of the evening shoppers it was hard to tell.

But then he drew closer. It was him. Then Richard, following her gaze, saw him too and his expression turned to one of astonished recognition. 'My God.'

Susan touched Nina's arm. 'Look …'

Michael Fellows was walking straight towards them.

Chapter 15

Silence seemed to have fallen on the High Street and all the cars and people had become invisible.

Even Susan and Richard had become quiet.

Michael shot her that crooked half-smile, a smile that after all the years was as familiar as if she had last seen him yesterday. 'Nina.'

It was all that she could manage to speak his name. 'Michael.'

He looked unchanged. Fifteen years later and he was the same young man of her memory. He was dressed exactly as she could have predicted: with easy style in good jeans and a worn brown leather jacket. Suddenly Nina felt self-conscious in her sober black suit and flat heels. She wondered if he thought she had aged. Surely she had?

His smile broadened as he regarded her. 'You haven't changed a bit.'

He turned to the others. 'Richard, Susan,' he said by way of greeting.

Richard gave him a sullen nod, but Susan came to life. She threw her arms around him. 'Michael! How fabulous to see you! Where have you been? What have you been doing? Are you staying?'

He allowed himself to suffer Susan's bear hug, then detached himself and without responding to Susan's eager questioning turned back to Nina.

'Would you like to go for a drink?'

'Good idea!' cut in Susan.

'Actually,' he said in that old understated tone, 'I meant Nina.' He had always had the ability to be very direct in a way that didn't appear overtly rude.

Nina felt stunned. It was the same feeling as being in a car crash: knowing that something utterly unexpected had happened but not quite believing it possible. At the back of her mind she had known that at some point Michael would return – but she had never for a moment imagined that she would be there to see it.

She looked at her watch. 'I ought to be getting back.'

He raised an eyebrow at her. 'A very small drink, then.'

'I really—'

He cut her off. 'A very small, very quick drink.' And then he offered Nina his arm as if to indicate that any debate about the matter had been concluded, glancing briefly from Richard to Susan. 'See you two later.'

Nina could do little else than take his arm and at Michael's brisk pace walk down the High Street. She wanted answers to all the questions that Susan had asked him – what he had been doing; was he staying? As for her plans to give Richard a further piece of her mind, they evaporated as quickly as her resolve to take Susan aside and apologise to her about dismissing her warnings about Sasha. It never seemed the right time to tell her family about the separation.

'I thought you lived in London now?' he began.

'I do. I had to come down here for a solicitor's meeting.' She had no intention of recounting the sordid details. It was embarrassing for one thing to admit that your own brother was defrauding your mother. Instead she said, 'Just routine. It's about the details of my father's estate.'

'I heard. I'm very sorry.'

'Thank you.'

'My father said the church was packed.'

She nodded. 'People were standing at the back.'

'I would have liked to have been there.' His voice tailed off.

She knew why he hadn't. To come back would have meant facing his father.

She knew where they were headed: to the Two Brewers in St Peter's Street, at the end of the road by the slipway to the river. It had always been his favourite place to go in the evening.

As they walked he asked her questions about her mother, Richard and Susan.

'My mother took it very hard. She hardly goes out.'

'It was the same for my father when my mother died. He's never recovered.'

Of course, that was the last time he had been back, for his mother's funeral more than ten years ago. By all accounts Michael had stayed just one day.

She was tempted to tell him about the meeting today – it would be such a relief to confide in someone – but instead she told him about her mother and the house and Richard and Kate's wedding. Then, 'They've got a daughter, Emily. And Susan's working at the farmers' market.'

'Susan hasn't changed a bit,' he laughed. It was a typically succinct comment.

At five thirty the Two Brewers was barely a quarter full and they were able to get a snug corner table under the low black beams, the walls painted in cream Anaglypta and a chalked menu listing potato wedges and chilli con carne as the specials of the day.

In the light now she was able to see him better. A little broader, his hair darker but just as full and when he turned round to bring their drinks she saw that his face was weather beaten.

He returned with a pint of Rebellion, the brew of the Marlow Brewery, and a gin and tonic.

'And you,' he said. 'How's married life?'

Her stomach lurched. She could put on a brave face in front of Susan and Richard – the old self-protective habits learned in childhood died hard – but lying to Michael was a different matter.

But she would try. 'Fine. The business is doing very well.'

He nodded. 'Whereabouts do you live in London?'

'Off the bottom of Kensington High Street. We have a flat there.' She was about to add that they had had a house in Gloucestershire, but stopped herself in time. She had no desire to explain recent events or Alex's murky business affairs. She had told him Alex's name in a letter sent shortly before the wedding. But he probably wouldn't remember that. She had never received a reply.

She needed to change the subject. 'I heard your father wasn't well.'

'He said you visited at Christmas.' He looked down at the table. 'It's pretty bad.'

'I'm so sorry.'

He shrugged. 'No one knows. He refuses to admit that anything's seriously wrong – keeps saying the bloody doctors are making a fuss about nothing. But I got a call from my sister. It may not be long.'

'And how are things between you?'

'Let's just say that it's not exactly playing out like the return of the prodigal son.'

'But he must be glad you're back.'

'If he is then he's making a good stab at not showing it. Apparently I need to spend the rest of my life making up for the fact that I abandoned the farm.'

She couldn't stop a rueful laugh. She could imagine Michael's father, a hard man who was short on emotion, saying just that. 'And will you? I mean, will you take on the farm?'

'I don't know,' he said shortly. 'I have a photography business in France.'

She knew that. Her mother had relayed the information to her – as told to her by Mrs Baxter, whose eldest son did occasional work at Fellows Farm during busy periods. However, since the departure of Mrs Baxter there had been no further news.

'And how is that going?'

'Well, it's not art. But the property boom in the south has been good for us. We do a lot of work for international estate agents, who want photographs for sales brochures for villas. Plus I pick up the occasional local job from press agencies. I've been lucky. I have good staff.'

Michael had always been self-deprecating, underplaying his achievements and giving credit to others. Having spent a childhood growing up alongside Richard's ceaseless boasting, Nina liked that about him. But she knew there was more to his life than that. He still did high-powered work. Only last year she had seen one of his pictures in the *Sunday Times* colour supplement illustrating a feature on British retirees in Brittany. She had never lost the habit, even after fifteen years, of glancing at the name of the photographer when she read an article. His name still appeared from time to time, though not as often as it once had.

He continued, 'Francine runs the office and there are two assistants.'

Who was Francine? He hadn't mentioned a wife or girl-friend or any personal information. 'And you have a house down there?' she prompted him.

'Hmm. In the hills above Antibes.'

There was so much more that she wanted to ask him. He wasn't wearing a wedding ring.

But he changed the subject abruptly at that point and started asking her about her business and they diverted onto the subject of *Capital Letter* and her catering work. Soon she was telling him about Lady Harnford's Christmas drinks.

'The menu has to include cheese cubes with a green olive on cocktail sticks and pâté on toast squares.'

'Sounds good to me.'

She wondered if he would suggest dinner, then stopped herself short. She was married, if only in name, and he was just visiting. He wouldn't stay. It was ludicrous to expect him to give up a life and successful business in France. No, after his father's death the farm would be sold, Michael would return to France and she would … She acknowledged to herself that she didn't know. Whatever Alex's past failings, he was making it very difficult for her to walk away: the emails, texts and calls continued on a daily basis.

What she was sure of was that neither she nor Michael could put the clock back fifteen years.

And yet for the first time since Alex had left she felt happy and expansive. In fact it was the first time for a long time since she had felt like this. Talking to Michael was so different from the distracted and business-centred conversations she had latterly had with Alex, her husband usually thumbing through the newspaper while he spoke. Looking at Michael she acknowledged that absence had not destroyed their comfortable familiarity, the unspoken understanding you can only have with someone who has known you and the events of your life for years. There was so much that didn't need to be explained or filled in.

Michael was talking about life in France. 'I go to Paris about once a month. Sometimes Milan and Madrid.'

'Did you ever think about setting up in London?'

'God, yes! There's nowhere I would rather be. But the costs are horrendous. And by then I'd been working with my European clients for a while. It made sense to be in France.'

She felt a small sense of satisfaction that he would have liked to have been in London.

Emboldened, she asked the question that she both wanted and didn't want answered. 'So how long have you known Francine?'

'Years now. I needed someone to help with the paperwork – by the time it reached the ceiling I knew I needed rescuing. Then she took on more and more of the office work. She's a fabulous organiser.'

'That must be a great help.' Nina hoped she sounded sincere. In truth she didn't want to hear that Francine was fabulous at anything.

But he hadn't finished. 'And of course it's always useful to have someone who's a native speaker. She keeps the books as well. She's got an amazing head for figures. It frees me up to do what I enjoy.'

Nina decided to change the subject before she heard any more about this dream partnership. 'Tell me about the farm.'

And then they were back on familiar territory: the crops, the offers from developers and the fraught life of the new farm manager who had used Edward's hospital absence to make some much needed changes. 'He's bought a computer with a proper agricultural accounting programme,' he explained. 'Dad's going crazy because he can't work it. He keeps fiddling with it. We've had to put a password in, otherwise he'd crash it.'

The Two Brewers was full now but they were tucked away in their secluded corner. At seven o'clock Michael looked at his watch. It felt as though they had barely been there for five minutes.

'I ought to get back. Francine's cooking dinner.'

And even though she understood then, even though the familiar tone he used to refer to her was not one that would be used about an employee, Nina could not stop herself. 'Francine?'

'Hmm. She's come with me,' he said, as if it was self-evident she would accompany him. 'It was time she met Dad,' he added casually.

She forced a smile and reached for her handbag. 'Well, I ought to be getting back to London,' she said brightly.

'I'm sure Alex will be wondering where you've got to.'

'Yes.' Her pride kicked in. 'I'm sure he will.'

It had come as an appalling shock all those years ago when Michael had finally told her the whole story. They had been walking the towpath from Marlow in the late afternoon, enjoying the last warm days of summer as they stretched into

September. At Bisham, Michael had gestured to the riverbank and they had sat down, watching the sailing boats tack back and forth amid the river traffic of pristine white motor boats cutting past the weatherbeaten hired cruisers. It was Nina's last week in Marlow before she left for college in London. But she hadn't seen why that would change anything between them. She would come back for the weekends, Michael would continue to work on the farm and pick up photography jobs and everything would continue more or less as it had before.

'I've been offered a job,' he said casually.

Naturally she had assumed it would be locally. He would hardly take a job to be further away from her.

'Great! Who with?'

'It's with Joan Perham Ford.'

She was amazed. '*The* Joan Perham Ford?' Instantly she felt stupid. There were hardly likely to be two. But Joan was a world-renowned photographer. At fifty-something, with a ground-breaking career behind her, Joan was at least as famous as most of the people she photographed. She appeared in the newspapers pictured at all the right parties and was the frequent subject of magazine profiles.

'How did you get it?' she asked, looking at him askance.

Michael leaned back on the grass. 'Jack put me in touch with her. He's an old friend of Joan's. He really liked the pictures I took of his properties. And it turns out she's looking for an assistant to start at short notice. She takes someone on every couple of years and trains them up. Apparently she's not the easiest person to work with. But she's good. And you get to make a lot of contacts.'

It was then that the first question appeared in her mind. 'When did you see her?'

'Last week,' he said, and she thought then that she detected a note of defensiveness in his voice. 'I went to her studio in Hampstead. God, it's amazing,' he said excitedly. 'The walls are covered with her work. I took my portfolio and she interviewed me – if you can call it an interview. She looked through my portfolio and asked me if I knew how to mix a Martini.'

Nina felt a churning in her stomach. He had not mentioned any of this before. 'Why didn't you tell me?' she said, now unnerved.

'I didn't think I stood a chance,' he said simply. He turned to her and she could see the excitement in his eyes. 'Hell, Nina. If I stay here I'll end up doing Saturday weddings and odd jobs for the *Bucks Free Press*.' He put his arm round her. 'It's like a dream come true.'

'So she's called to offer you the job?'

Michael was honest to a fault. 'Actually she offered me the job on the spot.'

That was a week ago! She frowned. 'Why didn't you tell me?'

'I wasn't sure—'

'About what?' she interrupted. 'What is there not to be sure about?' Despite her annoyance that he had kept this secret from her, she could see that it was fabulous news in every way. A wonderful opportunity for Michael and the chance for them both to be in London. It was almost as if fate had decided that they would be together. 'When do you start?'

'Next week. Her assistant is leaving at the end of this week.'

'Great!'

He pulled distractedly at the grass. 'Yep.'

'So will you live in Hampstead? Near to the studio?' The thrilling thought entered her mind that maybe they could even live together – provided her parents never found out.

For a few seconds he said nothing. 'The thing is it's not a regular assignment.'

'No?'

'No.' He took a breath. 'Joan's in the middle of getting divorced. She's met someone else.' Nina recalled now reading that Joan had a colourful private life. 'His name's Vladimir Cherenkov. He's the conductor of the London Philharmonic.'

'The one who defected?'

'Yes. Anyway, he and Joan met last year. She was sent to photograph him for a profile in the *New York Times*.'

Nina couldn't see what Joan's personal life had to do with Michael's job offer.

'He's been planning a major world tour with the orchestra,' he continued. 'Originally it was going to be to all the usual places: Paris, Berlin, Sydney. But Joan's persuaded him to go to places that the orchestra has never been before. Like Mexico City. And Calcutta. And they're going to play to audiences who've never seen a real orchestra. And meanwhile she's going to photograph the whole tour and the cities.'

Nina didn't want to believe what she now understood. So she said nothing in the fading hope that Michael's explanation might somehow lead somewhere other than to the obvious conclusion.

Finally Michael appeared to take his courage in his hands. 'So we're going to be travelling with the orchestra for a year.'

She looked at him hard. 'So you've accepted it.'

He looked away. 'Yes.' But then he turned back. 'Nina, it'll go really quickly! It'll fly by.' His voice rushed on. 'We can write. And telephone. And I'm sure I'll be able to get back.'

She sat stunned. If he had told her earlier it might not have been so bad. But she felt furious now at the way he had gone off to this interview without telling her, accepted the job without consulting her and was now presenting his decision to her without so much as asking her opinion.

It was exactly the way things were dealt with in her family. Her mother made decisions and then told them what they felt about them:

'Mummy's expecting a baby. That's nice, isn't it?'

'You're going to be starting a new school. It's very exciting!'

She had always believed that Michael was different.

He was still talking. 'I spoke to Jack about it. He thinks it's a great opportunity. He thinks I'd be a fool not to take it.'

But she wasn't listening. She felt overcome with furious

powerlessness. How could they be a proper couple, how could any of what had passed between them be true, if he could make such a momentous decision without speaking to her?

She had rounded on him, surprising herself at the vehemence of her anger. 'Why didn't you tell me any of this?'

He sounded defensive. 'I didn't know how to tell you.' He hesitated. 'And it's been difficult at home.'

She didn't care. 'Why?' she said dismissively.

'My father doesn't want me to take the job,' he replied heavily. 'He thinks it's a waste of time. He says I need to stay on the farm.'

She did not pause to consider how much pressure he must be under or to take in the fact that he had felt it necessary to turn to Jack Tyler for advice. All she could think of at the time was that he had kept quiet for a week, allowing her to breeze on in ignorance of what was going to happen to them.

She got up.

'Nina!' He sprang up after her and grabbed her arm. 'Nina, please. I love you. I want us to be together.'

She gave him a mocking laugh. 'And how are we going to manage that? What about me? I'm starting college, Michael. I have plans, too. And I'm going to be working in the holidays.'

'Look, it's only a year.'

That did it. She walked briskly away, tears filling her eyes, hurrying past the tourists and the young mothers holding the hands of their toddlers as the children threw bread to the ducks.

He followed her, talking to her back. 'Nina, it's a fantastic opportunity. What do you expect me to do? Turn it down?' With that last comment a note of anger had entered his voice.

She knew it was an impossible question.

'Of course not,' she said, even though that was exactly what she wanted.

His voice was accusing now. 'Joan's a legend. It's a once-in-a-lifetime opportunity. The type of thing I'll regret for ever if I don't go. It's only a year!'

But a year at twenty-one had felt to her like for ever.

At twenty-one, with all the fervour of first love and the selfishness of youth, it had been impossible to think beyond the moment.

At twenty-one all the intensity of her love for Michael collided with bitter disappointment that he had not shared any of this with her before now.

She had turned to him then. 'Leave me alone.'

And, bewilderment showing on his face, he said sadly, 'I thought you of all people would understand.' And then he had let her go.

Later they had made up. They had read Joan's itinerary and drawn up a plan. He had sworn daily letters and weekly telephone calls. She in turn had promised to wait for him.

That had been easy. 'Of course I will.' It was unthinkable that anyone could come between them.

Later she told him that she wanted to come to the airport to say goodbye.

He had looked uncomfortable. 'I don't think you can. I'll be with Joan. We'll have all the equipment ...'

It had been a bitter blow. Soon his promised daily letters arrived weekly, scrawled notes on hotel paper. In his calls he sounded like a different person, someone she didn't know any longer, excitedly telling her about his new life, the famous people he was meeting and the world of the orchestra.

'It's like a family. It's really close but there are also all these rivalries.'

Too soon he would ring off. Sometimes there had been no time to tell him about her new world. And besides, she was conscious of how dull it sounded in comparison. How did the first day of the Introduction to Patisserie course compare to a day spent following Joan Perham Ford into the depths of the Calcutta slums?

As for his letters, she would read and reread every line and torture herself thinking about the women he was spending time with.

Half the time she was out when he called and when they did speak, hastily across crackling lines, she could not contain her fears.

'Have you made any friends?'

'When will you be home?'

And then, a few weeks after moving into the Hammersmith flat, she had strolled down to the shops and into the Italian delicatessen and first seen the intriguing young man who from the very beginning fixed her with all his attention, pursued her relentlessly and made her feel that he would never leave her side.

As soon as their mother went to bed, Richard started. Susan could see he was beside himself. It was a wonder he had been able to contain his frustrations during the evening the three of them had spent together watching television.

'I knew it! I knew that Michael Fellows was tied up with this somehow. You're not telling me it's a coincidence he appears on the very day we go to see Kirkpatrick. God, they can't even wait a day before hooking up!'

Susan sat on the sofa in the drawing room with her feet up. It was ten o'clock and Richard showed no inclination to go home.

He was pacing up and down in front of the fireplace. 'It's all falling into place now.' He made a broad sweeping motion with his hand. 'It's a question of joining up all the little pieces to see the bigger picture. First Nina starts stirring up trouble with Mummy. Then Kirkpatrick brings up the idea of getting a court order. All of that was fixed.' He swung round to address Susan. 'Nina and Kirkpatrick planned that whole meeting in advance. Thank God Mummy wasn't there. They'd probably have got her to sign something there and then. And then – lo and behold! – Fellows appears. It's a plot.'

Susan thought all of this was highly unlikely. She'd heard something at the farmers' market the other day about Michael Fellows's father having recently come home from hospital. But she didn't mention this to Richard. It was more fun to watch him whirl.

He was beginning to sound quite nutty. 'They're all in it together: Nina, Fellows and Kirkpatrick. Probably Alex, too. They're going to swipe the estate from under our noses.'

He sat down on the edge of an armchair. 'It just shows I was right. You can't risk leaving Mummy alone for a minute. I wouldn't put it past Nina to kidnap her and take her back to London.'

Susan took a sip of Horlicks and leaned her head back. Earlier in the car on the way back from the meeting with John Kirkpatrick she had had to use all her powers of persuasion to stop Richard going off at the deep end.

'I'm going to tell Mummy everything,' he exclaimed, driving at breakneck speed. 'She needs to know the truth! Someone's got to tell her that she can't speak to Nina any more.'

'Richard, I think you should wait and see what happens. Nina may not do anything about a court order.'

'But what if she does? Then she'll have the initiative.'

'She can't do anything without a hearing. Cross that bridge when you come to it.'

The last thing they needed now was for their mother to takes sides. That would only fuel Nina's suspicions.

She tried another tack. 'The more worried Mummy gets, the more likely she is to do something unpredictable.'

This last point appeared to convince him. Reluctantly he said, 'All right. But I don't like it. We're entering dangerous waters!'

'Absolutely.'

When they got home, Susan had taken over. She spoke to her mother in a tone that implied the meeting had been a routine affair. 'It's fine. Everything's sorted out. There's nothing to worry about.'

'What did Mr Kirkpatrick say?'

'He said that you're very lucky to have three children who care so much about you and he couldn't see anything wrong with the bank statements.'

Her mother looked relieved. Susan put on the kettle. 'So it's all a storm in a teacup.'

Richard had made as if to speak, but Susan had quickly changed the subject. 'What would you like for dinner?'

Now, growing sleepy, she half-listened as Richard analysed John Kirkpatrick's likely motivation – 'Probably a backhander from Nina' – and Alex's part – 'Definitely money for the business!'

He moved on to consider the doctor's appointment to which Nina had attempted to take their mother. 'I knew that appointment was suspicious,' he said, shaking his head. 'Nina was probably going to get her something to make her more susceptible. Rohypnol! Yep, something like that.' He looked at her earnestly. 'We have to be vigilant.'

She nodded. 'Absolutely. I agree.'

It was significant that he used the word 'we'. She took another sip and stretched out her legs. It was 'we' for as long as it suited her. But next week she was off on the train to London for a surprise visit to see Alex – and after that things might well be very different. It came to her that this was the perfect time to sow the seed of the end of her alliance with Richard.

She cleared her throat. 'Richard. There's something else that I've been meaning to tell you. But I wanted to get the meeting out of the way first.'

He continued to look distracted. He stared out through the bay window – no one had bothered to draw the curtains – to their back garden and beyond to the darkness that was Fellows Farm. 'Michael Fellows is there now, scheming to get this house and the land. That's why he's come back.' His voice carried a bitter resolve. 'But he's damn well not going to get it.'

'Richard. It's about Kate.' She put down her mug of Horlicks, then sat up straighter to indicate the seriousness of what she was about to say. 'I met Kate in Cookham last week.'

'Mmm. She said.'

'She was with someone.'

Now she had his attention. 'With someone?'

'His name's Daniel. She said he was a colleague. He's young – about twenty-five I'd guess. He obviously has a very high opinion of Kate.'

'High opinion?' he repeated stupidly.

'Oh, yes. He was looking at her like a little puppy dog. Anyhow, Kate said they were colleagues.' Susan leaned forward earnestly. 'Richard, I think there's more to it than that.'

'How do you know?'

'You don't normally walk arm in arm with a work colleague on a Friday afternoon. They said they had just been to a meeting. But neither of them had a briefcase or anything like that. They were window-shopping.' She decided to embroider things a little. 'He was holding a carrier bag from one of those really expensive shops.'

'What?'

'Yes. Gosh, do you think he'd bought her a present?' Susan spoke as if this idea had just come to her. She leaned back. 'They looked like a proper couple.' She saw him flinch a little at that. 'But perhaps there's nothing to it. Anyway,' she said as if she was losing interest in the subject, 'you might want to keep an eye on the situation. Perhaps she's been calling him a lot – or seeing him while you've been distracted by this meeting.' It was vital to put the idea into Richard's head that he needed to spend more time at home. 'I wouldn't like for something to be going on behind your back.'

That did it. She saw it in his face. 'I'll look into it.'

Chapter 16

Nina stood surrounded by a gaggle of seated pumpkins, spiders, witches – and a plump Norland nanny holding a baby dressed as a bumblebee on her lap.

She leaned over a small goblin and put a plate of home-made breaded chicken-breast strips on the table. As she did so the goblin, his cheeks expertly painted in black and green, addressed her solemnly in a cut-glass accent. 'Excuse me. Are these goujons chicken or fish?'

'Chicken.'

The eighteen seven-year-olds were the politest clients she had had for a long time.

This was Beth Saltzman's annual Halloween party and it had been clear to Nina when she arrived earlier that afternoon at the Saltzmans' Upper Phillimore Gardens house, the most imposing in one of London's more exclusive streets, that no expense had been spared. A large netted cobweb covered the portico of the front door, the spacious stone-tiled hall was lit by dozens of suspended lanterns and the oak banister of the sweeping staircase had been draped in yards of ghost-like shapes. Beth Saltzman herself was dressed as a witch, albeit a man-eating one in a clinging black Lycra minidress, fishnet tights and what looked like a pair of black Jimmy Choos. She wore her blond hair up, a perky black velvet and diamanté witch's hat pinned atop her chignon. There was no sign of her husband, Joe, an entrepreneur famous for his daring deals and love of publicity. But as Nina knew, it was always touch and go whether Kensington husbands would be present at their children's events.

'I'm inviting all of my son's class – Josh is at Wetherby – and their parents,' Beth had briefed her. 'So I'd allow about fifty. Of course most of the men won't be home from work until later.' She had outlined her plans. 'I'm having carved pumpkin lanterns for the garden paths and my decorator is in charge of the house. Can you email me your menu ideas?'

Earlier there had been a treasure hunt in the garden, a game of apple bobbing and a not entirely successful improvised theatre session featuring a pair of children's workshop performers dressed as ghouls. Two of the more sensitive children had fled from the home cinema room in tears. Calm had been restored and now the children were seated for tea in the oversized basement kitchen, circled by their thin and fashionable mothers. Half were in costume, most of the rest in LK Bennett. They offered compliments on the food but did not touch it, instead sipping champagne flavoured with cassis – Beth had wanted purple drinks but guests had to make do with pink – or the non-alcoholic alternative of pomegranate and blueberry juice.

Nina picked up flashes of conversation: an appraisal of the senior colourist at Richard Ward, a discussion of the merits of the new BMW four-wheel drive and a headcount of who was going to the invitation-only Red Cross Christmas Fair opening party.

She tried to switch off. Work might be a tried and trusted remedy for easing emotional pain but the party was making her feel more raw and alone than ever. She was slap-bang in the middle of the comfortable world of Kensington families, a world from which she had never felt more excluded. These were women with husbands and children who took their family life for granted. After six thirty, when the husbands began arriving in black cabs from the City, the talk turned competitively to Christmas plans.

'We're off to Australia. We want to show the children the rainforest.'

'We'll be in Wiltshire. My parents have a farm outside Avebury.'

'Personally I think you can't beat Nevis.'

For Nina it also felt like everyone was leaving her behind: Alex, Susan … and Michael.

Susan had called her the day after the solicitor's meeting. 'Just wanted to make sure you were OK,' Susan said, appearing anxious.

Nina, icing a hundred miniature pumpkin cupcakes, had been in no mood to talk. 'I'm fine.'

'How was your evening with Michael?'

She was damned if she was going to tell Susan anything. 'We just had a drink.'

But Susan had more to say. 'Did you meet his fiancée?'

Her stomach had turned over then. 'No.'

'God, she's stunning! I bumped into them in Waitrose. She must have been a model. Or she could have been.' Susan's voice ran on. 'She had a fabulous engagement ring. Diamonds and rubies.'

Much as Nina didn't want to give Susan the satisfaction of being the bearer of bad tidings, curiosity got the better of her. 'What does she look like?'

'Really slim. Long dark hair. Gorgeous clothes. He probably buys them for her in Paris. He said he goes there for work. Anyhow, the wedding's next year. They were planning to have it in France, but now they've brought the date forward and they're having it in Marlow.'

Nina had had enough. 'I ought to be getting on. I have a party tomorrow night.'

'But I haven't told you my news!'

Nina inwardly sighed to herself: a new, wonderful, life-changing job no doubt. 'Oh?' she said.

'I'm having a baby.'

For a moment she had been struck dumb. 'Congratulations,' she managed to say as a flood of questions raced through her mind.

One of them was answered immediately. 'Gerry's thrilled. We both are.'

'When is the baby due?'

'March.'

And then Susan was off, launching into a monologue of which Nina supposed half was true: Anne was delighted; Gerry's children were excited and solicitous; Susan herself saw the baby as the natural next step in her new Marlow-centred life. Nina said all the right things in response. But as she replaced the receiver her first thought had been that this wasn't right. She was supposed to have a baby first.

Now, standing in the warm and crowded kitchen of Beth Saltzman's house, she felt her fears rising: of failure and aloneness, of being consigned to a guest role in other people's family events, of everything she wanted and believed she had slipping away from her. She was surrounded by women who would go home with their children, sleep next to their husbands and wake up to the warm rush of family life. She thought of her own flat, thank God occupied by Muffin, but quiet and still – and the prospect of another night alone, another lacklustre weekend stretching ahead.

She looked across at Beth, who for the first time that night was holding her baby. 'Isn't he darling? Josh adores him!' There was a murmur of appreciation from these women who were all members of the same club of married mothers.

And she made the decision that the next time Alex offered to take her to dinner she would accept.

Jemma sat down at Howard's desk, switched on the Anglepoise lamp and spread out their telephone bill in front of her. It was the Spanish calls she was interested in. There were twelve in total. Seven to Dimitri the gardener, one to the firm that delivered the propane gas – and two to Barbara and Brian's house, one six minutes long and the other thirteen.

She felt unnerved. Recently she had relaxed around Barbara – and of course Howard could be speaking to Brian. But the point was that he had not mentioned speaking to either of them. And when Barbara had called yesterday she hadn't mentioned any calls either. 'Hiya! We're back. We arrived yesterday. It's freezing here.' On and on she talked. 'We're coming to London next week for Christmas shopping and I was thinking we could have dinner at Nobu.'

Jemma had stalled. 'I'll have to check with Howard. He's very busy at work.'

It might be nothing. But then Nina came to mind: if ever there was a warning of what happens when you give your husband the benefit of the doubt ... It wasn't time for surveillance. But it was certainly time for some increased monitoring.

'You are having an emotional affair!'

Kate looked at Richard in disbelief. 'What?'

His expression was one of righteous indignation. 'An emotional affair. And this proves it.' He waved her mobile phone at her. Kate felt a shudder of apprehension. 'Yes, you might well look guilty,' Richard said pompously. 'I've read the text messages.'

'There's nothing to read,' she protested.

'*See you next Sunday. D.* And a cross which I take to be a kiss,' he quoted officiously. 'I assume that's your boyfriend, Daniel.'

'He's not a boyfriend! He's a work colleague.'

'That's not what Susan said.'

Kate felt her heart sink. She sat down on the edge of the bed. Minutes earlier she had come up to the bedroom to find Richard standing over her open handbag holding her mobile.

'What exactly did Susan say?' she asked wearily. 'And did you think about asking me about this before going through my things?'

'Susan said that you were obviously on a date with this Daniel person. She saw you last Friday. So I went and checked the AdTech calendar in the kitchen. It was a half-day.' He waved the mobile at her. 'What choice do I have? You've been deceiving me for months, carrying on behind my back, neglecting me and Emily.'

Listening to him, she felt suddenly drained of energy.

'Well?' he said aggressively. 'What have you got to say for yourself?'

And even though she knew at this point that she should put on the best front possible, somehow she lacked all will to do so. 'Daniel's a friend. We talk. Sometimes we have lunch ... That's all. Nothing's ever ... happened.' They hadn't after all slept together.

'Kate, it's a disgrace. You're a mother. You're always complaining about how hard it is for you to manage – no wonder if you're throwing yourself at this man.'

'I am not throwing myself at him.' It was unbearable to hear him talk about her and Daniel in that way.

'I forbid you to see him.'

It was almost laughable. He sounded like a character from a Victorian melodrama.

'Don't be so ridiculous,' she snapped back. 'I work with him. I can't avoid seeing him.' Even if I wanted to, she could have added.

She expected him to erupt at that. But instead he put down the mobile on the bedside table. 'Then you give me no option. I think I should move out for a while. That would give you time to consider your position.' It sounded as if he had almost rehearsed his little speech. Richard threw her handbag across the bed towards her and folded his arms as if to declare the conversation at an end.

It was incredible. 'You are completely overreacting.'

'I don't think so. And I think anyone else would agree with me. Let's face it, Kate, it hasn't been working for a long time. Nothing I can do will satisfy you. Maybe some time apart would do us good.'

Now, regarding her husband in his baggy jeans and

unironed shirt, she wondered if the idea of some time apart wasn't so bad after all. 'Where will you go?'

'My mother's.'

Of course. A missing piece of the puzzle fell into place. This wasn't all about Daniel. 'This is about that meeting with John Kirkpatrick, isn't it?'

'No,' he said angrily.

'Yes it is.' She got it then. 'You're afraid Nina's going to persuade your mother to change the will.'

Now he sounded defensive. 'We don't even know if she can change it. We don't know anything. That's because the bloody trust is secret. You should have let me find out.'

He meant that she should have let him continue to pester their neighbour, who worked at Carruthers & Kirkpatrick, for information.

'Oh, for goodness' sake ...'

He walked towards the door. 'I'm not going to listen to any more of this.'

She heard his footsteps on the stairs.

'What about Emily?' she called after him, running out on to the landing.

He stopped on the stairs and turned. 'I'll see her at the weekend.' Then he paused for a moment as if to consider the implications of this before continuing down and slamming the front door behind him.

Chapter 17

It was usual for Nina to wait for Alex. He would turn up half an hour late, issue a scant explanation about some crisis at work and then, omitting an apology, turn his attention to ordering a drink. But today he was already waiting for her, sitting at the back of the art deco surroundings of the Belvedere restaurant in Holland Park. In front of him were two glasses of champagne and as she walked to the table he rose to his feet. He looked nervous.

It was extraordinary. They had been married for years and yet as she drew near, Alex hesitated before resting his hand lightly on her arm and kissing her cheek. His touch and his kiss felt unfamiliar. With a jolt she realised how completely the intimacy between them had been destroyed. And suddenly she regretted coming.

Alex however looked happy to see her, gesturing for them to sit down and gallantly pushing in her chair. He hadn't done that for years. As soon as they were both seated he said unnecessarily, 'I ordered champagne, darling.'

'Thank you.' God, this felt stilted. But Alex had been so persistent. He continued to send her several texts a day and twice-daily emails, too.

'I know you don't want to see me. But we owe it to ourselves to talk. No strings attached. Just to talk ...'

And even though she raised a mental objection to so much that he wrote – she was not the one who had thrown it all away for lies and secret sex – gradually he had worn her down. Besides, she missed talking to him.

'So,' he said eagerly. 'How is everything? 'Your mother? Work? Is everything OK at the flat?'

'It's fine.' Since when had he cared about the flat? He left all that to her: going to the residents' meetings, disputing the service charge, writing the cheques for the bills.

'Good. And your mother? Any developments there?'

She had emailed him briefly to say that the meeting with John Kirkpatrick had been a disaster. Now she filled him in on the details. 'So Richard got himself out of it,' she concluded. 'And actually,' she added despondently, 'things are worse now because it's a joint account and he can do whatever he likes with it. Unless I go to court.'

'Do you want to?'

'John Kirkpatrick thinks I should. He called me the day after the meeting. But the problem is that I don't think Mummy will go along with it. She'll protect Richard come what may.'

He looked thoughtful. 'But you have the bank statements before Richard turned it into a joint account. You could go to the police.'

She had considered just that. But reporting her own brother to the police for theft felt like a step too far.

She shook her head. 'I could in theory. But can you imagine what the consequences of that would be?'

'It would certainly make for an interesting Christmas Day,' he said dryly.

They broke off to order. As he spoke to the waiter she took in Alex's crisply ironed shirt, the immaculate suit and recalled that in one email he had said that he was using the hotel laundry service. Alex was a far picture from the shamed husbands who fell apart without their wives. Somehow she wished he had fallen apart a bit. He was still wearing his wedding ring.

Alex had not finished with the subject of her mother. As the waiter left the table he continued, 'So what happened after the meeting? What did your mother say when you went back to the house?'

She was shocked. She had not expected that question. 'Oh. No. I didn't see her. I had to get back to London.' She broke her bread roll as a distraction. 'I had a work deadline,' she lied.

She found that she couldn't look him in the eye. Instead she focused all her attention on the white porcelain butter dish. God, this was what it must have been like for Alex all the time. But of course, after a while, he'd presumably got used to lying relentlessly.

He sounded surprised. 'Didn't you want to speak to your mother?'

She had. And ordinarily she would have gone back to the house, rather than leave matters in the untrustworthy hands of Susan and Richard – had she not encountered her ex-boyfriend on Marlow High Street and gone off for a drink with him.

She shrugged. 'I'm not sure it would have made any difference. Richard's there all the time. Mummy's only ever listened to him.'

She thought of a way to change the subject; a lighter topic was needed. 'Susan's having a baby.'

Alex appeared to do a double-take. 'Susan?'

'I know! It was a complete shock to me. Totally unexpected, of course.'

'Of course,' he echoed.

'But she says that Gerry's pleased about it. I suppose they'll move in together.'

He paused. The news seemed to have taken him aback. 'Any marriage plans?'

'Not that I know of.'

He appeared to consider this silently. When he spoke it was to change the subject and to talk about work. 'I ought to fill you in. We're fully let.'

Now, as he started talking animatedly about the latest

developments at work, he appeared to have forgotten all about the events following the Marlow meeting – and to have accepted her story. She understood that this was how she had behaved in the past, too. Since Alex's departure she had spent most of her mental energy running over the events of the past year. Sometimes she felt searingly angry with Alex, and at other times overwhelmed with self-reproach at her own stupid, blind acceptance of his lies. For months she had unquestioningly accepted the late nights, the weekend absences, his new habit of turning off his mobile when he got home – *The office gave out my number by mistake. I'm getting calls from tenants all the time.* And then there had been those late-night walks: *I need to clear my head.* That's when he must have checked for messages. Not to mention the way he closed the page on his email when she walked into the room.

And later, when her suspicions had grown stronger, still she had ultimately accepted his word. *There's absolutely nothing between us. I swear. It's just work.*

Now he was talking about Harriet and Marjorie. 'They've really knuckled down.'

She wondered if they were pleased that Sasha was gone. It couldn't have been much fun for them to observe her capture all of Alex's attention.

'I've set up a schedule to visit the properties and do the minor repairs. I've still got Sean for the big jobs,' he continued. 'But enough of me. What about your work?'

She started telling him about her diary, filled now with Christmas bookings, and the latest developments at *Capital Letter*. 'Things aren't too good. *Zut!* are way ahead on advertising revenue. Paula Nicholson is in a permanently foul mood. And each magazine has started running copy rubbishing the other. *Zut!* did a really nasty piece on Paula, making out she's some tabloid hack.'

'Hmm. I read it. I had a look through both of them. *Capital Letter* needs to spice it up a bit.' And then he was off on a critique of both magazines.

She could see that Alex was making a huge effort. But even as he lavishly complimented her on her gastropub reviews, her attention wandered. Sasha was the unspoken presence at the table. They had been sitting down for nearly an hour now, but neither had mentioned her. Nina's appetite had deserted her. She looked around the softly lit room and speculated as to how the two of them might appear to the other diners: a couple on a date? They had none of the easy familiarity of a married couple.

'Nina.'

She was aware of Alex speaking to her. 'Sorry?'

'You were miles away.'

And then she knew that she just couldn't do it any more. She put down her knife and fork. 'Alex, this feels so ... false. I'm not sure why we're even here.'

'Because we have to start somewhere,' he said firmly. It sounded as if he had anticipated her question. 'Of course it's going to feel strange. I'm living in a hotel, we don't speak ...'

You had an affair, she thought.

'But we have to try.' He took her hand. 'You're not wearing your wedding ring.'

He must have noticed that earlier. She looked away. 'Is there any point?'

'Yes! God, yes!' At the sound of Alex's exclamation a man on the adjacent table looked round at them. 'Yes,' he repeated more quietly, moving his chair closer to her. 'The point is that you're my wife and I love you and I want us to be back together.'

Everything he said had the effect of raising a red flag in her mind.

'Stop it! How on earth is that possible?'

'With time,' he said confidently. 'She's gone and she's not coming back.'

'So the court case has been settled?'

'It's all but settled. She hasn't got a chance.'

She felt her heart sink. 'Alex! It's still hanging over us.'

'No, it's hanging over me. I mean, it's not hanging over me. I'm dealing with it. It's nothing for you to worry about.'

She rolled her eyes. 'Since when has Sasha been nothing to worry about?'

'It's over,' he said insistently. 'And we can go on with our lives. We can use this to build a stronger relationship. You can be sure that nothing like this will ever happen again. We'll have a family. And we can live wherever you like.'

God, he had always been a fabulous salesman. And now he was selling her his vision for the future. But even so, she could not help but allow him to finish.

His voice ran on. 'I've got the business back on track; you don't have to worry about me making that mistake again either. Nina,' he said urgently, 'I can learn from my mistakes. I can come out of this a better husband, not a worse one. I swear to you I will spend my whole life making this up to you.'

Finally she looked into his eyes. The sincerity with which he spoke was mirrored in his expression.

'I know this isn't what you want to do now, darling. But I absolutely know that it's the right thing. Walking away might seem like the easy option. But how would that really work out for either of us?'

He paused. In the silence the figure of Michael Fellows entered her consciousness. She thought back to that too-brief evening at the Two Brewers, the easy laughter and the effortless conversation – the way he had made her feel nineteen again.

But she was not nineteen: she was married and Michael soon would be. It was time to close the door on the missed chances of the past, to accept the reality that Alex was her life and that whatever he had done wrong in the past there was some undeniable truth in what he was saying now.

She spoke hesitantly. 'What did you have in mind?'

He caressed her hand. 'Why don't we take it slowly? I'll stay at the hotel. We'll take things at your pace. But we could go for a walk on Sunday morning. Maybe have lunch, if you wanted to.' He squeezed her hand. 'Just like we used to do.'

It seemed a reasonable suggestion. 'OK.'

It was a dry, cold autumn day and as Susan waited on the platform for the Marlow to Maidenhead train she pulled her wrap closer. Mentally, she added a maternity coat to her list of purchases. After the train pulled in she boarded with a smattering of London-bound cheap-day-return shoppers, settling down in the near-empty carriage.

She had brought with her the latest edition of *Baby* magazine. She thumbed through it, pausing at the feature on Christmas fashion. The models, lean-limbed and glowing, were photographed at a country house hotel, an enormous illuminated tree in the background, wearing what were described as the festive season's most fabulous party clothes: cashmere tie cardigans, silk kaftan-style shirts, suede trousers and flowing low-cut black dresses. They were the type of clothes stocked by expensive maternity boutiques located in Primrose Hill and Parsons Green. Depressed, Susan turned to an article on how to deal with premature labour. These days she walked around with all her old clothes permanently unbuttoned, covered by voluminous jumpers.

Last week she had mournfully pointed this out to her mother. 'I've got nothing to wear.'

Her mother had reached for the *Bucks Free Press*. 'Here. Look through the classifieds. They often have ads for second-hand clothes.'

'I thought we could go shopping together.'

'Why ever would I want to do that? You know I can't walk far.'

Susan replaced the magazine in her bag. No, it was time for Alex to start playing a proper role in this baby's life. At Maidenhead she would change for Paddington and then onto the tube to Notting Hill. She had not been to Alex's office before, but she saw on the A–Z that it was a five-minute walk. Hopefully he would be in. Naturally it was better not to forewarn him of her arrival.

Susan stared out of the window as the train clattered past the expensive riverside houses of Bourne End and the pretty cottages of Cookham. At Cookham Station a young girl with a baby in a pushchair got on. Susan looked up, taking in the make of the pushchair – Phil & Teds – and the baby bag which she recognised from Mothercare.

These days she noticed babies everywhere, all accompanied by loads of expensive stuff.

It was a Monday and there were no markets today. In fact most of the farmers' markets had closed down now for the winter and many of the traders had packed up until the spring. The cheese man had previously told her on several occasions that he went to his gîte in Languedoc for the winter, purchased with the proceeds of his severance pay, and hinted that she might want to join him sometime.

Instead, Roger was sending her to Christmas fairs held in town halls. The Christmas fair stallholders were a different crowd and actually worse: loud middle-class housewives selling crafts who thought it was all really good fun and a super way to make some extra cash. Why they needed to, Susan didn't understand. Most of their kids seemed to be at private school. The housewives made dried-flower Christmas wreaths, beaded jewellery, velvet cushions embroidered with ironic sayings – 'I keep losing weight but it always finds me again' – and candle-holders out of anything at all. And the customers were picky Jaeger mothers and their grown-up snooty daughters, flooding in as soon as the doors opened at nine o'clock, which gave her no time to set up. Sometimes she didn't have time to open her book at all and she had worked three Saturdays in a row.

At Paddington she changed onto the Circle line after a stop in the ladies' cloakroom. It was a nightmare. She was constantly thirsty, hungry and in need of the loo. At work she was always having to ask people to watch the stall while she nipped off. All in all at five months pregnant it was high time for her to go on paid maternity leave. Especially as Roger was finding her extra jobs in December, including driving up to London to do Christmas fairs in Chelsea and Kensington. Last week he had come to check up on her at the Bourne End Community Hall.

Fortunately she had been at the stall, having nipped off earlier for a bathroom break and a cup of hot chocolate, and was actually in the process of serving someone. 'Come again!' she said cheerily to the customer, an annoying old bag who'd spent several minutes choosing one three-inch pillar candle.

Roger was dressed in his winter gear: a black duffel coat, brown cords and one of those Russian-style hats with furry ear flaps. His grey ponytail nestled in the hood of the duffle coat.

'Good news! I've managed to get you a table at Chelsea Town Hall at short notice. Of course the parking's a bit of a bugger around the King's Road. You'll have to get there early to get a place nearby. Before seven thirty.'

'Great! That's fantastic news.'

He pushed a box of cinnamon-scented candles below the table. 'It wasn't easy. Those stalls are like gold dust. I'm ordering in some Christmas stock from the States.' He lowered his voice. 'They make them in Vermont: Santa Clauses, Christmas trees and pies.'

'Pies?'

'Apple pie, pumpkin pie and lemon meringue.' He cupped his hands. 'They look like the pies, you see. As well as smelling like them.'

'Wow!' She backed away. Roger had told her that he made his own toothpaste out of baking soda and peppermint oil. It wasn't very effective.

Roger surveyed the stall, moving the boxes about. 'Pricey, but I reckon they'll go down a treat in Chelsea. You'll have to push them. The shipping's costing me a fortune.'

She nodded. 'I'll point them out.' Well, someone would. She would definitely have ditched the job by then.

She could barely get out of bed in the morning as it was, let alone at five o'clock. It wasn't fair. Other women had husbands who brought them a cup of tea in bed in the morning, massaged their feet at night and did the supermarket shopping at the weekend. She knew this from eavesdropping on their conversations at the antenatal clinic. One woman, blonde and thin with what looked like a real Hermès Birkin bag in lime green, had even reported on a surprise spa weekend that her husband had arranged.

'Massage, facial, manicure and pedicure! Oh, and a sip of champagne!'

Susan remembered that Caro Phillips had both a Hermès Birkin bag and a Constance. When she went out for the evening, which was at least three times a week, Susan used to dip into her La Prairie face cream and slip on her Rolex Oyster Perpetual, the dial set with twelve diamonds. Caro Phillips had it all. At Christmas she had given Susan a gift card to Bliss, just enough for a manicure without the tip. Two weeks later she went with her girlfriends for an all-day New Year top-to-toe makeover. 'Just what one needs after Christmas – it gets more stressful every year!'

Richard and her mother barely mentioned the baby, let alone offered to help. Richard's attitude implied that it was her problem.

'When are you going to move in with Gerry?'

'How are you going to manage financially?'

It was clear that Susan needed to take action. Emerging from Notting Hill tube she followed the A–Z to the mews where Alex's office was located. She was nervous, but this was overlaid by the pleasurable anticipation she felt at seeing Sasha again, if she was there.

Another girl from the party was seated at the reception desk.

'I'm his sister-in-law. He's expecting me.'

The girl looked flustered. 'Oh. It isn't in the diary.'

'It wouldn't be. I'm family, after all. I'll go on up.'

His door was open. She knocked anyway. 'Hi! Only me.'

Alex, seated at his desk, could not conceal the look of shock that crossed his face. 'Susan!' he said.

And she had not even unwound her wrap. She sat down uninvited.

'You were passing,' he said hopefully.

'No. I came up to see you.'

'Oh?'

'Alex, we need to talk.'

He interrupted her. 'Look, if it's about me and Nina then I don't think this is a good idea. Because,' he continued before she had a chance to respond, 'everything will work out. She didn't send you, did she?'

What was he talking about? Had they had a row? 'No. It's about you and me.'

'You and me,' he repeated, confused.

The moment had come. She leaned forward. 'Alex. I am going to be the mother of your child.'

She had never before actually seen someone's mouth drop open in surprise. He stared at her, transfixed and clearly unable to speak.

Then he said, 'What?'

She smiled at him. 'We're having a baby!'

For a moment he didn't react. His voice, when he finally spoke, was hardly audible. 'Nina said that you were having a baby.' He took a breath. 'You and Gerry.'

She shook her head. 'Not Gerry. You, Alex.'

He looked bemused. 'But what about Gerry?'

'You mean could Gerry be the father?' She shook her head dismissively. 'Absolutely not. Gerry and I don't have that kind of relationship.'

'I see.' He didn't sound as if he did. 'So you're quite sure?'

'It's impossible for Gerry to be the father,' she said firmly.

'And I'm quite sure I'm pregnant!' She stood up and cast off the throw. 'Look!'

He looked horrified.

'The midwife has confirmed my dates. There's no doubt.'

She had had no idea that he would be struck into this kind of mute shock.

'The dates match exactly with our time together in Gloucestershire,' she added confidently.

He looked up. 'What have you told Nina about this?'

'Nothing,' she said, wide-eyed. If he was thinking straight he would realise that it wasn't in her interests to make an enemy of Nina. 'The point is that you and I have to work this out. And I think it would be much better if we sat down like two mature adults and agreed things between ourselves. These things only get worse when lawyers get involved.'

'You've seen a lawyer?'

Suddenly, seeing Alex's alarmed expression, she realised that this was a very good point. 'Hmm,' she nodded. 'Only on an informal basis.'

'Not Carruthers & Kirkpatrick!'

'No. Someone else,' she improvised. 'But the point is,' she continued, anxious not to have to provide too many spur-of-the-moment details, 'that it would be much better if we agreed some points now.'

She pulled out her notebook.

'I've made some headings.' She began to read. 'Baby equipment and clothes.' She looked up. 'Obviously. That's things like the pushchair, cot, Moses basket, changing table, bouncy seat, car seat and nursery decor. Then daywear, nightwear and outdoor wear. Oh, and bedding.' She turned the page. 'Then there are general expenses. Housing, transportation, food, electricity, gas, telephone ...'

'Hold on. You're not expecting me to pay for all this.'

'Not permanently. Once the baby's older I'll go back to work and make a contribution. But there's no point me going back to work before then,' she said dismissively. 'With the cost of childcare, by the time I'd paid tax I'd actually be worse off. So it makes financial sense for me to stay at home. And I think a baby needs its mother. Don't you?'

He did not respond to this. 'But you have a home,' he objected, 'with your mother.'

'And I can stay there for the time being. But it's not fair on my mother to have to live with a crying baby.'

He looked askance at her. 'It's a huge house! There's plenty of room.'

Susan shook her head. 'I need a place of my own. I don't think that's unreasonable. Surely you don't expect my mother to take over your obligations as the father. She's not getting any younger and she's not well!'

He appeared to be recovering his composure. 'It's not a question of taking over my obligations,' he said irritably. 'It just doesn't make sense for you to get another place when you have a perfectly good home already.'

She had hoped that it wouldn't come to this. But Alex needed to be reminded that he was not negotiating from a position of strength. And while he was thinking on his feet she had had plenty of time to work out her position.

'Alex. Who's to say that I'm going to live in Marlow? I'm not sure that makes sense. After all, you live in London.'

He looked confused. 'And ...'

'It will be much easier for you to see the baby if I'm in London as well. I could live in Notting Hill. Then you could pop round in your lunch hour. Or after work.'

He sat back in his chair. 'You want to move to London,' he repeated flatly.

'It would cut down on travelling for you and the baby.' In truth, she preferred the idea of Marlow, but it was fun to wind him up.

'And how exactly do you intend to explain all this to Nina?'

'Me? I thought you'd be the one doing that. As far as I'm concerned this is just between the two of us.' She put her head on one side. 'Have you got any ideas of what you might say to her?'

Finally he popped. 'No! Christ, Susan. This is all a fucking big shock. Are you absolutely sure I'm the father?'

Now he was making her cross. 'I'm certain.' And this time there was no need to improvise. She had no doubts. 'But if you want to be sure then we can have the baby DNA-tested after it's born. I'll get the papers sent to you.'

'No! Don't send anything anywhere. You can't expect me not to ask for a test, Susan. You've got a boyfriend.'

'Yes. And in between his work and looking after the kids and working on his script there's precious little time for anything else. I worked out my dates. That's the weekend I got pregnant and I didn't sleep with Gerry that weekend or the week before or the week after. When we came down to Gloucestershire the kids were in our bed all night long.'

Alex nodded as if he recalled that the put-up bed in his study hadn't been slept in.

'If you want a test after the baby's born then that's fine. But I'm not going to manage on my own until then.'

He took a deep breath. 'Look. We'll deal with the issue of the test when the time comes. I'll do the right thing. All I ask is that we deal with this between ourselves. There's no need to involve Nina.'

She sat back. 'That's fine. Now.' She turned another page of the notebook. 'I've made some initial calculations.' She nodded to the calculator on his desk. 'Shall we add the figures up?'

He paused for a moment then reached over for an A4 lined pad and a pen. 'Very well. Go ahead.'

She beamed at him. 'And after we've done that we can look at property particulars. I've already been round the agents. There's plenty to choose from!'

Winter

Chapter 18

Anne lay in her bedroom in the semi-gloom of the early December morning. Through the gap in the curtains she could see the mist and the tops of the orchard trees and grey sky. The curtains were a fraction too narrow and had never closed properly. They were velour curtains bought from Caleys in Windsor, rich red when she and Archie picked them out, matching them to the torn piece of Sanderson pink climbing rose wallpaper they had taken with them. It was funny what she remembered. Now after twenty years the curtains were faded and striped from the sun.

There was always a morning mist here in the winter. Fellows Farm was damp, the house badly situated in the valley. She recalled Archie saying that to her when they came to look at this house. 'Better to be on the hill.'

Archie. At the thought of him a fleeting image came to her. It was on holiday, a week they had spent in Aldeburgh when the children were small, a recollection of him on a bench on the seafront eating an ice cream and reading a copy of the *Daily Telegraph*. And then before she could hold on to it, it was gone. She was so sleepy these days.

Her mouth was parched. She turned her head to look at the clock: six forty-five. Richard could be ages yet. Sometimes he didn't get up until nine or even ten. He stayed up till all hours on that new computer. And she needed to use the lavatory.

She tried to lift her head but failed. She had been in bed for two days now.

'You need to rest, Mummy,' Richard had said firmly. 'You've got a nasty bug. There's a lot of it going round.'

'I can rest downstairs!'

'Maybe tomorrow.'

She had always got up before Archie. People would be surprised to know that. But she had. So he had come down to a fresh pot of tea, a bowl of All-bran and a slice of toast and honey.

People thought all sorts about her and sometimes said so. There was that Scottish cow who did the accounts in Archie's office who'd probably thought that she was in with a chance when his first wife died. Every year at the office summer party she said something.

'You landed on your feet.'

'I don't expect you thought you'd be living in a place like this.'

Sometimes they didn't say anything because they didn't need to. You could see it in the way they looked at her. Mrs Baxter had been like that, though Archie of course wouldn't hear a word against her: 'Her mother worked for my mother.' Sometimes Anne would walk out into the garden and come across Mrs Baxter talking to Jim the gardener. From the way they fell silent she knew the conversation had been about her. She sacked Mrs Baxter the week after Archie died. Then she called for Jim and sacked him too.

People didn't know the whole story. Archie was no bloody saint, that was for sure. Another image came to mind: Archie pushing her back on his desk at work, lifting up her skirt, feeling hungrily for her, enjoying being with a woman who liked sex as much as he did. He never said so but it was obvious: his first wife hadn't enjoyed it. He still wanted it, right up to the end. And like many men who were charming and charitable in public, he could be a grouch when he got home. He'd sit in his study worrying about some client's business or piece of drafting or problem with the accounts. More often than not something to do with Jack Tyler. That's when she'd breeze in with a stiff Scotch and rub his shoulders and tell him that he was the best and he'd sort it all out. And later in bed she would do all those other things he needed, things he had never dared ask from another woman.

But she didn't miss all that any more. She missed Archie, though. Sometimes she saw a resemblance to him in Richard's expression or mannerism and felt a jab of pain. Over three years and it was still a sharp, miserable, shocking jab.

She never thought that she would be waiting to die.

She closed her eyes and listened to the silence of the house. One more Christmas would be all right. And Susan's baby ... it would be nice to see if it was a boy.

She needed the lavatory.

'Richard! Richard!'

There was no response.

'Richard! Richard!'

God, who would choose to live like this?

Nina had decided to deal with Susan first, then her mother, then Richard. And finally she would pay her visit to Edward Fellows.

She stood on the doorstep of the small brick block of flats located in the centre of the Old Brewery development and pushed the doorbell hard for the second time. Around her were neatly landscaped gardens and rows of expensive cars. Susan knew damn well that she was coming down because she'd left two messages on her mobile. And it was a Sunday so she definitely wasn't working.

There was no response from the entryphone.

It was infuriating. She pulled out her mobile and called Susan's number. After six rings it went onto the answer machine.

'Susan,' she said impatiently. 'It's Nina. I'm in Marlow outside your flat. I'll go up to the house and then come back. Call me!'

She slammed the phone shut and went back to the car.

The way things were going she wouldn't be at all surprised if Richard tried to bar her entry to their mother's house. Earlier that morning he had called to try to put her off.

'I really don't think that she's well enough to see visitors.'

'Richard, I'm coming.'

It made her blood boil. Since Susan had moved out, Richard had thrown a curtain of security around her mother. Half the time when she called he made excuses why she couldn't come to the telephone – her mother, it appeared, was permanently taking a nap – and now he was trying to stop her coming down that day.

It was appalling. Richard and Susan were running wild. It was hard to know which of them was worst.

Susan had called her out of the blue. 'I've got some news.' Susan's voice ran on quickly. 'I'm moving into a new flat.'

'Oh?'

'Yes, with Gerry. He got a promotion at work. And Roger gave me a huge bonus!'

When Susan began talking about money it always raised a red flag in Nina's mind. 'Where is this flat?'

'The Old Brewery.'

How on earth could they afford that? But Susan seemed to have anticipated that question.

'The stall is doing amazingly! We've never had so much business. I'm going to Chelsea Town Hall and all over the place.'

Susan had been happy enough to talk about the baby. But she had been reluctant to see Nina. 'Why don't you wait until we've got the flat straight?'

That did it. If Susan thought she would fall for some stupid story that Gerry and a market-stall candle business were paying for an upmarket flat in the centre of Marlow then she was very wrong. It was quite clear to Nina that Richard and now Susan were siphoning off money from that joint account. She was determined to get to the bottom of it.

She started the car. One result of her separation from Alex

had been a newfound willingness to look below the surface of what those nearest to her told her. It was an overdue loss of innocence. Take Alex and the priest, for example. She was now seeing Alex every week for lunch and a Sunday walk. But if he had hoped that his announcement would get him back home then he had been in for a shock.

They had been walking around Holland Park when he had dropped his spiritual bombshell.

'I'm having a weekly session with the priest at the local church.'

She couldn't help herself. 'You must have a lot to talk about.'

He had looked hurt at that. 'It's very serious, Nina. And very ... searching. I've realised that I need to put my house in order. I can't just go around creating chaos in other people's lives. I have responsibilities and I have to face up to them.'

'And what does your priest advise?'

'Well, for a start he says that divorce would be a terrible mistake.'

Neither of them had taken steps in this direction. But lately Alex appeared to have got nervous that she might. He had started cautioning her not to do anything rash and to be careful whom she spoke to.

'Susan, for example. Does she really have your best interests at heart?' he said earnestly.

But that was the trouble. Whenever he said these things, a variation on the same response automatically popped into Nina's mind: *How exactly did you have my best interests at heart when you were fucking Sasha?*

She had not said it. She understood that for them to have any chance in the future, she would have to forgive and forget. But she wasn't ready to do that.

So they had continued walking, Alex talking enthusiastically about his Bible study and set assignments. 'This week I'm writing about my family and the spiritual messages that were conveyed to me as a child.'

Despite her scepticism she was interested. 'And what were those?'

'I think there was only one: that business was the whole point of life and that everything else came second.'

It was true. And later Nina had realised that in Sasha, Alex had found someone who shared just those values.

Periodically he dropped hints about coming home. He had moved out of the hotel and taken a short let of a self-catering apartment near the Gloucester Road, telling her pointedly that he could give notice at any time. In the meantime independent life appeared to be taking its toll. Lately she noticed that he looked tired, dark rings under his eyes, and he appeared on edge.

But she diverted his comments. She was beginning to quite like living alone. It was peaceful. She didn't have to cook every night. She could watch exactly what she wanted on television. There was much less washing to do. And Muffin liked it on the bed.

The idea had even entered her mind that this might be a permanent arrangement. She had pondered this out loud on one of their Sunday walks.

'You could get a flat across the road. Living separately is quite the thing to do nowadays.'

Alex had been horrified.

A week later he reported back. 'I told Father Bernard what you said. He says it's unnatural for a man and wife to live apart.' Then he looked anxious. 'Why don't you come and meet him?'

'No.'

'Just for a chat.'

'No.' And then she had been overtaken by a sudden, vehement fury at his promotion of the idea. 'You had an affair! And now you expect me to forget all about it because Father Bernard says so!'

'No, that's not what I'm saying.'

'Yes, that is what you're saying. You think you can just say you're sorry and write a few essays and that's all it takes. But it isn't that simple.'

Sometimes she believed there was a chance – and other times that continuing with their marriage was an impossibility. Her time with Alex could be going so well and then – whoosh – some comment or triggered memory or assumption on his part would bring all her anger to the surface. And then she could see that he was so sorry and trying so hard that she felt obliged to give him a chance. Finally there were those occasions when he just wore her down.

Lately he had started pestering her about Christmas.

'Let's do something special. We could go away. What about the Caribbean?'

'Alex, no.'

'What would you like to do?'

She thought of a sure-fire way to put him off. 'Actually I think I ought to spend it with my mother.'

There was a momentary silence. But then he sprang back. 'Great idea! We can drive down, you can cook dinner and I can entertain your mother. We could take her for a drive in the afternoon!'

'I'll think about it.'

'I'll keep the day free.'

Now, she started the car engine and drove slowly out of the development, looking out in case she saw Susan drive in. But there was no sign of her. It had always been this way: Susan was adept at slipping away from awkward conversations and unpleasant consequences. As she got older she packed up and walked away from jobs, landlords and a clutch of creditors. Sometimes she gave Nina's number and left her to field the calls from the people she had let down. And in the past Nina out of some mistaken sense of loyalty had listened to the tales of out-of-pocket landlords and stranded employers. One woman had called at nearly midnight in floods of tears.

'You don't know me – my name is Caro Phillips.' There were gulps. 'Susan's been working as our nanny. I spent three months showing her the ropes.' The well-spoken voice hardened. 'And I made it crystal clear that I needed her to have sole charge while I went to Palm Springs.' The woman cleared her throat and Nina began to have an ominous feeling about where this story was leading. 'My husband works for a bank. It's their anniversary conference. I have to be there!' She rushed on, 'So today I was at the hairdresser and I got a call from a neighbour. Susan had left Hamish and Clemmie with her. She said she'd be back in half an hour. Well, she never came back at all!' She began crying again. 'I went to get the children, came home and found a note from her on the kitchen table. It says the job isn't for her. She's taken all her things.' The woman sounded desperate. 'We're booked to fly out tomorrow! I've spent all day trying to get a replacement – and I can't.' She hesitated. 'So I won't be going. I'm sorry to trouble you with all this. But the point is I've just discovered that there's some jewellery missing from my bedroom drawer. Do you know where she is?'

Nina truthfully didn't know. And even though she knew damn well that Susan had behaved dreadfully, still she had found herself defending her, just as she had done since they were children. 'I can only imagine she's going through some sort of emotional crisis. Let me take down your number and I'll call you if I hear from her.'

But Nina wouldn't be making excuses for her any more. This time Susan would be called to account for what exactly was going on with their mother's money.

After five minutes Susan got up from where she had been seated on the kitchen floor. Crouching, she peered out of the window. Nina's car had gone. She straightened up and went back to assembling the cheese and pickle sandwich she had been in the middle of making before the entryphone had sounded. She paused and then reached for another two slices of bread to make a second. That morning she had had two Shredded Wheat, a banana and a slice of toast spread with

Frank Cooper's thick-cut Dundee marmalade. It was nice buying treats from Waitrose.

From her vantage point of the floor she had had the opportunity to admire the sand-coloured stone floor tiles, the moulding on the kitchen cabinets and the rounded, bevelled edge of the corian worktop. This flat was the nicest place she had ever lived, the first time she had had a power shower, or a fitted wardrobe that spanned the width of the bedroom, or a fridge with a built in ice maker.

'You don't even have to fill it with water,' the letting agent had pointed out. 'There's a connection direct from the kitchen plumbing.'

The agent, a young girl, had looked at her enviously. 'If I could live anywhere in Marlow I'd live here,' she'd said.

And Susan had already seen enough poky cottages to know she was right. Besides, it had become necessary to move as soon as possible, since Richard's unheralded arrival at the house at ten at night carrying a sports holdall.

'I've left Kate,' he had announced baldly. 'She's been having an affair.'

Her mother had been full of concern – Susan, too, but for different reasons.

'Who with?' said Anne angrily.

'Some bloke at the office.' He had disappeared off to the kitchen at that point, reappearing with a can of beer.

Anne got up with some effort from her armchair and came and sat by Richard. She put her hand on his arm.

'So they're definitely having an affair?' Susan asked carefully. This was not at all what she had expected. Richard was supposed to be at home saving his marriage, not running home to Mummy. Inwardly she kicked herself: she should have at least considered this turn of events.

He shrugged and replied to Anne, 'Romantic walks, text messages, calls. All while she was complaining about how hard she had to work.'

Anne shook her head. 'Well, you've done the right thing.

Sometimes a cooling-off period is just what's needed.' She turned to Susan. 'Go and find some sheets and blankets for the spare room.' Then Anne patted Richard on the knee. 'You can stay the night, then work out what you want to do in the morning.'

He laughed. 'I don't think there's any reasoning with Kate. She always gets exactly what she wants.'

'I think it's very important, Richard, not to make any decisions in the heat of the moment,' Susan told him.

Susan noticed there was more washing-up than ever, more newspapers strewn all over the carpet. On Saturdays, Emily came for the day. Her favourite game was to play hide and seek with Richard, the two of them racing noisily round the house. On Sundays, Anne complained that they couldn't watch a nice film in the afternoon because Richard wanted the football on. And she'd come down one morning to find no milk for their morning tea because Richard had polished it off on a bowl of cereal before bed.

If Susan hadn't been in the middle of it all, it could almost have been quite amusing, watching Richard and her mother start to bicker like an old married couple. Anne had even been driven to start saying nice things about Kate. 'She's probably regretting the whole thing. She's a very good mother. Think about Emily!'

But Richard merely grunted and each day more of his stuff appeared at the house. Every time a new LP arrived from eBay they would endure it being played over and over at top volume on the record player Richard had installed in his bedroom. Downstairs there was now a PlayStation linked up to the television, a computer in the dining room and a sandwich toaster that Richard never cleaned in the kitchen.

In blissful contrast the flat was all so clean and quiet and new. It was like living in a show home. The cream walls were spotless, the windows gleaming and best of all was the oatmeal carpet. Not a pulled thread or worn patch or the slightest mark to be seen anywhere. On the first night Susan had just walked barefoot from room to room. The bed was king-size and so was the television and the bath. The wardrobe even came with loads of proper wooden hangers.

'The owner works overseas,' the agent said. 'It comes fully furnished. Unless you want your own things.'

Susan appeared to consider this. 'No. I think we'll keep them in storage.'

At the viewing she had made her mind up on the spot.

'I'll take it.' How good that had sounded.

But the agent had cleared her throat. 'The only thing is,' she said, giving a nervous laugh, 'you're having a baby. And the owner has specified no children.'

'Oh, that's fine,' said Susan. She would cross that bridge when she came to it. In her experience landlords forgot all about you, as long as you paid the rent. 'We only need it temporarily. Once my husband comes back from overseas we'll be looking for a house to buy.'

'Oh, fine.' The agent looked reassured. She made a note on her clipboard paper. 'I know the owner's keen to let the property.'

'Can you make sure the lease is in my husband's name? Alex Burnett.' As the agent drove away, Susan had called Alex from the steps of the block. 'Good news! I've found somewhere.'

'Where?'

'The Old Brewery in Marlow. I changed my mind about Notting Hill.'

'What? That place is top of the range.'

'Yes, it is. Let me give you the agent's name. Then she can bike the lease to you to sign.'

'Wait. Hold on. Where else have you looked? And why can't the lease be in your name?'

Because she had a tricky time getting past the credit checks, that was why – on account of several county court judgments and a couple of debts that weren't down to her at all but nonetheless had been unfairly put on her record.

She snapped at him, 'Because it's your responsibility. Like I said, I'll have the lease biked over.'

He sounded resigned. 'Just give me the agent's number.'

Presumably he wanted to organise a confidential signing.

But he wasn't going to get the final word. 'By the way, I told her you were my husband.'

She rang off before Alex could protest. In the event, the lease had come back not in Alex's name but under some company she had never heard of. Maybe he had formed one especially? He was certainly being very careful to cover his tracks. So far he'd only given her cash.

Naturally, Nina had wanted to visit the flat. That posed more of a problem. Nina might be gullible but she wasn't a complete fool. She might start asking awkward questions about how Susan could afford somewhere quite so luxurious and what exactly was this new job and why hadn't Gerry moved in?

'Why don't you wait until I've got it all straight?'

Now she took her sandwiches to the living room, sat on the sofa and clicked on the television with the remote. There were hundreds of satellite channels. She'd never had those before, either.

Nina didn't worry her. In fact, juggling all the stories to the different characters was fun. Nina thought Gerry was paying; Gerry thought the family trust was paying; and Richard and her mother didn't appear to care. It sounded complicated, but all she needed to do was keep them apart. So she would hold Nina off until she broke off with Gerry, which would probably be just after Christmas.

Can you believe it? He's moved all his stuff out! I feel so alone. What am I going to do?

She wanted a present, after all, and someone to hang out with over the holidays other than Richard and her mother. And most pressingly she still didn't have a car lined up for when she jacked in Roger's job, which she planned to do as soon as possible.

Besides, Gerry was being pretty good at the moment. Now that he had finished the script he had more time. He'd insisted on coming to the scan and at the sight of the grainy picture on the screen she had seen tears well up in his eyes.

'It's a little person,' he had said, squeezing her hand.

He'd also been useful helping her move.

'Nice flat!' he'd exclaimed. 'I wish I had a family trust!'

And last weekend he'd even come with her to Mothercare and bought some baby clothes.

They had stood in the busy Saturday queue at the till and he had placed his hand gently on her stomach. 'Our baby,' he'd beamed.

She had returned his smile. 'Yes, our baby.'

Edward Fellows sat on the rocking chair in the farmhouse kitchen. Nina felt reassured. He was thinner but with that same restless vibrancy – and his manner was as it had always been.

He turned to Michael. 'Go and check on the gates.'

Michael opened his mouth to protest.

'Go and check.' His father dismissed him with his hand.

From the doorway, Michael shot Nina an exasperated glance and disappeared into the porch where she could hear him whistling for the dogs and pulling on his jacket.

The door slammed shut.

'So you've come to see the old man before he dies.'

She was pulled up short. 'I heard you weren't well.'

He grunted. 'Well, I'm still here.'

'Michael tells me the doctors say you're doing very well.'

'Doctors. What do they know?'

He sounded like her mother. Did all old people develop these depressing opinions?

He regarded her. 'You look good. You were always the best-looking one. What have you done to your hair?'

She touched it self-consciously. 'Oh, I had some colour put in it. And a different cut.'

He nodded. 'Suits you. Don't take any more off, though. Men don't like it.'

Whether this was true or not he said it with the assurance of a fashion editor. She had also bought some new clothes during an unexpected shopping trip with Maria on a rainy Sunday afternoon. 'You need a makeover,' Maria had announced, taking her arm and steering her into Zara. Maria had picked out black jeans, which Nina was wearing today with knee-high Boden black embroidered boots, an ecru cashmere V-neck, which was lower-cut than she had worn for years, and a fake-fur gilet.

He looked her up and down. 'And you've got new clothes. Good.'

She couldn't think of anything to say to this: it seemed a double-edged sort of compliment. But in any case his train of thought had moved on. 'How's that sister of yours?'

'Fine. She's expecting a baby.'

'I know. And no wedding ring.' He caught her expression. 'Oh, I hear things. I keep my ear to the ground. What about your mother?'

She was torn between a desire to confide in him and embarrassment at the antics of her family. Though to be fair, her visit that afternoon had been uneventful. Her mother had been in the drawing room watching television and Richard had gone off to 'spring-clean the house because it's obvious Susan didn't do anything while she was here'. He had avoided her and with it any awkward conversation.

Now, sitting with Edward Fellows, she decided to draw a veil over Susan's unplanned pregnancy, Richard's matrimonial problems and her suspicions that the pair of them were defrauding their mother.

Instead she searched for a non-contentious reply. 'She needs to get out more.'

He nodded. 'She doesn't care. Not without Archie. That's how it is when you've been married your whole life.'

Nina felt a rush of failure. It seemed as though there was

a good chance that she wouldn't know what it was like to be married to one person your whole life.

'People talked,' he continued. 'But they were happy in their own way. And he took you two on.'

Old people had a way of being incredibly blunt. But it was impossible to take offence. After all, everything he was saying was true.

He shot her a hard glance. 'And what about that husband of yours? The Italian.' He said this in such a way as to imply that this was not a characteristic in Alex's favour.

She was used to fielding questions about Alex by now. 'He's fine. The business is doing very well.'

'Why haven't you got any children?'

She was lost for words. 'We plan to,' she came up with lamely.

He looked unimpressed. 'What's the point of waiting to have children when you're too old to look after them?'

She decided to change the subject. 'How are things with Michael?'

'Well, he's here. And not before time.' And then he was off. 'Why would you choose to live in France when you've got a perfectly good home here? This land isn't going any-where. They can't build on it. There's covenants.' He said this proudly. 'Rock solid covenants. Jack Tyler tried to break them – bought that bottom field off me and thought he'd make a killing. Then he found out he couldn't build! Tried all sorts, running up to London to see fancy lawyers. Ended up selling it back to me!'

Nina had heard the story from Archie. Edward Fellows was one of the few people ever to get the better of Jack Tyler in a business deal.

He was reminiscing now. He shook his head. 'Jack was the devil. Racing them cars up the Henley Road. He took a Caterham over my hedge one time.' He paused. 'But it was the cancer that got him in the end. All those cigars, silly bugger.'

Nina wondered what it must be like to lose all those people you had spent your life with – and to know that you were the next to go.

There were so many questions that she wanted to ask him: had he made up with Michael? What did he think of Francine? Where was Francine, come to think of it? And how did these old people manage to stay married for so long?

But he hadn't finished with his questions. 'He brought some French woman back with him. What do you think of that?'

'I hope they'll be very happy.'

He shot her a devilish smile. 'She's Madame Bossy Boots!' He grunted. 'What's the matter with the pair of you? Italian! French! My wife lived in Bisham and my father thought that was far enough.' He leaned forward. 'I don't think he loves her, you know. He should have married you.'

And even though it was ridiculous, at his words she felt a surge of pleasure. She shook her head in denial.

'You were the daughter-in-law I never had. You would have done all right on this farm, the two of you.'

He sat back. 'Forty years we spent here, me and my wife.' He gave her a hard look. 'Do you want to know the secret of a happy marriage?'

She couldn't stop herself. 'Yes.'

But just then the front door swung open.

Michael's voice rang out: 'All those bloody gates were shut.'

Edward winked at her. 'Did you double-check them?' he called out in response.

'Yes!' he said, exasperated, walking into the kitchen. He turned to Nina. 'Has he driven you mad yet?' He strode over to the sink and began filling the kettle with water, the dogs running round him excitedly.

Below the commotion of the dogs and the clank as the water pipes started up, Edward Fellows leaned over and whispered to her, 'The secret of a happy marriage is to pick the right one in the first place.'

Then he called over to Michael, 'You need to get that joint in the oven.' He turned back to Nina. 'That girl puts herbs on everything. I wouldn't wonder if she put them on her toast. Now,' he concluded, 'you're staying for dinner.' His voice made any argument impossible. 'I'm just going to have a lie down.' Slowly he got up. Michael came over to help him.

'I'm all right. Leave me alone.' He nodded in Nina's direction. 'Never mind that tea. If you want to make yourself useful, pour the girl a drink.'

And with that he was gone.

Michael shot her a grin. 'Sorry about that.'

'It's no problem. My mother's exactly the same.'

'Do you think that's how we're going to end up?'

'Probably,' she laughed.

He had gone out into the lobby. 'There's a case of pretty good Corbières in here.' He came back with a bottle. 'Dad won't drink it, of course. It's foreign,' he said, in a good impersonation of his father's gruff voice. He pulled the cork. 'We ought to let it breathe, but we won't.' He poured two glasses and handed her one. 'Cheers. Here's to …'

'Your father,' she said.

'Thanks. He's doing pretty well. There was a time we didn't think he'd make it until Christmas.'

'Are you going to be here for Christmas?'

'Yep. Francine's going backwards and forwards but we'll spend it here.'

She made an effort to sound disappointed. 'She's not here?'

He shook his head. 'She had to go back to the office. She's the only one who can sort out the computer stuff. Besides,' he said, taking his father's vacant seat, 'a week with my dad was more than enough.'

She said nothing, hoping he would elaborate.

'Dad manages to make his feelings very clear.' He paused.

'And Francine isn't the type to back down.'

She wondered if there had been rows. She felt awkward and unsure of what to say next. Maybe it would help to get the subject out of the way. 'Susan says you're getting married in Marlow.'

'Hmm. We were thinking that we might have to do it in January at the register office, but Dad's doing so well we've set it for March at the church. Francine's been making all the arrangements.' He took a drink. 'I've decided to stay here to look after Dad.'

It was like being on a particularly unpredictable roller-coaster, one that she knew perfectly well she shouldn't be riding at all: first shocked at the possibility of a January wedding, next buoyed up by the delay until March, then dismayed at the obvious influence of Francine and finally delighted that he was going to be in Marlow for the winter.

'She still hasn't sorted out the reception. Believe it or not everywhere's booked. I thought everyone got married in September.'

She had had enough. 'Tell me more about your father.'

His features lightened. 'Unsurprisingly, he's confounding all expectations. They got all the tumour and he's responded really well to the chemotherapy. Initially they were saying six months at the outside but now they're not making any predictions.'

'That's fantastic news!'

'Yes. Of course he can't work. He wants to, but he gets tired so quickly. That's when he has his tantrums.'

He got up and began taking vegetables out of the old-fashioned larder next to the kitchen door. It was natural to get up to help him and soon they were preparing dinner side by side. 'I'm trying to find things for him to do, but it's a no win. Either he finds them too easy – like writing the cheques, moaning that I'm treating him like a child – or he can't do them, like helping repair the yard fence. He gets demoralised, blames me for using the wrong tools and storms off.'

'I'm sorry.'

He shrugged. 'We just have to keep going. He likes having visitors.'

Nina thought out loud. 'I'll suggest to my mother that she comes over. Of course, she'll probably depress him even more.'

'No.' He shook his head. 'He's never happier than when talking about how the world is going to hell.'

'And how are you finding it back here?'

'Drink helps,' he said, grinning at her and raising his glass dramatically. 'And I'm probably a whisker away from starting smoking again. Apart from going quietly crazy in the evening watching his soaps, I'm fine.' He replaced his glass. 'But I am going to try to pick up some work while I'm over here.'

'To keep your hand in?'

'To make some money! There are all of Dad's little treats to buy. He likes his Burgers' cream cake every afternoon.'

'My mother's the same. She's developed the biggest sweet tooth.'

'They're all the same. There must be a switch in the brain that gets flicked when you hit sixty-five. Dad's latest thing is not to buy him a Christmas present ...'

Nina finished the sentence for him. 'Don't tell me! Because he won't be around to enjoy it.'

They continued in the same vein, swapping parental notes as Michael refilled their glasses. She was about to say no, but then the thought came to her that she could always stay at her mother's. So she accepted and put on a saucepan of potatoes to parboil. 'By the way, if you did want some work I could ask around at *Capital Letter*. The budget's a bit tight there at the moment, but they might have something.'

'Thanks!' He sounded genuinely enthusiastic. 'Anything. Magazines, commercial work ...'

She thought out loud. 'It's a shame I can't ask Alex. He has loads of business contacts.'

As soon as the words left her mouth, as soon as she saw

the quizzical frown cross Michael's face, she realised her slip. Whether it was caused by the wine or the feeling of being more relaxed than she had for ages, it was not an admission she had planned to make. Of course she could cover her tracks: Alex doesn't mix personal contacts with business dealings.

But for some reason she couldn't lie. 'We're separated.' She was not sure where these words were coming from, but she was definitely the one speaking them.

He did not look as shocked as she had expected. 'I'm sorry.'

She felt relieved and foolish at the same time. She sat down heavily. 'Alex had an affair. With his secretary,' she added, staring into her glass of wine. She didn't want to meet his gaze. 'It's over. But we've been living apart.'

He shook his head. 'I'm really sorry.'

'It's so stupid. Everyone was warning me, even Susan. But I just didn't want to believe it.'

'I think that's normal, isn't it?'

'Maybe if I'd been more alert ...' She let her voice trail off.

He came and sat down next to her. 'Nina, I spent fifteen years avoiding the farm and my father and everything I left behind. Fifteen years pretending to myself that I could walk away. It's human nature to avoid what we don't want to see.'

'It's all such a mess. Alex wants to get back together.'

'And you?'

'Sometimes. And other times I can't face it – that whole thing of recovering from an affair. Apparently it takes years and even then you can't be sure things will work out.'

'Do you have to make a decision now?'

'No. But Alex is making a huge effort. I feel I ought at least to try.'

And at that he nodded. He got up and strained the par-boiled potatoes into the sink. 'I suppose so,' he said sombrely. 'If that's definitely what you want.'

Chapter 19

Lady Harnford's drinks party was going swingingly. Nina's two long-time waitresses were distributing hot sausages with barbecue dip and mini vol-au-vents filled with coronation chicken. The guests, mainly an older crowd, seemed to love this Fanny Craddock-inspired menu. Meanwhile Nina poured the wine. All of the guests had arrived, including the Canadians, who had asked for bottled water.

All Nina had to do was keep from bursting into tears.

All the humiliation, rawness and outright misery had returned. Not that Lady Harnford had appeared to notice anything amiss with her caterer. But then she was an unlikely reader of *Zut!* – not least because she never travelled by tube. When Lady Harnford needed to get about she called a little man from a Battersea minicab company.

It was Maria who had called her yesterday.

Immediately from Maria's tone, Nina had known something was very wrong.

'Nina? Have you seen today's edition of *Zut!*?'

'No. I haven't been out all day. I've been cooking for Lady Harnford. It's her party tomorrow.'

'The thing is, there's something in it about you.'

Still Nina had not been unduly worried. The sniping between the two magazines had intensified with frequent barbed comments from each publication about the other's inadequacies.

'About one of the restaurant reviews?' Had a chef or owner complained about an unfair assessment?

'No.' Maria cleared her throat. 'It's about Alex. And the court case.'

'Oh, my God!'

She knew then with a sickening shock what was coming. 'What does it say?'

'Are you sure you want me to read it out? I mean, you don't have to read it.'

'Yes I do. What does it say?'

She heard Maria sigh. 'It's in that column where they print bits and pieces of gossip.' She paused and then began reading. '*Capital Letter*'s novice restaurant reviewer Nina Burnett likes to pass judgement on other people's kitchens. But Nina has troubles of her own brewing at home. Her husband, London property developer Alex Burnett, is soon to face an ex-employee in court in a claim for sexual harassment. The employee, a young woman whose name remains confidential, allegedly underwent a year-long ordeal at the hands of the London businessman. Despite suffering flashbacks and panic attacks the woman is determined to speak out and protect other women, according to her lawyer.'

Nina sat down at the kitchen table unable to speak.

'Nina. Nina!' Maria's voice came urgently down the line. 'It'll be all right. No one's going to believe her. From what you've told me it probably won't even go to court.'

'But even if it doesn't the damage has been done,' Nina responded distractedly. She felt as if all the fight had been knocked out of her. 'This is what everyone will remember.' She understood that all their neighbours and friends would see this and that even people who didn't know her would discuss her behind her back.

Maria sounded more worried than she had at any time in this whole saga. 'Nina, I know it's none of my business. But haven't you suffered enough?'

Later that evening, Alex had called. To his small credit he wasted no time in getting straight to the point. 'Have you seen it?'

'Yes,' she said dully, still too stunned even to be angry.

He sounded beside himself. 'Christ! That fucking bitch. She was smart enough to keep her name out of it. She obviously made that a condition of giving them the story.'

'Is there anything you can do?' she asked, even though she knew there was nothing.

'Well, I'm not fucking giving in to her,' he said furiously. This was the true Alex, the street fighter who'd built up his business from nothing.

'And what about me, Alex? What about when she starts giving interviews to the papers?' An image of a double-page spread in the *Daily Mail* flashed through her mind.

'That isn't going to happen. I promise.'

She shouted at him now. 'You're not in a position to promise anything! You can't control her. She's always been way ahead of you in the game.'

There was a pause at the other end of the line. 'Maybe.'

'Alex. Why don't you just settle with her? Make her a generous offer.'

He sounded outraged. 'Why should I give her a penny?'

'Because it's not worth it. No amount of money is worth living like this. What's the alternative?'

'My lawyer says she'll settle on the steps of the court. With her record she won't dare go into court.'

'But you can't be sure, can you?' Nina persisted angrily. 'She's mad enough to do anything. God, she might see you at the court and decide to go ahead just for the fun of torturing us some more. She might call me as a witness.'

'That won't happen.'

'It could.' She was sick of the pretence that he had any control over the situation.

'Nina, you have to trust me.'

That did it. 'No! I don't have to trust you. In fact, I don't have to do anything. How much more do you expect me to put up with? Everyone is going to know now. The whole story of your affair is going to come out. And I don't have to live with that.'

'Nina,' Alex's voice sounded desperate, 'I'll deal with it. I'll stop it all.'

'I don't think you can.'

She rang off.

Now she stood in Lady Harnford's kitchen unwrapping a platter of smoked-salmon sandwiches. Thank God her restaurant review didn't carry her picture. All around her were laughing, happy, intimate, normal married couples. She felt a surge of depressed loneliness.

Maria had implied that it was time to take steps to get a divorce. She felt a wretchedness now, a feeling that they would never be free of Sasha. It was clear that divorce from Alex was the only way to put a stop to all of this, to put the past behind her and to move on with a new life. She thought back to dinner with Michael, the ease of their conversation and her eventual departure at two a.m. Then she reminded herself that the evening was a pleasant interlude and nothing more than a distraction from the reality of her daily life. He had walked her back over the dew-covered field up to the house, their way lit by moonlight, and embraced her in a brotherly fashion by the door.

After a little while she had pulled away. 'Thank you for a lovely evening,' she had said formally.

Mirroring her, he took a step back. 'My pleasure.'

And then she had turned swiftly away. There had been too many lies and too much pain already. Michael was engaged to be married and she would respect that: whatever else she would do with her life, she would never, ever behave like Sasha; she would never do to another woman what had been done to her; she would never tempt Michael in a fleeting moment made up of memories and too much wine to make a decision he would regret in the morning.

Mechanically she served the food for the rest of the party, barely noticing the chitchat of the waitresses and the couple of guests who popped their heads round the kitchen door to compliment her on the food.

She felt like a shadow of her former self, going through the motions every day, and realised that she had begun to feel like that from the time she had suspected Alex was having an affair. Where had all the joy and laughter and spontaneity gone from her life?

At the end of the party she let the waitresses go early, preferring to clear up on her own. After the last guests had gone, Lady Harnford breezed into the kitchen.

'Wonderful spread, Nina!'

'Thank you.' She concentrated on packing the platters and glasses into boxes.

'Is everything all right?'

'Oh, fine.'

'You don't seem yourself, dear.' So Lady Harnford, who Nina always knew was a shrewd old lady, had after all noticed something was wrong.

Maybe it was the unexpected nature of Lady Harnford's enquiry or the sheer stress of the last couple of days but Nina was sick of pretending. 'Actually I'm having one or two problems at home. My husband.'

'Oh,' said Lady Harnford, 'I see.' Her tone was relieved, as if she had expected something more serious. 'Another woman?'

Nina was surprised. 'Yes.'

'It usually is once you get to the bottom of it.' Lady Harnford gave a small laugh. 'Boys will be boys!'

Nina looked up from where she was closing the lid on a box of wine glasses. 'I'm sorry?'

Lady Harnford looked unconcerned. 'All men are like little boys in a sweet shop. They can't resist dipping their hand in the jar now and again.'

Nina was incredulous. 'And that's it? We should just let them?'

'No, dear. But as long as it's just a fling and they don't

bring her home then one should turn a blind eye. It all blows over; you'll see. I used to draw the line at taking a girlfriend to the theatre. It can get so awkward in the crush bar if one's friends are present.'

'I just don't think that I can forget about it. It went on for such a long time.'

'Well, that's your mistake! You should have nipped it in the bud. A word in the ear is all it takes.'

Nina had thought that no one held these opinions any more. 'But ... but what about my husband? He's the one to blame.'

'Yes, dear. But that's the nature of the beast. You married him because he was full of life, didn't you? That's the problem with wives nowadays. They expect to marry a lion and turn him into a pussycat!'

'So you think I should take him back?'

'I think you should think about whether you would rather be without him. In my experience people get divorced and they're just as miserable as they were before. You could go off, marry some other chap – and it could happen all over again. That's if you find a decent one.'

Lady Harnford went out towards the door. 'Now, dear, I'll get my chequebook. Lovely cheese straws, by the way!'

'Have you heard anything from Nina?' asked Howard.

Jemma hesitated. 'I'm seeing her next week for brunch.' She looked at Howard, but his expression gave nothing away. 'Why?'

They were having dinner at their local Chinese. The Mandarin was Howard's favourite, a down-to-earth set-price menu restaurant with unchanging staff and red and gold decor where the waiters always remembered to bring Howard a knife and fork.

'Just wondered.'

Just wondered indeed! Something was up with Alex. Jemma knew this because she had checked Howard's mobile on a regular basis and last week there were two received calls from Alex and two outgoing from Howard.

'What's going on?'

'Nothing.'

She put down her chopsticks. She was on edge. She had the feeling that Howard was up to something behind her back.

'Nothing? Don't give me that.'

'Alex called last week.' He picked at a piece of sweet and sour pork. 'But that was business.'

'You mean selling his business to you?'

Howard shook his head. 'He seems to have got back on the straight and narrow.' He took the last piece of the pork, which she had had her eye on.

'So what did he want?' she said impatiently.

'He wanted to know if I was interested in a little joint venture. Something to help him with his cash flow.'

She was uneasy. The mention of Alex made her think of Sasha, which in turn made her think of Barbara. She didn't want Howard hanging out with blokes who thought it was OK to play away. 'What kind of business?'

Howard thought for a moment. 'Leisure.'

'And are you going to do it?'

'No. Not my area of expertise. But I put him in touch with someone who might be interested.' Howard looked at her. 'Jem, it's nothing to worry about. You need to ease up, girl.' He took a drink of his lager. 'Maybe we should go away for a few days. I know the weather's not great, but how about spending New Year in Spain?' He spoke as if it was decided. 'I'll book the flights tomorrow.'

Sasha double-checked the image on the screen of the entry-phone. Yes, it was definitely Alex. She felt an uncharacteristic twinge of uncertainty. Common sense told her not to let him in. But since when had the rules of the game been dictated by common sense?

She decided to play for time. She spoke into the entryphone. 'Alex. How lovely to see you.'

'We need to talk.' He sounded curt.

'You can communicate with me through my lawyer.'

'I want to make you an offer.'

She thought for a moment. If it was a very good offer, he might well have to cut some corners to raise the cash – corners that he wanted kept private from his advisors.

Besides, if he were planning to hurt her he would hardly risk coming to her flat to have his image recorded on the security system on his way in.

And she really wanted to hear what he had to say. 'Come on up.'

She opened the front door and walked out into the lobby area by the lift door. As the doors opened he looked startled to see her standing there.

She gestured to the camera mounted in the corner of the lobby. 'Just so you know you're on camera,' she said coolly. 'We have the best firm in London. The tapes are reviewed every week.'

He nodded. 'Understood.' He was carrying a black briefcase.

She led the way into the living room and gestured to the sofa. 'Drink?'

'Thanks. I'll take a beer.'

That was a good sign. He was clearly nervous. She went into the kitchen and returned with a glass.

'Now, how can I help you?'

He looked gratifyingly tense as he sat on the edge of the sofa. She opted to sit opposite, reclining back and crossing her legs. It was a shame she was wearing jeans, even if they were Joseph.

'I want to end this,' he said earnestly. 'I want to make you an offer. It's very generous. You know as well as I do that there's no point in continuing with this.'

She pushed her hand carelessly up into her hair. 'Oh? Why not exactly?'

There was a flash in his eyes. 'Because you can't go into court, that's why. Because you have a record of extortion from rich men.'

She was unfazed. 'No. I have a record of untrue accusations made against me.'

He waved his hand. 'It's a pattern that we can use to destroy your credibility as a witness.'

'So why don't you do just that?'

'Because I don't want my name in the papers again.' He clicked open the briefcase and pulled out a foolscap folder. He handed it to her. 'At the front there's an A4 manila envelope. The offer's in there.'

Quickly she took out the envelope and removed the two-page typed document. Then she took her time reading it: the numbers were good. Very good. The confidentiality clause – lifelong and covering all media worldwide – she had expected.

But the final clause was the problem. She laughed. 'You want me unconditionally to withdraw all the accusations I have made and to agree in writing that they were without foundation.' She took the paper and replaced it in the envelope. 'Did you really think that I would agree to that?'

He looked confident. 'Sasha, that's more money than any court would ever award you. The clause is what I need in return.'

'No,' she said crisply. She put the envelope in the folder and slid it across the coffee table towards him.

'Don't you want to see the rest?' He gestured at the folder. 'It's the payment details.'

'I'm not agreeing to say that what I said was untrue.'

'Even if it is.'

'That's what you say, Alex.' A sudden thought came to mind. 'By the way, if you're recording me it's inadmissible. The tape has to be made with my knowledge.'

He rolled his eyes. 'I'm not recording you. I know that.' He took a long drink of his beer and sat back. 'Look. I don't understand what there is left for you here. You've made your point. You've even got the case into the papers. What I'm offering you is a very good outcome – there's nothing to say that if you did take this into court you would win. And you'd end up paying your costs and mine as well.'

She knew this full well. So she bluffed him, looking him straight in the eyes. 'I'm prepared to take that chance.'

'Sasha,' he looked frustrated, 'this is a good deal.'

'For who? For you, you mean. I sign some paper saying it was all untrue and you get away scot-free.'

'Christ, Nina's thrown me out. I've hardly got away with anything.'

'She'll take you back,' Sasha said confidently. 'Nina is the stand-by-your-man type.'

'I wouldn't be so sure,' he said with feeling. 'Have you any idea of the damage you've caused?'

'The damage I've caused,' she repeated, injecting incredulity into her voice. 'And what was your role in all of this?'

He took another drink. 'God, Sasha. It's not that unusual. People have affairs. It happens all the time. They don't set about ruining each other's lives afterwards.'

'No. But plenty of them would like to. They just don't have the guts. All I've done is stand up for myself, Alex.' Now she spoke with real feeling. 'I refuse to be misled and lied to for a year and then sacked.'

He shot back in a tone that implied he didn't understand what all the fuss was about, 'You knew the situation. You knew that I was married.'

'And you knew that I was a person with feelings. Or maybe you didn't. Perhaps you thought that I was some piece of nothing that you could use until you were ready to throw me away.'

Now he changed his tone. 'I didn't mean to do that. And if I misled you I'm sorry.'

She had to give him credit. Alex was the first man ever to apologise to her and appear to actually mean it.

'But that's why this is a good deal,' he continued keenly. 'It's more than you could hope to get through the lawyers.'

That put her on alert. 'I see. You thought that you could come here and sweet-talk me into signing that paper without checking it with my lawyer first.'

He looked caught out. 'No. I just thought that if we sat down together we could put an end to all this. You know as well as I do that it's not in the interests of the lawyers to settle this; the longer it goes on, the more fees they get. Why not take that money for yourself?'

She knew he was right. But she wasn't ready to stop playing yet. 'Alex. I have a very good case. And I'm not ready to settle.'

'And everyone else has to suffer in the meantime!'

Her patience snapped. 'You mean Nina? It's a little late in the day to be worrying about your wife, isn't it?' She gestured in the direction of the bedroom. 'She wasn't on your mind when you were in there with me.'

He exhaled. 'Christ. You never let go, do you? What are you getting out of this?'

How could she possibly describe to anyone, let alone her prey, the excitement of the chase, the elation at the exercise of her power, the thrill of always being one step ahead? Nina might have got Alex, but Sasha had snatched victory straight back. Alex was living in a hotel and Nina looked as if she was falling apart. For as long as the game lasted there would be no hope for them: no cosy weekends away, no baby-making, no couples' dinner parties. As far as Sasha could tell, observing the flat from a distance, Nina didn't even let him in. And the longer the court case lasted, the more likely it was that their separation would be permanent. The court case and all the other torments she had devised for Nina occupied her totally, made all the other anxieties of her life disappear and when she woke up alone in the mornings gave her something to get up for. And in between times she forged ahead with her plans for Miami – the flat, the car, the sports clubs – all paid for by Alex.

So instead she said, 'It's not about me. It's about making you face the consequences of your actions.'

'Of course.' He sounded resigned. 'I should have realised that there was no point trying to reason with you.'

He got up. And then she felt a pang. She didn't want him to leave just yet. Who knows after a few beers what might happen?

She backtracked. 'OK. Maybe you're right. Why don't you stay for another drink?'

He paused to consider this for a few seconds. 'OK.'

She took his glass to the kitchen, wishing she had a stronger beer in the fridge. 'Would you like a whisky with that?' she called back.

'OK.' Then, 'Can I use your bathroom?' he asked.

'Of course.' That was interesting. Alex was playing for time. She recalled how Tony, after the police had dropped the investigation, had turned up asking to 'collect a few things'. After two bottles of wine they had ended up in bed together. That was the thing with men: very few of them let a grudge stand in the way of a good screw. He'd left in the middle of the night when she was asleep. In the morning she found the note: *For old times' sake. Thanks, Tx.*

Thanks! She hadn't liked that at all. It was demeaning. It was definitely patronising. It felt very much as if he was trying to get the last word. So she'd posted the note, and a photo of the two of them taken by the harbour in Monte Carlo, to his wife.

From the open-plan kitchen she observed Alex get up from the sofa and walk towards the bathroom leaving his briefcase behind him. Time for a quick look? But then, as he was almost by the hallway, he turned back to get it, word-lessly picking it up.

She went into the kitchen and poured him another beer. After a couple of minutes he was back.

She offered him the glass, but he shook his head. 'Look, on second thoughts I think I ought to be going.'

'One beer won't hurt.'

He shook his head. 'I think we've been there before. Best not to. Like you say, I've misled you in the past. There's no excuse for doing it again.'

She felt a surge of disappointment and a grudging respect for him.

He walked to the front door. As he reached it he turned. His voice had taken on an enticing edge. 'Sasha, won't you at least think about it?'

In his voice she heard that old charm and remembered all the reasons why she had fallen for him. If he had slept with her she might even have agreed.

She waited before replying, letting his hopes rise. He couldn't get away with rejecting her. She turned to face him, arranging her features so that her expression was blank. 'No. This is going to go all the way, Alex.'

Unable to conceal the dejection from his face, he opened the door and walked to the lift.

Chapter 20

Every year Nina's school had hosted an exchange visit with a school situated in a Paris suburb. As was the case with French schools, the girls did not wear uniform. And so for one week the Marlow school corridors would be scattered with girls who made their English sisters vow to diet for ever: slim-hipped, clear-skinned, lightly tanned, their lush hair always freshly washed, and dressed in a way that suggested they had thrown on the jeans and the white shirt and had paused only to tie an Argyll lambswool sweater casually round their shoulders. It was a style that could be copied but never truly imitated.

Looking at Francine as they stood in the study of MP David Stratford's country house, Nina was reminded of these girls. She and Francine, she guessed, were about the same age but Francine still had the figure of a fifteen-year-old and the ability to wear the same clothes. But today she was clearly dressed for work in a pristine fitted honey silk shirt and a pair of chocolate velvet slightly flared trousers that showed off her flawless figure. David Stratford, despite the occasional presence of his wife as she came in with cups of coffee, couldn't take his eyes off her.

Stratford was being photographed for a piece *Capital Letter* was doing on up-and-coming Tories tipped for the leadership of the party. On the telephone, Diana, the features editor, had been apologetic. 'I know it's very short notice. The photographer who was booked has called in sick. But we don't want to cancel – apparently Stratford can be a bit difficult.'

Francine was currently fixing a pair of arc lights to

compensate for the grey sky outside, Michael was adjusting his digital camera and Stratford was staring at Francine like a puppy dog.

From the moment she arrived Nina regretted coming. She felt like a spare part and she looked hopelessly overdressed. Her new suit – a well-cut, up-to-the-minute number in soft tweed that had looked bloody good in Peter Jones – had the effect, seen next to Francine, of making Nina look a frump.

Michael, though, had been pleased to see her. They had exchanged a few lowered words in the hallway. 'Thanks for the booking.'

'I'm sorry the money's not great.'

He shook his head. 'No problem. I really appreciate the work.'

'Michael!' An accented female voice had rung out. At that Michael had ushered Nina into Stratford's study and introduced them. 'This is Nina from *Capital Letter*.'

David Stratford was tall, debonair, dressed as if for the weekend in a Viyella checked shirt and brown cords. His previously bored expression now became more attentive. 'Are you writing the piece?'

'No.'

Michael covered for her. 'Nina's just here to keep an eye on us.'

Then he had introduced her to Francine, the owner of the voice. There was a brief and formal hello before Francine touched Michael's arm. 'You must excuse us, Nina. We must work now.'

Nina stood back and observed them. They were a smooth team, each knowing their part. Francine deftly set up the lights and white panels to achieve the right effect. Wherever Nina stood she seemed to be in the wrong place.

Francine was polite but firm. 'You must move, please. For the light.'

Stratford's study was at first sight that of a typical country house: book-lined shelves, a large antique mahogany desk and silver-framed photos of his children. But when she looked more closely Nina saw that the oak shelves looked brand new and most of the books were pristine and presumably never opened. It had a staged feel to it.

Eventually Michael was ready to begin. But first Stratford held up his hand. 'Let's go over the brief, shall we? This is a piece profiling future leaders of the party. So I want to look relaxed but in control.'

Michael nodded.

'Frankly I would rather have done this in my offices at the Commons. That would have been more professional—'

Francine cut him off. 'Do not worry! We are the best.' She came over to him, took his face and lifted his chin slightly. 'There. *Bien!* This is better for the neck – makes you look younger.'

David Stratford was struck dumb.

Michael shot him standing, sitting and in every possible pose and background. Nina felt initially surprised and then almost proud of Michael: he was so clearly at ease and proficient at his work. After a few minutes Nina could see that Stratford had let his guard down. The two exchanged some banter and as the shoot progressed his expression became more natural, less posed in a statesmanlike expression and truer to his real self: confident to the point of arrogance and with a hard touch to the eyes. The only break in the flow of pictures was Francine occasionally interrupting, 'Stop!' and rushing forward to twist Stratford's head up, down or around. Nina couldn't see that her input was anything but a distraction at this stage, breaking the rapport between the two men.

After half an hour Michael put down his camera. 'We've got enough. I'll email you the thumbnails.'

Stratford nodded. 'Thanks.' He shook Michael's hand. 'Perhaps you'd be interested in doing some work for me – some private family pictures.'

'Sure.'

Francine was now busy packing up – 'Excuse me!' – and

Nina felt she had more than outstayed her welcome. She raised a hand to Michael, who was talking to Stratford, and mouthed, 'I must run!'

He looked up as if to say something, but was interrupted by Stratford. 'Michael, let me show you the garden. I think there are some rather special locations we could use.'

Nina slipped out into the hall, pausing briefly to locate her car keys in her handbag. At that point she heard the bang of a door somewhere in the house and the sound of David Stratford's voice growing more distant.

There was a sharp clip of heels behind her. Nina hoped that it was Mrs Stratford, but knew it wasn't.

'Nina!'

She took a deep breath. 'Francine.' She turned. Looking over Francine's shoulder, she saw through the far window the two men striding across the lawn. She was well and truly stranded.

Francine had come up close. She got straight to the point. 'This shoot is not a good idea.'

It was an entirely unexpected comment. 'Oh.'

Francine shook her head definitively. 'No. It is a distraction for Michael. He is here in England for his father. His father is very ill.' She said this in a way that presumed Nina didn't know this. 'Our work is in France. Please do not be getting more bookings.'

Nina, thoroughly annoyed, protested, 'I think that's up to Michael!'

Francine ignored this. 'You are the ex?' she said smiling, but her eyes were unfriendly.

'An old friend,' she corrected her.

'No.' Francine shook her head. 'Michael has told me all about you. You are the ex.' She was utterly sure of herself. 'It is natural you want an excuse to see him.' She looked at Nina's hand. 'You are not wearing a wedding ring. This is hard at your age: you are all alone and you have no children.' Francine looked over Nina's clothes at that point and there was a slight purse of the lips as if to suggest that Nina's dress sense was a further problem for her. 'I understand this. But you must face facts, Nina. We are soon married. It will be better for you if you do not live in the past.'

She turned to leave but not before securing the final word. 'So, no more bookings. Understood? Thank you.'

Jemma stared at the screen. She had almost not bothered to log on to her college online learning profile, assuming that the department wouldn't post the end-of-term results until the New Year. The Department of Management and Accounting had not so far impressed her with its efficiency.

But in front of her, in three neat rows, her grades were displayed. 'A plus' was marked on each of her end-of-term assessments.

She felt a surge of delighted surprise. She would be able to sign up for Accounting Module 2 now.

She logged off and thought about calling Howard. He would be pleased, of course. But not in the way that she was. Not in the way that someone who deep inside doubts their ability to do something feels when they pull it off. So she sent a text message to Nina, instead. A call would have looked like boasting. But Nina understood how much it meant, how this was about so much more than a paper qualification. And then, filled with new confidence, she reached for the telephone and made the call that she had agonised over for days now. The call to the travel agent to cancel their flights to Marbella for the New Year. Why should she go if she didn't want to? She had plans now: she needed to get ahead with her coursework for next term; she didn't want to see Barbara – and she was damned if Barbara was going to see Howard.

Howard might not like it, but he'd better get used to it. Things were going to start changing around here.

Susan set off on her morning walk, turning out of the Old Brewery and on to Marlow High Street. It was brilliant to live somewhere so central. Since she had given up work her walk had become a daily routine: a stop at Burgers for a loaf of bread or something sweeter – she had a craving for the apple turnovers lately – and then up to the newsagent for the paper. Last week she had met up for coffee in Starbucks with some of the antenatal crowd: since they'd found out where she lived, their attitude towards her had become markedly friendlier and less condescending. Previously, admitting that she lived with her mother had made her sound like a promiscuous teenager. It was so much better to live with her partner in a luxury flat. Sometimes she took in the library or the florist and more often than not she popped into Waitrose for some bits and pieces. Not today, though. Waitrose on Christmas Eve would be packed to the seams, with checkout queues stretching halfway up the aisles.

Instead she strolled up the High Street, tastefully decorated with wreaths and lights that came on at dusk, admiring the elegant window displays in the town's boutiques and gift shops. Around her the women shoppers wore the Marlow winter ensemble of sheepskin or ski jacket with very well-cut jeans and boots. Beside them were their children, miniature versions of their mothers in OshKosh and Ralph Lauren.

Susan pulled her new maternity coat around her, a black wool wrap bought online from Seraphine. It went with her new black leather boots and the maternity jeans, nice ones though, in distressed dark denim.

She had finished her Christmas shopping; not that she had really done any at all. Plenty of sales reps cruised the craft fairs handing out samples. As long as she looked enthusiastic and confirmed that she was the owner of Valley Candles they were happy to oblige. So her mother was getting an assortment of fruit-scented tea-lights, Richard was getting coffee in an unglazed clay pot from somewhere in Africa and Nina was getting a selection of handsewn Venezuelan felt and lace Christmas tree ornaments.

She had handed in her notice to Roger after he left for

India. Really she had wanted to go before then, but it had been necessary to wait until Roger left for his winter trip – and paid her up to date. Otherwise he might be round for the van and she needed it because Alex was being somewhat sticky about a replacement vehicle. The Osho commune in Pune, Roger had told her several times, was a place where he went to recharge his spiritual batteries. When she called him she hoped that Osho banned mobiles – leaving a message was always so much simpler in these circumstances – but unfortunately he not only answered but also sounded crystal clear.

'It's Susan,' she said, trying to impersonate a very tired pregnant woman.

'Susan!' He sounded recharged already. 'How's it going?'

'Fine. Can you talk?' She hoped that he couldn't.

'No problem. I'm in the guesthouse. God, it's so wonderful to be back.' His voice took on a sudden worried tone. 'Did the Vermont stock come in?'

'Yes.' God, all twenty boxes of candles had been delivered to her flat and were currently stacked in the spare room.

'And they included the snowmen?'

'Yes.' The portly candle snowmen were clad in luxurious navy scarves and red coats, a wick sticking out of their little black Pilgrim hats.

'Good. Cost a bloody fortune. Make sure you push them. And the pies.'

Roger, though avowedly a spiritual person, never entirely took his eye off the bottom line.

'That's what I'm calling about, actually. I'm afraid I won't be able to go to the fair at Chelsea Town Hall.'

There was a silence. 'What? Why not?'

Susan assumed her most regretful tone. 'It's the baby, Roger. I went for my check-up. I've been put on total bed-rest. I'm only allowed to get up to use the bathroom.'

He appeared not to have heard. 'Oh, for fuck's sake, Susan! You can't just let me down like this. I've got a fortune in that stock. And it's perishable – it's proper organic wax with natural dyes. It'll discolour before next year.'

'You could sell it for Easter ...'

'Pumpkin pies and fucking Christmas trees! Susan, you have to go. Or find someone else.'

'I've tried. I really have. But it's Christmas, Roger.'

He sounded really worked up now. 'I know it's Christmas. That's why I employed you.'

Roger wasn't remotely interested in her health crisis which, if it had been true, would have been really hurtful. She began to feel quite resentful. It was often the case, in her experience, that people who preached universal love and tolerance displayed the opposite of these characteristics when they didn't get their own way. The woman who owned the Swansea café had a tattoo on her right upper arm – Live, Laugh, Love – but that hadn't stopped her, as soon as the environmental health officer left, turning red with fury and screaming at Susan that she was a stupid bitch who could have single-handedly ruined her business.

Now Roger, who owned a sweatshirt with the serenity prayer scripted on the back, sounded as if he was going to keel over with anxiety. 'You can't just leave me in the lurch.' He obviously had a thought at that point. 'And what about Henley?' he began to gabble. 'And Maidenhead Town Hall?' His voice had reached a new pitch.

'I'm sorry. Like I said, I have to stay in bed.'

'This is my busiest week. Christmas accounts for half of my annual sales!'

'Well, maybe you should be here, then.'

He lost his temper at that point. 'That's why I employed you! Susan, I relied on you. I even gave you a bloody bonus! Why didn't you mention this before I left? I could have made alternative arrangements.'

'I didn't know,' she said, sounding hurt and confused. 'I have to put the baby first.'

From the tone of his voice she had the impression that he

didn't believe her. 'You'd be sitting down all the time,' he said nastily.

She decided to adopt the high ground. 'I think it's time we ended this conversation,' she said haughtily. 'I'm sorry it was under these circumstances.' It was a phrase someone had used years ago when they'd fired her and she had repeated it ever since in difficult situations.

'Drop the van back at my house. And put the keys through the letterbox.'

She flipped the phone shut, which meant she hadn't heard that last part.

So she had her pay and the surprisingly generous Christmas bonus from Roger. In addition there was Alex's money for December. She stopped, as she had done for several days now, outside the window of Lily's. The window was still draped in white silk and bordered by birch twigs, the three mannequins simply clad in cashmere wraps in red, cream and pink. But the floor was now deep in fake snow and dotted with delicate miniature Christmas trees, the decorations solely silver and white, and a canopy had been added from which hundreds of crystal snowflakes had been hung. It looked amazing, one of the best displays in the High Street. She looked up and saw the offices of Carruthers & Kirkpatrick above, the firm's name painted in copperplate on one of the two first-floor windows. The other window said, *Established 1960*. Looking at the lettering filled her with a sense of entitlement: she was a Carruthers, too.

Then she pushed open the door. It was time to buy her Christmas present, time to enter a shop that for years had seemed forbidden to her – a closed club for the rich and glamorous, for those women who thought nothing of spending in one trip what it took her weeks to earn. Women like Nina and Jemma and Caro Phillips.

She stepped inside, smelling the aroma of expensive orange-spiced room scent. Behind the counter on a high shelf burned three Diptyque candles. Lily herself, made-up, manicured and coiffured, stepped out from behind the counter, elegant in a jade-green silk print wrap dress and black suede kitten heels. 'Can I help you?'

'Yes. I'd like to see the cashmere wraps. The ones you have displayed in the window.'

Kate let her hand rest on the telephone. She was in two minds about calling Richard: any contact with him invariably provoked an argument between them and so it was tempting to let sleeping dogs lie. But on the other hand it would be irresponsible not to postpone Emily's Christmas Eve visit. Dawn, the childminder, had called at lunchtime reporting that Emily's morning snivel had worsened and Kate had had no option but to take the rest of the day off work.

'Emily's running a temperature. And it's going to her chest. Half the town's going down with the flu. You'll have to come and get her, love. I can't have her around the others.'

Sitting at her desk, a stack of papers still to be dealt with, she had thought quickly. Her parents were in Oxford at a friend's lunch party – which left Richard. Three times she called his mobile but there was no reply.

The doctor's surgery at one o'clock on Christmas Eve had been hellish. A handwritten notice on the sliding window at reception announced that due to staff sickness the surgery was running with half the usual doctors. 'Please be patient. Alternatively the nearest Accident and Emergency service is located at Wycombe General Hospital.' Kate couldn't imagine that would be any better. Instead she had taken a number and waited for two hours to be seen, Emily wriggling and complaining on her lap. After an hour the waiting room had reached capacity: people began sitting on the floor and the collective mood, amid the sounds of crying babies and irritable toddlers, was one of frustration. 'This isn't what I pay my taxes for!' said the woman sitting next to her with a hacking cough. 'I tried calling. Even if you can get through you just get put on hold. In the end I decided to come down and wait.'

After their five-minute consultation with an exhausted-looking young woman doctor, Emily was prescribed amoxicillin for her sore throat, cough mixture and bed-rest. 'The virus just has to take its course. Take her to the hospital if her breathing gets laboured or her temperature goes up.'

Now, safely back home, Emily asleep in her bed, Kate knew she had to speak to Richard.

He answered his mobile on the last ring. In the background she could hear the television blaring out. Raising her voice, she explained Emily's poorly condition and their gruelling trip to the surgery.

'So I don't think she'll be well enough to come later. Why don't you take her on Boxing Day?'

Immediately she knew this last suggestion had been a mistake.

Richard sounded riled. 'Don't tell me when I can see my daughter! We agreed Christmas Eve, and that's how it's going to stay.'

'I know that's what we agreed. But she's not well.'

'She'll be better after she's had a nap. Wrap her up warm – it's not as if we'll be going out.' He started to get more worked up. 'I'm bringing her over here whether you like it or not. My mother wants to see her – she has a right, you know.'

'Yes. That's not the point—'

But his voice rode over hers. 'This isn't about what's convenient for you, Kate. I suppose you've got plans to see Daniel.' He spat out the name. 'Of course. Boxing Day would give you the whole day together.'

'No, I haven't!' And even if she had, Daniel wouldn't have minded staying in: he was a natural with Emily.

'I wish I could believe you,' Richard said accusingly.

Kate struggled to keep her cool. 'Richard, this is about Emily. She's not well.' She felt a surge of resentment against

334

him. He hadn't replied to any of her messages. 'Didn't you get my messages? I had to leave work. I'll have to go in over the holidays to get my desk straight.'

'That's not my fault. I was working.'

She didn't believe him for a moment. She had, after all, called him at lunchtime on Christmas Eve. Even though she knew it was pointless trying to change his attitude, still she felt compelled to try to get him to understand the situation. 'I had to wait two hours at the surgery! You can't even get through on the phone to make an appointment; it's constantly engaged. Or you're put on hold and forgotten about. You just have to turn up and wait. It's completely chaotic. Half the doctors are off. It's a really nasty bug and everyone's got it.' A sudden thought occurred to her. 'Anyway, your mother shouldn't be exposed to it. It may be the flu. Emily's probably infectious.'

'Since when have you cared about my mother? Look, let's get this clear. As the father I have rights. I'm coming round. And if you don't hand Emily over as we arranged I shall make it clear when the divorce goes through that you've stopped me seeing my daughter. And I shall ask for extra time to make up for that.'

Kate felt a shudder run down her. The last thing she wanted was an all-out battle with Richard over custody. So far neither of them had taken any steps to end their marriage: her instinct was to let things drift for a while in the hope that Richard would find himself a job or a girlfriend or hopefully both. The worst thing she could do right now would be to provoke him.

She sighed. 'All right. I'll put her in lots of layers and blankets. You'll have to keep the engine running.'

'I can assure you I'm perfectly capable of taking care of Emily. Just make sure she's ready.'

Chapter 21

It was a cold, crisp Christmas Day, the sky clear blue and the sun bright enough for sunglasses. At ten thirty in the morning the M4 was close to deserted as they left the London suburbs and headed west. Alex was at the wheel, powering down the outside lane.

They had been late leaving London because Alex had insisted on coming up to the flat.

'I'm not giving you your present in the street. Come on.'

In the flat he had handed her a gift-wrapped box. He looked unsure of himself, watching her as she sat down on the edge of the sofa to unwrap it.

She felt disarmed. 'Alex,' she said, untying the ribbon to reveal a Theo Fennell box, 'you didn't need to do this.'

'I wanted to. You deserve it, darling.'

She pulled out a gold bangle set with small diamonds at intervals. 'Alex!'

'Do you like it?' he said anxiously.

'Yes. It's lovely.' She looked up at him. 'It's too much.'

'No, it's not,' he said firmly, 'and it's yours whatever happens. I don't care even if you divorce me and you never want to see me again. I want you to have it.'

He reached forward, took the bracelet from her grasp and slipped it over her wrist, clicking the metal clasp shut. It was the most intimate contact they had had for six months. And it was both comforting and disturbing to her. She pulled away.

'Thank you. Your present's in the car.' She had bought him

a Brora cashmere sweater – not least because if she didn't buy him a present no one else would.

He shrugged. 'That's not important.'

It was true. Alex had always looked uncomfortable unwrapping presents. He had told her that when he was a child his mother had piled them at the end of the bed after he went to sleep and he had been left to open them on Christmas Day on his own.

Now, as they passed Windsor Castle, Nina sat staring out of the side window pondering her options for the day. She still hadn't decided whether to confront Susan with Richard present.

She turned to Alex. 'I'm determined to get some straight answers out of Susan.'

'Susan! I thought you said she wasn't going to be there.' He sounded surprisingly put out.

'Well, she is. There's been a change of plan. Apparently Gerry's spending the day with his children at his ex-mother-in-law's. Anyhow, the point is that I just know that she's getting the money from Mummy. It's impossible that she's paying for that flat herself. It's a luxury development.'

'It is?'

'Yes. And all the flats in that block are two-bedroom. I checked with one of the local agents.'

'You did?'

'Yep. And the rents are astronomical!'

'I'm sure.'

She had assumed that Alex would be all for getting to the bottom of this. He was the one after all who had urged her to speak to John Kirkpatrick. But instead Alex sounded lukewarm about her plan. 'All the same, Nina ... are you sure this is the right time and place for that kind of discussion? It's Christmas Day. And you don't want to spoil it for your mother.'

'Of course not. I'm going to wait until the afternoon.'

As they turned off the dual carriageway and drove through

the winding Bisham Road lined with picture-postcard cottages, Nina admitted to herself that she still had mixed feelings about spending Christmas Day with Alex. If she was honest, one of the main reasons she had given in was to continue to avoid telling her family about the separation. She remembered a neighbour they had lived next to in Wandsworth who, one night after a few drinks, had miserably told Nina what she had long since worked out for herself – that her husband had left a year ago.

Besides, Alex had worn her down. Two weeks after the *Zut!* piece about her had appeared, he had insisted on meeting up.

'I've done what you wanted. I made Sasha an offer.'

'And has she accepted it?'

'She will do.'

At that, Nina was about to object, but he cut her off.

'Believe me. When she reads between the lines she'll accept it. There isn't going to be a court case.'

'How do you—'

He raised his hand. When he spoke he sounded very sure of himself, as though he had regained the initiative. 'It's over, Nina. Wait and see.'

On their arrival at the house Richard took an age to open the front door. There was no sign in the house that it was Christmas.

'There didn't seem any point putting up a tree for the two of us,' Richard said offhandedly as he showed them in. Their mother was waiting for them in the drawing room. It was a mess: newspapers piled up on the coffee table, dirty mugs on the side tables and the carpet didn't look as if it had been vacuumed for weeks. Only a small fire burning in the grate lent any cheer to the room.

Her mother ignored Nina and turned to Alex. 'When I heard you were coming I told Richard to light a fire in here.'

Alex was always good with her. 'And you've put on the red velvet.' He went forward to kiss her. 'Happy Christmas!'

Her mother sounded positively coquettish. 'As I said, I heard you were coming!'

Incredibly, her mother was wearing her faithful red Windsmoor and black tights and Nina thought that she detected a hint of blusher and lipstick. As far as her mother was concerned, bringing Alex had been the right thing to do.

Alex sat down beside her. 'How about a drink?'

'What a good idea!' said her mother.

At that, Richard slumped onto the sofa and switched on the television.

Their mother snapped at him, 'Turn that off! And get everyone a drink.'

Richard looked like thunder.

'It's OK,' Nina stepped in. 'I'll do it,' she volunteered, gathering up a clutch of dirty mugs.

She set to work in the kitchen opening a couple of bottles of wine – one red and one white – from the coolbox and looking for bowls to serve smoked almonds in. The cupboards were a mess; saucepans piled on top of serving dishes, plates stacked anyhow and tea-stained mugs that looked as though they hadn't been washed properly for weeks piled higgledy-piggledy in the spaces in between. Finally she found a couple of cereal bowls.

Having served them wine – Richard commenting that the white needed to be chilled properly – she started on lunch, beginning by clearing a pile of washing-up from the sink. Clearly Richard's enthusiasm for spring-cleaning hadn't lasted long. There wasn't time to cook a whole turkey so she had brought a huge turkey breast and several bags of prepared vegetables, and made a pan of stuffing and a dish of potatoes boulangère.

Nina could hear her mother fawning over Alex. 'Now tell me all about that business of yours.'

And then he was off with anecdotes about the tenants and his plans to buy a run-down block of bedsits in Earls Court.

'I always said to Archie you'd go far. Isn't that exciting, Richard?'

Richard didn't sound excited. 'So what's happening with all that trouble you had with the police?'

Having put the lunch on, Nina turned her attention to the dining room. It was filled with Richard's stuff – a laptop on the table and papers strewn over every spare surface. Cardboard boxes were lined up along the oak sideboard in what appeared to be an ad hoc filing system. Strangely, equipment for picture framing was stacked up against one wall.

She called out to him, 'Richard, you need to clear the dining room.'

He appeared within seconds. 'I thought we could eat in the kitchen.'

'It's Christmas Day!'

'So what? Mummy won't care.'

God, he made her blood boil. 'Don't you want to make it nice for her?'

'I live here!' he retorted. 'Anyone can make an effort for one day.'

'Why don't we ask her where she wants to eat?' As soon as this comment left her lips, Nina realised that they sounded like children, running to their mother to settle yet another squabble.

'Anyway,' she said, gesturing to the table, 'what is all this?'

'Paperwork. Business paperwork.'

'We can just pile it on the floor.'

'I'll do it,' he said quickly. Too late Nina realised that she had missed the chance to see what he was up to.

If it hadn't been Christmas Day she would have confronted him there and then. It was obvious he wasn't working. Every time she called he was at home. Who was paying for him?

'Well, go on then,' he said irritably. 'Let me get on with it.'

She stood by the door. 'Are you seeing Emily over Christmas?' she asked.

'I saw her yesterday. Anyway, she's not well. Feverish.' His expression grew worried. 'I hid some crackers but she wasn't up to looking for them.'

Nina's heart sank. She was sorry the little girl was ill, but she'd hoped that he would go for at least part of the day and she would get some time alone with Susan.

At half past twelve, too late to help with lunch, Susan appeared. Nina had not prepared herself for the sight of her pregnant sister – or the totally unexpected and overwhelming surge of envy that it provoked. At the meeting with John Kirkpatrick Susan had looked merely heavy, encased in several layers. Now there was no mistaking her pregnancy. She was wearing a black jersey dress, cut low with the fabric draped over her bump. Around her shoulders she had a silk shawl. She looked exactly as pregnant women were supposed to look – glowing and full. Susan's former lithe body had been transformed into something more lush and beautiful.

For a moment she had been struck dumb.

Then Susan had thrown herself at her. 'Nina. God, this is so fabulous! Everyone together. Just like old times!'

Nina wasn't sure what old times Susan was thinking of. Past Christmas memories included her mother ordering them to get out of the kitchen, blood running out of the newly carved turkey, and Richard twisting the head off Susan's showjumper Barbie doll.

It didn't feel like old times at all, because Archie wasn't there to put the star at the top of the tree and hand out presents and shoo them off on a Christmas cracker hunt. As on so many occasions, she now appreciated how much he had done for them all.

Susan, who had never had any interest in food, was eyeing the lunch hungrily.

'God, I'm starving.'

'Good. You need to eat.'

And then Susan was off on some detailed explanation of the recommended calorific intake for pregnant women, the development of the baby at six months and how all that advice about eating for two was old hat now.

'They weigh you to make sure you're not gaining too much or too little. You also have to watch out for diabetes.'

It was remarkable. Susan actually sounded grown-up for the first time in her life. She picked at a carrot baton. 'Of course, you take special vitamins too.'

'Really?'

It was a club of pregnant women, of which Nina was not a member.

And if she and Alex did get divorced it would seem unlikely that she ever would be. She was thirty-six, and next April she would be thirty-seven. That, according to a crop of alarmist articles that had recently appeared in the papers, gave her very little time to find a man, marry him and get pregnant. She had begun to read other articles that she had previously ignored as irrelevant – the ones about getting your eggs frozen or making the decision to have a child alone.

'And how's Gerry?'

'Oh, he's amazing!'

Even though she had sworn to herself that she would wait, Nina could not help herself. 'He must be. Paying for that flat. I came round, you know.'

'Oh. Yes. God, I'm sorry. I only got your messages later.'

'It's a very nice development.'

'Hmm.' Susan headed for the door. 'Anyhow, I ought to go and sit with Mummy. She'll be wondering where I am!'

And then she was off, leaving Nina to cook lunch and create order out of chaos in the kitchen.

It was Alex who came to the rescue, finding her marooned over a stove of steaming vegetables. 'Come and sit down.'

'God, this cooker is filthy! I feel I ought to clean it all up.'

'No. You are not doing that.' He led her away from the cooker. 'It's Christmas Day and you are not turning into Mrs Baxter. Here,' he reached for her glass of wine, 'drink this.'

And then he took over: laying the dining-room table,

shepherding her family in, carving the turkey breast with as much flourish as was possible. Their mother had insisted that Alex was at the head of the table. Richard had positioned himself next to their mother, Nina was at the foot of the table nearest to the door and Susan was on her own on the other side. Finally he served everyone wine, except for Susan. When it came to her turn he whisked her glass away.

'I don't think half a glass would matter,' Susan said plaintively.

Alex shot her a warm smile. 'Better safe than sorry. I know you mothers don't like to take any chances with what's best for the baby.'

That shut her up and started their mother on a stream of reminiscences about when they were younger. 'In those days the doctor told you to give the baby its medicine in a spoonful of sherry. Of course, those were the days when you could get a home visit. That Dr Hayley, he was a nice man. His wife got leukaemia.'

Alex headed her off before she began her inventory of the town's terminal illnesses. 'Nina tells me that you used to get the tree from Henley Market?'

'Archie would send Jim for it the day before. People didn't have all this tat up weeks before like they do now. We decorated the tree on Christmas Eve. Oh, it was beautiful!'

Artfully steered by Alex, her mother embarked on what seemed to Nina to be largely fictional accounts of white Christmases, sunny family holidays and delightful car rides in which Archie kept spirits up with a non-stop regime of singalongs and car games. Where were the tedious journeys of Nina's memory, her mother commanding them to be quiet and Richard pinching them both in the back seat? Each of her mother's accounts ended with an unfavourable comparison with the way things are today. 'Now in those days everything closed on Christmas Eve lunchtime. There was none of this running out on Christmas Day if you forgot something. People were organised or they did without.'

As the lunch wore on, Nina felt more and more disgruntled. What was the reality behind the family gathered around the table? Her brother was a liar, her sister was the same and her husband was an adulterer.

But everyone else seemed determined to pretend that it was otherwise. Her family had always assumed an air of superiority over other people. Susan was talking about Gerry. 'I'm really disappointed that he can't be here. He has to spend it with his children. But I can't complain. That's one of the things I admire about him – his sense of responsibility to his children. These days so many men don't have that.'

'I agree,' chimed in her mother. 'They go around fathering these children and then expect the taxpayer to support them.'

Susan spoke next. 'Hmm. What do you think, Alex?'

'Absolutely.' He got up. 'I'll go and check on the fire.'

Nina had had enough. They were hardly the perfect family themselves. 'So, Richard, have you and Kate come to any decisions?'

He shook his head. 'Kate refuses to discuss the situation. She's got her mind on other things.'

Her mother cut in. 'I always said that she was a flighty one. Not at the time – you have to let your children make their own decisions.' Involuntarily, Susan and Nina exchanged glances at this point.

'Surely there's something you can do?' Nina persisted. 'How about trying mediation?'

Richard cast her a resentful glance. 'That costs money, you know. We can't all spend our way out of trouble.'

'What do you mean?'

He jerked his head in the direction of the drawing room where Alex could be heard putting logs on the fire. 'Well, he's not in prison, is he? If you know the right people you can get out of anything.'

'Alex did nothing wrong!' she protested.

Richard raised his eyebrows. 'Really?'

'Anyway, we're not talking about Alex. We're talking about you. You could go to the Citizens' Advice Bureau.'

He looked unimpressed. 'I don't want some busybody knowing my business.'

At that point Alex returned and for the first time in months Nina was genuinely pleased to be in his company. After any length of time in her family's presence she felt weighed down. It seemed that they were never happier than when criticising other people or relaying their misfortunes.

Susan decided that it was all going very well. Her mother was doing most of the talking, Nina and Richard were working up to a row and Alex couldn't look her in the eye. As for Gerry, she had expertly fielded her mother's initial query about his absence.

'So where's Gerry?' said her mother. 'Doesn't he want to spend the day with you?'

Susan made an effort to sound insouciant. 'He's with the children at his ex-mother-in-law's. I'll see him tonight.'

The exact truth was that at that very moment Gerry was on his own in his flat. His ex-wife had let him go over for an hour that morning to watch the kids open their presents. He would spend the rest of the day alone until the evening, when he could come over to her flat to give her her present. It had been much too risky to let him come to the house for lunch. The last thing she needed was Nina, Alex and Gerry in the same room.

So she had put him off. 'Darling, I know this is going to sound weird. But my family are weird. Anyhow, Nina wants it just to be the three of us. Me, Nina and Richard.'

'Why?'

'Because Mummy's so confused at the moment and she's worried that lots of extra people in the house will make it worse.'

'But your mother knows me!'

'But you know what a control freak Nina is. She's kind of insisting on it.'

'What about Alex? Will he be there?'

'He sort of counts as family.'

Gerry looked woebegone. She had had no idea that he would get so into this father thing. 'But it's Christmas Day! Technically it's the baby's first.' He rubbed her stomach. 'There's a little person inside there, you know.'

God, he could be so irritating. 'Yes. Technically. But we'll be together in the evening.'

'All right then,' he said reluctantly.

Now, as they started on Marks & Spencer Christmas pudding, Susan congratulated herself. Admittedly there had been a few tricky moments but nothing that she couldn't handle.

Nina had zoomed in on the subject of Gerry and their future plans. 'So, Susan, when are you going to set a date with Gerry?'

That had set her mother off. 'Good question! I keep asking her and I never get a straight answer.'

'Really?' Nina had given her a hostile glance. 'Why don't you tell us, Susan?'

'We'd like a spring wedding,' she had been forced to concede.

But overall it had been fine. Susan was on top of things. Nina hadn't come close to landing a punch. She couldn't prove anything. Nina might be able to get hold of her mother's bank statements, but she couldn't get hold of hers. Meanwhile Gerry was in the dark and Alex had no choice but to do what she wanted.

It was vital that Nina didn't find out. If she did, Alex would have no reason to pay large sums of money to stop Susan telling her.

Susan had, from time to time, nonetheless toyed with telling Nina that her doting husband was the father of her sister's child. Like now, watching Nina across the table so smug and sure of herself. She looked at the gold bracelet on her sister's wrist – with all those diamonds it was obvious that Alex could pay much more. Those were the times when it was so tempting to tell Nina that she had nothing to feel superior about.

But then she recalled the reality of the situation, a reality she had been made uncomfortably aware of since meeting Libby at antenatal yoga classes at the Marlow Sports Centre. Libby was, like her, six months pregnant by a married man. But Libby's married man had made it clear that he wasn't willingly going to give her anything.

Listening to Libby, Susan had worked out that legally Alex wasn't obliged to give her money until the baby was born. Legally he was well within his rights to wait until the results of the DNA test. And legally she wouldn't get much after that. Libby's most optimistic assessment of what she might get from her baby's father would barely cover Susan's Waitrose bill.

'That's if he pays it,' Libby said hopelessly. 'He's got his own business, which makes it harder.'

'Oh. Why?'

'He'll just fix his accounts to show he didn't make any money.'

Susan had felt a chill run down her spine. 'Why don't you threaten to tell his wife?'

Libby looked at her flatly. 'I did tell his wife. She said she'd rather see him go bankrupt than give me anything.'

So Susan resolved to keep her mouth shut. That was the important thing about lying. Whatever the situation the essential thing was to stick to the plan and never under any circumstances admit the truth. When she was fifteen, Archie, in the presence of Mrs Palmer, had gone on and on at her.

'We found the money in your bag!'

'No. That was different money.'

'So where did you get it?'

'I found it.'

'Susan!'

As Nina would discover, suspecting something was amiss and proving it was an entirely different thing.

All the same she had had enough. She pushed the remains of her Christmas pudding away. She wanted to grab the sofa before Richard got there. So she stood up and arched her back melodramatically.

'I need to lie down.'

'Of course you do, dear.' Their mother was always nicer to them when other people were around. 'I think I'll do the same.'

Both of them rose heavily to their feet, Richard rushing round to pull back their mother's chair and usher her out of the room.

Susan stretched. 'I'll help with the clearing-up later.' There was little chance of this: Nina would zip through it in no time. Alex was already clearing away the plates.

Before Nina could reply, Susan slipped into the kitchen on her way to the bathroom. It was then, pausing to get a glass of water, that out of the kitchen window in the dimming light of the afternoon she saw Gerry coming up the garden path.

She felt a cold shudder run down her body.

But before she could get to the front door and head him off, she heard Alex at her shoulder. 'Hey! Gerry's here.' He moved close to her. 'Isn't that a nice surprise, Susan!' He lowered his voice. 'You'd better pull this off. Or life will get very unpleasant indeed.' Then his voice was quieter still. 'Believe me, if Nina finds out I will make it my business to make sure you don't get another penny.'

Gerry was behaving very oddly. Nina had come out into the hallway to greet him, only for Gerry to take an involuntary step backwards at the sight of her.

Now he was standing, still wearing his coat, shifting uneasily from foot to foot and regarding Nina with an expression of nervous hesitation. 'It's OK. I'm not staying.'

Nina decided to ignore this strange behaviour. 'You're

very welcome. Have you eaten? There's plenty left over. I can make up a plate.'

He shook his head vigorously. 'Oh, no. I don't want to cause any trouble.'

'It's no trouble at all.'

'I was just driving past and I thought I'd call in with your mother's present. But I won't stay.'

'I expect you need to get back,' added Susan.

'Actually I was just about to make some coffee,' said Nina.

Gerry's face was a picture of confusion. It was almost as if he felt that he wasn't welcome. Nina, perplexed, took him by the arm and physically steered him into the drawing room. 'Stay for a cup.'

Having left him on the sofa, Nina went into the kitchen and began to make coffee in their mother's ancient percolator. Above the rumbling she could hear Alex working hard to make conversation with Gerry. To give Alex his due, he was making more effort with her family than ever before.

'So. How's the writing?'

'Oh. Great! Actually I've had some good news. I expect Susan mentioned it.'

'I don't think so.'

'I've been shortlisted for the BBC New Scriptwriters' Prize.'

'Gerry's in the last fifty,' Susan explained without much enthusiasm.

'Terrific!'

When Nina brought in coffee Gerry made to get to his feet. 'I don't want to cause any confusion.'

Why was he talking to her like this? 'Gerry. You're very welcome. After all, you're part of the family now. Why don't you take off your coat?'

He looked relieved and allowed himself to slip off his jacket.

There was an awkward silence.

Then Alex spoke. 'Congratulations on the baby. Great

349

news!' He looked from Gerry to Susan. 'You must be very proud.'

'Thanks! Of course, Susan's doing the hard part.' He gave a nervous laugh.

There was another awkward pause. Susan said warmly, 'So how were Harry and Samantha?'

He shrugged. 'They seemed to enjoy it. Harry got a bit over-excited.'

Nina, observing the scene, felt a growing sense of irritation. First lunch and now this pretend banter.

Now Susan was trying to persuade Gerry to go for a walk. 'Exercise is good for the mother and the baby.'

Nina knew Susan's game. She'd get Gerry out of the house and the next thing they'd be in the car and off.

It was time to seize the moment. She cleared her throat. 'Now that Mummy's having a nap I think it's time that we had a talk about the way things are round here—'

Richard interrupted her. 'It's Christmas Day. I don't think it's the time or the place for anything like this.'

'And Gerry's nothing to do with it either,' added Susan.

'It's as good a time as any. And Gerry's about to marry into this family.' She looked across at him. An expression of shock had crossed his face at this last statement. She put this down to his general state of agitation and pressed on. 'He needs to know what he's getting himself into.'

Gerry put down his coffee cup. 'Into?' he repeated anxiously.

She addressed him. 'There have been some discrepancies in my mother's bank account lately. Money has been used for purposes that are nothing to do with her.'

'That's what you say,' said Richard.

'It's what I know, Richard. I've seen the bank statements.' She was getting into her stride now.

But Alex cut her off. Incredibly, he seemed almost to be on their side. 'Perhaps Richard's right. This isn't the time or place.'

'Yes it is!' She was determined to break through this conspiracy of silence. She shot Susan a hard stare. 'You've just moved into a very expensive two-bedroom flat in the centre of Marlow.'

Susan went to open her mouth.

'And don't tell me any different. I called three agents.'

'Which ones?' interrupted Alex.

Why did that matter? Nina pressed on. 'They told me that all the flats in your block have two bedrooms. And they also told me the monthly rents. I wrote them down.' Anticipating some lie from Susan, she reached into her handbag for her notebook.

Alex spoke up. 'I'm sure we can take your word for that.'

Nina raised her voice to Susan. 'How are you paying for it?'

'I told you.'

She hadn't told her anything. 'Told me what?'

'I don't have to account to you!'

'Then you can account to the police. You know damn well the money in the trust is for Mummy. It's not for Richard and it's not for you.' She turned to Gerry. 'I have good reason to believe that Richard and Susan are taking money from our mother's bank account to pay for their own expenses.'

At that Gerry looked horrified. He swung round to face Susan. 'That's not what you told me. You said the trust was paying and the solicitor had agreed it.'

Nina felt a surge of triumph run through her. 'God help you! This is what I've known all along. You're both stealing!'

'No I'm not!' shouted Susan. 'God, who do you think you are? Coming in here with your holier-than-thou attitude. You think you know it all.'

Above the uproar Alex could be heard. 'Let's all calm down. Maybe you should get some fresh air, Susan. All this excitement can't be good for the baby.'

But Susan looked in no mood for an afternoon stroll now. She was staring daggers at Nina. 'What about you? You sit there like you're whiter than white. Why don't you tell us all about your cosy meeting with Michael Fellows?'

Nina felt stunned and angry at herself for not anticipating that a cornered Susan would fight dirty. But it was too late now. Susan had taken the initiative.

Susan turned to Alex. 'Didn't Nina mention it? She and Michael went off together after our meeting with John Kirkpatrick.'

'What? You didn't tell me he was back!'

'I didn't know he was.' Nina felt herself flush red. 'I didn't go off with him. I bumped into him by accident in the High Street and we went for a drink. A very quick drink.'

'Oh, come on.' Richard sounded scathing. 'You're saying that you just happened to meet Fellows on the very same day that you were plotting to get control of the trust.'

'I haven't been plotting anything!'

Richard sneered at her. 'You and Fellows have always been thick.'

It was outrageous. But before she could defend herself Alex turned to her accusingly. 'Is this true? Have you been having secret meetings with him?'

She stopped herself just in time from saying that he was in no position to point the finger. As she took a moment to muster her defence, she heard Gerry speak to Susan. His voice was calm and quiet.

'So who is paying for the flat?'

Distracted from her own thoughts, Nina observed Gerry looking at Susan with an expression of sad intensity.

Quiet had fallen on the room as Richard and Alex listened, too.

'I think we should take a break,' said Alex firmly.

But everyone ignored him.

'Who is paying for the flat, Susan?' Gerry repeated slowly.

Susan said nothing.

'Is it the trust?' he persisted.

She shook her head. 'No.'

There was an awful pause. Then Gerry said slowly. 'Is it someone else?'

She nodded. 'Yes.'

'The father?'

'Yes.'

He hung his head. Nina could barely hear him. 'Well, who is it?'

Susan lifted up her head and wiped a tear from her eye. She clasped his hand. 'I'm sorry. I'm so sorry. I wanted it to be you, I really did.'

At last he sounded angry. 'Who the hell is it?'

Susan looked at each of them in turn, her eye falling on Nina, then Richard – and finally Alex.

'I'm sorry. But I can't do this any more.' She ran her hand through her hair. 'What's the point? It's all going to come out in the end.' At that her voice broke. 'It's Roger.'

Chapter 22

Maria was horrified. 'Who the hell is Roger?'

'Susan's boss,' Nina explained. 'None of us have met him.'

They were sitting at the back of the Scarsdale Arms in Edwardes Square. At lunchtime the normally packed pub was quieter than usual, its Kensington clientele presumably out of London until after the New Year. It was a genteel sort of pub, with an open fire, a restaurant area at the back and Methuselah champagne bottles lining the mantelpiece and high shelf that ran around the interior wall.

Nina relayed what Susan had told her. 'He spends a lot of time overseas. He used to own a shop, but now he sells candles at these stalls.'

Maria continued to sound appalled. 'And what did Gerry say when he found out?'

'He was devastated.'

Nina recalled the scene. Gerry had got up from the sofa ashen-faced. 'When were you planning to tell me?' He had cast Susan a disdainful glance. 'Were you ever planning to tell me?'

Susan had fallen silent.

It had been left to Alex to break the silence. 'Would you like a drink, Gerry?' he said gently.

'No. I'd better go.' Gerry had pulled on his coat. He looked down at Susan and when he spoke his voice was one of bitter sadness. 'I'll leave your things in a bin bag on the doorstep.'

As the front door slammed, Nina rounded on Susan. 'How could you lie about that?'

'I didn't! I made a mistake.'

'Oh, for God's sake. If Roger's paying for that flat, he must be damned sure.'

Susan said nothing, sinking into a surly silence as Nina threw a barrage of questions at her.

'How old is Roger?'

'Is he married?'

'Where does he live?'

'Why did you have to involve Gerry?'

At that Susan looked up as if wounded by an unfair accusation. 'I didn't! He just assumed he was the father. I was trying not to hurt his feelings!'

'Well, you didn't make a very good job of that.'

Susan began slowly to get to her feet. 'I'm tired. And I'm feeling sick. I think I'd better go home.'

'I think we should leave this for another time,' Alex had agreed. He had looked from one to the other. 'It's been a long day for everyone.'

Now, Nina put down her drink. 'At least my mother wasn't there.'

'Does she know about Roger?' asked Maria.

'I'm sure Richard's told her.'

Maria paused. 'So were you glad to have Alex there?'

Nina thought for a moment. 'Yes. I was. Actually, he was in his element. He's always been good in a crisis.' She gave Maria a half-smile. 'He wants to move back in.'

In the car on the way home Alex had begun talking as soon as they pulled out of the driveway. 'Nina, this is crazy. Let me come home and I'll prove to you that it's the right decision. And I don't like this business with Michael Fellows.' There followed a host of quick-fire questions: when, where and why had she seen him?

She had been grateful to be in the car, where Alex had to keep his eyes on the road. 'I told you – it was a coincidence. I bumped into him.' Though he was in no position to find fault with her, she wasn't going to tell him that they'd had dinner, talked several times on the phone and met up at the David Stratford photoshoot.

'So there is no business with Michael Fellows,' she concluded curtly.

'Then why didn't you mention it?'

'Because there was nothing to mention.'

But Alex had claimed the moral high ground for the first time in a long while and she could see that he wasn't about to surrender it. 'So you have your secrets too, Nina.' At that they had fallen into an uncomfortable silence for the remainder of the journey.

Now, Maria was clearly choosing her words carefully. 'Are you going to let him?'

'Maybe.'

Maria said nothing and Nina took her silence for disapproval. 'Well, just make sure you don't take him back before New Year's Eve!'

'Maria, I really don't know if it's a good idea.'

'You agreed! It'll be fun. I thought we could go and buy you something.'

'Buy me something?'

'Yes! You need a proper dress. The men are going to be in black tie.' She looked closely at Nina's face. 'You might want to hop on a sunbed, too.'

Nina could feel her spirits sinking. But before she could object Maria launched into her sales talk.

'It's a group event – a New Year's Eve ball,' she said grandly. 'So there's no pressure. And they're one of the best events organisers in the business.'

'Singles' events organisers,' Nina corrected her.

Maria ignored her. She had recently paid an extortionate joining fee and seemed determined to prove to herself as much as Nina that this new approach to finding a husband would succeed where all others had failed. 'It's not like a dating agency. They do dinners, days out and even holidays – sailing and country house weekends. Because it's a group thing, if you don't like someone, you can make your excuses. It's very upmarket, Nina. There's a champagne reception and then a sit-down dinner.'

'What if I'm sitting next to someone I don't like?'

Maria ignored this, too. 'And afterwards there's dancing. The tickets cost a fortune, which is good because you know the men are serious. It's not like online dating where any loser can sign up. They vet them to make sure they're not married.'

'But I'm married!'

Maria brushed this aside. 'You're my guest, so you don't have to be vetted. It's exclusive,' she pronounced definitively. 'Anyway, I've bought the tickets.' She finished her drink. 'It'll be good for you. Besides, you don't want Alex to think you're too available. Nina, we're going. You might not want to meet a man but I damn well do.'

'I told you it was going to be too much for you.' Richard sighed heavily. 'But you wanted everyone here on Christmas Day. And look where it's got you.' With that he crossed the room to close the curtains.

'I don't want them closed.'

'You need to rest.'

Anne had been resting all day. In fact, she had been in bed since Boxing Day. She had started to feel hot and cold on Christmas night, but it was not her visitors on Christmas Day who had caused the problem – the problem was Kate and her wretched germs. She felt a surge of resentment towards her. To be precise she had caught it from Emily, the little girl red-faced, sneezing and feverish throughout her visit on Christmas Eve, falling asleep on the sofa soon after she had opened her presents. But Richard had said that Kate had it first – she probably got it from her fancy man – so it was tantamount to the same thing.

Richard had been gone for ages.

'Where have you been?'

'Boots,' he said, holding up a carrier bag. 'Shopping for you.'

Admittedly she sometimes lost track of time. Without her glasses she couldn't see the face of the clock on her bedside table. But she felt sure it was afternoon and Richard had left before lunchtime. He had brought her some mashed-up Weetabix before he went. Now she was hungry.

'I want to get up.' She felt terrible, very short of breath and wheezy. But she may as well feel terrible downstairs in front of the television with a nice cup of tea and a piece of cake. Her head throbbed, every bone in her body ached and her throat was sore. It was impossible to get comfortable: burning up one minute and shivering the next.

'Shh. It was getting up and rushing around that made you ill, didn't it?' He took out the contents of the paper bag. 'I've been down to Boots and got you some vitamin C pills and some more paracetamol. They'll help with the temperature.'

She watched as he unwrapped the containers of pills and placed them on the bedside table where all her pills were laid out.

'Here.' He came and sat down on the edge of the bed holding a glass of water. 'Open wide.'

He popped the one large pill and then the two paracetamol into her mouth. Obediently she swallowed.

He put down the glass. 'Now,' he said cheerfully, 'I'll go and get you something to eat.'

She knew what that meant: a tin of tomato soup and some bread and margarine followed by supermarket macaroni cheese. Privately, she wished that Nina were here. Nina would get her up and make her a proper meal. Nina would light the fire and they would watch television together. She had asked Richard about getting a television for the bedroom. She knew people did that these days, but he said there wasn't an aerial socket.

Christmas Day had been a real treat. She had forgotten what a proper home-cooked meal tasted like. She could ask

Nina to bring some home-made chicken soup and maybe a nice bit of stewed lamb. And an apple crumble.

But it would hurt Richard's feelings if she asked for Nina. He was doing his best. He was the man of the house now and it would be a snub if Nina came and took over. With that thought, a more ominous one took hold. Nina might also suggest calling the doctor, who in turn might insist on all sorts of tests and second opinions and who knew where the fuss would end: very possibly she would find herself stuck on a hospital trolley for days on end and God knows when she would see her home again.

That settled it: whatever happened, however bad she felt, no matter how tight her chest was, one thing she was certain of – she was never leaving this house.

She turned to Richard, who was straightening the covers. 'Yes, dear. You make some lunch. Whatever you think is best.'

Chapter 23

Sasha put down the telephone and made a note to call her bank as soon as they reopened. Next she wrote down the funds to be wired to the agent. She had, after days of internet searching, finally decided on a thirty-fourth-floor Miami beachfront condominium, telephoning Gloria the agent to secure it.

Gloria, who talked fast in a Brooklyn accent, had been brisk. 'You'll love it here. I've been in Miami twenty years. I'd never go back.'

Maybe she wouldn't either.

For a start, it was great to do business on New Year's Eve when the world was getting ready to party. Gloria had provided Sasha with her office, home and 'cell' numbers. Her office was open as normal for business, while here in Britain the country had gone into a two-week-long hibernation. Annoyingly, the gym didn't open for another two days.

Pat had invited her over for a meal of gammon and bubble and squeak but one meal of mushy green sprouts and greasy roast potatoes was more than enough. The best thing about Pat's Christmas dinner had been the Fortnum & Mason Christmas pudding that Sasha had brought. Instead she had decided to hit the West End sales. She got up from the table and looked at her watch: it was lunchtime. She had had to wait in until it was morning in the US, though Gloria had no objection to being called at seven a.m. In fact she had been insistent that Sasha call her any time.

She walked to the bedroom to change out of her tracksuit.

It was time to move on: a new country, a new history and a new wardrobe. She had told Gloria that she was a London property developer who, tired of the grind of London living, had decided to spend three months in the sun.

She would leave in a couple of weeks, settling the case just in time for Alex's payment to be transferred so that it would be waiting for her on her arrival in Miami. She had her eye on a Corvette, which she would use to tour a shortlist of private membership-only country clubs, the type of place where a uniformed porter sat marshalling cars in and out of the long driveway leading past sprinkler fed golf greens to a white colonial clubhouse. In return for a ten per cent increase on Alex's offer she would even sign his confidentiality clause. Her time as a PA was not something she would be alluding to in her new life anyway.

As she stood in front of her built-in wardrobe selecting what to wear there was a ring on the doorbell. Her first thought was that it was her neighbour. But everyone was away. So that brought Alex to mind. She flung off her tracksuit and, remembering that she had looked overly casual on his last visit, pulled on her long black silk La Perla robe.

At the door, she peered through the spyhole.

Two uniformed police officers and two men in suits, their faces turned to the side so that she could not see them clearly, stood outside.

Shocked, she stepped back, instinctively placing herself with her back to the wall.

Immediately there was a pounding on the door. 'Sasha Fleming, we know you're in there.'

Then there was a second voice. 'Angie, we've been watching the flat.' This second voice sounded vaguely familiar, but she couldn't place it.

The first voice spoke again. 'Sasha Fleming, we have a warrant to search your flat.'

For a moment she felt paralysed. 'Wait a minute,' she called.

The voice was more urgent. 'No. Open up now! Or we're coming in.'

Coming in! God, he must mean that they would break the door down. The thought of being physically invaded in her flat, her sanctuary, was unbearable. 'Stop! I'll open the door now!'

As she did so, she recognised the detective who greeted her with a self-satisfied smile. 'Hello, Angie. Detective Sergeant Cannon. What a pleasure! I told you we'd meet again. Let me introduce you.' He gestured to the other suited man. 'This is Detective Inspector Henshaw.'

Henshaw looked like a criminal himself with close-cropped hair and a suit that strained to cover his bulky frame. She knew straight away that he was a man who could look after himself in a fight and who didn't necessarily play by the rules – one of her own kind.

Behind him she saw now that there were not two but three uniformed officers – a young WPC stood to the rear of the group.

'What do you want?' she snapped at Cannon. 'It's New Year's Eve.'

'No need to be like that. We like to work with an element of surprise.'

The other officer, Henshaw, spoke up. 'I'm in charge of the investigation. DS Cannon is here as an observer.' She picked up his East End accent, ironed out but still present. Cannon had been promoted from constable since their last meeting.

'I didn't want to pass up the chance to see you again,' Cannon chipped in.

Henshaw handed her a sheaf of papers. 'This is a warrant to search the premises. You'll find it's all in order.'

She unfolded it. 'There must be some mistake.'

'I don't think so.'

She was feeling nervous now. 'What do you want? Is this some kind of joke?'

'Let's go in,' he said in a tone that allowed no argument.

There was no option but to stand aside. As soon as the five of them were inside the flat, Henshaw issued brisk instructions to the two older uniformed officers. 'Start on the bathroom. Then the bedroom.' He turned to the fresh-faced WPC. 'You stay here.'

The last remark was the most ominous. The presence of a WPC could only mean one thing.

Watching the policemen head off, she felt a rising sense of panic. These people were going to be handling her possessions. 'You're not touching my things.'

'Oh, it's perfectly all right,' Cannon said easily. 'They wear gloves.' He walked confidently into her living room as if he owned the place. 'I was telling DI Henshaw all about you.' He looked around nosily. 'Nice pad.'

'What are you doing here?'

Henshaw followed them into the living room. 'We're acting on information received.'

'Who from?' she demanded.

'I'm not at liberty to say.'

She could have predicted that. 'Is this about the court case?'

'No.'

She felt another chill. So he knew about that. Henshaw scared her: a thief set to catch a thief?

'I want a lawyer.'

Henshaw was staring out of the window with his back to her. 'Fine. Make the call.' He turned round to face her. 'Do you think you need one?'

He walked over to the dining-room table and scanned the papers on her desk. He looked totally in control of the situation. 'Tickets for Miami? Planning a getaway, Sasha?'

She forced herself to calm down. Mentioning a lawyer straight off the bat was a mistake. It had made her look guilty. She would wait to see what they had on her. In the meantime she made an effort to sound nonchalant. 'It's not a crime to go on holiday.'

He nodded in agreement. 'No, it isn't.' He went back to looking at the papers. She noticed that he was being careful not to touch any of them. 'You're renting a luxury condo. And planning to buy a car. How long is this holiday, exactly?'

'That's none of your business.'

He looked up and his voice took on a harder tone. 'I think you'll find it is.'

Cannon chipped in, 'We heard you were about to make a move.'

It was then that the taller of the uniformed officers came out. In his gloved hand he held at the top corner an A4 manila envelope.

'I think this is what you're looking for, sir.'

Henshaw stepped forward. From his pocket he pulled out a pair of latex gloves. Then he carefully extracted the contents from the envelope, handling it as little as possible. Inside was a clear plastic freezer bag, the resealable kind with a plastic zipper. It was full to the brim with white powder.

He looked across at Cannon, who was staring at the package transfixed. 'Cocaine.'

'It was in the bathroom, sir. We unscrewed the bath panel,' the uniformed officer explained.

She could hardly speak. 'That is nothing to do with me,' she rasped.

Henshaw ignored her. He was weighing the plastic bag in his hand. 'Our source told us this is one hundred per cent pure.' He addressed Detective Sergeant Cannon. 'We'll need to send it to the lab. Assuming that's right, the street value could be twenty times what she paid for it wholesale. Once she'd cut it.'

She was regaining her power of speech. 'Cut it! That isn't mine. It's nothing to do with me.'

He carried on as if he hadn't heard her. 'They use all sorts. Glucose, baking powder ...'

'I am not a drug dealer!' she shouted.

He looked at her coldly. 'We found it in your flat. And if

it's got your fingerprints on it we're good to go.'

'It hasn't! I've never seen it before.'

And then her eye fell on the A4 manila envelope. An envelope identical to the one that Alex had handed her on his visit to the flat. Except he hadn't handed it to her. To be precise, he'd handed her a folder out of which she had taken the envelope.

Who else had been in the flat? Who had repaired the loose bath panel? Who had the means to set her up – and a fucking enormous motive?

She felt a desperate, sinking feeling. 'I've been set up.'

Cannon gave a hollow laugh. 'You're telling us you're the victim in this?'

'Yes!'

He turned to Henshaw. 'See what I mean? She's a piece of work. Caught red-handed and she still won't give up.' He turned to Sasha. 'You must be caught up in something pretty big. DI Henshaw's one of the Drug Squad's best officers. He's got the record for the most convictions.'

'Oh, shut up!'

Cannon surveyed the room, gesturing at the view from the window. 'You're not telling us that you paid for all this on a secretary's salary.'

Henshaw nodded sagely. 'It all fits.' He looked at her contemptuously. 'With your contacts you were in a perfect position to run drugs to all your high-class friends. OK, let's go.'

'Go?'

'To the station. You'd better get dressed. Good job you had a shower. I think you get one once a week where you're going.'

'What?'

'We'll oppose bail.' He pointed at the envelope. 'And with that amount we'll win.' He spoke to Cannon. 'Best case she'll be spending six months on remand. Of course, if she's part of a wider ring it'll take longer.'

'I'm not part of anything!'

He didn't appear to be listening. He spoke to the WPC. 'Go with her. Don't let her out of your sight.'

'I am not having her watch me getting dressed!'

Cannon took a step towards her. His voice was slow, deliberate and slightly threatening. 'Angie, you might as well get used to it. It's three to a cell and communal showers where you're going.'

Kate placed Emily's overnight bag in the hallway. Negotiating her daughter's choice of clothes had been tortuous, Kate eventually dissuading her daughter from taking her red velvet party dress in return for being allowed to pack her entire Barbie collection. Later that afternoon she would drop Emily with her parents to stay the night, return home to change into a new and rather sexy cocktail dress and wait for Daniel to collect her. He had spent Christmas with his family. But he was driving back today, already calling her to confirm their arrangements for the evening.

'I'll be round at six thirty with your present. And put on your dancing shoes!'

Upstairs, in her bedside cabinet drawer, she had his Christmas present: a small model sailing boat she had bought in an antique shop in Amersham. Then they would be off to the Upper Thames Yacht Club New Year's Eve Dance – Daniel had two tickets for the dinner and dancing which went on until two a.m. She couldn't remember the last time she had been out for the evening or felt such a sense of excited anticipation or spent quite so long wondering if she would or would not wake up alone on New Year's Day.

'Have you ever visited Aberdeen?'

Not for the first time that evening Nina felt her mind go blank. She was seated next to Graham, a Scottish actuary, and across from Phil, who was something in financial services. Phil had been vague about the details of his work beyond saying that he should have set up as a consultant years ago and he didn't miss the office grind at all.

She knew she had to make an effort. 'No. But I'm sure it's a wonderful city.'

Graham nodded appreciatively. 'It's got its own beach. Not many people down here know that.'

She half listened. The New Year's Eve Ball dinner was being held in the tired dining room of a minor London gentleman's club off Pall Mall. Worn royal blue curtains hung listlessly from the high windows, the carpet was threadbare in places and the food was upgraded school dinner. Her lamb cutlets were close to inedible.

Thanks to the champagne reception, however, and a good supply of wine at dinner, the mood amongst the guests was voluble. Nina and Maria had arrived to be ushered by one of the club staff into an anteroom and greeted cheerfully by Tessa, who wore a tight red cocktail dress and a name badge with 'Guest Co-ordinator' on it. Nina noticed that there was nothing on the invitation to indicate that this was a singles' dating event. Tessa had handed each of them a label with their name printed on it. 'It helps break the ice!'

Once in the reception, Maria had taken a quick glance round the room and turned to Nina with a resigned expression on her face. 'It's always the same.'

'What is?'

'More women than men.'

Nina looked around and saw that this was true.

'They say events will be balanced,' whispered Maria, 'except that they never actually guarantee the same number of men to women.'

Not only were there more women, but they were also a cut above the men: tanned, toned and in long, glamorous evening dresses. Nina realised that her fears of being overdressed in a new black chiffon number were unfounded and that she should have taken Maria's advice about the sunbed.

'Let's mix,' ordered Maria. 'Best foot forward.' She had

367

marched off in her clinging midnight blue to approach a group of six standing by the window. Two steps behind her, like a maiden aunt on chaperone duty, Nina followed.

She stood slightly back, admiring Maria's confidence as she went up cold to a short man in what had to be a rented tuxedo. 'Hi! I'm Maria! How did you hear about tonight?'

He did not get a chance to reply. A sharp-eyed redhead standing next to him spoke first. 'The six of us met over the summer at the Isle of Wight sailing weekend.'

Maria ignored her. 'This is my friend Nina.'

While Maria forged ahead undaunted with the men, Nina struck up a conversation with a friendlier member of the group, Vicky, a heavyset woman in a three-quarter-length washed-silk dress that looked to be from Laura Ashley several years back.

'I just like to get out,' Vicky confided. 'The men lose interest when they find out that you've got four children. My mother's looking after them tonight.' She took a good drink of champagne. 'Still, Becky likes me to come with her,' she said, gesturing at the redhead. 'She's never been married,' she added, in a tone that suggested this was an advantage.

Maybe, Nina thought to herself, never being married gave you a stronger killer instinct, too. Here the women were the hunters and there weren't nearly enough prey to go round. The men, none of them especially good-looking, stood happily while the women circled. Maria was now working the room, shamelessly butting into *à deux* conversations. Nina, meanwhile, felt like going home.

Over dinner, they were seated side by side, Maria dividing her attention between Phil the financial consultant sitting opposite and on her other side a taciturn man who was something in property management. Nina had endeavoured to avoid further conversation with Phil after he had found out that she lived in a flat in London. His eyes had glinted hungrily. 'You might want to consider releasing some of your equity and putting your money in one of our new guaranteed-return investment vehicles. Here's my card.'

Graham the Scottish actuary was nice enough, though, topping up her glass and commiserating about the food. He had wasted no time in confirming that he owned his own home, a three-bedroom detached in Esher. 'It's so important not to stay in rented accommodation after you get divorced. You get left behind on the property ladder.' Then he had got straight to the point finding out about Nina.

'Where do you live?'

'What do you do?'

'Have you got any children?'

He had nodded at her answer to this last point, as if to indicate that her childless status was to her credit. 'I've got two. I see them every weekend and I coach football for my son's team on Saturday mornings.'

It was another world. Belatedly Nina realised that a new partner would very possibly involve a ready-made family.

'My daughter's thirteen,' Graham continued. 'Heather's certainly got a mind of her own!' He gave a nervous laugh, which Nina felt sure hid a bigger story. An image of Susan at that age came to mind. It was not a pleasant thought.

By the time pudding was served she needed a break. Her throat hurt from shouting above the rising noise levels in the room, her face ached from the fixed attentive expression she had tried to maintain all evening and she suddenly felt painfully homesick for Muffin, who would no doubt be asleep on her bed. She felt tired – but more than that she had an unanticipated sense of emotional vulnerability as a result of being not very subtly judged on her attributes as a future partner. It was eleven o'clock. She stood up.

'Excuse me.' Maria looked up at her questioningly. 'I need to make a call,' she explained.

She stepped out into the chill night under the clear sky. The traffic was sparse, every taxi taken. From the distance in the direction of Piccadilly came shouts of London revellers. She took out her mobile and called her mother's number.

Richard answered suspiciously, 'Hello?'

'Happy New Year!'

'You're a bit early.'

She ignored this. 'I wanted to speak to Mummy.'

'Too late,' he said. 'She's gone to bed.'

'Oh.' Her mother had in the past stayed up to watch whatever Scottish celebrity was presenting the Hogmanay television special.

'You should have called earlier.'

'Tell her I'll call tomorrow.' A thought came to her. 'And I'll try and come down.'

'There's no need.' And with that Richard put the receiver down.

She clicked shut her phone. She had no desire to call Susan. Alex would probably call anyway at midnight.

And it would not be appropriate to call Michael. He would be at the farmhouse now, his father insisting on watching BBC 1 – he had never got used to television with advertisements – with Francine by his side. Michael's future was happily settled. Francine, for all her brusqueness, had been right when she had told her that she couldn't live in the past. But tonight had been a glimpse into the future and Nina was sure that she didn't want that either. So she was left with her own imperfect, scarred but possibly salvageable present. It was, as Alex kept saying, surely time to give him a second chance.

It was night-time. Anne knew this because the crack where the curtains didn't meet showed the clear night sky. She was hot and damp, the sheets soaked with her perspiration. She tried to lift herself up, as she had done since waking, but it was hopeless. At the effort, she struggled for breath and, feeling her chest tighten and taking a desperate gulp of air, she felt an awful foreboding. That was the worst way to go – fighting for every hopeless breath.

'Richard.' Even to her own ears her voice sounded weak and barely audible. Her mouth was parched. She wanted water and for the covers to be lifted off her so that she would be cool. She had lost count of the days she had been in bed. A week? Maybe longer?

She knew she was dying. She had wanted to die for so long, to leave all this – and maybe to see Archie again. But did she want to die right now?

'I think you need to see a doctor,' Richard had said worriedly that afternoon. He had given up feeding her the cream of mushroom soup after she shook her head and turned away from him. He had placed his hand on her forehead. 'I'm going to call the surgery now.'

Before she had had a chance to object he had left the room, returning ten minutes later. 'I can't get through,' he said and she caught the note of alarm in his voice. 'The line's permanently engaged.' He paused. Then, 'I should take you to the hospital.'

'No!'

'Mummy—' he began, but she cut him off.

'I said no.' She mustered all the authority she could. 'I'm your mother. Don't tell me what to do!'

He sounded chastened. 'But you're not getting any better,' he said quietly.

'These things take time. You have to let them run their course.'

'Mummy. You have to let me look after you—'

'I'm not going to the hospital and that's final.'

Now she knew that she needed to fight. She needed to call out for Richard again, to reach over to the bedside lamp and bang it hard against the table, to summon every ounce of strength in her body to shout and call and cry.

But did she want to fight? The sleeping tablets stood in the bottle on the bedside table. She could choose not to. She could decide not to go to some fluorescent-lit ward, not to be washed and dressed and ordered about, not to be sat on a bedpan and put in a bath, not to have her cigarettes taken away from her and her meals chosen for her – not to be told what to do and when to do it.

She could keep her independence. She could choose to live as she had always done: according to her rules, her desires and with no one telling her what to do. She thought back to the day of the accident with Monty, the moment when she knew that he was about to throw her, and recalled why she had loved him so much: no one was his master.

She could leave her present suffering behind and avoid that to come. She felt for the bottle of sleeping pills and then for the glass. Please God let there be some water. There was. Quickly she began to take them, one after the other, before she had time for any second thoughts, until the water was gone. She lay back, all her energy spent.

And then there was nothing but silence. She began to feel sleepy, but not the normal kind of sleep. This was heavy, the drug pulling her under with its power.

Then she saw the white light. Was that Archie's voice calling to her?

Spring

Chapter 24

Sasha had watched enough television drama to have some insight into what prison life would be like: meals on metal trays, cramped cells, queues for the telephone. Communal showers. But what television could not convey was the indescribable smell and the constant, echoing noise. Even at night there was noise: doors banging, women shouting – sometimes screaming.

She waited at a small square table in the visitors' room of the prison's remand section.

'You've got a visitor,' the officer had told her. 'I've been looking all over for you.' Sasha got up from her seat in the library and put down her book – *What University Degree?* There was a delay while the visitors were presumably searched and then let in at two p.m. Then there would be more noise – chairs scraping, shouts and exclamations and the whining of all the bloody kids. Belatedly she had realised that one of the many things money bought was quiet: cars with engines so smooth you would hardly know they were running, hushed first-class airport lounges and high-rise triple-glazed Miami apartments. She had told Pat to come alone next time. On her last visit she had brought their father. He had sat, broken, tears falling down his face. 'We'll wait for you, Angie.'

Pat had looked devastated. 'How long are you going to be here?'

She had lied. 'I don't know. Not long. My lawyer's working on it.'

Actually the lawyer had already put a proposal to her from the other side. 'Five years if you plead guilty.'

'No.'

'It's a good deal, Sasha. With good behaviour you'll serve half that and with the time you've spent here you could be out in two.'

'And the money?' She meant the law forfeiting the profits of a drug deal.

'There's nothing we can do about that.' The police had traced most of the payments that over the years she had faithfully deposited. 'Unless you can show that you came by them legally.'

There was no chance of that. She could ask Sir Christopher, Tony and all the others to swear an affidavit that they had voluntarily given her the money, but they were unlikely to agree. So she was stuck with being charged and convicted for a crime she did not commit and never would have done – drug-dealing was for sordid, stupid people who took risks. She was none of those.

She had told Pat to bring her cigarettes. She had resisted the impulse to start smoking again, though most of the women here did. Instead she needed some as currency. Beverley, a hairdresser in for a third drink-driving offence in which she had mown down a traffic policeman, had said she would do her highlights. Fortunately for Beverley and the policeman he had survived, but she was looking at three years minimum. In the meantime, each week Sasha watched the dark roots that lined her parting lengthen. Most of the women had also put on weight. So she exercised on the cell floor, doing press-ups and lunges and sit-ups. Prisoners on remand had more privileges, like wearing their own clothes and supposedly having access to the gym, but since her arrival a sign on the door said that due to staff shortages the gym was closed until further notice.

Finally, ten minutes late, the door swung open and the visitors came in. Sasha scanned their faces, looking for Pat. But it was not Pat she saw. It was Alex.

He came and sat down. He was wearing a suit and expensive camel overcoat. He looked like a visitor not from London but from another planet.

She felt acutely self-conscious. No make-up, not even a trace of lipstick, her hair in need of a wash and tied back in a ponytail, her nails cut short and unpolished, her jeans and grey sweatshirt the same she had had on for three days now. He had never seen her like this. Hell, she had never seen herself like this.

Her sense of disadvantage made her aggressive. 'Come to gloat?'

'No.'

She was caught unawares by the power of the scent of his aftershave. It was hard not to stare at him. He looked so clean. 'Then why are you here?'

'Because you wrote to me and asked me to come,' he said reasonably.

Fuck! She had forgotten about that. In the first week she had been here she had written to him, a desperate, pleading letter in which she had thrown away her pride.

Please, please whatever I have done I am SO SORRY. I know you think I deserve this but PLEASE can we work something out.

Now she shuddered at the thought. Nearly three months later and she had clawed back her courage and her self-assurance and her fighting spirit. The others looked up to her. When there was a complaint with the staff or a dispute between the prisoners, it was Sasha who was called upon to intervene. Sometimes she almost enjoyed herself.

Anxious to forget about that letter she moved the conversation on. 'Why did you do it?' she asked, even though she knew the answer.

He looked at her evenly. 'I think you gave me little choice.'

She nodded. After her arrest she had had no option but to drop the court case.

'I was going to end up paying you a hundred grand to settle,' he continued. 'And at the end of it I had no guarantee that you wouldn't trash my reputation anyway.'

'I would have signed the confidentiality clause.'

'So you say.'

She let it go. 'So how did you get the coke?'

'A friend of a friend.'

She had had a lot of time to think about it. 'That man Howard?'

He nodded as if to acknowledge her guess. He was being very careful, selecting his words with precision. 'He's not involved in the drug trade himself. But he knows people who are – people at a very high level. He didn't know the details; he just gave me a name and number.'

It was strange, but she didn't blame Alex. If anything she blamed herself. It was her own foolish stupidity, combined with mind-blowing arrogance, that had allowed him into the flat. He had played the game so well that she hadn't even known that he was doing it. She had come to realise that she had underestimated Alex.

And he had covered all the bases.

In explaining the story to her lawyer, she had told him enthusiastically about the security camera located outside the flats. 'Alex will be on tape coming into my flat carrying a briefcase!'

The lawyer had looked unconvinced. 'But this man, Alex, was your boyfriend.'

'Ex-boyfriend.'

'Whatever. He was a regular visitor to your flat. And he's got absolutely no criminal history and no involvement with drug-dealing.'

'He's got a friend who was accused of smuggling cigarettes!'

The lawyer had looked at her as if she was grasping at straws. 'I think it's unlikely that this friend is going to admit to supplying Alex with a wholesale quantity of cocaine. Sasha,' he said patiently, 'even if Alex is caught on tape coming to your flat it doesn't prove anything. Your fingerprints are on the envelope. The cocaine was found in your bathroom. As far as the prosecution is concerned, it's an open and shut case. But I'll check anyway.'

He reported back a week later. 'I spoke to the company owner. The tapes are reviewed weekly. If there's nothing suspicious they're wiped and reused.' He paused. 'He did say that a man had rung about a month ago asking the very same question.'

Now Alex leaned forward. 'I want you to know that I don't take any pleasure in this.'

'Really?'

'No.' He had lowered his voice. 'The fact is you gave me no option. Did you really think that I would sit back, watch my marriage and my business reputation go down the pan, and pay you for the privilege?'

A lesser woman would have pleaded with him then. All the things that she had thought of to say to him during that first terrible week as she had lain awake on the hard, narrow bed of her cell came back to her. *Tell the truth, Alex! Please! Tell them it was all a lover's revenge that went too far. What's the worst that can happen? Wasting police time? I'm looking at five years here! I'll pay you every penny I've got, I promise you.*

Now was the time to throw herself on his mercy.

And in doing so to break the first rule of the game: don't play if you can't afford to lose.

There was a pause. Finally she spoke. 'I don't think there's anything else to say. Except, perhaps, congratulations. You won, Alex.'

He shook his head. 'No. I don't think so.' He stood up. 'You got too ambitious, Sasha. But something tells me you'll survive.'

She held his look. 'Oh, I'll do more than survive. I'll prosper. And when I come out I'll be even stronger than before.'

Susan brushed her hair and slowly applied eyeshadow, mascara and eyeliner. It was hard to get close to the bathroom mirror. It was another two weeks until the baby was due and if she got any bigger she would pop.

She longed for it to be over. She was suffering from an aching back, indigestion, swollen ankles and the impossibility of getting a good night's sleep. She slept with her bump bolstered by pillows, waking every two hours in need of the bathroom.

She was wearing the only outfit she could still fit into that was suitable for that morning's meeting with John Kirkpatrick at the Marlow offices of Carruthers & Kirkpatrick, a hideous plum-coloured Jersey dress that she had ordered online, using her new laptop, and forgotten to return in time for a refund. At least it fitted, the huge folds of purple material draped over her so that she looked even bigger, like an upholstered whale.

Richard had already telephoned. 'Now remember what we discussed. We have to be alert. God knows what Nina and Kirkpatrick have been cooking up between them.'

In the weeks immediately following their mother's funeral in January, Richard had barely spoken to Susan, hiding himself away from everyone and spending most of his time in the pub. But lately, with the meeting looming, he had taken to calling by her flat unannounced to discuss the trust. 'Why is it taking so long?'

The meeting and its implications had become his only topic of conversation. He had reported back on his frequent calls to John Kirkpatrick. 'He says that the trust has to be wound up before any information can be given out to the beneficiaries. Apparently there's a provision in the trust that says so – or so he says. Something to do with preventing uncertainty and arguments. Ha! More like giving Kirkpatrick time to swindle us.'

Richard's mood swung alarmingly. At times he was

optimistic. 'Dad would have written that trust so it was watertight. They can try all they like, but it's going to have to be settled the way he wanted it.' At others he was unsure and spoiling for a fight. 'They won't fight fair. We have to be ready to appeal. I've already researched the law and drafted some arguments.'

Susan picked up her handbag. Personally she didn't believe there was any sinister motive behind the delay. Lawyers always took ages. No, what would happen today was that the trust would be divided between the three of them. Richard would throw a fit because he thought he should get more and John Kirkpatrick would tell him patiently that there was nothing that could be done.

All that was at stake was how much the trust was worth. At the very least the value of the house and land, and probably a good deal more if Archie had savings and stocks and shares stashed away.

At any rate it would be enough to buy Susan her freedom. A flat, a car and the option to tell Alex and Nina exactly what she thought of both of them. And if Nina continued to behave as she had since their mother's death, there was no guarantee that she would continue to protect Alex.

For a start, Nina had been a real cow about their mother's funeral. She had totally taken over, organising the whole thing, acting as though she was the only one who was really upset. They were all upset, but Susan had to think of the baby. The fact was that Mummy was not very happy and she had had a good life.

Richard had telephoned Susan on the morning he found their mother. 'You'd better get over here.' He had sounded distraught. 'Mummy's died.'

She had dressed as quickly as she was able to and driven over.

Richard opened the kitchen door as she drove up in the van, hurrying out. 'I found her this morning.' He sounded beside himself. 'I can't believe it!' They went into the kitchen, where he paced up and down, shock consuming his features. 'Do you want to see her?'

Susan shuddered. 'No.'

'It's all right,' he said softly. 'She looks very peaceful.'

Susan shook her head. 'Have you rung Nina?'

'No. The doctor's on his way. Let's get that out of the way first.' His eyes flickered away and Susan realised that he was putting off telling Nina. Was he afraid that Nina would blame him for what had happened?

After the doctor had come downstairs from examining their mother's body the three of them had convened in the kitchen. Now in the presence of the doctor, a locum, Richard seemed even more upset. 'I called the surgery twice yesterday to ask for a home visit. The first time the line was engaged. The second time they said someone would call me back but they never did.' He went on the offensive. 'The calls will show up on my itemised phone bill!'

The doctor, a young locum, had looked worried. 'We're very stretched at the moment. It's the flu.'

'Well, that's what she had.' Richard reeled off the symptoms. 'And then there was her emphysema and her weak heart. But you'll know that from reading her notes.'

The doctor did not respond. Susan had the suspicion that the doctor wasn't familiar with Anne's medical records. He frowned. 'Perhaps you could have taken her to Accident and Emergency.'

'I suggested that! She wouldn't go.' Richard sat down at the table and put his head in his hands. When he spoke his voice was close to breaking. He looked up at the doctor. 'Why? Are you saying she could have been saved with medical attention?'

'No.' The doctor appeared to backtrack. 'No, she was elderly with – as you say – a heart condition and emphysema. I would be inclined to issue a death certificate saying it was death from natural causes.'

Richard looked at him as if not totally convinced, then sighed. 'Well, you're the doctor.'

And then he had called Nina. From that point on, Susan had stayed well out of it. After that Richard barely spoke in those first few days, inhabiting the house like a ghost, spending hours in Anne's bedroom sitting on the bed staring out of the window. Nina organised every aspect of the funeral, from the flowers to the readings and guest list.

After the funeral Nina had insisted on having everyone back to the house for a drink and something to eat. Naturally, Susan had felt tired and gone into the drawing room to put her feet up on the sofa.

'Can't you do anything to help?' Nina had hissed at her.

'I need to rest! I'm pregnant!'

'The baby isn't due for another three months!'

Actually it was two and a half. Since then Nina had been down every week, nosing around at the house and making a big list of all the contents. She was already dropping hints that things were missing. 'Where's Mummy's ruby ring?'

On the day Mummy died, Susan had taken all that stuff, made a list and put it in a safe-deposit box at the bank.

'I don't know! Ask Richard.'

And Alex had started getting really funny, too. After she posted him the bill for the baby's nursery he'd had a fit on the telephone.

'For God's sake. What is this shop?'

'It's in Cookham. They sell really nice French baby stuff. And hand-painted furniture.'

'What's wrong with Mothercare?'

Eventually he had paid up, but not without a lot of grumbling. If this was how it was going to be then frankly, after she'd got all the stuff she needed for the baby, she may as well kill two birds with one stone: tell Nina and cut Alex loose.

*

Nina had come alone. Richard had already made it clear that he would object to the presence of Alex in the meeting. 'It's family only. And he's not family.'

Richard's behaviour since their mother's death had become increasingly unpredictable. Initially he seemed too shocked to speak or act. Then, beginning a few weeks after the funeral, he had made several late-night calls to her, his speech slurred, in which he veered between outpourings of grief and a determination to dwell on every detail of those last days.

'If I hadn't taken Emily over there none of this would have happened. Mummy would still be alive today.'

'Richard, you don't know that. Mummy had an awful lot of health problems.'

He did not appear to be listening. 'Do you think we should sue the surgery? Someone should have come out.' He sounded close to tears. 'I should have taken her to the hospital.'

She had tried to reason with him. 'Richard, you can't think like that. You couldn't make her go against her will – she would have resented you for that. Besides, I could have done more. You were there with her and you did your best.'

'Did I?'

He would ring off abruptly and there would be days when she could not get hold of him. Coming down to Marlow, she would find him sitting silently in the unlit house.

Today's meeting, however, appeared to have provided him with some distraction from his introspection. Lately he had become more aggressive. It was no more than Nina expected. Richard, brought up by Anne as the favourite, naturally assumed that he should gain more benefit from the will. At these times, Nina thought that Anne had not merely spoiled Richard – she had ruined him.

Now the three of them sat opposite John Kirkpatrick, who had just finished making a very gracious speech about their mother.

'She was one of the old school and she will be much missed at the firm,' he concluded.

'We'll all miss her,' said Richard, with feeling.

'Thank you,' Nina responded.

'Now, we come to the matter at hand.'

Nina felt her stomach tighten. He turned to a thick folder on his desk and opened it. 'The details of the trust,' he added unnecessarily.

Beside her Nina saw out of the corner of her eye that Richard was leaning forward. On her other side, Susan fidgeted.

'The trust was set up by your father one year before his death. You should know that at the time he wrote it he was aware that his illness was one from which he would almost certainly not recover.' He looked at each of them in turn. 'He took a great deal of time and trouble with the details. His principal concern was to safeguard your mother's financial future and to ensure that adequate funds were available to support her in her old age.'

At this point John Kirkpatrick paused and took a sip of coffee.

'His second concern was to safeguard the future of the firm. But,' he looked up at them, 'that is a point to which I will return. First we should examine the provisions of the trust as they apply today.' He cleared his throat. 'The trust provides that on the death of your mother the assets should be divided equally between the three of you.'

Immediately, Richard interrupted. 'I will want to challenge that.'

Susan and Nina spoke simultaneously. 'What?'

Richard ignored them and addressed John Kirkpatrick. 'I have assembled a great deal of case law on this point. I believe that as the only legitimate heir I have a good case to take to the Chancery Division of the High Court.'

Nina supposed that she should have expected this, but all the same it was bloody annoying. She exchanged glances with Susan, who rolled her eyes and spun her index finger next to her head to indicate her opinion of Richard.

Only John Kirkpatrick seemed unconcerned. 'That, of

course, is your prerogative. However, in all litigation you must consider whether the costs of taking action outweigh the potential gain.' He turned another page. 'At today's date I should tell you that the trust property comprises the contents of the house and outbuildings. Your mother's jewellery and personal effects are to be divided between Nina and Susan.'

There was a catastrophic silence.

'What?' Richard choked. 'Contents? What about the house? And the land? What about the orchard?'

John Kirkpatrick looked at him evenly. 'Those are not part of the trust.'

Richard had flushed red. 'Well, what are they a part of?'

'On the death of your mother, under the terms of the estate, they pass to Edward Fellows.'

'Fellows,' Richard gasped. 'How? That's not possible. Are you saying Mummy altered the trust?' His voice ran on. 'How did he persuade her to do that? She can't alter the trust. It's set in stone.' He was unstoppable. 'Fellows is trying to swindle us.' He turned to Nina and then Susan as if to appeal to them. 'Don't you see? It's all a conspiracy to rob us of our rightful inheritance.'

Nina was utterly confused.

She put a restraining hand on Richard's arm. Then she addressed John. 'Can you explain to us what this means?'

John Kirkpatrick cleared his throat. 'I said earlier that I would return to the subject of the firm. Carruthers & Kirkpatrick is now a successful firm. But at the end of the 1980s it very nearly went bust.'

'Bust!' Nina could not help herself. 'I thought the firm was solid.'

'It is now. Archie built up a fine reputation in Marlow. But for many years Archie's biggest client was Jack Tyler. Jack, you will recall, was a property developer. Archie did all of Jack's legal work. And as was common at the time, Archie allowed Jack generous terms of credit. Often he needed it until the houses he was building were sold. Until they were sold, Archie often guaranteed the bank loans for Jack, too. For years the arrangement worked well: Jack pulled off the deal, Archie got repaid and they both made a good profit to boot. But then came the property crash of the late 1980s.'

Nina knew what was coming. 'And Jack Tyler went bankrupt.'

'Yes. Jack owed hundreds of thousands of pounds to creditors, including Archie. It looked like the end of the firm. My father and Archie sat down and made plans to declare bankruptcy.'

Nina exchanged glances with Richard, who looked stunned.

'We had no idea!' Nina exclaimed.

'No. You wouldn't have. Archie kept it secret. I don't think your mother knew, either. But just as it looked as if the firm was going to have to be wound up, a guardian angel stepped forward in the guise of Edward Fellows.' He cleared his throat. 'This was the deal. Fellows gave Archie money to pay off the firm's creditors. And he also agreed that after your father's death he would pay an annual income – an annuity – to your mother until her death. In return he would get the house and all the land when your mother died.'

'He's a bloody crook!' Richard exclaimed.

'No. From your father's point of view it was a generous deal. Thanks to Edward Fellows he saved his home, his business and provided for his wife.'

'So what happens now?' Richard asked more sombrely.

John Kirkpatrick sighed. 'You have to think back to the time of your father's death, when he drew up the trust. I believe that you were studying for a law degree then, Richard. Your father believed that in time you would join the business – by the time of your father's death making a good living – and that your financial future would be secured by you working here.'

Richard appeared to have been struck dumb.

'As for the girls, your father was an old-fashioned man. He

thought it was important to provide Nina and Susan with a safe and regular income. So it was agreed with the firm that in return for your father giving up his share in the firm on his death, the rents from the shop lease – currently let to Lily's – would be paid to Nina and Susan.'

John shot Nina a wry smile. 'He made a good deal. At the time that was a modest amount. Of course, since then shop rents on Marlow High Street have soared.'

Richard recovered himself. 'So you're saying I get nothing,' he said, almost to himself. 'Who gets the profit from the firm?'

'The partners. As I say, Archie gave up his share.' Nina thought she saw the trace of a smile play on John Kirkpatrick's lips. 'For you to share in the profits, Richard, you would need to work here.'

He looked back at Nina. 'By the way, when the current shop lease runs out, you might want to consider applying to the planning department for change of use to a restaurant. That would give you even more income.'

He closed the file. 'Are there any questions?'

There were a hundred questions in Nina's mind, but none that John Kirkpatrick could answer. Before she could frame a response she was distracted by the sound of Susan beside her. She was laughing. A loud, unrestrained, full-of-life laugh.

Susan turned to Richard. Her voice was euphoric. 'Richard, I have to tell you this is more than I could ever have hoped for!'

Chapter 25

It was a relief when Michael answered. Nina had been worried on the walk across the fields that Francine might open the door of Edward Fellows's farmhouse. He greeted her with a half-smile. 'Dad's been expecting you.'

Nina managed a small laugh. 'Am I that predictable?'

'No. Dad just hasn't got anything else to think about.' He ushered her in and shut the front door. 'He knew the meeting at Carruthers & Kirkpatrick was this morning.'

'He knew about it?' she said, surprised.

'Mrs Baxter was round last week,' he added, which was all the explanation that was required. He took her coat and lowered his voice. 'How are you?'

She shrugged. 'Shell-shocked, I think. First Mummy. Then all this business with the trust ...' Her voice trailed away and she felt herself begin to choke up. It was natural for him to embrace her. As he did so she had the horrible thought that Francine might be lurking within. So she pulled away.

Michael had come with Francine to her mother's funeral. She had turned heads in a close-fitting black suit and over-sized velvet hat. Her presence – and that of Alex – had made it hard for them to talk. It had been a bitter January day, the icy wind cutting across the churchyard. Alex, it had to be admitted, had been a tower of strength: marshalling the small congregation, dealing with the undertaker and keeping Richard calm. A few days later Michael had called, but she had cut it short, aware that with his father's illness and the wedding plans, he was in no position to take on her troubles, too. In defiance of Francine she had secured him another booking with *Capital Letter* but avoided the shoot itself.

'How's the wedding?' she asked brightly. It was a week away. 'Steaming ahead. Francine's gone into Marlow with her parents for some shopping.'

She wondered how Edward was getting on with Michael's future French in-laws.

Michael anticipated her unasked question. 'Dad's behaving appallingly. Complaining about the food, mainly. Or pretending that he can't understand what they're saying and turning up the television. When I try to reason with him he blames the drugs and says he doesn't know what he's saying.'

At that moment a voice rang out from the direction of the kitchen. 'I'm not deaf, you know!'

Michael raised an eyebrow. 'Come into the dragon's lair.'

Edward was in his usual position next to the Rayburn, the newspaper on the floor next to him. Nina came in and pecked him on the cheek. He looked frail – he had not been able to attend Anne's funeral – and he sounded uncharacteristically worried. 'Where have you been? Your meeting finished hours ago.'

'I went up to the house.'

He nodded. 'You look washed out.'

She felt it. 'I went for a walk. I sat in the orchard for a little while and then I packed up some more of Mummy's stuff.' She sat down on the opposite chair.

'Is Richard still living at the house?'

She nodded. 'I suppose he'll stay there for the time being, until the paperwork's completed. He disappeared after the meeting. I think he went down the pub.'

'Mrs Baxter says he spends every lunchtime in the Crown, and most nights, too. If he's not careful your brother will end up drinking himself to death.'

'Dad!' Michael, who was leaning against the kitchen table, interrupted. He looked askance at Nina. 'I'm sorry,' he said.

'I'm not. The truth will out,' Edward declared. He might look weak, but his opinions were as strident as ever.

'How did Richard take it?' asked Michael.

'Not very well.' She had no energy to describe Richard's furious complaints. He had stormed down the stairs of Carruthers & Kirkpatrick shouting that he would be telephoning the Law Society immediately.

Edward had more to say on the subject. 'He should have joined the firm like Archie told him to.' He turned to Michael. 'But he thought he knew better than his old dad.'

Michael looked exasperated. 'Nina doesn't want to hear your opinions about her family.'

Edward leaned towards Nina. 'You'll be all right with that shop. You want to try to get restaurant use. Of course the council are trying to stop all that, but you can have a go.'

She must have looked taken aback by his insight.

'Oh, just because I'm old doesn't mean I'm stupid.'

'I didn't mean ... What are you going to do with the house?' she asked, keen to move on.

He spoke firmly. 'The house should go with the farm,' he said firmly. 'This one can be rented out. It'll always be damp; doesn't matter what you do with it.' He looked as if there was more that he wanted to say.

'Archie always said that our house should be the farmhouse.' She paused. 'I want you to know that I don't mind about the house. Or the land. John Kirkpatrick said that without you, Archie would have gone bankrupt.'

'Jack Tyler was always bad news. But you can't speak ill of the dead,' he added without irony. 'It all worked out.'

'Did my mother know?'

'No. Archie kept it all from her.' He looked at Michael. 'Couples back then didn't think you had to talk about everything. Or be business partners.' He shook his head at Nina. 'That's what that French girl calls herself. A business partner.' Then he glared at Michael. 'A man looked after his family.'

'I had no idea. We had no idea.' She began to feel

overwhelmed at the memory of Archie and the thought of his solitary struggles. 'I feel so bad! Archie had no one to talk to.' Michael moved closer to Nina and put his arm round her shoulder.

'He did have people to talk to!' Edward objected. 'He had Kirkpatrick. They were partners. What good would it have done bothering his wife and children?'

Her voice ran on. 'And Mummy! It all happened so quickly. I should have done more to help her. I was at a party the night she died!' She broke down then. 'If I had done more, she would probably be alive today.'

'You don't know that. You can't think like that.'

'I should have been there!'

'Who's to say you could have made any difference?' His voice was resolute. 'And what if you had? I don't think that your mother wanted to grow any older, sitting in front of the television, or deaf and half-blind in some home. That wasn't her. Anne was one of a kind – a free spirit – and she wouldn't be told what to do by anyone. She liked to put on that Shirley Bassey woman and dance. You could hear it on a summer's evening, the music coming out of the window across the valley.' He paused. 'Look at me, Nina. She had a good life. She loved Archie. And now she's with him.'

'Do you believe that?'

'Yes,' he said firmly. 'Yes, I know so.' He bore down on the handles of his chair. It was clear that he had said his piece. 'I'm having a lie-down.'

Michael came forward to help him and Edward made an effort to stand up straight. He took a step towards her, reached forward and held her shoulder. 'The past is gone, Nina. Enjoy the present while you can.' Then he turned back to Michael. 'Let go of me. I can manage.'

For a few seconds after his departure Michael and Nina said nothing.

Finally Michael broke the silence. 'Hell, Nina, I had no idea.'

'About the house?'

He nodded. 'Dad's only just told me.' He ran his hand through his hair. 'Will you be all right?'

'Financially? Yes. Susan and I get the shop rent. If anyone causes trouble it'll be Richard.' She felt compelled to defend him. 'The trouble is, he spent his childhood being told by my mother that he would inherit the firm.'

He shifted. 'I didn't just mean financially.'

'Yes,' she said firmly. It was now or never. She knew that if she delayed a second longer she might not tell him. 'I'm thinking of asking Alex to move back in.'

He said nothing, as if to invite further explanation.

'He's desperate to come back. When Mummy died everything between us got put on hold. But I can see that he's trying really hard. He's been working with someone at the church.' She looked up to gauge Michael's reaction to this, hoping for some sign of approval from him. But his face was expressionless. 'And he's been a huge support – he helped me with all the funeral arrangements.' Her voice trailed off. 'I feel I owe him a second chance.'

Michael did not speak for a few moments. 'Even after he had an affair?'

'Yes.' She sounded more positive than she felt. 'Even after that.'

She paused so that she could present her arguments for taking Alex back: because it felt as though she could not delay the decision any longer; because the past in everything that it represented was gone; because she wanted a baby with a desperation that she could never before have imagined; because by some miracle Sasha's past had finally caught up with her and she could never trouble them again; because of the aloneness that had engulfed her after her mother died – because right now it felt like the only option.

She started to try to explain this to Michael, the only person in the world who might truly understand. 'I feel ...'

But at that moment Nina's mobile rang.

She glanced at the number and quickly answered. 'Calm down. I'm coming straight away.' She stood up. 'It's Susan. She's having the baby.'

Michael responded immediately. 'I'll go and get the car. You won't be able to drive; you'll need to look after her.'

'I want an epidural! Now!'

The midwife ignored her. 'You're nearly there.'

Susan looked around for the gas and air. They had started taking it away from her. Nina was holding the mask with one hand, the other supporting Susan in a hold under her right shoulder. Michael Fellows grasped her on the other side as she knelt on the floor. It was the only position that helped, not that it made the pain even close to bearable.

Michael had tried to leave, several times, but Susan had grabbed him. 'Help me squat!'

God, you lost all your dignity doing this, she thought.

Now she eyed the gas and air hungrily. 'Give me that,' she ordered Nina.

Nina looked at the midwife, who appeared to be about eighteen. She shook her head. 'You've had too much, Susan.'

No, no, no. She hadn't had nearly enough.

This wasn't turning out a bit like Flower in the antenatal yoga had said it would. Flower, addressing the group at the end of each session in female warrior pose, had promised that in childbirth each sister would be awed at her own mother-power and psychically bound to the generations of women who had laboured before her. Susan just felt hot, sticky, exhausted and miserable. No one told you how much it hurt or how long it took or how disgusting it was. And the scented relaxation oil recommended by Flower had made her feel sick. Nina had dumped the bottle in the bin outside.

It was the middle of the night and they had been there for hours. Arriving at the hospital, Susan had felt sure she was about to give birth.

'Three centimetres!' the midwife had proclaimed.

The midwife must have got it wrong. It was absolutely impossible to be only three centimetres and for it to hurt so much.

'I want an epidural.'

The midwife laughed. 'Oh, you're not far gone enough for that.'

She had been put on a ward, Nina rubbing her back and spraying her with Evian while Michael Fellows tried to get the hospital pay-as-you-view television to work.

And even when she had got into the proper delivery room and they told her that the baby would come soon, still it had gone on and on.

'I want an epidural!'

'Now come on, Susan. Focus on your breathing.'

She still couldn't believe this was happening. It was another two weeks until the baby was due. She had returned home from the meeting with John Kirkpatrick feeling ebullient, experiencing the kind of high that only knowing you never, ever have to go to work again can produce. Then she had settled down with a plate of Marmite on toast to watch a rerun series of *Knots Landing*. Two hours later her waters broke all over the cream carpet of the flat.

Was this what they meant when they said a baby changes everything? Susan had felt a flush of fear wash over her: the fear of the inevitable, of there being no exit route, for the first time in her life no escape from the consequences of her actions. She was going to have to give birth to this baby and she couldn't run away or get someone else to do it for her.

Soon after that it started to hurt. She didn't want to be alone so she had called the only person in the world that she could rely on. Nina had arrived with Michael Fellows.

He looked awkward. 'We thought you might need some help getting down to the car.'

Nina could have brought the fire brigade for all she cared. She must be having a really quick labour. Surely it couldn't hurt this much at the start?

Nina had said all the right things – focus on your breathing, try to find a position that's comfortable – while Michael Fellows had tried to work the stopwatch function on his wristwatch to time the contractions. Nina quickly set about doing all those things that Susan was supposed to have done already, locating the hospital-supplied list and packing her hospital bag, most of the stuff still in carrier bags with the labels attached.

It was comforting, as if all that had passed between them ceased to matter.

Now in the delivery room Nina was consulting with the midwife. 'Will there be any complications because the baby's early?'

The midwife frowned, then opened her notes. 'No, she's spot on. It's actually her due date.' She closed the file. 'They dated the baby at the scan.'

Nina turned back to her and gave her an exasperated grin. 'You were always hopeless with dates.'

Was she? Susan didn't know anything any more. All she knew was the pain, each wave worse than the last, her body consumed by it and her mind fighting not to be broken down. She had taken advantage of Nina's distraction to grab the gas and air, shoving the nozzle into her mouth and gasping in huge gulps until Nina took it away from her.

Now she felt angry and light-headed. She wanted an ice-cream. 'Give that back! I want a Cornetto.'

Nina's voice sounded distant. 'In a minute.'

'Now!'

She wanted to stop giving birth. She wanted it to be over or, better still, never to have begun. Why should she have to go through this? It wasn't her fault!

She was having trouble thinking straight. 'This is Alex's fault,' she slurred. 'Not my fault.'

'Alex?' Nina sounded shocked.

'Yes.' Susan thought it was obvious. 'He's the dad.'

The midwife spoke quietly to Nina. 'Is that her boyfriend?'

She heard Nina reply, bewildered, 'No, it's my husband.'

The midwife laughed. 'Oh, they say all sorts. It's the gas. It gets them confused.'

She wasn't confused! She tried to speak but another contraction caught her.

Nina caught hold of her shoulder.

'Oh, God,' she cried out. 'I need to push!'

'Hold on,' the midwife said urgently.

'I can't.'

'Come on,' Nina said encouragingly. 'Do what she says.'

'Fuck off.'

And then it was all just a God-awful nightmarish fight – a visceral, bloody struggle which nothing could ever have prepared her for, until she was so desperate for it to be finished that finally she took every ounce of her strength and, in a force of will, heaved the baby's head out. After a few more pushes, it was all over.

Michael cheered, Nina hugged her and the midwife held up the baby.

'Do you want to hold him?'

Susan barely had the energy to shake her head. She wanted only to be sure that the pain had finished. She needed to be sure this birth was absolutely over. She didn't feel elated, triumphant or in any way keen to bond with the baby. She just felt exhausted.

So the midwife took the baby over to the transparent plastic cot accompanied by Nina. After a few moments, Nina called over her shoulder to Susan in a voice that betrayed more than a hint of confusion.

'He's a little redhead! Just like Gerry.'

Howard pushed a piece of sweet and sour pork disconsolately around his plate.

Jemma reached over. 'If you don't want that, I'll have it.' And she deftly picked it up with her chopsticks and popped it in her mouth.

Even the top-price set menu at the Mandarin couldn't lift his spirits. Howard had been down in the dumps since last week's meeting with the brief. Beforehand he had been confident.

'He's the best. If he can't get me off, no one can.'

Afterwards he had adopted the look of a condemned man. 'Two years!'

The barrister, who was posh but no fool, had given it to them straight. 'The prosecution can prove a pattern of smuggling from Spain to Britain going back over several years.'

Privately Jemma had expected as much. Howard had looked woebegone when he came clean to her. Detective Inspector Taylor, who had arrived at their house with two uniformed officers, had let them have five minutes together before he took Howard to the station. They spoke in quick, hushed tones in the conservatory.

'They're doing me for the cigarettes.'

'You told me you stopped all that!'

He shrugged. 'The money's so good, Jem.'

She had slapped him hard around the head for that. 'How could you? How could you risk everything?'

But there was more. When he recovered his balance he added, 'And they're going to charge me with art fraud.'

'Art fraud!'

He sighed. 'Barbara's been forging these paintings. Little pictures on bits of wood.' He held up his hands to demonstrate. 'They're only small. Pictures of saints with those gold rings round their heads.'

'Halos?'

'Yeah. Halos. There's a big demand, Jem.' He could not, even after his arrest, conceal the excitement from his lowered voice. 'People want these paintings from Eastern Europe. From the churches, like. Only you're not allowed to take them out of the country. So Dimitri thought Barbara could make them instead.' Howard made forgery sound the obvious solution. 'He showed her some photos from Russia and she copied them. Then she suggested that we put them on the yacht to bring them to Britain.' He adopted his how-could-I say-no expression. 'She said she really needed to make some money fast – something about Brian finding her credit card statements. Jem, they go mad for them in Chelsea! They pay top-whack prices.'

When the police had come to arrest Howard it was clear that they were satisfied that they had a watertight case. Later Detective Inspector Taylor had spoken to her at the station.

'We've charged him with cigarette smuggling and art fraud. He might not get bail on account of you having a second home in Spain.'

She had looked him straight in the eye. 'You're sure about all this?'

He had sounded almost apologetic. 'We didn't forget about your husband after the Gloucestershire raid. We carried on with the surveillance. We've got tapes, phone records and the photographs of the contraband found on the yachts.' He hesitated. 'And my guess is that Barbara and Dimitri will try to make a deal.'

Howard had made bail but he had had to surrender his passport and he wasn't allowed to leave the house except to go to the office. Lately she had begun to wish they'd kept him in the station cells. He hung around the house like a black cloud, veering between bouts of self-pity and bursts of self-justification. 'It was all Barbara's idea. She's the brains behind the operation.'

Even by the time of their meeting with the barrister, Howard still seemed to be in a state of denial. In response to the barrister's last points he leaned forward in his chair.

'What if I say I didn't know about it?' Howard interrupted.

'You own the yachts. And unfortunately Barbara and Dimitri have sworn affidavits saying you did know all about it. There are phone records to show a pattern of contact

– somewhat more than would be required to discuss the pool-cleaning schedule,' the barrister added, anticipating Howard's next objection. 'And then there is the small matter of the religious paintings.'

The paintings. Jemma didn't care about those. She had been so convinced that Howard was having an affair with Barbara – sulking about not going to Spain for New Year – that the news of the paintings had come as a relief. The pair of them had been keen to get together not for a romantic tryst but to discuss their joint criminal activities.

Thus Howard would be doing time not only for cigarette smuggling but also international art fraud. Meanwhile, Barbara would be marooned in a Spanish prison and Brian, who called Jemma one night drunk to trade notes on their law-breaking spouses, was talking about divorce.

'If she thinks I'm going to believe that her and that slime-ball Dimitri were just friends then she's got another think coming.'

Now Howard looked up to get the bill. Later on he had scheduled another computer lesson for her. He had gone into overdrive, bombarding her with information, all of which she already knew, and interviewing for someone to run the business in his absence.

But Jemma had other plans. There wasn't going to be a manager. As soon as Howard was safely locked up she was going to sack the new manager and run the businesses herself: the car showrooms and the restaurants and everything else, too. She'd watched Howard for twenty years and it wasn't difficult.

For Howard prison was, admittedly, a catastrophe. But every cloud has a silver lining. There had been no affair with Barbara. There would be no affairs – or come to think of it any contact with any other women for the next two years. And Jemma would finally get to do something constructive with her newfound accounting knowledge. She was one of those women she had spent years reading about in magazines, starting a new career when everyone else was retiring.

Howard downed the last of his lager. 'Will you be all right without me?' he said for the umpteenth time since his arrest.

'I'll manage somehow.'

Chapter 26

Alex ushered Nina onto one of the benches that overlooked the small lake of the Kyoto Garden in Holland Park. In summer the garden would be ablaze with azaleas and orange-red acers. For now the foliage was in hibernation. Nina looked out on to the small faux beach composed of large round stones, the minimalist slab walkway across the lake, the elegant stone pagodas and the small waterfall cascading gently down.

'I think we should go on holiday. In fact, I have a plan.'

'Alex ...'

He raised a hand. 'A complete getaway in the Bahamas. I think it's just what we need.'

And then he was off, describing the hotel: the beachfront bungalows, the gym and watersports, the spa and the choice of three restaurants.

At ten o'clock on a Sunday morning the park was quiet. A young father with a small boy in a pushchair parked next to them. Nina watched as he pulled a bag of bread from his rucksack. The two of them went hand in hand to the water's edge and began feeding the ducks.

'If we went in a month that would give me time to give notice on the apartment and get settled back in. And you can get your meeting out of the way.'

Later that week she and Susan were going to see John Kirkpatrick to discuss the running of the shop.

He took hold of her hand. 'Darling, we're doing really well. We see each other all the time.' This was true. Since

Anne's funeral they had dinner together two or three times a week, often shopped at the weekend – Alex, noticing her new wardrobe, had looked discomforted and insisted on taking her clothes shopping – and had even attended a few social events. They had gone to their neighbours Sally and Jonathan's recent dinner party and nothing ill had passed between them. 'It's the obvious next step.'

She said nothing.

'I know you have concerns about me moving back. That's natural. But we have to take the plunge sometime.'

Her mind turned to sharing a bed. A magazine article that Maria had clipped for her said it was quite normal for it to take a year or even longer for a couple in their position to resume their sex life.

He put his arm round her. 'We have to move forward,' he said conclusively. 'This is the right time. It's not as if divorce is an option,' he added, almost as an afterthought.

She looked over to the small boy, who was dressed in bright blue wellingtons and a red quilted jacket, a matching striped navy and red scarf tucked into his coat. He lifted his arms up to be held and his father swung him high up in the air with swooping motions as if he was an aeroplane. It was impossible to think of Alex ever doing that. He would be a dutiful father, never anything less than a good provider and a diligent attendee at school events when his work schedule permitted.

The holiday he proposed was in a month – plenty of time for him to finish refurbishing Earls Court and let the flats.

The life he proposed was exactly as it had been before.

She turned to him and her heart was pounding. 'Alex, I think divorce is an option.' She paused to summon up her courage. 'That's what I want.'

For a moment he seemed unable to speak. She hardly dared look at him, but forced herself to meet his eye. He looked astonished, searching her features as if to detect some sign that she was joking. 'What?'

She could not hold his gaze. She looked away, out on to the still water. 'Alex, this isn't going to work.'

'Yes it is.' It was an emphatic statement, almost as though he felt that by sheer force of will he could persuade her. 'We can have a good life – and children. I've already conceded that.'

She shook her head. 'Conceded that,' she repeated, turning to him. 'That's the right expression. This is a marriage, not a deal. I don't want to bring up our children on my own while you live at the office. I don't want to feel that this baby is a concession you've made. I want a marriage, Alex.'

How could she explain it to him? 'I want to feel that I live with my partner, my equal, someone with whom I can share my every thought and feeling and dream. And you are not that person.'

'Is this about Michael Fellows?' he said angrily.

In a way. 'No. He's getting married next weekend.'

'Have you been seeing him?'

Not recently – or at least not on purpose. The hospital drama didn't count. 'No.'

He ran his hands through his hair. 'I just don't under-stand.'

'Alex ...'

How could she tell him that she should never have married him, that Edward Fellows had been right when he said that the secret of a happy marriage was to pick the right one in the first place? How could she tell him that no amount of counselling and compromise, no amount of working at their relationship or rebuilding trust, was going to fix the fundamental problem between them? She didn't love him any more. She had once, as much as it was possible to, but not now.

'Why?' he said, bewildered. It was heartbreaking to watch him and it would have been so easy then to backtrack, so easy to slip into all the good and sensible reasons why they should stay together.

There had been no moment of blinding revelation; no

point in time when she realised it was over between them. But when she thought about spending the rest of her life with him it filled her with a dull depression, a sense of settling for second best, of continuing to live her life in the safe, slow lane. At some level she had known but tried to ignore the voice telling her that if she went back she would always regret it.

She realised now, too late, that she had made the wrong choice fifteen years before. She had tried to deny it, to make the sensible decision, to pretend otherwise. But she felt it every time she went to the farmhouse, every time she saw Michael, in every easy moment they spent together. She thought back to when they had been at the hospital together, the way they could communicate without speaking, how each could sense the next move of the other, the intuitive dance by which they could draw near.

She had made the wrong choice fifteen years before – but that was no reason to repeat the mistake.

He was angry now. 'I know I've made a mistake, a terrible mistake. But I've worked really hard to repair the damage.'

'I know. But this isn't all about Sasha.'

'Yes it is! If she hadn't come along you wouldn't be saying any of this.'

She nodded her assent. 'But she did come along, didn't she?'

She believed Alex now when he told her over and over again that he had never loved Sasha. She also believed that this was one of the reasons why the relationship between the two of them had worked, why their sex life had doubtless been so electric, why he had kept going back for more. Sasha had provided excitement and counsel but never demanded intimacy of him. Alex had a part of his heart that was closed, a part of his soul that was shut down, and she didn't believe that however long they spent together he would ever truly open himself to her. He would be loving and attentive but never completely unguarded: he couldn't be.

What he offered was a modern marriage of convenience.

He stood up. 'This is ridiculous. I'm not going to accept it, Nina. You're obviously …' he stopped to search for the right word, 'still upset by losing your mother. That's fine. I can wait.'

And then, as if fearing that he would lose control, he strode off in the direction of Kensington High Street. Still seated, she watched him leave. As he reached the pathway and disappeared from her sight she had an involuntary impulse to stand up, run after him and call out, 'I was wrong.'

But she stayed seated. She wasn't wrong; she was alone. The little boy was running up and down now, chased gently by his father, laughing helplessly at the pleasure of the game. He looked carefree and happy, all the choices in his life still to be made, all the consequences still to be faced.

Susan could not remember the last time she had been so furious. It was just like when they were children. Archie thought he had been so clever leaving the two of them the shop rents, but it was abundantly clear to Susan that bossy Nina was going to team up with miserly John Kirkpatrick and she would be outvoted on every point regarding the shop. In silence she descended the stairs from the Carruthers & Kirkpatrick offices where they had just finished their meeting with John to discuss Lily's.

On the pavement Susan rounded on Nina. 'You never listen to me!'

Nina looked at her impatiently. 'Yes, I do. Susan, this is just the way it has to be. It's good business practice.'

'You know I need the money now. It's all right for you.' She was walking very fast now in the direction of the flat, where her friend Libby was looking after Zak.

Nina was trying to keep up with her as they weaved in and out of the weekday shoppers. 'We can talk about this. Let's go for a walk.'

Reluctantly Susan slowed down. Perhaps if Nina heard

how difficult things were for her she would be a bit more reasonable.

At that morning's meeting Susan had fully expected to be presented with a large cheque and for the whole thing to take about five minutes. Instead it had gone on for over an hour – and she had barely got anything at all. She had sat bored as Nina and the solicitor had made a list of expenses that had to be provided for before either of them could get any money.

'Legal fees for updating the trust; provision for business rates; service charge for the building as a whole; buildings insurance and the sinking fund.'

'What's that?' Susan had asked irritably.

Nina answered, 'You set aside money every month to provide for large items of expenditure in the future.'

God, she was so patronising.

'But I need some money now!'

Kirkpatrick had exchanged glances with Nina, which had made her even more cross. It felt like Susan was five years old again. He spoke as if he was doing her a favour. 'I can give you an advance and send you the balance when we've set aside the expenses.' He had gone off to write her a cheque. As he handed it over she saw it was much less than she needed. And there was more bad news. 'That's the gross amount.' He had looked hard at Susan. 'You'll need to set aside a percentage of that for tax. An accountant will be able to advise you.'

More expenses! Susan, who had spent her life paid in cash, had always been a strong supporter of taxing the rich. Now she was beginning to have second thoughts. No wonder all these wealthy people hid their money overseas – who could blame them?

'Let's walk to the lock,' Nina suggested. As they turned left into Station Road they fell into a normal walking pace. Susan turned over the events of that morning in her mind. It was clear to her that Nina was at the heart of her problems. Nina would make all the decisions about the shop with John Kirkpatrick, Nina would get half the money – and Nina didn't need it! It was just the same as it had always been since they were children: Nina was always in charge.

She began to seethe with resentful thoughts. Susan, after all, had Zak to think of now. Archie should have written the trust so that anyone with children got more money. Susan had had nothing from Alex since Zak was born. He had called her a couple of days after she got home from hospital. He did not offer his congratulations.

'Nina's told me everything. I assume you're not going to pursue this any further? We're in agreement that Gerry is in fact the father?'

She had said nothing to that.

'Good. Susan, I'm prepared to be reasonable. I'll pay the rent on the flat until I can give notice on the lease – there's a six-month break clause, fortunately. Provided you are prepared to be discreet, I won't require repayment. That will give you and Gerry time to make other plans.'

So she wasn't homeless yet, but she was penniless. Gerry had been to see the baby but had stalled at paying any money.

'But you were a runner-up in the BBC competition!' she had shouted at him. 'And you've got an agent now! And they must have given you money for the pilot!' Gerry had been noticed by one of the judges, who had put him in touch with an agent. To Susan's further amazement a contract with an independent production company had followed.

He had stuck his hands in his pockets. 'Susan, it's just six episodes. Who knows if it'll even get made? I need that money to live on.'

Of course. Gerry had, as soon as the ink was dry on the short-term contract, jacked in his job to 'follow his dream'.

'And I have to pay maintenance for Harry and Samantha,' he said resignedly.

Nina was talking now as they walked down St Peter's Street. 'Look. This is just a problem of cash flow. In the long run the shop will give you a comfortable income. It'll pay for somewhere to live and a car.'

Comfortable! Susan had expected so much more than that. What about clothes, holidays and all the little luxuries?

Nina continued, going on and on about budgeting and how she needed to write down what she spent in a notebook and how important it was not to run up credit cards because that only cost more money in the long run.

'And when you get a job that'll give you spending money,' Nina concluded.

The whole damn point of the shop was that she never had to work again! By the time they reached the lock, Susan had had enough of Nina's financial lecture.

It was deserted, the cold March morning air dissuading any walkers. There was no sign of the lock-keeper: only a few boats came through at this time of year. In the summer the buttercup-yellow lock-keeper's cottage would be decorated with overflowing hanging baskets, the pavement packed with tourists, but now they were the only visitors.

On the curved walkway bridge that spanned the river Susan stopped. 'Oh, shut up! It's all right for you. You've got a business and Alex to support you. You don't even need to work.'

Nina looked at her with incredulity. 'So you think you should get it all?'

'I think I need it more than you do. I've got Zak.'

'Susan, you chose to have Zak. Surely you thought about how you would manage before you decided to do that?'

Who did that? Priggish, smug, boring people like Nina no doubt.

'You wouldn't understand,' Susan countered dismissively. 'You don't have children. All you and Alex have to do is spend your money on yourselves.'

'That's not true!'

'Yes it is. You've never known what it's like to struggle. Dad always looked after you more than me.'

Nina looked frustrated now. 'Oh, for God's sake. Is that what this is all about – Dad? He treated us the same, Susan.'

'No he didn't. I had to make my own way.'

Nina gave a bitter laugh. 'Like you had to steal and lie? You made him sick with worry.'

It wasn't that simple. 'You don't know anything.'

Nina sounded as if she was making an effort to control her temper. 'Look. Have you ever thought about all the good things in your life? You have a lovely baby, a nice flat and a guaranteed income for the rest of your life.'

'So have you! Alex can look after you.'

'No, actually that isn't the case. Alex and I are ...' Nina hesitated, 'going our separate ways.'

Susan was stunned. 'Because of Sasha?'

Nina sighed, looking out towards the fast-flowing weir. 'I'm not going to go into the details, Susan. It's a very complicated situation.'

That did it. Even when she was totally in the wrong, still Nina had to pretend she was right!

'I told you about her! And you ignored me.'

'I know,' Nina said flatly. 'I should have listened to you, I'm sorry.'

'Sorry!' Nina needed to apologise properly. 'You spend your whole life acting like you're better than me and now you think you can just say sorry.'

It was as though a fury had overtaken her. All the stress of the baby, all the late lonely nights, all her frustration that things had not worked out exactly as she had planned, spilled over.

'You bitch, Nina. Alex was screwing Sasha and you just can't admit that I was right.'

Nina flinched. 'Do you think this is easy for me?'

Susan was screaming now. 'What about me?'

But Nina began to walk away. 'I'm not going to listen to you any more.'

That was how it always was: Nina would go to her room and her mother would turn to Susan and tell her irritably not to make a fuss or be a cry-baby or pester her big sister because she had her important homework to do.

But now there was no one to tell her to be quiet or read quietly or go into the garden and play.

Susan shouted, 'I screwed him, too, Nina.' She ran behind her. 'At your weekend party, I came downstairs and found Alex in the drawing room and we fucked each other.'

Nina stopped.

'It was Alex who paid for the flat.' She laughed. 'Think about the dates. Didn't you guess? And he paid for all the baby things. He thought he was the father.' She could not stop herself. 'We fucked, Nina. Don't you get it? And all the time you thought you were living your perfect life with your wonderful husband.'

Nina turned round and walked back towards her. Instinctively Susan took a step back, glad all of a sudden that they weren't standing on the footbridge.

'What the hell are you talking about?'

And then Susan began to feel just a little scared. 'It's true,' she said quietly. 'I'm just telling you the truth.'

Nina stared at her for what seemed like for ever. Finally she nodded. When she spoke it was calmly and very quietly. 'Why are you telling me this?'

Susan faltered. No words came to mind.

Nina shook her head. 'Do you really hate me that much?'

And in an instant Susan realised that she didn't hate her sister – she wanted to be her. 'No! I just ...' Her voice petered out. Nina's silence, the hurt that consumed her face and her pose of utter stillness was much, much worse than any shouting. Susan had the feeling of just having made a really terrible mistake. 'It was nothing. We were drunk. It didn't mean anything ...'

But Nina had already begun to walk away.

Chapter 27

Nina drove across Marlow Bridge into the town, deliberately avoiding looking at the church to her right. It was unfortunate timing. She had had no option but to come back down to Marlow the day before Michael and Francine's wedding: Richard had organised the auctioneers to come in to appraise the furniture: it had seemed the simplest way to prevent the arguments that would otherwise arise about who got what: sell the lot of it and split the money.

It was a cold but sunny day and she had spent the journey listening to Bach in a not entirely successful attempt to calm her nerves.

Earlier in the week she had turned off her mobile, tired of the stream of messages. First there had been a contrite message from Susan: 'I'm sorry. We need to talk.' She erased it. Then Susan had clearly been in touch with Alex because four calls, none of which she answered, arrived in quick succession. He had not tried to deny it. It was all, apparently, a terrible drunken mistake.

As for clients, the last thing on her mind right now was miniature sushi. They would have to wait.

She pulled up at Orchard House armed with a pad of paper and a pile of sticky notes. The best that could be hoped for was that Richard would keep quiet, but she had little hope of that. She parked, went round to the back door and walked into the kitchen. It was piled up with cardboard boxes on every kitchen counter. Richard came down the stairs. He was still living at the house. Edward had been very reasonable about giving them time to pack up, but she needed to tackle him about his plans.

He caught her by surprise. 'Susan told me what happened. I'm sorry.' He sounded genuine. He shook his head. 'Sleeping with your sister's husband. That's about as low as it gets. She's really done it this time.'

'I agree.' It still felt like a punch, a blow that you never saw coming, which makes you think at the time that you'll never get up. She was unsure if she would ever rebuild a relationship with Susan – or even if she would try. As for Alex, in his fourth message he signalled the beginning of his acknowledgement of defeat. 'I suppose you'll be seeing a lawyer. Let me know what you decide. Let's just try to be civilised, shall we?'

Richard put on the kettle. 'Cup of coffee?'

'Thanks.' There was something different about him, but she couldn't work out what. 'So,' she said as casually as possible, 'what are your plans?'

He looked up. 'I went to see Edward. I'm going to rent the house for a couple of months. It's OK – we can still go ahead and sell the furniture. I don't need much. Then I'll take my share of the money from the contents and put down a deposit on a flat.'

She saw then that he had shaved. And he was wearing a shirt and tie.

'And then what?'

He hesitated. 'Let's sit down.'

Her spirits sank as he led the way into the drawing room: she had the unwelcome feeling that Richard was going to ask her for money.

Sure enough his opening words were as she anticipated. 'I have an idea.' He looked across at her almost nervously. But the next sentence was a surprise. 'I'm going to start a record stall.' He stopped abruptly. 'What do you think?' He seemed to be seeking her approval.

She was caught off guard. 'Records?'

'Hmm. LPs. Vinyl. Buying and selling. Lots of people still want that stuff. Hell, I know most of them. When Susan told me how much Roger makes selling candles I figured I had to do as well as that.'

His voice was now filled with enthusiasm and she realised that it was his demeanour as well as his appearance that had changed. Where had this newfound resolve come from?

'I've wanted to do this for years. I know as much as the local dealers – probably more. I could even start a website and sell on that. I could trade worldwide.'

She was pleasantly surprised. 'I had no idea you would want to do that.'

He shook his head. 'Can you imagine what Mummy would have said? She only put up with me doing the building because I told her it was temporary and I made good money. The only thing she wanted was for me to join the firm.' A new note of bitter regret had entered his voice. 'Even when I was little Mummy used to come up to my room and tell me to work hard at school and one day I'd go into Daddy's office and do what Daddy does.'

'She did!'

He nodded. 'Except I never wanted to. I liked being out and about. I hate all that book stuff. But I felt I had to. I tried to tell her, but she didn't want to hear. Christ, she made me feel so trapped. I was her little boy and I felt I had to make her happy.' He looked over at her and his expression was sheepish. 'I didn't drop out of law school, Nina. I failed the first-year exams.'

'I had no idea!'

'That's between you and me. Well, Kate knows, too. Don't tell Susan,' he said, rolling his eyes.

'Of course not.' It had never occurred to Nina that being the favourite might be a burden. 'You and Mummy always seemed so close,' she commented.

He shook his head. 'I used to envy you. You had the freedom to go and do what you wanted. She made me feel guilty when I moved out. I was twenty-one! When I flunked my degree I went into building thinking at least I could make some money and impress them that way. I never wanted to do it.'

It was a revelation.

He looked up at her. 'I know I've been a prick, Nina. I know I need to get my act together. I can't spend the rest of my life in the pub. But up to now I've felt so ...' He was clearly searching for the right word.

'Unmotivated?' she hazarded.

'Yes! Like I was doing things because I had to. It made me feel permanently pissed off.' He slowed his voice. 'I haven't always done the right thing. I know that. And I'm going to have to live with that.' He put his head in his hands. She had the feeling that he was talking about the last days with their mother. He seemed to be on the brink of telling her something but was holding back.

'Richard,' she said gently, 'what is it?'

He gave a deep sigh. 'Nina, there's something I haven't told you. Something I haven't told anyone,' he corrected himself. He was speaking very quietly. 'I think Mummy took sleeping pills.'

Nina felt a jolt of shock. 'On the night she died?'

'Yes. Not all of them. But I'm sure there were some missing.' He looked at her and his expression was anguished. 'And it's all my fault! I left them next to her on the bedside table. All she had to do was lean across and take them.'

Nina was struggling to take it in. 'Are you sure?'

He nodded. 'Don't you see? If I had put them out of her reach she would still be alive today.' He looked as if he was about to break down.

Seeing his distress, Edward Fellows's words came back to her. Anne was one of a kind, a free spirit, and she wouldn't be told what to do by anyone.

Quickly she got up and went over to where Richard was sitting on the sofa. She took hold of his shoulders and turned him so that he was facing her. At that moment the years dropped away – she was the eldest and he was her little brother. 'Now listen to me, Richard. Even if she did take those pills, there was nothing you could do about it. Once Mummy made her mind up about something, nothing stood in her way. She was a fighter; she would have got to those pills on her hands and knees if she had to.' She touched his cheek. 'Don't you think I've asked myself the same sorts of questions? I wasn't even here. You were with her and you did your best.'

'I should have made her go to the hospital,' he objected.

'Against her will?'

He said nothing.

'Richard,' she continued, 'she's gone. And if she went on her own terms then that was exactly how she lived her life, too.'

For a while they sat side by side saying nothing. Then Richard spoke. 'I miss her, you know. I miss talking to her and watching television. I never guessed I'd miss her so much.' Then he continued as if choosing his words with care, 'But now – now that Mummy's gone – I've realised that I can make a fresh start. I feel so guilty saying that. You must think I'm a complete bastard.'

She understood then. Richard too was claiming the present. 'No. I don't think that at all.'

'I've got nothing left to lose,' he said simply. 'Mummy's gone. Kate's going to want a divorce. I've lost everything, Nina.' He looked around the room. 'For what?' He gave an empty laugh. 'But in a way that makes everything simpler. Can you understand that?'

'Yes. You can get so wrapped up chasing things, or trying to hang on to what you've got, that you forget what you really want.'

'I really think I can make a go of the record stall,' he said earnestly. 'And I know I can be a good father to Emily.'

'I'm sure you can. And I'll help in any way I can.'

'Will you?' He was clearly pleased in a way that touched her. Then a thought seemed to occur to him. 'What do you think will happen between you and Susan?'

She shrugged. 'God knows. I don't know how we can come back from that.'

'Maybe after a bit of time,' he said cautiously. 'I mean, it's just the three of us now, isn't it? We're still family.'

She had yet to think of it that way, the three of them as a united family. They had always seemed so fractured.

But now Richard looked painfully anxious. 'Just don't make any hasty decisions.'

She could almost laugh: Richard, the hot-head, advising caution.

He regarded her with a concern that she had rarely seen before. 'And what about you? Are you going to be all right?'

She was still the eldest. 'Yes. I'll be fine,' she said cheerfully.

In truth she had no idea. In truth she felt that she was stepping out into the unknown, into a cold new world where none of the previous certainties that had supported her life existed any longer. She cast her gaze around the drawing room. In this house she had always felt safe, never doubting that there was an order to her world, blithely assuming that she would grow up and get married and have children just as Anne and Archie had done. In this gilded world she had believed that infidelity and betrayal and all its ugly aftermath would escape her.

And she had believed that in doing the right thing, a good outcome would prevail.

She still believed that. Which was why, even when it had been so tempting, she had not called Michael. To contact him, with the purpose of relying on him for support as he prepared to marry another woman, would make her little better than Sasha. It would be the ultimate betrayal, the betrayal of her own values, to come between Michael and Francine for her own selfish ends.

The time for contacting Michael had been fifteen years ago, not today.

Now, speaking to Richard, she continued with her optimistic tone, endeavouring to sound more upbeat than she truly felt, 'I expect Alex and I will sell the flat and split the proceeds. I'll buy somewhere smaller.'

'In Marlow?' he said hopefully.

'I haven't really thought about it. I might go travelling for a while.'

'Oh.' He looked taken aback by that. 'I didn't think you were the backpacking type.'

Nina laughed. 'I'm not sure what my type is any more. Maybe that's what I need to find out.'

Richard got up. 'I'll make that cup of coffee.' But before he had a chance to go into the kitchen his gaze was caught as he looked out of the drawing room window. He turned back to her. 'On second thoughts, I think you're needed outside.'

Of course, the auctioneers. They must be starting in the outbuildings.

'Shall we go together?'

He looked puzzled. 'No. You go on your own.'

She stepped briskly outside, but no one was there. She walked round to the driveway, but saw no car or van. Thoroughly confused now, she traced her steps back towards the kitchen door. It was then, when she glanced in the direction of Fellows Farm, that she saw him. He was walking across the near field, his stride hampered by the wet pasture, traces of the morning dew still thick on the ground. She stared at him hard to be sure that it really was Michael. It was. But he was the last person she had expected to see that day – there must be a hundred and one errands to be completed before tomorrow's wedding. She stood still and watched as he climbed the fence and walked towards her across the lawn.

He sounded almost annoyed. 'Why didn't you tell me you were coming?'

'I came to see the auctioneer,' she said, confused. She had declined her invitation to the wedding.

'Oh.' Michael seemed nonplussed. 'I was worried about you. Not that there's anything to be worried about,' he added quickly.

He wasn't making any sense.

'Nina, you don't bear any responsibility. None at all,' he said slowly. 'I don't want you to think that.'

The thought came to her then that something terrible had happened to his father: some shock brought on by the revelations about the trust and her last visit?

'How's your father?' she asked.

He looked puzzled. 'Elated. He even opened some of the champagne earmarked for the wedding.'

'Why?'

He looked at her, still more confused. 'Didn't you get my messages?'

She felt foolish. 'Actually I switched my phone off.' She had no intention of going into the reasons why.

He looked at her now more closely, not speaking, clearly making connections in his mind. 'You don't know, do you?'

'Know what?' she said, unable to conceal the trace of impatience in her voice.

He looked away, towards the farmhouse, and then back to her. 'The wedding's off,' he said quietly.

'Why?' was all she could manage to say.

'Because it was the wrong thing to do,' he said simply. 'Because I forgot what I really wanted.'

Nina was finding it impossible to take in. Images of an empty church and a wedding reception with no guests filled her mind. 'How's Francine?'

'Steaming mad,' he said, and from his tone she could imagine the scenes that had followed his decision. 'She left for France, but not before telling my father that he'd put a spell on me and it was all his fault. I'm not sure the studio will be standing when I get back.'

'Oh, my God!'

'It's OK. I'm going to come back and work here, anyway. I'm going to do what I always wanted to do – photograph people. David Stratford put me in touch with some political contacts. I never wanted to do houses.'

The fact that the house brochures had been Francine's idea hung in the air unspoken. Michael seemed to be searching for the right words. 'Francine isn't a bad person. We were a good team. But I finally realised that that isn't enough. Does that make sense?'

'It makes perfect sense.'

'And Dad's finally worn me down. He's persuaded me to work freelance and have a go at the farm. I've agreed as long as we keep the manager.' He looked away, not meeting her eyes. 'I know you're going back to Alex. And I understand that. You mustn't think ...' His voice trailed off.

She did not respond. Instead she turned to look at the house. Her bedroom window with its view of the valley looked empty now, the curtains taken down. The drawing room where Anne and Archie had lived and partied was stacked with boxes, the furniture rearranged in preparation for sale. The garden was ragged and overgrown. The days of childhood play and children's parties, Jack Tyler's Rolls pulling up on the driveway, Jim carrying in the Christmas tree and Mrs Baxter cycling to the kitchen door, Monty grazing in the distance and Archie putting up the badminton set – all of it was gone.

She turned back to Michael. 'I'm not going back to Alex,' she said bluntly.

'You're not?' He looked at her as if trying to establish whether she was serious.

'Going back would have been easy, but it wouldn't have been right.'

They stood for a moment in silence, as if to acknowledge what existed between them, neither wanting or needing to articulate what they both instinctively understood.

He did not press her – did not demand answers or explanations. It was as it had always been between them. Instead, he took her hand. 'Come and have a cup of tea with Dad. He says he feels a new man.'

Side by side they crossed the lawn. He helped her across the fence, away from the house and then they walked down the sloping field to the farmhouse in the valley.

WITHDRAWAL

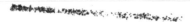